UNHIDDEN PILGRIMS

KAREN PETIT

WestBow Press books may be ordered through booksellers or by contacting:

WestBow Press
A Division of Thomas Nelson & Zondervan
1663 Liberty Drive
Bloomington, IN 47403
www.westbowpress.com
1 (866) 928-1240

ISBN: 978-1-9736-0053-4 (sc)
ISBN: 978-1-9736-0054-1 (hc)
ISBN:978-1-9736-0035-0 (e)

Library of Congress Control Number: 2017913480

Print information available on the last page.

WestBow Press rev. date: 08/30/2017

Acknowledgements

My loving family has been supportive throughout my life. My thanks go to my children (Chris and Cathy), to my brothers and sisters (Ray, Rick, Margaret, Carl, Sam, Bill, Dan, and Anne), and to my nieces, nephews, cousins, and other relatives.

My thanks are extended to my many friends and colleagues at Phillips Memorial Baptist Church, the Fitness Studio, The Dancing Feeling, the Community College of Rhode Island, Bristol Community College, Bryant University, Massasoit Community College, New England Institute of Technology, Quinsigamond Community College, Rhode Island College, Roger Williams University, the University of Massachusetts at Dartmouth, the University of Rhode Island, Worcester State University, and the Association of Rhode Island Authors.

I also thank WestBow Press for supporting me and many other authors. Historically and today, publishers have been expanding the literacy skills of our world.

I am most thankful to Jesus Christ, my Lord and Savior, for his constant loving presence. He has helped to change the many nightmares of my life into positive realities. With his help, my best dreams have become my reality.

Contents

Contents

Preface

Freedom of religion and freedom of speech are both key components of the First Amendment of the United States Constitution: "Congress shall make no law respecting an establishment of religion, or prohibiting the free exercise thereof; or abridging the freedom of speech, or of the press; or the right of the people peaceably to assemble, and to petition the government for a redress of grievances."[1] The creation of this amendment was a result of the journeys of many hidden and unhidden Pilgrims: people who initiated the prolific use of movable-type printing, free speech, and religious freedom. Through the inclusion of historic information about such freedom initiators as Johann Gutenberg, William Brewster, and Gregory Dexter, *Unhidden Pilgrims* connects our past history to our present society.

The creation and use of Gutenberg's movable-type printing press helped to make printed books more affordable and numerous. Religious reformers could then send ideas to more people in different countries, resulting in debates about how to respect, worship, and love God. More printed books also meant that people had more freedom to communicate and debate various opinions, including the appropriateness of their government's actions.

The modernization of printing had other effects, such as to help standardize language. "Gutenberg's printing press ensured that supply was better able to satisfy demand, simultaneously assisting language's journey to standardization."[2] With more books being printed and distributed to more people, vocabulary, spelling, grammar, and other linguistic components of language took on more standardized forms.

The effects of this standardization helped people to more effectively write, read, learn, think, and communicate with one other.

For centuries, freedom and censorship have been practiced in the printing world. In the seventeenth century, William Brewster and Gregory Dexter were both very helpful as printers and religious leaders. While in Europe, they sometimes printed censored materials. They then had to flee authorities and journey to the new world. Even though they did not own printing presses in New England, they helped to establish our country's freedom through their ministry, their communication, and their other activities.

People in the twenty-first century exercise freedom and censorship through such mediums as printed writing, the internet, social media, dialogue, body language, home decoration, clothing, possessions, codes, abbreviations, computer software, images, and symbols. These methods of speaking to others are visible in many sections of *Unhidden Pilgrims.* Both hidden and unhidden elements of modern and historic communication are displayed by the characters in this novel.

In today's world, as well as in earlier centuries when our democracy was being created, people often had to run, hide, and fight. Hopefully, people today will not just run, hide, and fight, but like the Pilgrims also did, they will stand their ground, become visible, and share their faith and their love.

Heidi Hiding in a Dream

Heidi tried to open her mouth, but it remained closed. She moved her hand onto her mouth and touched some duct tape, which was holding her lips together. Her hand slid horizontally along the tape and then vertically from the top of her nose to her chin. She had just made the sign of a cross on her face. Her hand moved sideways again, trying to remove the tape, but a nurse grabbed her hand.

"No, you can't talk right now."

Heidi stared at the nurse, who was wearing a mask. Even while wearing the mask, the nurse was still able to talk clearly and said, "You'll have to pay me some money before you can be free to talk."

In the middle section of the nurse's blouse was a blood-red name tag. The too-bright color made the nurse's name impossible to read. Only a single straight line and one curvy line were visible in the middle of the tag.

Heidi managed to pull the nurse's hand away. Heidi then tried to open her mouth again, but the tape was still firmly in place. She could not separate her lips even slightly.

The nurse moved her hand to the tape that was keeping Heidi's mouth closed. Heidi tried to lift her chin, but the nurse's hand stayed put, keeping Heidi's chin frozen in the same position with the tape covering her mouth.

"Do you have any money?" the nurse asked.

Heidi pointed to her purse, sitting on the table near her bed. The nurse went over to the table, opened Heidi's purse, and pulled out a billfold. There was only a single dollar inside.

The nurse asked, "Do any of your credit cards have fifteen hundred dollars of available credit?"

Heidi tried to say "yes," but she was unable to speak because of the tape, so she nodded instead.

The nurse moved the purse over close to Heidi, who immediately pointed to one of her credit cards.

"Okay," the nurse said. "I'll use that one, but it better work." She took out her cell phone and typed in some information about Heidi and one of the credit cards. After waiting for a few seconds, the nurse looked at her phone, showed it to Heidi, and smiled. "The charge has gone through okay." She ripped the tape off of Heidi's mouth. "You're now free to speak."

"It's not fair that you're charging me to speak," Heidi said as she rubbed her lips. "We have free speech in this country."

"You're only free to speak at appropriate times." The nurse looked behind her left shoulder. Three police officers and a doctor were standing behind her; they nodded in agreement. Like the nurse, they were wearing masks, and their other clothing further hid their identities. The doctor was wearing a dark suit, and the end of his stethoscope was covering his name tag. The police officers had no badges or other means of identification.

"I can't believe I'm being charged money so that I can talk," Heidi said. "Are you for real, or am I dreaming?"

No one answered her question.

"I'll try a reality check." Heidi looked at the clock on the wall. It was four o'clock. She closed her eyes and then opened them. The clock was missing. She closed her eyes, waited a few seconds, and opened them again. This time, the clock was back on the wall, but the time had changed to two o'clock.

"I guess I'm dreaming, so all of you must be unreal."

The doctor shook his head and said, "We really are real."

"Are you saying yes or no?" Heidi asked.

"We're in your memory, so we have to be real." The doctor waved his hands at the other people in the room.

"I don't remember ever seeing anyone who was dressed like you are."

"Don't you remember being in the hospital?" the doctor asked.

"Yeah, I was, but the doctors and nurses weren't wearing masks and strange clothing."

One of the officers unhooked some handcuffs from his belt and waved them at Heidi. "What happened?" he asked.

"I can't tell you," Heidi said.

The officer raised his eyebrows, showing his surprise. "Why can't you tell us? We're the police."

"I just can't."

"You wanted to have the freedom to talk. You now have no tape on your mouth, and you're trying to hide the truth from us," the officer said.

"I know, but I need to keep silent about this."

"We're not charging you any money right now to talk to us. Your speech is free."

"You already charged me money, and it was just so I could have that tape removed from my mouth. That's not free speech."

"No, I didn't charge you that money; the nurse did."

Heidi looked at the nurse, who smiled while saying, "I needed the extra money. Plus, removing that tape from your mouth was a medical procedure."

Heidi frowned and looked at one of the police officers. "If you want me to tell you secrets, I should be the one getting some money for talking."

The officer moved his pair of handcuffs close to Heidi's left wrist. "We're the police. You have to tell us."

Heidi stared at the handcuffs as she swallowed and pressed her lips together. After a few seconds, she said, "Being silent is sometimes a part of my job."

The officer looked at the doctor and asked, "Does she have any mental problems, or is her memory messed up in some way?"

The doctor walked over to Heidi and placed his hand on her forehead. "Does this hurt?"

Heidi blinked several times. "Yeah, it does," she said in a nervous voice.

The doctor moved his hand away and stared at Heidi's eyes. He then shone a light into each of her eyes and examined them closely.

Heidi blinked continuously. Her eyes did not like the bright light. After the doctor was finished examining Heidi's eyes, she asked, "Am I okay?"

The doctor said, "I think so, but why can't you tell us what happened? Did you forget everything?"

"No, I remember lots of things." Heidi paused before adding, "Actually, I remember too many things. That might be why I have a headache."

The police officer grunted, moved two sets of handcuffs onto Heidi's left wrist, and locked them together tightly. "You need to tell us what happened."

"It's a secret," Heidi said.

She sighed while closing her eyes. She inhaled deeply and exhaled slowly before opening her eyes again. Everything was dark until a beam of light appeared. Heidi found herself now standing with two men inside an elevator. The beam of light was moving around the walls, doors, ceiling, and floor.

"Turn that thing off," one of the men said in a low, demanding voice. "You know we're trying to save the batteries."

"Okay," the other man, with a nagging, medium-toned voice, responded. "I just wanted to see if anything was different. It's all the same."

"Of course it's the same."

"With my cell phone's light turned on, we know for sure that everything's the same." The nagging voice paused and then added, "We're still stuck inside this elevator."

The light turned off, and the elevator seemed even darker than it had been just a minute before.

"Help!" Heidi screamed.

"Be quiet!" the demanding-voiced man yelled.

"If I scream, people might hear me and rescue us."

"They'll be rescuing us pretty soon anyway."

Heidi began to jump up and down.

The man with the nagging voice turned on his cell phone light again and pointed it at Heidi's face.

The other man asked Heidi, "Why are you jumping?"

"It might help the elevator to move."

"No, jumping won't help. It'll just make the elevator fall down the shaft," the demanding-voiced man shouted.

Heidi jumped up and down several more times. With each jump, the elevator floor shifted slightly.

The man with the demanding voice put his hands on his hips and stepped closer to Heidi. He then waved one of his hands toward the other man's cell phone, indicating he should turn off the light. The elevator immediately became dark.

Heidi kept jumping. Suddenly, something hit her head, and she fell to the floor. After a few seconds, she put her hands on the cold metal floor and started to push herself up into a sitting position.

The light turned on again as the nagging voice asked, "What just happened?"

Heidi immediately laid back down on the floor. She positioned her eyes upward and tried to look like she was unconscious, though she could still see and hear everything that was happening.

When the beam of light from the cell phone was directed at her face, Heidi's eyes were already closed again. After a few seconds, the light moved up and was shining above her head. Heidi partially opened her eyes. A shadow from a hand moved into the beam of light.

"You must have done that to her," the nagging voice said.

"No, I didn't do that," the other man said. After a pause, he added, "Besides, how can you claim I did something if you didn't even see me do it?"

The first man laughed. "Just because it's dark in here doesn't mean I didn't hear anything."

"We both heard her jumping up and down, so it's obvious that she's the one who did it. She hit herself in the head and then fell." A threatening look shot out from the second man's eyes and landed on the first man's face.

After just a few seconds, the light shifted as the first man stepped backward. "Okay, you're right," he said. "She did it to herself."

"Of course she did. She's also likely to be very quiet about this anyway."

"Why do you think that?"

"She's a spy."

"Is she really?"

"Yeah, she is. That's why she happened to be in this elevator. She was following me."

The light turned off again.

After staring into darkness for a few minutes, Heidi fell asleep. When she woke up a short time later, she was in her office. She looked at her watch. Her eyes widened when she realized that she had jumped back in time to three days before the elevator scene.

The computers were all displaying some people of interest in video feeds on the screens. An alarm suddenly sounded from one of the computers. Heidi and some other people in the office went over to look at the computer screen. In the video feed, a criminal was letting himself into a bright yellow car. The car's owner had left the car unlocked, and a key was in the ignition.

The thief was just turning the key when the computer in Heidi's office automatically sent a message to the yellow car. A few seconds later, the car received the message and immediately turned off its engine.

Heidi said, "In this office, we have some great spyware. It's doing all kinds of crazy things that I never thought would be possible in reality."

A message for Heidi appeared on the computer screen that had sent the message to the yellow car: "You're dreaming. Your reality is different."

"Thanks for letting me know," Heidi said as she looked at the video feed that was again on the computer's screen. Because the computer now had control over the car's actions, the car's bright yellow color was much paler. The thief was still in the driver's seat, but he was unable to start up the car again. With each attempt to turn the key in the ignition, electricity exited from the ignition into the criminal's hand. After a minute, he stopped trying to start up the car and exited from the driver's door. His hand was bright red. Police cars pulled up close to the pale yellow car. The officers arrested the thief and returned the key into the car's ignition.

Heidi said, "This video has been saved on our computer, and it'll be great evidence at a future trial."

One of the other employees said, "I love the spyware on our computers."

"Is it really called 'spyware'?"

"Of course it is."

"I thought 'spyware' was used by hackers, rather than by honest companies like ours."

"To keep our society safe, we need to watch criminals through their cell phones, computers, and other devices." The employee paused for a few seconds and then added, "I like the 'spywear' that you're wearing."

Heidi looked at her clothing. Her jeans had mirrors on the knees, small computer screens on the thighs, and at least ten pockets in different places. Two of the pockets had guns in them. One pocket had a knife in it. Another pocket contained a wrench, a hammer, scissors, and screwdrivers. Her blouse was covered by a bulletproof vest, and her head was safe in a helmet. Her purse looked more like a backpack than a purse. Heidi also was wearing her spy glasses, which could be used to take pictures and videos, as well as to send and receive text messages.

Before Heidi had a chance to talk some more with the employee who liked her clothing, her boss was handing her a folder.

Heidi pointed to the picture on the front of the folder and asked, "Is this the guy we're after?"

"Yeah, he sent some emails to a known terrorist."

Heidi opened the folder and asked, "Where are the emails?"

"You're looking at them."

Heidi stared at the papers inside the open folder while saying, "You're right. I am looking at them."

"Should I hold onto some of those papers for you?" Heidi's boss asked.

"No, thanks, I can hold onto all of them while reading each page." Heidi silently began to read the first printed page. After carefully examining several of the pages, she said, "Okay, something's being planned. What should I do?"

"Follow him."

"Who is he, and where is he?"

"We'll soon be getting information about his identity and location from his cell phone."

Heidi looked at the next page in the folder. It was blank, and then it started to change. Some bright blue, green, and red lines were appearing on the page. The paper now looked like a picture that was being colored by a child. A child's hands grabbed tightly onto the coloring page. As Heidi continued to watch the hands that were holding the paper, the hands became her own. She was now a child, who was drawing a picture of the *Pilgrim Maiden* statue at Brewster Gardens in Plymouth, Massachusetts. The picture included the fountain that was in front of the statue.

Partially blocking the fountain was a lady who was talking to several children about the statue. One of the children, Maul, was the lady's son. He was standing near his mom while making faces at Heidi.

Maul's mom said, "In 1922, the *Pilgrim Maiden* statue was created by Henry Hudson Kitson. Two years later, it was dedicated to 'those intrepid Englishwomen whose courage, fortitude and devotion brought a new nation into being.'[3]"

"People today have courage, too," Heidi said.

Maul grimaced before saying to Heidi, "You don't have any courage."

Heidi opened her mouth to reply, but a leaf flew onto her lips. She tried to brush it off, but it seemed to be glued to her face. She was unable to talk.

Maul stepped forward and dropped several of his crayons on top of Heidi's picture. Heidi looked at Maul while his laughing face was staring at her picture. One of the crayons that he had dropped was now making a glazing mark on her drawing. No one was holding onto the crayon; it was adding color to the picture all by itself.

Maul grabbed a crayon and drew some negative symbols on Heidi's drawing.

Heidi tensed up her right arm in anger; she was still unable to brush the leaf away from her mouth. She closed her eyes and prayed: "Dear Lord, please help me. Whenever I'm upset, I have problems speaking. I stutter, and my throat is dry. In Jesus's name, I pray for your help, Amen."

Heidi was immediately strong enough to brush the leaf off her mouth. Her throat felt normal, and she asked Maul, "Why are you messing up my picture?"

Maul ignored her question and asked, "Why were you just praying?"

"I always pray a lot."

"Why were you praying silently, Heidi? Were you too scared to pray out loud?"

"No, I wasn't scared. I just have problems talking if I'm nervous, but I know there's a God. I go to church to worship Him, and He always helps me."

Maul laughed. "I think you were just hiding, Heidi. You're always hiding. It's a part of your name."

"I don't hide all the time. Especially if I'm thinking about my faith, I like to share it."

Maul made a face and then moved the crayon in his hand across Heidi's coloring page. "I'm fixing your picture, so it's now more creative."

Maul's mother stepped closer to Maul and Heidi while saying, "I like what Maul just added to your drawing, Heidi."

Maul smiled at his mom and then said to Heidi, "You're really bad at coloring."

"No, I'm not. I got an 'A' on my last picture."

"I don't believe you. Everyone knows you're a liar." Maul tried to grab onto Heidi's picture, but she quickly moved it sideways and out of his reach. While moving her picture behind her back, Heidi yelled, "Leave me alone!"

Maul yelled back, "Shut up! I don't even like talking to you!"

"Why are you being so mean?" Heidi asked.

"You're the ugliest girl I've ever seen!" Maul threw the crayon in his hand onto the ground.

Maul's mother moved over close to Heidi, looked at her face, and told her, "You can't say such bad things while we're in Brewster Gardens."

Maul squeezed himself between his mom and Heidi. He then said, "I can say whatever I want to say. In our country, we have freedom of speech."

Maul's mother glanced at Maul as she said, "I was talking to Heidi." The mother then turned to Heidi and said, "You shouldn't say Maul is mean."

"But he really is mean. Even his very name shows his meanness."

"No, it doesn't. Maul was named after my father," Maul's mother said.

Maul stared at his mom in disbelief. "Your father really was mean. He went to prison for assaulting people."

"He had good reasons for what he did."

"What were the reasons?"

"I can't tell you about that stuff here."

With an angry face, Maul said loudly, "I already know about all of that stuff. He did a whole bunch of bad things, like hurting people and cheating on his taxes." Tears formed in Maul's eyes. After he wiped his eyes with his index fingers, he said, "I just don't understand why you named me after such a bad person."

Maul's mom frowned, sighed, turned to Heidi, and said, "You're being mean by telling Maul that he's mean."

"He messed up my picture and keeps saying my picture is bad." Heidi stared at her drawing before adding, "Plus, I'm a descendant of William Brewster. He's one of my ancestors. How can anyone say that my picture of his garden is bad?"

Maul's mom said, "Brewster has been called 'the most lovable of all the Plymouth "Saincts."[4] You need to be nice and lovable, like he was, while we're in his garden area."

"Maul needs to be lovable, too," Heidi said.

Maul's mom frowned at Heidi. "Maul's my son. I know he's being lovable."

Heidi moved her drawing forward and said, "Brewster was loved by so many of the people who knew him." Heidi looked at Maul's mother, who walked away and crossed the Town Brook Bridge. Maul's mother then turned to watch the children from the other side of the brook.

Maul said to Heidi, "You can't draw anything."

"William Brewster never attacked people, like you're doing right now. You really are a meanie!"

"I'm not attacking you, and I'm not being mean. I'm telling you the truth."

Tears appeared in Heidi's eyes as she stood up. Eight children had formed a circle around her and Maul. They all began to yell.

"You can't talk!"

"Your voice is even uglier than your nose is!"

"Your speech yesterday was so bad!"

"We all laughed at you."

"Even the teacher laughed."

Heidi opened her mouth and tried to say something, but no words came out. This time, no leaf was covering her mouth; the problem was entirely due to her own inability to overcome her fear. She cleared her throat while looking up at the Pilgrim Maiden statue. The strength of the bronze statue as it stood on its granite rock made Heidi breathe deeply. After a few seconds of added oxygen, Heidi was stronger, but still weak. She said softly, "Nearly everyone's scared of doing speeches, especially in our class."

One of the girls in her class said, "You shouldn't be so scared of just talking to people."

Heidi tried to say something, but her voice was not working again.

Maul said, "You keep claiming your ancestors are Pilgrims. You should have more courage, just like they did."

Heidi deeply inhaled and exhaled as she again looked at the Pilgrim Maiden statue. The bronze Pilgrim lady climbed down from her rock, took several steps forward, jumped over the fountain, and walked over to stand next to Heidi. The statue then shook hands with Heidi before turning around and going back to stand on her rock behind the fountain.

Heidi stared at the statue for a minute before saying, "I know about the Pilgrims. Around half of them died in their first winter in Plymouth. They were still thankful about their colony and about their lives in the new world." Heidi looked down at the ground and put her hands over her eyes. As she moved her hands back and forth, trying to wipe her tears away, her nose was hidden.

"Your hands are even uglier than your nose," Maul said. He and the other children laughed loudly.

After a minute of continuous laughing noises, a new voice yelled, "Stop bullying her! You must be nice to your classmates."

Heidi opened her eyes to see her teacher from the sixth grade. A tear dropped from Heidi's eye down into her mouth. Heidi then stuttered a couple of unintelligible words, cleared her throat, and said nervously, "I'm okay, Miss Janet. They're not bullying me." Heidi's voice sounded scratchy, as if she was trying to stop herself from talking while her words were making themselves heard.

Miss Janet said, "I listened to some of the things they said to you." After pausing for a few seconds, she added, "I know you're scared, but I'm still going to deal with the students who were just bullying you."

"They'll only blame me for their punishment."

"The school's policies must be followed," Miss Janet said.

"Can't this time be an exception to the rules?" Heidi asked.

"No, it can't be. Even if others misbehave, we should still act correctly and do what is right," Miss Janet said.

Heidi closed her eyes, placed her hands on top of her head, and tried to hide. Moving sideways, she stepped into the Town Brook's water. When her head went beneath one of the gentle waves, the tears were washed away from her face. Her eyes stayed closed until an alarm began to sound. Then her eyes opened.

Drive-through

Heidi sat up, rubbed her eyes, and turned off the alarm clock. She quickly got ready for work and drove to the newly rebuilt Pilgrim Office Building. After pulling into the wide driveway, she parked in the lot behind the building, got out, and waved at a lady who had just parked a car next to hers.

The lady asked, "Do you always get here this early?"

"Yeah, most of the time, I do," Heidi said. "What's your schedule like?"

"I usually get here a little bit later, but I wanted to see how the traffic was if I left fifteen minutes earlier."

"Was it a better drive for you this morning?"

"It definitely was. I might be changing my schedule permanently."

As Heidi and the lady began walking toward the building, Heidi said, "I love what has been done to this building."

"I only started working here a few weeks ago, so I don't know too much about the old version of the building. Were you here before the bombings happened?"

"Yeah, I was."

"What's different?"

"Some of the new offices and stores are more creative in their design."

"In what ways can an office be creative?"

"One office has some escalators, and another one has a giant slide." Heidi paused and then added, "I think the different designs are saying something about the different products and services in each place."

"How can a slide say something?"

"It's in a store that sells amusement park rides."

"Oh, I'd love to visit such an office," the lady said as her eyes jumped around to different windows in the office building. She was obviously looking for the amusement-park office. After a few seconds of silence, she asked, "What's the name of the company?"

"I think it's called 'Amusement Plus.'"

The lady smiled and then asked, "Which office has escalators?"

Heidi thought for a few seconds before saying, "I don't know which one has the escalators. Someone told me an office had escalators in it, but I never found out where this office is located."

"Maybe the office is hidden away somewhere, so people won't keep on going to visit it."

"I think more people might keep on visiting Amusement Plus because slides will be more interesting than escalators."

"You're right about that. If I knew where one or both of those two offices were, I'd probably visit them this morning."

"The lobby has a listing of all of the companies."

"I guess I'll be reading a listing in a minute or two." The lady looked at the building's foundation before adding, "The building looks safe."

Heidi shook her head in agreement. "It's much safer than it used to be. There are a lot more security cameras."

"Are there other safety measures?"

"Yeah, there are. For example, most of the doors now turn inward."

"Why is that safer?" the lady asked.

"People can put chairs and desks in front of the doors to keep them closed, so criminals in the corridor won't be able to come in."

"Can't employees just lock the doors?"

"Locks can be broken," Heidi said.

"Oh, you're right."

The lady looked at the top of the building. "Were you working here when the bombs went off?"

"Yeah, I was trapped in one of the elevators."

"Oh, no, that must have been awful."

"It was." Heidi frowned and cleared her throat.

"Can you tell me about what happened, or will it make you too anxious?"

Heidi sighed. "I'm used to telling people about what happened, so it doesn't really stress me out too much."

"So, what happened?"

"I was stuck in an elevator with two thieves. They actually knocked me out, but I woke up after a while. We were rescued, and I completely recovered from my injuries. The whole experience taught me how to cope with my fears."

"What were you scared of?"

"Like a lot of people, I was scared of elevators."

"Are you still scared of elevators?" the lady asked.

"No, I'm not. Now, I usually take an elevator, rather than walk up the stairs."

"That's so wonderful."

"Yeah, it is," Heidi said.

"I'm so glad you lived through that experience."

"Every day since then, I'm really thankful to just be alive."

Heidi and the lady were now at the back of the building. They shook hands with each other and said "good-bye." Heidi turned to the left; the lady moved to the right.

In front of Heidi, at the left rear corner of the building, was a drive-through office area. A large sign on the building's wall had the company's name: "Drive-through Technology." Next to the sign was a drive-through window. People could go up to the drive-through window or over to one of the large plastic tube areas. The plastic tubes were much larger than the ones used at banks.

A gray sedan pulled up, blocking the lane leading to the drive-through window. A man slowly stepped out of the sedan, looked around, and walked up to the window. He was wearing sunglasses and a cap pulled downward. The cap was slanted and hiding more of the left side of his face than anything else. Next to the bottom of his cap, under his left ear, was a dark line, which may have been the bottom section of a scar or a tattoo. Even though he had moved into a shaded area, he kept his sunglasses on and touched his cap, making certain that it was pulled down. When a section of the drive-through window slid open, the sunglass man just stood there, looking closely through the window and into the interior of the office area. He was not looking at the employee, who was wearing a shirt with images of futuristic computers on it. The sunglass man was instead staring at the office's walls, furniture, and other objects.

Inside the Drive-through Technology office, the employee who had just opened the window said, "This is a drive-through area, sir. What are you doing outside of your car?"

Rather than answering the employee's question, the sunglass man asked a different question: "What's your name?"

"Jim. What's yours?"

The sunglass man did not respond, but instead used his cell phone to take some pictures of the drive-through window area.

"What are you doing?" Jim asked.

The sunglass man walked up closer to the drive-through window. After moving his cell phone upward and inches away from the window, he took some pictures of the interior of the office area.

"Why are you taking all of those pictures?" Jim paused and then added, "If you don't tell me, I'll have to call the cops."

The sunglass man frowned before finally saying something: "I work for a company that's going to build its own drive-through area. My boss asked me to take some pictures of some different kinds of drive-through lanes and windows."

"That's interesting." Jim hesitated before asking, "Can you tell me your identity or where you work?"

The sunglass man turned away from the office window and took several steps toward one of the large tubes. Heidi slowly moved in his direction. While the sunglass man took some close-up pictures of one of the large tubes, she also took pictures of him by touching her security glasses multiple times. She then walked back away from the man and watched as he stared at the tubes. Inside of each tube was a large steel box. The boxes were open; straps inside of each steel box were visible. People could tie the straps around items placed inside the boxes. A computer, a printer, or even a small TV could be attached to the inside of one of the boxes.

Jim noticed Heidi and then said to the sunglass man in a loud voice, "Excuse me, sir. I understand that you need to take pictures, so you need to do some things differently from other people. However, this is not a walk-up window. You should either stay in your car or move it out of the way. I don't want you to block customers from coming in."

The sunglass man said, "I like the set-up here. I'm also really curious about the kinds of equipment you have in your store."

"We help customers repair their laptops, cell phones, and other items." Jim pointed to a listing next to the window. "These are what we fix."

The sunglass man took a picture of the listing. He then asked, "Do you replace hard drives in computers?"

"Yes, we often can do that. We also fix other problems with computers."

"Can you put new batteries into my cell phone?" the sunglass man asked.

"Yes, we do replace batteries, but there might be other problems besides the batteries."

"How do I leave my cell phone or laptop with you?"

"You're supposed to stay in your car, explain to me what repairs are needed, place your items in the plastic container, and send the container through the drive-through tube. You can also bring your items to this window. I then will give you some paperwork to sign. After we have done the repairs, you will pay for the work."

"How much does it cost, and how long do the repairs take?" the sunglass man asked.

"It depends on the kind of technology and the kind of problem."

"Can you give me an example?"

As Jim explained some of the cost possibilities, the sunglass man's eyes kept moving around to different sections of the drive-through office.

"Are the repairs done here?" the sunglass man asked as his eyes stared at the structure of the window area.

"We have different employees who stop by this drive-through window, pick up items, and then go to an appropriate place to do the repairs," Jim said.

"Then this is really a drive-through window for a drive-through office."

"Yeah, it is. Customers and employees all use this drive-through window or a plastic container that they send through one of the tubes."

"I'll have to stop by with my laptop in a day or two," the sunglass man said.

"We should be able to help." Jim shook his head as the sunglass man got into his car and drove away.

Another car pulled up to the Drive-through Technology office. Jim said to the driver, "Hi, Justin. We have several devices for you to fix."

"That's great!" Justin said. "I even have a lot of time today to do repairs."

Jim sent multiple items through the drive-through tube. Justin took each item and carefully placed it into his car. Seatbelts were attached to a laptop and a computer monitor.

After the items were all secure in Justin's car, Jim started to tell him about the needed repairs. Justin listened to Jim for a minute and then appeared to be getting bored. After glancing at a few of the cars driving into the parking lot, Justin looked at the small electronic items in the passenger seat of his own car. He picked up one of the cell phones needing repair. Opening up his glove compartment, he pulled out some small metal tools. Every few seconds, Justin glanced at Joe, who was still talking about the needed repairs. Justin was obviously still listening to Jim while beginning to fix the cell phone. In just a few minutes, Justin had taken the back panel off of the cell phone, replaced the battery, and turned the cell phone on; it was working again.

Jim asked, "Do you have that phone fixed already?"

"Yeah, I do. My car is set up like an office, so I actually do a lot of work in here."

"Oh, you must be one of those people who text while driving."

"I don't want to cause any accidents, so I only text while stopped at red lights or in places like this drive-through lane." After taking a sip of coffee from his travel mug, Justin said, "I like working in my car. I can drink coffee, listen to music, send emails, do texting, and even repair some small electronic devices."

"Can you also fix laptops and computers while you're in your car?" Jim asked.

"They're a little bit tougher to fix in such a small space. I usually fix those at home."

Justin placed the repaired cell phone back in the tube and sent it to Jim. After signing some paperwork, Justin also sent the paper forms through the tube to Jim. Finally, Justin started up his car's engine.

A dashboard message appeared: "Service engine soon."

Justin stared at the dashboard message, frowned slightly, and then pulled away from the drive-through office. While driving toward one of the exits from the parking lot, he typed a message onto an electronic device. The words "Thanks a lot, Jim" appeared in the back window of his car.

Jim waved at Justin, who used the same messaging device to change the words appearing across his car's back window to "good-bye."

Heidi walked up to the drive-through window and asked Jim, "Do you know how that driver managed to write words across the back window of his car?"

"I think the words were written in the air in front of the window, which made them look like they were written on the actual window."

"That kind of writing would be great to use. That driver just shouldn't have been writing while driving."

"It's interesting that—while his car was not moving—he was reading a dashboard message from his car, but then he wrote a message to me while driving."

Heidi laughed. "I know we shouldn't be texting while driving, but I'd love to talk to some of the drivers on our roads and not just talk to my friends."

"If you were going to say something nice, then I'd love to see texting to other drivers happen. However, if you were going to say something negative, there's already too much road rage."

"I'd be nice—at least most of the time."

"If more drivers had that device, I'm guessing most of them would be saying bad things to each other."

"You're right. Hopefully, that driver who just left this drive-through window is not using his writing-in-the-air device to say negative things to other people, including other drivers."

For a few seconds, Heidi and Jim both watched as a different driver was leaving the parking area. This car did not have any messages written across its windows, but a flyer was hanging on its rearview mirror.

Heidi said, "That flyer is a nice way to say something to other people about an upcoming event, but the flyer is a little large."

"Yeah, the flyer's blocking too much of the driver's view."

"In our country, though, we do have free speech."

"You're right. We do." After pausing for a few seconds, Jim asked, "Do you need help with anything?"

Heidi took out her identification card and explained to him that she worked for a security firm in their building.

After looking at her card, Jim said, "For safety reasons, you really should be in your car, rather than just standing in a drive-through lane."

"I know, but I'll just be here for another minute."

"Can I help you with something?" Jim asked.

"I was wondering if I could help you with something."

"Are you trying to get a job here?"

"No, however, thanks for asking. I'm just wondering about that guy who was here earlier."

"That man who was writing in the air actually works for our company."

"I was thinking about the guy who was here before that—the one with the hat and the sunglasses. Did you get his name?"

"He didn't answer my questions, so I didn't find out who he was."

"Do you have any cameras here that took pictures or a video of that man?"

"No, we don't have any kind of cameras."

"That's interesting. Most companies in this building have at least one camera."

"In this office, we don't have a lot of items that thieves would want to steal. Because we're a drive-through work office, our employees have the tools to fix things in their homes, rather than here in this office."

"Can you step aside, so I can better see the inside of your office?"

"I can definitely do that." Jim moved to his right, and Heidi took a step closer to the drive-through window. As she was looking inside the window, Jim's eyebrows moved upward in surprise. He pulled on Heidi's hands while saying, "Jump inside with me, right now, really fast."

Because of Jim's facial expression, Heidi jumped up, leaned her upper body inside the window, and grabbed onto Jim's shoulders. He pulled her the rest of the way into the interior of the office. He then waved his arm and said, "Come on back here where we'll be safer."

Heidi started to run after Jim, who was standing in the corner of the room that was furthest away from the drive-through window. Before she could reach the room's corner, a loud banging noise came from the window. Heidi turned around and saw a gray sedan with the sunglass man as the driver. The car had banged into and tried to drive through the drive-through window.

Heidi took pictures by pressing one of the buttons on her glasses several times. She then ran up to the window and tried to take a picture of the car's license plate number, but the car had no license plates. The car was also moving quickly as it backed away from the window area.

Heidi reached into her pocket and withdrew a small pistol. She aimed at one of the car's tires, but too many people were near the sedan. Most of them started to move quickly away from the car. However, a few of the people were completely stunned; they were standing still with horrified expressions on their faces. It was now almost eight o'clock, and a lot of the employees were trying to get from their cars into the building and up to their offices.

Heidi waited for a chance to shoot at one of the sedan's tires, but the car spun around and moved quickly onto the road in front of the office building. Once it was out of sight, Heidi could no longer shoot its tires. She sighed, put her gun away, and turned around to speak with Jim.

"Are you okay?"

"Yeah, I am. How are you, Heidi?"

"I'm fine. Thanks for asking."

"You're welcome."

Heidi took out her cell phone and sent a text message to several people about the drive-through window event. She then said, "Thanks, Jim, for seeing what was happening. You might have saved my life."

"Thank you, Heidi, for trying to catch that guy. Do you know why he did that?"

"I took some pictures of him with my security glasses a little while ago. I'm guessing he noticed what I was doing. That's probably why he tried to drive through the drive-through window. He just wanted to run me over and destroy any pictures that I had."

"After what happened, I'm going to be thinking of that window in an entirely new way."

Heidi smiled. "Driving though a drive-through window is the type of event that has probably happened before today."

"It probably has."

"It's also interesting that, when you wanted him to use his car, he didn't. However, when I wanted him to not use his car, he did."

"I'm so glad you have some pictures of him."

"The pictures might help a little bit. Since he was wearing sunglasses and a hat, though, the pictures also might not be too helpful."

"Will you let me know if you find out any information about that guy?"

"Yes, I will. Do you have a business card?"

Jim and Heidi traded business cards. Heidi then left Jim's office by climbing out of the partially destroyed window. After taking some pictures of the damage, she waved good-bye and carefully walked along the drive-through lanes and over to the sidewalk.

H.I.D.E.

FOR THE NEXT TEN minutes, Heidi walked around the outside of the building and looked for the gray sedan. She then paused at the front entrance into the building. After glancing quickly at her watch, she went through the first set of doors. Without any hesitation, she walked over to the elevators and stepped into the first elevator that opened its doors. She then pressed the button for the eighth floor. Before the elevator doors closed, a man in a gray suit entered. He stared at Heidi while saying, "Eleven, please."

Heidi pressed the appropriate button on the elevator's control panel. The gray-suited man said, "Thanks."

"You're welcome."

The man was still staring at Heidi as he asked, "Do I know you from somewhere?"

Heidi glanced at the man's face and shook her head from side to side.

The man was still staring at her as he said, "I really think I know you."

"No, we don't know each other."

"I see you're getting out on the eighth floor. Do you work in that small clothing store?"

Heidi ignored his question and looked down at the floor.

After waiting for a few seconds, he asked another question: "What's the name of that store?"

Heidi took out her cell phone and began to read an online news article. When the elevator arrived at her floor, she stared at the slowly-opening doors.

The gray-suited man said, "It was nice meeting you."

Without replying, Heidi stepped out of the elevator. She walked quickly past several offices and paused beneath an exit sign above a stairway.

"Did you get off on the wrong floor?"

Heidi turned around to face the voice. It was the gray-suited man from the elevator. She frowned at him while saying, "No, you got off on the wrong floor. Are you following me?"

"Of course not!"

"Then why did you ask me to press the elevator button for the eleventh floor?"

The man's eyes moved downward as he said, "I just noticed that I'm here too early. I thought I'd buy something in that clothing store."

"The store's in the other direction." Heidi pointed backward beyond the elevator.

"Oh, you're right. Thanks for showing me." He took a step toward the store, paused, and asked, "I'm still curious. Why did you get off on this floor if you don't work here?"

"I sometimes just like to take the stairs."

"Then why were you in the elevator?"

"I like a little bit of exercise, but I don't want to walk up too many flights of stairs at one time." Heidi looked at her watch. "I really need to run."

"What floor is your office on?"

Heidi took out her cell phone, hit three buttons, and said, "I'm dialing 911." She then glanced at the man; he had turned around and was quickly walking away from her. Heidi had not yet hit the phone icon on her cell phone, so her 911 call had not been initiated. She put her phone away, exited through the doorway, and walked up the stairs to the next floor. Pausing, she looked down the stairwell. The gray-suited man was nowhere to be seen. Rather than walking to the door leading into the corridor, Heidi went over to the beige wall and placed her hand in the center section. She pushed the center wall panel backward and slid it sideways. The center panel was now behind the right section of the wall. She stepped through the open space into a narrow corridor with metal walls. She followed the corridor, which turned to the right twice. After walking about halfway down the corridor, she paused briefly to look at some of the paintings on one of the walls. Sighing, she said softly, "I love these paintings and the 3D version of the flag."

Heidi began walking again. She quickly arrived at the end of the corridor. On the top left section of the wall was a security camera. Heidi waved her hand and smiled. The back wall opened up, and she walked through into a reception area. The top section of a large sign displayed the company's name as "H.I.D.E." Below the word "H.I.D.E." was the full name: "Helpful Investigative Defense, Etc."

At the first desk, a lady waved.

Heidi walked up to the lady's desk and said, "Good morning, Jane."

"Good morning to you."

"Whenever I walk in here, I love thinking about our company's 'H.I.D.E.' name. I know the 'E' is an abbreviation for 'Etc.' However, the whole idea of hiding—or classifying—the real meaning of the 'E' by using 'Etc.' is very creative."

"I like the use of abbreviations generally; they're faster to write down, so they're sort of like shorthand," Jane said.

"Speaking of being fast, were you able to find those paper files yet? I know going through stacks of paper files takes a lot longer than looking at the electronic ones."

"Yeah, I found them. Here they are." Jane gave Heidi several files, as well as a flash drive. She then said, "You're also going to need that USB flash drive."

"What's the flash drive for?"

"It has some content for a pamphlet that we need printed. Once Kevin has decided which printer we should contact, you'll probably have to talk to a company about our printing needs."

"Okay, thanks so much." Heidi opened up the top folder. Attached to the first page was a picture of a man. At the bottom of his left ear was a scar that might have been the same as the sunglass man's. "This is really interesting. I should speak with Kevin as soon as possible. Do you know, Jane, if he's busy right now?"

"I think he's in his office."

"That's great. Thanks." Heidi went to the back of the reception area and into a circle shaped corridor. Inside of the circle was a conference room. Outside of the circle were multiple offices; none of the office doors contained people's names or other identifying information.

Heidi knocked three times on one of the doors and asked loudly, "Kevin, are you busy right now?"

His voice from inside the room said, "Please come in, Heidi."

She entered. Kevin was sending a text message. After he hit the "send" icon, he said, "My parents want me to stop by tonight after work."

"Are they okay?"

"They're fine. They're just having a birthday party for my brother."

"I know what you'll be singing tonight." Heidi smiled and then added, "I love spending time with my family."

"I do, too. One of these days, I hope to get married and have kids." Kevin stared at Heidi, and she stared back at him. After about ten seconds of connecting silently with Kevin, Heidi took off her glasses and asked, "Guess what happened this morning?"

"In our world, there are so many possibilities."

Heidi laughed. "I guess I should just tell you." She described the actions of the sunglass man and then pointed to her glasses. "That's why I took some photos this morning with the camera lens in my glasses. I even remembered to zoom in this time."

"That's really great!"

"The photos might or might not help. The guy was wearing sunglasses and a hat. Plus, the hat was pulled down low on the left side of his face."

"He was obviously trying to hide something."

"I know he was. Even so, I could see there was something on the left side of his face. He had a tattoo or a scar."

"If there's a scar or a tattoo, your photos might help us to figure out his identity."

Heidi shook her head in agreement. She then raised the folder that she was carrying upward and showed it to Kevin. "The photo of the man in this folder is interesting."

"Can I see the photo?"

"You've probably already seen it, but here it is." Heidi showed the picture that was inside the folder to Kevin. She then said, "It's interesting that this man has a tattoo of a hundred-dollar bill on the left side of his face."

"A lot of criminals like money, but they don't all display their desires in such a bold fashion."

Heidi laughed. "That man must be really stupid."

"Yeah, he is. If he ever goes on a job interview, most employers will never hire him."

"Maybe a bank would hire someone like him," Heidi said.

"I don't know about that. Bank employees would worry about someone like him stealing their customers' money."

Heidi put her glasses in front of the folder and said, "I've noticed some similarities between the man's photo in this folder and the man whose photos I took with my glasses."

"What similarities did you notice?"

"In addition to the scar or the tattoo on the left side of their faces, I think their chins and necks are about the same."

"Seeing the ears and noses might help, too."

"I'm uncertain about how much of the man's face will be in the photos on my glasses, but I'm hoping at least one of the pictures will be helpful."

"Maybe we'll be able to see a part of the tattoo."

"That would be really nice." Heidi handed her glasses to Kevin and then opened up the folder again. "It says here that the guy's name is Joe Smith. Do you think that's his real name?"

"Anything's possible, but the guy's name is probably just a part of his fake identity."

"It's strange that someone trying to hide from the police would have a tattoo on his face."

Kevin said, "He might have gotten the tattoo before he was a criminal, or he might have gotten the tattoo because he wanted to hide a scar."

"I guess the marks on his face could be a tattoo, a scar, or a tattoo hiding a scar."

"Whatever the marks are, I'm just so glad you were able to take some pictures." Kevin waved Heidi's glasses up and down before asking, "Did you have to shoot your gun?"

"I wasn't able to because of all the people in the area."

"Okay." Kevin looked at Heidi's glasses. "While I think of it, let me show you the messaging system on your glasses."

"I was wondering about that."

Kevin gave Heidi her glasses, and she put them back on her face. He then showed her how the glasses would vibrate when a message was being sent to her. He used his cell phone to send her an actual message. As soon as a vibration was felt, Heidi pressed the top center part of her glasses' frame. A written message appeared on the inside of the lenses of her glasses: "After work, possibly tomorrow night, would you like to go out to dinner with me?"

Heidi's facial expression showed her surprise at the content of the message. She moved the glasses up onto the top of her head and away from her eyes. She then stared at Kevin while asking, "Are you thinking of this as a real date or as just two colleagues hanging out with each other?"

His eyebrows were slightly raised upward as he replied, "I'll be happy with whichever one you prefer."

Heidi took her glasses off her head and asked, "How can I reply by using these buttons on my glasses?"

Kevin showed her different possible responses by pressing a button on her glasses: one push for a "yes," two pushes for a "no," and three pushes for a "maybe." He then showed her how to send a text message on them.

Heidi put her glasses on and pushed one of the buttons a single time.

Kevin smiled joyfully when he received her "yes" response on his own phone. He then said, "We'll need to figure out a nice restaurant, possibly one with an outdoor area."

"Outdoors would be so great at this time of year."

"I agree. Do you have any preferences?" Kevin asked.

"I'll be happy with wherever you want to go."

"Would you like to eat right after work, Heidi, or would you like a later time?"

"Right after work would be really great."

Some footsteps were heard outside of Kevin's office. Jane, the administrative assistant from the front office, stepped into the doorway and asked, "Are you two going out to eat?"

Heidi turned around and smiled nervously at Jane. Keeping her mouth firmly closed, Heidi looked at Kevin.

He said, "We're talking about eating dinner somewhere tomorrow night." After pausing for a few seconds, he asked, "Do you want to go with us?"

Jane laughed. "I really don't want to be the third person at your table."

With an unusually blank look on his face, Kevin said, "We're just going out as co-workers. We haven't been dating or anything like that."

Heidi, with an even blanker look on her face, shook her head in agreement. "We know about the H.I.D.E. policy of not dating a colleague."

Jane laughed again. "Everyone knows you two have been staring at each other."

Kevin said, "I just like Heidi's facial expressions. We haven't yet been on a single date."

Jane looked back and forth between Kevin and Heidi as she asked, "So, will tomorrow night be your first date?"

Kevin tried to keep a blank look on his face, but he was unsuccessful. After smiling briefly, he asked, "Do you really need an answer to that question?"

"No, I already know the answer. You told me what's going on with your happy face," Jane said. After pausing for a few seconds, she added, "I won't tell anyone—or at least not anyone who will say something to our boss."

Waving good-bye, Jane turned around and went back into the corridor. After a few steps, she stopped, turned again, and came back to the doorway. "Kevin, I forgot to tell you about the real reason why I needed to talk to you."

Heidi asked, "Should I leave, or is this something I need to know, too?"

Jane looked at Heidi and said, "You have to stay, Heidi."

"Why?"

"I was just going to tell Kevin that you've been approved to do some field work, Heidi. I'll obviously need to tell you, too," Jane said.

"That's so neat," Heidi said.

Kevin said, "Congratulations! I know you've really wanted this upgrade for quite a while."

Heidi smiled. "Thanks, Kevin. I wonder if my first case will be related to Joe Smith's activities."

"I'm sure you'll find out within a day or two," Jane said. She took a step out into the corridor, paused, and then took a step back into the doorway. "I hope you two have a great time tomorrow night."

Heidi and Kevin looked at each other for a few seconds. Kevin then said, "Thanks so much, Jane. I hope you also have a good night."

Jane waved good-bye and went back into the hallway.

Kevin and Heidi stared at each other until the sounds from Jane's footsteps could no longer be heard. Kevin raised his right hand up to his ear and smiled. "Now we can say whatever we want to say, and no one will hear us."

"What do you want to say?"

"Are you still okay with going out tomorrow night?"

"Of course I am." After pausing, Heidi added, "I've wanted to date you for quite a while."

Kevin smiled back at her. "I've wanted to date you ever since we first met."

For a few seconds, Kevin and Heidi stared at each other. Heidi then took her glasses off and gave them to Kevin. "You need the pictures on these, right?"

"Yes, I do. Thanks so much."

"You're so good at analyzing things, Kevin. Within an hour,

you'll probably have some more information about that guy with the sunglasses."

"You're also good at analysis, Heidi. I'm so glad that you've been approved to start doing some field work."

"I'm really happy about this change in my job." Heidi paused for a few seconds before adding, "Working outside the office will obviously be tougher in some ways, but the work will be more interesting. Plus, the pay will be so much higher."

"You're right about the higher pay." Kevin smiled as he put Heidi's glasses on his desk. "I'll download the pictures and try to get your glasses back to you quickly."

"Thanks so much, Kevin."

"You're welcome, and thank you for being alert enough to notice something strange going on."

"Another strange thing happened this morning."

"You seem to be having an interesting day, and it's still early."

Heidi smiled. "Well, this second guy might have just been trying to ask me out, but he seemed a little bit too pushy."

Kevin's eyes widened. "You didn't tell him 'yes,' did you?"

Heidi grimaced. "There's no way I'd ever go out with that guy."

The brightness in Kevin's eyes showed his happiness as he said, "I'm so glad about that."

Heidi smiled. "I'm really glad that you're glad.

"So, what happened?"

"Even though I ignored that guy and did other things, he was still really pushy. Hopefully, he won't try to kidnap me or something weird."

Kevin stared at the upper part of Heidi's right arm. "You're strong enough now to be able to fight anyone off. Those biceps of yours are beautiful."

"Thanks for being so nice." Heidi clenched her fist, punched up at the ceiling and then twisted her hand down at the floor. "You're right; with all of the training here over the last few months, my biceps and wrists are strong enough for almost anything."

"We'll have to keep going to training sessions together on Saturday mornings."

"I've been enjoying those exercise sessions so much."

After shaking his head in agreement, Kevin asked, "Did anything else happen with that strange guy?"

"He lied about some things and tried to remain anonymous." Heidi gave Kevin some more details about what had happened with the gray-suited man.

"Do you have any pictures of him on your glasses?"

"I didn't bother to take pictures because I thought the elevator's camera would take at least one photo of him." Heidi thought for a second and then added, "I probably should have taken his picture. I was just trying to ignore him."

"I'll check the elevator's photo files."

"Thanks, Kevin. I'll see you later." Heidi went to her own office, located just two doors away from Kevin's. After reading some of the files, she retrieved her laptop from the vault and her glasses from Kevin's office. At three o'clock, she had read several files, completed some paperwork, went to three meetings, and was about to start working on another file.

Someone knocked on her door by hitting it twice quickly, pausing, and then hitting it a third time. Heidi recognized the knock. "Come on in, Kevin," she said.

He immediately walked into her office; he was carrying another folder. "Do you want to do some field work right now?"

"Yeah, I'd love to."

"I need someone to go with me on a short visit to an office in our building."

"I'd love to go out with you."

Heidi and Kevin stared happily at each other for a few seconds. Heidi then asked, "Is anything major happening?"

"There's just a small problem about some vibrations."

"What kind of vibrations?" Heidi asked.

"People are moving things or using some kind of new machinery."

"That sounds like some interesting activity. Maybe a 'person of interest' is involved," Heidi said.

"We might be able to find out, especially if we go and talk to people," Kevin said.

"Since those thieves set off bombs in this building a few years ago, a lot of people have been immediately reporting anything unusual."

"In this case, there were actually reports of the vibrations at three different times."

"It doesn't make sense that people would keep on moving things around, so it's probably some kind of new equipment."

"We'll find out in a little while." Kevin looked at his watch. "You should have enough time to get one of these new watches. They just came in two days ago."

Heidi stared at Kevin's watch as she said, "Your watch appears smaller than the other ones."

"Yeah, it is smaller, so now it looks more like a normal watch."

"I'll read this file later. Right now, I'll stop by our equipment office for one of those watches," Heidi said.

"You can ask Warren if there's anything else he suggests for you to wear."

Heidi reached up to her neck and pulled at her silver necklace. "I'm already wearing one of those necklaces."

Kevin's eyes moved from Heidi's face downward. He was now staring at her neck. "Is that the one people are using as a handcuff?"

"Yeah, it is." Heidi moved her other hand upward, so both of her hands were resting on the necklace. "Some people are actually wearing two of these at the same time."

"You can see what Warren thinks would be appropriate," Kevin said.

"Yeah, I'll talk to him. He might even have something else that's new, besides the watches."

"Right now, I need to run back to my office and finish my emails."

"I'll check with Warren about one of those watches."

"Then we can talk to the people in that store about those strange vibrations."

Heidi smiled. "Your plan sounds perfect."

After Kevin left, Heidi picked up her laptop and purse. She pressed several security buttons to lock her office. She then dropped off her laptop into the computer lock-up room before walking over to the equipment office. This room was always locked, even when someone was inside.

Heidi rang the security bell. Nothing happened. She rang it again before noticing a sign that said "Will return in ten minutes."

Sighing, Heidi pulled her cell phone out of her purse. Before she had a chance to send a text message to Kevin, a man walked up to her, pressed his finger into the security device, and opened the door.

Heidi said, "Thanks so much, Warren."

"I'm sorry about not being here when you needed me. I had to leave for a few minutes."

"That's okay. I actually had only been at the door for a minute. You arrived at a good time, especially since I need one of the new watches."

Warren laughed. "Whenever someone needs a watch, time is always the issue being discussed."

"You're right about that." Heidi looked around the room. There were five different cabinets, a table with four chairs, and a desk. Multiple doors leading into walk-in closet areas were closed, but one of them was open. Inside the large open closet was a variety of bullet-proof clothing.

Warren walked over to one of the cabinets and pulled out a tray of watches. "Do you need any specialized watch, or is the usual one okay?"

"What does the usual watch do? Is it the same as the older, larger version, like the one I have right now?" Heidi raised her left hand out toward Warren and showed him her silver watch with a leather band.

"The new one has the same features as the one you're wearing. It's just a smaller size, so it looks like a normal watch."

"Does it still have a small camera inside, so it can take pictures and videos?" Heidi asked.

"Yeah, the new watch can do that, and now the resolution is actually a little bit higher."

"That's really nice."

"Inside the watch's back panel is the same tiny knife."

"I love that little knife. I've even used it before."

"Were you fighting?"

"No, I just needed to cut the shipping tape on a box."

Warren laughed. "Well, I guess using the knife to cut anything is okay; you'll then be experienced in using it."

"That knife is really tiny, but it still works. It just takes forever to cut anything."

"The size of the knife was discussed a couple of months ago. Obviously, we can't make the knife larger and still fit it into the back of a watch, especially a watch that was just made smaller," Warren said.

"Couldn't you create a folding knife?"

"There isn't any available extra space. The watch still needs to have its working parts, like the wheels and the batteries."

Heidi frowned. "You're right. There wouldn't be much available space. I wasn't even thinking about the parts of the watch and how much space they'd need."

"We also wanted to still have enough empty space for one or two small pills."

"Should I tell you what kind of pills I need to have inserted inside the case?"

"In each watch, I'm automatically including two pills that will put a suspect to sleep in under ten minutes. However, if you want something different, I can easily change things."

"I'm happy with the usual two pills." Heidi looked at the tray of watches and pointed to the one in the top right corner. "I like that silver one with the black leather watchband."

"That watch is the most commonly requested style."

"Can I just have the watch on that tray, or do you have to get another one from the warehouse?"

Warren picked up the watch, inserted two pills inside, handed the watch to Heidi, and said, "Here you go."

While trading her old watch for the new one, Heidi said, "I really like the design and size of this one. Thanks so much."

"You're welcome." Warren smiled and then asked, "Is there anything else you need today?"

Heidi pulled the end of her necklace upward. "Do you have another necklace like this one, so I'll have a pair of handcuffs?"

"Yeah, I do." Warren pulled out a drawer from the middle cabinet. "This one might look nice with your current one."

Heidi tried on the second necklace, which was a little bit longer than the first one. It was stainless steel, just like the first necklace. "These two will look really great together."

"They do match each other."

"Do you have a mirror?"

Warren walked over to one of the closed closet doors and opened it up. The closet contained umbrellas, luggage, shoes, boots, purses, and billfolds.

Heidi said, "I love this closet."

"Do you need any of these items?"

Heidi's eyes moved around the closet for a few seconds. "No, I don't think so. I already have most of these things."

"Isn't there a single item you need?"

"No, I'm really all set. The items that I don't have, I don't want or need. For example, I don't need a man's billfold."

"Okay, but I do know one thing you need right now."

"What's that?"

"The mirror will be helpful, so you'll know how you look while wearing those two necklaces." Warren pointed to the back of the door.

Heidi moved close to the mirror and smiled. "Yeah, these two necklaces go well together."

"Do you need anything else today?"

"Is there anything new that's come in during the past week?"

"The watches are the only new items." Warren pulled out some paperwork from his desk, filled in most of the blank spaces, and had Heidi sign two forms.

After looking around at some of the other items, Heidi said, "I'll check back with you in a day or two about another gun. Even though I already have a small pistol and a Taser, it's always nice to have an extra one."

"Now that you'll be working in the field, you probably should have at least four guns and some extra ammunition."

"You're right." Heidi thought for a few seconds before adding, "I'll figure out what I need and then get back to you. Enjoy the rest of your day."

"Thanks." Warren opened the door, and Heidi walked out into the corridor. She went over to Kevin's office. He must have heard her coming because he opened the door before she knocked on it.

"You're fast," he said.

"Thanks, but you're even faster."

Kevin showed Heidi a picture and asked, "Is this the guy who was bothering you in the elevator?"

"Yes, he is. Who is he?"

"His name is supposedly Moe Smith."

"Does he have a record?"

"He's under investigation for a bank robbery. He also has some connections to Joe Smith."

"So, was he harassing me, or was he doing something else?"

"We don't know for sure yet, but he and Joe are doing some kind of surveillance of this building."

"I didn't see Moe taking pictures like Joe was," Heidi said.

"We checked out the photo files for all of the elevators. Moe actually was taking pictures. He just wasn't doing it when people were around. He also seemed to be trying to find our office."

"If I see him again, I'll try to get some information from him."

"That sounds like a plan." Kevin paused and then added, "Just stay safe."

"I will." Heidi smiled at Kevin.

He smiled back before asking, "Are you ready to go to Amusement Plus?"

"I think so. Have you ever been in that store before?"

"I haven't yet been inside, but I've often walked past it and thought about checking it out. Have you gone inside yet, Heidi?"

"No, not yet, so today should be a lot of fun."

"You're right about that. The Amusement Plus store should be so amusing that we'll have some fun while doing our job there."

Amusement Plus

HEIDI AND KEVIN LEFT the H.I.D.E. office, walked down the hallway, and entered the elevator. Kevin pushed the "four" button and then stepped closer to Heidi. When the elevator doors were partially closed, a man's hand appeared between the doors. The doors opened, and a man with a briefcase stepped into the elevator. He said "hi" to Kevin and Heidi before pressing the "three" button.

When the elevator began to move downward, Kevin and Heidi did not talk with their voices, but instead communicated with their eye and face gestures. With furrowed eyebrows, Kevin stared at the man with the briefcase and then moved his eyes sideways several times. He was obviously saying that he did not want this man on the elevator right now.

Heidi shook her head in agreement. Her eyes then jumped back and forth several times between Kevin and herself. She was saying that she wanted to be alone on the elevator with him.

Kevin smiled, and Heidi responded with a smile. Kevin moved his hand close to Heidi's hand, but before they had the chance to connect their hands together, the elevator arrived on the fourth floor.

The man with the briefcase moved sideways; he then waved for Kevin and Heidi to walk out of the elevator. Heidi followed Kevin as he stepped out into the corridor; they waved at the briefcase man and then walked over to the Amusement Plus store.

The glass windows and front door of the store had interesting photos of the company's products and services. The words "fun" and "lifestyle" were intermingled with the photos on the store's windows. Many of the photos showed the fun lifestyles of happy customers using the company's products. One photo depicted children playing cell phone games while riding on swings. Several other photos showed families being together on different amusement park rides. A large photo directly in front of Heidi and Kevin illustrated a man and a woman riding down two parallel slides at the same time; their hands were joined, and they were looking at each other, rather than at the bottom sections of the slides.

Heidi pointed to the picture of the sliding couple and said, "We'll need to try that someday."

"We definitely should," Kevin said.

"I like slides." Heidi paused and then added, "While we're at work with people watching us, though, we probably can't hold hands and slide down two parallel slides."

"Amusement Plus only has one slide in its store, but we can possibly still do something similar."

"What are you thinking of?" Heidi asked.

"You could slide down a slide while I stand at the bottom. When you arrive at the end of the slide, I'll be able to reach out, grab your hands, and help you to stand up."

"That's an interesting idea. You could look like you were holding my hands to keep me safe when you would actually be holding my hands for another reason."

"Keeping a reality hidden is something you and I are both good at doing," Kevin said.

Heidi laughed. "I sometimes really love my job." After pausing, she added, "I actually meant to say that I almost always love my job."

"You said exactly what I was thinking."

Heidi shook her head in agreement. She then looked through one of the store's glass windows. She was able to see the interior of the store while still standing in the outside corridor. Inside were some recliners with customers seated on them. The customer nearest the door was reclining and being massaged by the chair. The next customer was rocking back and forth. The third customer had a seat belt on and was playing with the control panel on the arm of his recliner; when the chair began to move up and down continuously, he relaxed and seemed very happy with the movements.

Near the recliners, a four-foot square hole suddenly appeared in the floor. A chair with a lady on it came up through the hole. The lady had her seat belt on and was frantically pressing a red button on the arm of the chair. After a few seconds, the chair stopped moving. The lady hesitated and then pressed the green button. The chair turned around in a circle before going back down into the hole in the floor.

Kevin said to Heidi, "When we get inside this store, we'll have to watch where we're walking."

"If we want to ride a chair down onto a different floor, maybe we shouldn't watch where we're walking."

"A surprise ride on a chair might be fun, but what we already planned on the slide might be even more fun."

"You're right about that."

Kevin smiled and then put his hand on the door. "I'll do most of the talking. You can just relax and watch."

"Maybe I'll notice a few people's body language as they slide around into different levels of honesty."

"Do you mean levels of honesty or levels of dishonesty?"

Heidi laughed. "I think I mean both of them."

Kevin pushed the door and held it open for Heidi. Once they were both inside, they walked up to the front desk, where a lady was seated. She was wearing a nametag with "Mira" printed on it. Her gray dress was similar in its color to the mirror that she was holding. She was carefully examining her face. Her brown eyebrows were scrunched; her eyelashes were long, but fluttering up and down. Her mouth was frowning slightly. She was obviously unhappy about something, so she did not notice Kevin and Heidi standing in front of her until Kevin said, "You're very beautiful. You don't have to worry about how you look."

Mira smiled at Kevin, put the mirror in her desk drawer, stood up, and said, "Thanks so much."

"You're welcome," Kevin said.

"How can I help you?" Mira asked.

Kevin looked around at the customers and then spoke in a low voice. "We're from a federal agency." He pulled out his identification card and showed it to Mira.

"Why are you here? Has something happened?"

While still speaking softly, Kevin asked, "Can we talk over there?" He pointed to the right front corner of the room, where a small round table had four chairs around it. No customers were seated there, and no one was within ten feet of the area.

"Of course we can talk over there." Mira walked over to the corner table and sat down in one of the chairs. Kevin and Heidi followed her.

Kevin said, "A company on a lower level than yours reported a large number of vibrations yesterday and today. We need to check out all of the companies in this section of the building to see if anything unusual is happening."

A horn sounded from the far left corner of the room. A small train began moving slowly across the back wall. Four people with laptops were seated on benches in the back half of the train.

Kevin asked Mira, "Are the people in that train customers or employees?"

Mira turned around, looked at the train, and said, "They all work here, but you can have a ride, too, if you want one."

Kevin glanced at Heidi. She was shaking her head sideways and obviously saying that she did not want a ride on the train. Kevin said to Mira, "No, I don't think so, but thanks for asking,"

One of the people on the train screamed "Yahoo!"

Another train rider yelled "Yippee!"

Kevin asked Mira, "Why are they yelling words like that while at work?"

Mira said, "We're supposed to use positive, exciting words while on the rides at work. Especially when customers are in this section of the store, seeing and hearing the fun of amusement park rides might result in a sale."

Heidi said, "That's interesting. I guess people in different stores and offices have different ways of marketing their products and services."

Kevin said, "The vocabulary is different in different fields, too. For example, I'm sure we use the word 'identification' more often than Mira does."

Mira laughed. "I think you're right about that. When we ask to see someone's identification, we usually ask for some form of 'I.D.'"

"You probably also check customers' credit cards," Kevin said.

"We do. Even more than we ask for an 'I.D.,' we ask to see a customer's credit card. We then check the signature on the back of the card. Sometimes there are pictures we can check, too."

One of the workers on the train yelled again.

Kevin looked at the train as he asked Mira, "Those employees on that train, are they actually working, or are they taking a break?"

"They're really working. The train's motion makes them happy, so they can do their jobs better."

"That ride looks like a train, but is it really a train? I don't see any tracks," Kevin said.

"There aren't any train tracks. Plus, what you're looking at is not really a train, but rather a small truck shaped to look like a locomotive. The attached vehicle for the passengers is actually a trailer with eight wheels on it."

Kevin watched the train slow down, stop, and move backward across the same wall. "I would be too distracted to ride a train while typing things on a laptop."

"I would be, too, but they're used to riding and typing at the same time." After a few seconds of watching the train, Mira added, "So, what can I help you with?"

"Can we look around your store to see if anything new might be making the vibrations?" Kevin asked.

"We don't have anything new in this store. The most recently bought equipment was received more than three months ago," Mira said.

"Is it okay if we look around?" Kevin asked.

Mira hesitated before saying, "Of course it is. I'll get someone to help." She walked over to her desk, picked up the phone, dialed an extension, and said, "We have some visitors who need to be shown around our store." After listening for a moment, Mira said, "Thanks, Nira. I'll see you at my desk in a minute." Mira hung up the phone.

Kevin and Heidi went from the corner of the room over to Mira's desk.

Kevin asked, "Is Nira a member of your family, Mira?"

"No, we just happen to have very similar names." Mira tried to avoid eye contact by looking down at her desk. She then sighed. "I guess I should be telling you guys the truth."

Kevin smiled. "We already have some information about both of you. I was just wondering if the owner of Amusement Plus knows that you and Nira are sisters."

Mira laughed softly and then looked around. The customers seemed to be too busy with their chairs to notice what was being said. From a doorway at the back of the room, a lady entered. She was wearing a sleeveless dress with roses and vines intertwined closely together.

The lady walked up to Mira's desk and stood so close to Mira that their elbows were touching.

Mira said, "This is Nira. She'll be happy to help you two."

Kevin said, "Thanks. Is there anything we should know about this room?"

Nira walked over and stood close to Kevin. As her hand touched his wrist, she said to him, "You can already see the great amusement park rides in here. Do you need to know their prices?"

"No, we were more interested in anything that might be vibrating more than it did in the past. Are there any new rides?"

"A couple of these came in a few months ago, but they're exact duplicates of items that were sold. In other words, we haven't started to carry any new rides that we never had before," Nira said.

"Can you show me how you make them work for customers? We might be able to find some possible problems," Kevin said.

"Okay." Nira showed to Kevin and Heidi some swings, flying chairs, a small Ferris wheel, a carousel, and a small child version of a roller coaster. In the right rear corner of the room was the top part of a slide. It was placed inside of a hole in the floor.

"Is this slide new?" Kevin asked.

"No, we've had it for more than six months," Nira said.

Kevin stared at the top of the slide and the floor circling around it as he asked, "Have you changed its position?"

"We did after the first couple of months, but it's been in the present position for at least three months now," Nira said.

One of the employees got off of the train, walked over to Nira, and asked, "Can I take a break now?"

"Of course you can, Bera."

Bera walked over to the slide and sat down on its top edge; she then slid downward and out of view.

Kevin walked closer to the slide. "Does everyone or just some people go down this slide to take a break?"

"Many of us use the slide. However, a few people prefer the stairs." Nira pointed to a small stairway that was right next to the slide. The stairs looked more like a set of stairs in a house, rather than a stairway in a store.

Heidi said, "It's interesting that your store has its own stairway."

Nira shook her head in agreement. "I don't even think our set of stairs is included on the map of this building."

Kevin said, "Those stairs are actually being hidden by the slide. People coming into this store might not notice the stairs. Even if people came over to this section of the room, the slide would attract their attention, so they might not see the stairs."

"You're right," Nira said.

"Can we go down the slide and see what's in the lower-level area of your store?" Heidi asked.

"Of course, let's all go down on the slide. It's a fun ride," Nira said as she moved closer to the slide. She slid down the slide first. As soon as she landed, she turned around and waved up at Kevin and Heidi. They waved back at her.

Kevin stared at Heidi for a few seconds before going down the slide. He then stood a few feet away from the bottom of the slide, waved at her, and smiled. Heidi smiled back as she started to go down the slide. When she arrived at the bottom, Kevin clasped onto her hands and slowly helped her to stand up. He then kept on holding onto her hands while he and Heidi stared into each other's eyes.

Nira suddenly asked, "Are you okay? Do you need any help?"

Kevin slowly let go of Heidi's hands while he said, "We're both fine."

Heidi glanced at Nira and then started to look around at the lower level of the store; it was much smaller than the upstairs section. There were some cupboards, a couple of restrooms, a refrigerator, a microwave, three computers, some chairs, and several eight-foot round tables.

Bera was seated at one of the tables. She was reading a newspaper while drinking a can of beer.

Kevin asked, "Can people really drink while they're at work here?"

Nira said, "As long as we do our work, we can drink whatever we want to, especially if we're on a break, like Bera is. Because we have so much freedom in this store, everyone's always happy."

Another lady came down the slide. Nira said to her, "Hi, Gama."

The new lady waved, went over to the refrigerator, and took out a soda. In one of the cupboards, she found some candy and chips, which she brought over to the same table where Bera was seated.

Bera said, "Thanks so much, Gama. It's been a long day, so I really do need some sugar and salt right now."

As Bera ate a piece of candy, Gama took out her cell phone and started to play a game.

Bera held out some candy to Heidi and Kevin. Heidi waved her head sideways, indicating that she was not interested. After Kevin waved his head in the same manner, Heidi said, "Thanks anyway, Bera."

"Don't you like chocolate?"

Heidi said, "I actually love chocolate, but whenever I'm having a tough day, I wait on eating comfort food until I'm relaxing at home."

Bera smiled. "Chocolate always helps me to feel better, even when I'm at work."

Heidi shook her head while saying, "People react to stress in different ways."

"You're right. People really do act differently." After pausing for a few seconds, Bera added, "Even when people are happy, they act differently."

Heidi smiled at Kevin; he smiled back at her while saying, "Sometimes, happy people act in the same way, just like we're all doing right now."

Bera asked, "What are we all doing that's the same right now?"

While smiling at Kevin, Heidi said, "We're all smiling at each other."

Suddenly, the floor vibrated slightly.

Kevin asked, "Did you all feel that vibration?"

Heidi, Bera, and Gama shook their heads up and down, indicating that they had all felt the vibration.

Heidi looked over at the slide. Mira was standing on the floor directly in front of the slide. Heidi asked her, "Did you just jump off of the slide?"

"Yeah, once I get to the bottom of the slide, then I jump. I'm trying to practice some of the moves normally done in my exercise class," Mira said.

"Do you jump around in your exercise class?"

"Yeah, we jump up and down on some steps."

"Are these stairs in a stairway?"

"No, they're heavy plastic aerobic steps that everyone uses."

"Oh, so you go to a step-aerobics class."

"Yeah, I do. I decided that practicing jumping at work would help me to become better in my aerobics class."

Heidi and Kevin looked at each other. Heidi then said, "That might explain the vibrations."

Mira asked, "Am I really the one who's making the vibrations?"

Kevin said, "Yes and no. I think something's happening with the slide and the floor connection. When you jump at the bottom of the slide, the connection logically should be okay, but it doesn't appear to be so. You should stop jumping until the connection section is checked out and repaired."

Mira sighed. "If there's a possible problem with how the slide's connected to the floor, we should probably all stop using the slide until it's fixed. We'll close it down." After pausing for a few seconds, she asked, "Can you please let me know if there are any more complaints about vibrations?"

Kevin smiled. "We'll let you know if anyone tells us about any more vibrations or something similar."

Kevin and Heidi said good-bye to everyone. They then climbed the stairs up to the main level of Amusement Plus. After they exited the store, Kevin said, "Since I need to stay at work for a little longer tonight, I'll do the report about our visit to Amusement Plus. You can look at the report tomorrow and just sign it, unless you want to change anything."

"Thanks a lot, Kevin. I actually was trying to figure out how things should happen if both of us needed to sign the report."

"It depends on the situation."

Heidi and Kevin walked down the corridor to the elevators. Kevin pressed the "up" and "down" buttons. When the first elevator arrived, it was going down. Even though Kevin was going up and Heidi was going down, Kevin stepped into the "down" elevator in order to be with Heidi. Several other people were already there. Kevin and Heidi stood near each other and communicated with their eyes.

Heidi began their eye conversation by making her eyes jump back and forth between the up and down buttons on the elevator's control panel. She then widened her eyes to show her surprise that Kevin was going down with her.

Kevin's eyes stared at the down button and then sparkled, showing his happiness to be with Heidi.

Heidi's eyes glanced up at her glasses' frame and then strongly blinked once, which was the code they used on their glasses to say "yes." She was obviously saying that she was happy about Kevin being with her.

Kevin shook his head, looked at his watch, and blinked his eyes a single time, which meant that he agreed with the idea of being together for an extra couple of minutes.

Heidi and Kevin both stared at each other with sparkling eyes, conveying their happiness about being with each other.

When the elevator arrived too quickly on the ground floor, Heidi frowned, sighed, and shrugged her shoulders. She then got off the elevator while Kevin pressed the "nine" button. Finally, they waved good-bye and stared at each other wide-eyed until the elevator doors had completely closed.

Heidi exited the building, got into her car, and left work. She drove onto North Main Street in Providence, Rhode Island. She soon was stopped at a red light. Her cell phone rang, so she pulled over to the side of the road, picked up her phone, and said, "Hi, Kevin. Is anything happening?"

"Tomorrow, we'll need someone to talk to people in the printing shop on the tenth floor of our building."

"Will this be about our need for a printer or about something else, like a security problem?"

"We just need a printer for some secure documents, Heidi. I think you already have the first one that we need printed on a flash drive."

"Yeah, I do. I'll check with people in the printing store about their prices and policies."

"Since they're so close by, Heidi, I'm hoping we'll be able to use them for most of our printing needs."

"I agree with you completely on that." Heidi paused before adding, "If the shop is open early enough, I'll stop by on my way to work tomorrow."

"The company's website says the shop is open at seven-thirty."

Heidi laughed. "I know where I'll be tomorrow morning before eight o'clock."

"I'll plan on watching my cell phone. If you need to text any questions to me, I'll try to answer them quickly."

"I'll see you tomorrow, Kevin."

"That sounds great."

"Good-bye for now." Heidi turned off her cell phone and placed it in her purse.

Hiding in Dexter's House

As Heidi touched her car keys with the intent of starting her car, she heard a sound on the window next to her left shoulder. A man in a gray suit was knocking on the window of her car. He was the same man who had followed her as she had walked out of the elevator inside her office building that morning.

Heidi opened her car's window slightly and asked, "What are you doing here? Are you following me again?"

The man was staring at Heidi as he said, "No, I live nearby." He pointed to the next side street.

"Then why did you stop here?"

"I was just curious. You looked like the same woman whom I met earlier today in the Pilgrim Office Building."

"Well, now you know; I am the same woman whom you were bothering earlier today." Heidi reached up to her glasses and pushed the camera button twice.

"What are you doing?"

"I'm just adjusting my glasses. What are you doing?"

"I was curious about what time you usually leave work."

"Now you know from seeing me here."

"Does everyone else in your office leave at the same time?"

"No, they don't." Heidi paused and then asked, "How about in your workplace? When do people leave?"

"They often have to work overtime."

"Your name is Moe, right?"

Moe's face tensed up as he asked, "Why do you think that's my name?"

"I heard it somewhere. Maybe one of your friends called you 'Moe.'"

"Now that you think you know my name, what's yours?"

"I don't know you well enough yet to tell you that."

"I wanted to ask you out on a date."

Heidi glanced at her watch before saying, "I have no time right now, but if you give me your contact information, I can call you later."

"Are you free tomorrow night?"

Heidi asked, "What if I am? Where will you want to take me?"

The gray-suited man raised his shoulders up high, pulled his cell phone out of his pocket, and turned the phone toward Heidi's face. Before he could take a picture, Heidi placed her right hand between her face and the man's phone. She then used her left hand to close her car's window.

While running back and forth next to Heidi's car, the man took multiple pictures of the driver's front and side window areas. After a minute, he stopped running, looked at the pictures on his cell phone, and started laughing in a sarcastic, loud fashion. He then pointed at one of the pictures and waved his camera in front of Heidi's face. On the man's cell phone was a picture of her face as she was trying to hide. Even though her right hand had hidden one of her ears, the picture still clearly showed her frightened face.

Heidi opened her mouth, but she was unable to talk. Her throat was all dry and scratchy. She positioned her right hand at her side and touched a Taser that was inside a holder attached to her belt. Her index finger moved upward and touched a cross that was carved into her belt. She said a silent prayer for the Lord's help.

The man moved his head downward until it was just two inches away from the driver's side window. Heidi's lips softly said the word "Amen" right before she opened the window. Her throat now felt better, so she was able to talk. She asked, "Can I see that picture?"

The man held his cell phone in front of her face.

Heidi looked at the phone and said, "I can't see the picture. Is it still there on your phone?"

The man stood up straight, turned his phone around, swiped at the screen, and smiled. He then bent forward again and started to turn the front of his phone toward Heidi's face. She pulled her Taser out of its holder. In less than a second, she had shot the man with electricity from her weapon.

He was in pain as he fell slightly sideways and landed on the hood of her car. While Heidi closed her car's window, she noticed another man running toward her. He was wearing sunglasses and looked like Joe Smith, the man who had driven through the Drive-through Technology office that morning.

Heidi glanced at the man on her car's hood; she then looked in her rearview mirror at the sunglass man, who was now about ten feet away. Sighing, she jumped out of her car and reached for her Taser. It was neither in her holder nor in her hand. She started to run across the street. The house on her left was the Jeremiah Dexter house. She glanced briefly at the front door of the house before running to the door on the side. When Heidi knocked, a lady immediately opened the door and asked, "What's going on?"

Heidi said softly, "I think someone's chasing me. Can I please come inside?"

"Of course you can." The lady held the door open and asked, "Should I call 911?"

"Yes, please do so, and I'll call my boss." Heidi stepped inside and then added, "Can you please lock the door?"

The lady was looking out into the street. "Someone's on top of a car."

"I know. We need to lock this door and call 911."

The lady frowned. "I've had CPR training. If that guy's injured, I might be able to help him."

Heidi glanced briefly at the lady while dialing Kevin's number. Heidi then waved her hand at the door, indicating that it should be closed, as she began talking into her cell phone: "Kevin, please send some officers out here right now. Possibly both of those men from this morning are following me and might be trying to get my personal or work information."

The lady listened intently to Heidi and then closed and locked the door.

Heidi still had her cell phone turned on and pressed against her ear as she asked the lady, "Did you notice anything happening out there in the street before you closed that door?"

The lady's voice was slightly jittery when she said, "The guy on top of the car just climbed down off of the car's hood. Another man helped him."

"Was the other man wearing sunglasses?"

The lady thought for a second before saying, "I don't know for sure, but he probably was. Nearly everyone is wearing sunglasses today."

Someone outside of the Dexter house knocked on the side door. The lady inside the house took a step toward the door before she turned and looked at Heidi, who shook her head sideways.

Heidi picked up a metal rod that was standing next to a fireplace. With her right hand strongly gripping the rod, Heidi walked into the room to her left and waved her empty hand, indicating that the lady should follow her.

The lady asked, "Are you thinking of using that fireplace poker as a weapon?"

Heidi grabbed more tightly onto the metal rod as she said, "I might have to."

"That's an historic item."

"I'll only use it if I really have to."

The lady's fast breathing and facial expression showed her fear as she quickly walked into the room and stood next to Heidi. The lady then dialed 911 on her cell phone and said softly, "We need police at the Jeremiah Dexter house in Providence, Rhode Island."

Before the lady could explain to the 911 person more about what was happening, a loud series of knocks came from one of the doors. A thundering voice from outside the house then said, "Open up, or we'll shoot through this door."

Heidi walked back into the first room, but she did not walk too close to the door. She yelled, "We just called the police. They should be here any minute."

The noise of a siren in the distance was heard. After only a few seconds, the siren was quite a bit louder. The police car sounded like it was within a block of the Jeremiah Dexter house.

Heidi stepped over to one of the windows and looked outside. No people were visible. There was some traffic in the street, but her car was the only one that was parked near the Dexter house. Heidi walked to a different window. A police vehicle with bright lights and a blaring siren drove through the red light and stopped in front of the Dexter house. Two police officers—with their guns drawn—got out of their car, ran up to the front door, and knocked.

The lady let them in. Heidi introduced herself to the officers and showed them her identification. She then put the fireplace poker next to the fireplace and started to explain what was happening. One of the officers turned on his cell phone, held it in front of Heidi's face, and said, "You're also talking to some other officers who will be here in just a minute."

"That's great," Heidi said. "The persons of interest have probably left in one or more cars, but it'll be nice to have everything checked out."

"Criminals often leave evidence behind at a crime scene."

Heidi smiled. "I know that happens a lot."

The officer laughed. "Yes, with your job, you have to know a lot about evidence and crime scenes."

"You're a police officer. You also know a lot about solving crimes."

"Thanks." The same officer asked Heidi and the Dexter-house lady for more information about the suspects and their actions. Both officers then began looking around the house. When the first two officers went upstairs, four more police officers came to the front door. Two of them came inside; the other two stayed outside to search in the yard and to talk to people in nearby houses.

Heidi and the lady stayed downstairs in front of one of the fireplaces. The lady said to Heidi, "I'm glad you told the officers your name, Heidi. Now I also know what your name is."

"What's your name?"

"I'm Providence Williams."

Heidi and Providence shook hands. Providence then asked, "Would you like to look around the house?"

"I'd love to." Heidi paused before adding, "While the officers are upstairs, we should probably stay down here."

"That sounds like a plan."

Heidi walked over to the fireplace and touched its brick surface.

Providence said, "More than one fireplace is in this building."

"Yeah, I noticed another one when I first walked in." Heidi pointed to the fireplace poker. "I should have placed that poker near the other fireplace. I'm sorry. I just realized now that I put it back into the wrong place."

"Don't worry about that poker. I'll put it back into its right position later."

"Thanks so much, Providence."

"You're welcome."

Heidi looked around the room as she said, "This is a great example of a colonial farmhouse."

"Have you ever been here before?" Providence asked.

"My parents brought me here when I was a teenager."

"Did they tell you, Heidi, about this building also being the office area for Preserve Rhode Island Headquarters?"

"Yes, Providence, they did. I still remember them talking about that. It's so neat to have people like you working for the preservation of history in an historic building."

"Your last name is Dexter, right?"

"Yes, it is." Heidi smiled. "I'm a descendant of Jeremiah Dexter. He was descended from the Reverend Gregory Dexter."

"Did you know your relatives, Jeremiah and Gregory, were both printers?"

"Yes, I've learned a lot about my ancestors by my parents telling me about them." Heidi paused and then added, "I'm also a descendant of William Brewster, so I've always thought of printing and religion as parts of my past, present, and future life."

Providence shook her head in agreement. "You have a lot of interesting connections in your life. You and I are also connected together."

"How are we connected?" Heidi asked.

"I'm a descendant of Roger Williams, so one of your ancestors printed things for one of my ancestors."

"That's so neat." Heidi's face showed her happiness. "Gregory Dexter was the printer for Roger Williams. After printing *The Bloudy Tenent of Persecution,* Dexter had to flee from England."

"Just a little while ago, you also had to run away."

Heidi looked down at her feet. "At least I only had to run for a short distance. I didn't have to run away from England and then travel on a boat all the way to New England."

Providence laughed. "You're right about that. You also had this house to run into and a cell phone to talk into for some extra help."

"Your ancestor, Roger Williams, also had to run away and hide," Heidi said.

"I know. He was banished. Then in January 1636, to avoid being arrested, he had to leave his home in Massachusetts during a blizzard." Providence's face showed her sorrow.

Heidi pointed her index finger at Providence. "You're the one who really helped me when I needed it. Thanks so much for letting me come into this house while those men were chasing me."

"You're welcome. I'm just so glad everything's worked out okay."

Heidi shook her head. "I think it's so wonderful that a descendant of Roger Williams helped a descendant of Gregory Dexter, just like Williams helped Dexter to escape back in the seventeenth century."

"Roger Williams really helped the Reverend Gregory Dexter by giving him some land in 1636. This house stands on a part of that land."

"When was this house built? Was it when Gregory Dexter was still alive?" Heidi asked.

"No, it was built in 1754 by Jeremiah Dexter, the great grandson of Gregory Dexter."

"I'm a descendant of both Gregory and Jeremiah Dexter," Heidi said.

"It's so neat that you're in this house today and talking about your ancestors."

Heidi said, "You're talking about your ancestry, too."

"I am. My ancestor, Roger Williams, gave this land to your ancestor, Gregory Dexter. Then Dexter and his ancestors owned the land for over three hundred years. In 1977, his ancestors gave the Dexter house to the organization that I work for: Preserve Rhode Island," Providence said.

"Like your ancestors donating land, Roger Williams's family also donated land," Heidi said.

"You're right." After pausing for a second, Providence added, "In 1871, Betsy Williams donated the land for Roger Williams State Park to the city of Providence."

Heidi said, "I love driving past the Roger Williams statue in the state park every day while I'm going to and from work."

"Roger Williams helped so many people, and his legacy is still helping so many people."

"Not only did Roger Williams help Gregory Dexter, but Dexter also helped Williams by publishing a book that he knew people in England wouldn't like," Heidi said.

"I know. *The Bloudy Tenent of Persecution* wound up being one of the books that were ordered to be burned."

Heidi looked at the fireplace and laughed. No fire was burning, but a teapot on its floor appeared to be waiting for one to be started. "I wonder where they burned the censored books. Was it inside of fireplaces or somewhere outside?"

"Books were often burned publicly in places where large groups of people could see what was happening. Occasionally in history, whole libraries were even burned," Providence said.

"That's interesting."

"What I think was even worse was when people were burned with their books." Providence frowned as she added, "For example, in 1553, Servetus was burned at the stake with some of his writings tied to his waist."

Heidi and Providence both stared at the teapot in the fireplace for a few seconds. Then Providence took Heidi on a tour of the first floor of the house. In addition to some historic items, modern-day office equipment was present: a laptop, some file folders, a bookcase, lamps, tables, and chairs.

The police officers came downstairs; they began to examine the doors and windows for evidence. Heidi and Providence went upstairs and looked around. A few minutes later, they came back down to the first floor. After Heidi and Providence filled out forms for the officers, everyone exchanged contact information and said "good-bye."

Heidi watched as the officers were driving away. Kevin's car then pulled up in front of the Dexter house. Kevin quickly exited his car and ran over to the front door. Heidi let him in.

"Are you both okay?" Kevin asked as he stared at Heidi's face.

"We're fine," Heidi said. She ran her right hand through her hair.

"You look beautiful, Heidi."

"Thanks, Kevin. You look beautiful, too, but in a handsome way."

Kevin smiled, reached forward, and held onto Heidi's hand. After a few seconds of silence, he said, "The police told me that you had to run, hide, and fight."

Heidi said, "I guess I did, but in a different order. I first did a little fighting near my car. Then I ran over to the side door of this house. Finally, I hid inside with Providence until the police came."

Kevin said, "You were so great today. You acted in a very logical way for the situation."

Providence shook her head, looked at Kevin, and said, "I thought the words 'run, hide, and fight' were used for interacting with terrorists."

"We have to run, hide, and fight in many difficult situations, not just with terrorists." Kevin sighed and then added, "Trying to stay safe is just a part of our lives in this world."

"Sometimes negative events have positive outcomes," Heidi said.

Providence's eyes widened, showing her surprise. "Why do you think that?"

"We both did some really great activities today. We were helping each other," Heidi said.

"You're right. You really did help me today. Thanks so much," Providence said.

Heidi let go of Kevin's hand and shook Providence's hand. "I thank you, too, Providence. You helped me even more than I helped you. Even though men were chasing me, you let me come into this house and stay with you."

"You're welcome." Providence looked at the unlocked door and said, "Whenever the Dexter house is open, people are always welcome here. My job includes letting people come in and telling them all about this historic house."

Heidi shook Providence's hand again while saying, "Like one of the Pilgrims, you stood your ground and did your job as an employee in this historic home."

Kevin also shook hands with Providence. He then squeezed Heidi's hand and said, "You both did a really great job today."

Heidi said, "Thanks, Kevin. You're also really great. You've helped me so much with my training at work."

"You're welcome," Kevin said.

Heidi and Kevin stared at each other.

Providence watched them silently for a moment before saying, "I'm so thankful about the police officers. They got here really fast."

Kevin kept looking at Heidi while he said to Providence, "I know they did. I was so happy when I found out that everyone was safe and uninjured."

Heidi was still staring at Kevin as she said, "Let's say a prayer to show God how thankful we truly are."

Providence said, "I think that's a great idea!"

They all closed their eyes and folded their hands. Kevin thanked their Lord and Savior for His continuous presence, His eternal love, and His help to turn negative events into positive endings.

Kevin, Heidi, and Providence all said "Amen" at the same time.

"That was a nice prayer," Heidi said.

"Thanks." Kevin smiled at Heidi and Providence. "It's so nice to be able to share our faith and our love with one another."

Heidi sighed in a happy way. "It is. I would again go through my run, hide, and fight activities, just so I could have this wonderful time together with a new friend and a colleague from my workplace."

Kevin and Heidi silently gazed at each other.

After a few seconds, Providence asked, "Are you two dating?"

Heidi glanced over at Providence and then looked down at the floor; she was obviously trying to hide her facial expression. After a few seconds, Heidi said, "We haven't been dating. We just love working together."

Providence laughed. "I should take a picture of you two while you're staring at each other. I think you would then realize that you really are dating, or that you should be dating."

Heidi pulled her hand away from Kevin's and said, "We might get into trouble if anyone finds out about us wanting to date each other."

Kevin opened his mouth and then closed it very firmly. He was trying to silence himself.

Providence said, "So, you two are hiding your love for each other from other people, rather than openly sharing your love?"

Heidi turned her face toward Providence, cleared her throat nervously, and changed the subject. "While I didn't like being followed by those men, I really enjoyed visiting with you this afternoon in this historic Dexter home."

Providence shook her head in agreement. "I really loved talking about our ancestors and the printing done by your ancestors."

"Printing was so important in debating ideas back then. It helped to initiate freedom of speech," Heidi said.

Kevin's face showed he was happy with the idea of free speech. He said, "I've been reading a book about printing and its effects on society."

Heidi asked, "What's the book's name?"

"It's called *The Printing Press as an Agent of Change: Communications and Cultural Transformations in Early-modern Europe.*"

Heidi said, "I read that book before. It says a lot about how printing had cultural effects."

Kevin held out his cell phone to Heidi while saying, "Here's a quote from that book. I was going to send it to you in a text message last night, but I got too busy with other things."

Heidi read the quote that was on Kevin's cell phone: "Since their commodities were sponsored and censored by officials as well as consumed by literate groups, the activities of early printers provide a natural connection between the movement of ideas, economic developments and affairs of church and state."[5]

Kevin said, "I love the whole idea of how printing helped to move ideas around to different people; printing also has helped with matters of economics, church, and state."

Heidi shook her head. "Whether an idea has been published in a book or is being read on a cell phone, it's still being communicated to different people."

Providence, who had been silently watching Kevin and Heidi talk to each other, said, "I love the different forms of communication, but I especially love watching two people—who are madly in love with each other—communicate with each other."

Heidi said, "I guess you love 'love.'"

"Everyone loves 'love,' especially people who are in love," Providence said as she glanced back and forth between Kevin and Heidi.

They both looked at Providence for a few seconds before focusing on each other with sparkling eyes and smiling lips. Their lips then parted slightly and moved outwards; they appeared to be kissing each other while being separated by more than a foot of space.

Providence asked, "Should I leave the room for a few minutes?"

While still staring at Heidi, Kevin said, "I know you're trying to help us, Providence. Thanks so much."

"You're welcome." After pausing, Providence added, "In fact, you're so welcome that you can stay right here for a little while and look for some evidence of those criminals."

Providence began walking toward the closest door, but before she had exited the room, Kevin and Heidi both turned to look at her. Kevin cleared his throat, and Providence turned around to look at him. From his shirt pocket, Kevin took out a small notepad, a business card, and a pen. He waved the business card at Providence, who walked back to stand close to him and Heidi.

Kevin gave the business card to Providence and said, "We should exchange contact information."

"Thanks for your card. Heidi and I have already traded email information, so Heidi can share that with you." After hesitating for a second, Providence added, "I'll write it down for you, too, Kevin."

"Thanks."

Providence glanced at Heidi and said, "I'm really curious. Please tell me when you two actually go out on a date together."

Heidi said, "If that happens, I'll send you a text message. However, it'll be sent as a code, so no one will be able to say for sure what's happening."

"What will the code be?" Providence asked.

"Love connection." Heidi looked at Kevin. "I'll obviously have to make certain Kevin's okay with me sending such a message before I actually send it."

Kevin smiled at Heidi. "I would love for you to send that coded text message to Providence. We'll be talking more about our first date sometime soon."

Before Kevin and Heidi had a chance to further discuss their love in front of Providence, Kevin's cell phone vibrated. With a frown, he answered his phone. He said "okay" a few times before turning off his phone.

Heidi asked, "Was that someone from our office?"

"Yeah, it was. The photos that you took were checked out. There weren't enough visible details to identify the man who said he was Joe Smith."

"Oh, so he could have been Joe Smith, or he could have been someone else."

"You're right." Kevin hesitated and then added, "They also couldn't find more information about that strange guy in the elevator, but was he the same guy who followed you out here?"

"Yeah, he was the same guy." Heidi smiled. "This time, I took a picture of him."

"That's so great. You can give me the photo right now, and I'll bring it back to our office."

Heidi touched her glasses, looked over at Providence, and then said to Kevin, "Can you also give me that other pair of glasses you were talking about?" She was obviously trying to hide from Providence the fact that her glasses contained a camera and a photo.

"Yeah, I have your other pair of glasses right here." Kevin took them out of his pocket. He and Heidi exchanged glasses.

After Heidi had put her new pair of glasses on, Kevin said, "I really want to stay here with you, Heidi, but I have to leave right now. I have to do some paperwork about what happened here. Plus, I'll be checking on the photo that you took."

"Are you also still going to your brother's birthday party?"

"Yeah, I am, but I'll see you early tomorrow morning." Kevin waved to both Heidi and Providence; he then walked out the side door, got into his car, and drove away.

Providence said, "I'll need to lock up in a minute."

"I also should get going." Heidi paused and then added, "It's strange how some things can't be too easily hidden. Even if Kevin and I had a lock and a key for our feelings, I think some of them would still be visible."

"Have you really never been out on a date with Kevin before?"

"We actually just know each other from work." After hesitating for a few seconds, Heidi said, "Kevin's been staring at me a lot lately, and I think he sometimes has made up excuses just to see me for an extra minute or two at work."

"You're in different offices?"

"Yeah, we are, but our offices are fairly close together." Heidi smiled and then said, "I love the location of my office."

"You'll have to text me when you actually start dating."

"I will."

Providence looked down at her watch. She then headed toward the side door, and Heidi followed her.

In front of the door, they paused. Heidi looked around the room before saying, "Even though I love where my office is located, you have a nice office, too. This house has such a great history. You must love working in an environment that connects directly to your job."

"I do." Providence opened the door and added, "Please feel free to connect yourself to your family's history by visiting this house again."

"I will. Thanks again for your help." Heidi and Providence waved good-bye to each other. Heidi then got into her car, went to a store to do some shopping, and drove to her apartment in Warwick. She made a microwave meal, watched TV, and read a few pages from a book. She then said out loud, "It would be so nice to dream about Dexter and the history of printing tonight. If I focus on that idea, I might even dream about it tonight." After silently praying for a few minutes, she fell asleep.

Hiding in a Dream with Gutenberg, Brewster, and Dexter

Heidi felt like she was lying on a floor, instead of in her bed. She opened her eyes and then gasped in surprise. She actually was lying on a floor under a bed. She slid out from under the bed's frame and found herself inside a large wooden chest. She opened up the top of the chest and climbed out. She was now hidden in the back section of a fireplace. A large pot and a pile of logs were piled in front of her, so she could not see anything in the room.

After she pushed the pot aside, climbed over the logs, and stared at the room, Heidi said out loud, "This can't be real. I must be dreaming."

The room appeared to be from a different century. Multiple slanted wooden tables with chairs were arranged in a square inside the room. Long-haired, bearded men in robes were seated in the chairs in front of the tables. They were very slowly making handwritten copies of pages from books. The pages in the books, as well as the papers being used to copy them, were really thick. Discoloration was making some of the words tough for Heidi to see, but the men were not having any problems.

Heidi tried to read the words on one of the papers and then said, "Those words look like Latin, and the letters appear to be some kind of shorthand or an antique font."

The paper with the unreadable words on it shook itself slightly, showing its agreement with her comment.

A breeze came through an open window and picked up the paper. As it flew through the air, the paper was hit multiple times by the sun's rays. With each stream of light, the words and appearance of the paper were changed. Finally, the paper arrived in front of Heidi and stopped changing. She said, "Oh, now you're written in modern English in a normal font, so I can read everything."

The words written on the paper were: "He said to them, 'Is a lamp brought in to be put under the bushel basket, or under the bed, and not on the lampstand? For there is nothing hidden, except to be disclosed; nor is anything secret, except to come to light. Let anyone with ears to hear listen!'" (Mark 4:21 – 23 NRSV).

"I love those verses. Jesus is telling his disciples to share their faith, instead of hiding it." Heidi looked back across the room at all the scribes who were still busily copying words onto new pages. "You're all sharing faith because you're making copies of the Bible."

One of the scribes said "yes" by shaking his head up and down.

"Are those papers really paper? They look a little bit too thick. Are they some kind of early version of paper, such as parchment or papyrus?"

No one answered her question. The tallest scribe moved to a table in the back of the room. Another man gave a completed paper to the tallest scribe, who compared the newly written paper to the original one. Errors were being looked for, so they could be fixed. No errors, though, were found. Then an illustrator drew some pictures and other designs in the blank sections of the page. Finally, one page was completed.

"This process is taking forever," Heidi said. She glanced over at the one window in the office. The sun had initially been in the window, but now the moon was there. As Heidi watched, the sun and moon changed position multiple times. After weeks went by, some more papers were finished. Once enough pages were completed, the papers were arranged and bound together inside of a leather cover.

"Too many months are passing. Not enough books are being made for people to read. Plus, the cost of the books will be too high for most people back then to buy."

Pieces of gold and silver started flying in and out of the window. Heidi said, "This money is talking to me. It's trying to say that, before the Gutenberg printing press, the cost of these books was definitely too expensive."

The process suddenly changed. Everything was still being done in slow motion, but the men were now carving words and pictures into wooden blocks. The completed blocks were used to put ink onto pages, which were then bound together into books. As Heidi watched, some of the older-looking blocks became cracked and had to be carved again from fresh pieces of wood.

"This process is still taking forever," Heidi said. "I know that books were very expensive before Gutenberg, but I never realized how expensive and how slow the whole process really was."

The sun outside of the office's window paused briefly in its shifts with the moon. Bright beams of light drew some words across the sky: "We're in the middle of the fifteenth century."

A wooden rectangular table appeared in the center of the room. A man was experimenting with some ink, paper, parchment, and different parts of a printing press, including a giant wooden screw and a handle to press the screw down on top of some paper. On another table were some movable metal letters, numbers, and images.

Heidi said, "You must be Johannes Guttenberg, the inventor of the Guttenberg printing press."

Guttenberg asked, "Is anyone here?"

"Yes, I'm here, and my name's Heidi."

Guttenberg sighed. "I thought I heard something, but I guess it was nothing." He noticed the window was open, walked over to it, looked outside, and then closed the shutters. "I need to be really careful and keep my invention secret, so no one steals it."

Heidi told him, "There weren't any copyright laws back then, so you had no choice. You had to be quiet about your invention."

Another man suddenly appeared in the room. He introduced himself by saying, "I'm Johann Fust." He and Gutenberg talked for a while and then came to a financial agreement. Fust loaned some money to Gutenberg, who agreed to produce copies of the Gutenberg Bible and then to pay back the loan to Fust.

Fust and Gutenberg left the room. Heidi opened the window and saw many sun and moon rotations. Then Gutenberg appeared outside the open window. He was in a different building and making copies of the Gutenberg Bible.

Before Gutenberg was finished producing the Bible, Fust needed his money back and took Gutenberg to court. The court decided that Fust could have Gutenberg's presses, as well as the almost-completed copies of the Gutenberg Bible.

A modern book flew out of the sun and moved through the air toward Heidi. Right in front of her face, the book opened itself up. On one of the pages, Fust was quoted as claiming himself and Schoffer, rather than Gutenberg, to be the inventors of the printing press: "The present copy of the Psalms … was so fashioned thanks to the ingenious discovery of imprinting and forming letters without any use of a pen and completed with diligence to the glory of God by Johann Fust, citizen of Mainz, and Peter Schoffer of Gernsheim."[6]

Heidi said, "Even though Fust and Schoffer claimed to be the inventors of the printing press, Gutenberg really was. He was eventually given appropriate credit for his invention. 'The court documents from the lawsuit … later served to give credit to Gutenberg for his invention.'[7]"

Beams of sunlight flowed through the room until they landed on the rectangular table in the middle of the historic office. A completed copy of the Gutenberg Bible now lay in the middle of the table.

Heidi said to the Bible, "I heard that 'several years' were needed for '20 workers to print about 175 copies of' the Gutenberg bible.[8]"

The Bible on the table sent multiple beams of light toward the open window. The streaks of light went flying out the window and over to other copies of the Bible.

"Well, I guess a lot of tables, bookcases, museum displays, and churches have the other copies."

The Bible moved itself up and down on the table, showing its agreement to Heidi.

She then said, "One of my favorite Bible verses is about the word of God. The verse says: 'Your word is a lamp to my feet and a light to my path' (Ps. 119:105 NRSV)."

The Bible lit up again with beams of light flowing from its interior.

Heidi said, "Even with my eyes being sensitive to light, I completely love the brightness of your light."

The Bible became even brighter.

"I guess my eyes are sensitive to light in a very positive way because they are always trying to look for you, my God. Whenever I see light, it's like my soul becomes happy, resulting in even more light," Heidi said with a big smile on her face.

The Bible fluttered its 1,282 pages at Heidi.

"According to *Historyofinformation.com*, Gutenberg's 42-line Bible had 1,282 pages,[9] so you must be that Bible, right?"

The Bible fluttered several of its pages up and down; it was saying "yes" to Heidi's question. The Bible then sent a beam of light out through the window. The light beam connected to the sun, which then changed positions multiple times with the moon. A light ray beamed back into the room, landing on an old pine chest that was in one of the room's corners.

Heidi asked, "Are you the chest that William Brewster brought over on the *Speedwell* and then on the *Mayflower* in 1620?"

The keyhole on the front of the chest moved up and down; it was saying "Yes."

Heidi walked over to the front of the chest and said, "I'm a descendent of William Brewster."

The keyhole became bigger and wider until it looked like a giant smile. It seemed very happy to meet her.

Heidi said, "For years, I've heard so many wonderful things about my relative and your owner."

The keyhole curved outward slightly on one side, so it now looked like an ear that was listening to Heidi as she said, "I've read about Brewster being 'a student among radicals at Cambridge, a witness to the power plays of the Elizabethan Court, a postmaster at Scrooby, a printer of forbidden books in Leyden, … and … the single most important individual in the formation and development of the group of settlers known as the Pilgrims.[10]"

The chest moved its top up and down, making clapping noises. It was showing its agreement about the importance of William Brewster.

"When he left England to go to Amsterdam in 1608, he was trying to avoid prosecution for his religious views. He really wanted to worship God as one of the separatists," Heidi said.

The chest agreed again.

"When Brewster secretly published forbidden books, like *Perth Assembly,* he was showing his desire for political freedom and free speech."

The Brewster chest made more clapping noises.

Heidi turned on her smart phone, searched online, and then read out loud some information from the Pilgrim Hall Museum's website about Brewster's printing press: "Between 1617 and 1619, this press, known informally today as the 'Pilgrim press,' printed and distributed controversial religious books. These books were banned by English law and had to be smuggled into the country."[11]

The Brewster chest opened up the top part of itself. Some books were inside, but they appeared to be partially hidden in a shadow.

"I know some of the books published back then were hidden from some people. However, a lot of them were distributed to the general public. Distributing forbidden books back then was a great way to have political and religious debates. It was also a way to be put into prison. That's why Brewster had to go into hiding for a couple of years; he didn't want to be found and put into prison."

The Brewster chest changed its shape into a bed and then some papers fell onto its top.

Heidi thought for a few seconds before saying, "You're trying to show me that you were used as a bed and a desktop, in addition to being a chest with needed storage space."

The chest changed back into its original shape as a rectangular wooden chest.

Heidi looked inside the Brewster chest and said, "Brewster had so many books and so much going on that he needed something like this for his 1620 journey on the *Mayflower.* He also became the church elder for the Pilgrims until he died in 1644."

The Brewster chest again made clapping noises. Then its books jumped out of the chest, flew across the room, and landed on a bookcase, which was standing between a fireplace and the open window.

"Whose bookcase are you?" Heidi asked.

One of the books in the bookcase lay down on its side and then opened up its cover. Words on the open page appeared cloudy and then changed into real words: "I think I'm yours."

"Are you really? My books and bookcases look a lot newer than you are."

The words on the cloudy, open page changed to different words that asked Heidi a question: "What's your name?"

"I'm Heidi. I'm a descendant of William Brewster and Gregory Dexter."

A different cloudy page of the book flipped itself open and showed these words: "You must really love things like printing presses and books."

"I also love bookcases. My house has four of them."

A picture of a library appeared on the cloudy page with these new words added: "Your house must look similar to William Brewster's library."

"I know about his library. It had hundreds of books, which, according to the Reverend Ashbel Steele, showed some important aspects about Brewster's mind and activities. Brewster's mind 'acted upon all the various agitating questions of the time, not only respecting their own colony, but those around them, and in connection with the Indian tribes, and respecting changes abroad, that required corresponding action at home.'[12]"

The cloudy page now looked sunny as it said to Heidi: "Brewster was very respectful of everyone."

"He really was a great person. Even in the last seven years of his life, 'he continued to be the wise and experienced counselor, the conciliatory medium in matters of debate, and active assistant in matters of legislation.'[13]"

The cloudy-turned-sunny page turned toward the other books on the bookcase and then said, "Brewster must have loved reading his books."

Heidi said, "Some of the books in the Brewster library were forbidden ones; the authorities in England didn't want people to read them, but Brewster obviously read them anyway."

The open book closed itself and stood back up among the other books in the bookcase. A different book—one printed more recently—opened itself up; its name was *Gregory Dexter of London and New England 1610-1700;* its publication date was 1949.

Heidi said to the book, "Oh, you have some information about my other ancestor: Gregory Dexter."

The book turned its pages until it arrived at a section titled "A Printing Job for Prynne."

Heidi said, "I've read this part of the book. It talks about Dexter and two other printers; all three of them were charged in court with printing some books for Prynne. Dexter told the court that he had done the printing, but he also said that he had wrapped the books inside of some paper. Instead of distributing the books to the public, he had carried them—hidden in the paper—to a house. He then printed an epistle for Prynne."

A question appeared in the air above the open book. "What's an epistle?"

"It's a formal letter. Prinne's was eight pages long. His epistle was supposed to be a secret without the printer's name on it. "As soon as they had finished one perfect proof Dexter threw the original copy into the fire, ... he had been directed by Prynne's letter to take this precaution."[14]

When Heidi picked up the book to place it back into the bookcase, the left side of the room became warm. She looked in the direction of the heat. The fireplace next to the Brewster chest now was alive with a crackling, noisy fire. The fire yelled, "I'm the censor here. Whatever I don't like gets burned!"

Heidi asked, "Are you burning pamphlets and books printed by Dexter?"

"I'm burning up whatever needs to be kept secret and away from people."

Heidi put the book that she was holding into the bookcase.

The fire said, "Sometimes, I've been burning up books for people like Dexter, who was hiding his publication activities to stay out of jail. At other times, I burn up books that governments want me to censor, like that one." The fire's flames pointed toward one of the oldest books in the bookcase.

"Is that book by Roger Williams or William Prynne?"

"I don't know, but it's one that I have already burned up."

"Then why is it still on the shelf of a bookcase?"

"When I burn up books, sometimes additional copies of the books are out there somewhere."

"I know that William Prynne was publishing things for the Puritans. He started to do this in 1627."

"Yes, I've had a lot of fun burning up some of his pamphlets."

"In 1633, Prynne was put into prison. A year later, parts of his ears were cut off."

"Even with his ears being chopped off, he didn't listen to the government's censors."

Heidi laughed. "Maybe he couldn't hear them too well."

The fire crackled. "He had the inner parts of his ears left. He could hear fine."

Heidi looked at her cell phone, which was making noises. She swiped the screen and saw an online encyclopedia article. After she read the article, she said, "Even being in prison with parts of his ears missing, Prynne still said what he wanted to say. He just had to hide his identify. According to one of our modern encyclopedias, while in prison, Prynne "issued anonymous pamphlets attacking Laud and other Anglican prelates, resulting in further punishments: the stumps of his ears were shorn (1637) and his cheeks were branded with the letters S.L., meaning 'seditious libeler'—though he preferred 'Stigmata Laudis' ('the marks of Laud')."[15]

The fire crackled again. "The censors put some letters onto Prynne's cheeks, but Prynne didn't even listen to the meaning of those letters."

"I think the censors were the ones with incorrect meanings. They should have chopped off their own ears."

The sides of the fire's flames indented slightly inward. The fire now looked like its own ears had been chopped off. Even so, it was still able to throw some words into the air: "The censors are the ones who carved the letters into Prynne's cheeks. They created the letters, so they had the right to say what the letters meant."

"Prynne was a Christian and was comparing his wounds to the ones done to Jesus Christ. With Prynne's publications, he was just trying to say his religious views. The anti-Puritans shouldn't have censored him."

"Censors are good for society. They help to maintain order."

Heidi thought for a few seconds before saying, "I agree with you partially about that. Sometimes censors are needed, so people don't say lies or other hurtful things about each other."

"Have you been bullied before?"

"Yes, when I was a kid, there were several bullies who kept on trying to hurt me." Heidi sighed. "A censor would have been nice."

"There are other times when censors are needed, too."

"I know. Sometimes, there are security issues, so some documents are classified." Heidi hesitated and then added, "Some people believe in free speech for everything in this country."

"Would you want a credit card company to use free speech and yell out your personal information to the whole world?"

"No, I'd never want that to happen." Heidi inhaled and looked over at the bookcase. "Today in our country, things might not be too bad. However, historically, censors have done some extremely inappropriate things. They have often tried to stop people from discussing correct and good views on different topics."

A book on the top shelf of the bookcase started shaking and fell down to the floor. Some papers flew on top of the book and wrapped themselves around its exterior. The book's title, author, and publisher were now completely hidden. Heidi lifted up the book and tried to remove the papers, but they were stuck firmly onto the book's cover. She was not even able to open up the book and read any of its interior pages. After glancing over at the fire, Heidi placed the book behind her back, so even the paper wrapped around the book was now hidden.

The fire's flames glared too brightly in the direction of the hidden book. "I know where you are, book! You might be hiding yourself from your audience, but you can't hide yourself from your censor."

Heidi laughed. "That book really is hiding from its censor. It's inside of some paper and behind a person."

The fire's flames changed from yellowish red to a completely red color. "Heidi, you must be the publisher or the author." The fire's flames grew so large that they exploded outward from the fireplace.

Heidi moved back several steps. Some of the flames blazed close to Heidi while others jumped toward the bookcase.

Heidi screamed. Tears flew out from her eyes and landed on one of the fire's extended flames. The water from her tears made the fire pause in its forward motions.

Heidi said, "Get back into your own space, Mr. Fire."

"I can go wherever I want to go."

"No, you can't be all over everywhere. You're a censor. Your place is inside the fireplace."

"No, it isn't." The fire reached out close to Heidi, who refused to move backward away from the censoring flames.

Heidi said, "If you censor everything, there will soon be nothing left for you to censor. Lots of people will cry and spit at you. I don't think you'd want all of that water to take away your life."

The fire's flames paused.

Heidi stepped forward and spit at the fire. Its flames hesitated and then went back into the fireplace.

Heidi turned her back to the fire. She was trying to ignore its flames while replacing the hidden book onto its own shelf in the bookcase. Heidi then looked at some of the other books. She picked up one that was published by Dexter in 1643 and written by Roger Williams: *A Key into the Language of America*. "I love this book's information about the language and culture of the native people. I also love the poems and the vocabulary listings."

Heidi opened the book to the 'Introduction' section and read out loud: "A little Key may open a box, where lies a bunch of Keys."[16]

The fire was still inside the fireplace as it asked, "What did Roger Williams need a key for?"

"He wasn't talking about a real metal key. He was rather using a metaphor in which he was comparing language to a key."

"How is language like a key?"

"It can open a box, which will then contain a lot of other keys. Then people can open up other boxes with the additional keys."

"What are the other keys?"

"One example of these other keys is mentioned in *Roger Williams in an Elevator:* 'his use of the word "key" showed that he was trying to unlock knowledge about culture, as well as about language'.[17]"

On the shelves of the bookcase, multiple books opened and closed their covers, sounding as if they were clapping in joy over the idea of more knowledge within themselves, as well as within each other.

Heidi said, "Look at all of those books. I guess Roger Williams's book did result in a lot of other books."

One of the books opened itself up to a page that said "1643." It then tilted itself forward toward Heidi, inviting her to notice the page number.

Heidi frowned. "Are you saying only 1643 other books were published? I don't believe that."

The book fluttered its pages toward the sun that was outside of the window. The sun suddenly changed into the moon, and the book fluttered its pages some more. It then opened again to the page that said "1643."

"Oh, you must be talking about 1643 as a year."

The book moved itself up and down; it was trying to say "yes" with its version of body language.

Heidi said, "You're right about the year. Even back in 1643, many people loved *A Key into the Language of America.* They liked having the knowledge to help them communicate with the native people in New England."

The fire in the fireplace became smaller. Heidi said, "I guess at least one book by Roger Williams—*A Key into the Language of America*—was safe from the fires happening in England."

One of the books on the bookcase opened up to a blank page; these words then appeared: "Other writings by Roger Williams were burned, though, including perhaps his most famous book: *The Bloudy Tenent of Persecution*."

The fire in the fireplace became large again and sent a flame outward toward the book. Heidi moved her left hand in front of the book. She managed to block the censoring fire from burning her copy, but her hand turned red from being burned.

The flame wove past Heidi, grabbed onto a second copy of the same book, and burned it.

"How can you do something like that?"

"I'm a fire. Even in a fireplace, I have enough heat to jump forward and burn up books."

"You burned me, too."

"That's because you connected yourself to the book."

"I'm thankful not all copies of this book were burned." Heidi smiled as she gripped her copy tightly with both of her hands.

"Back in the seventeenth century, many people wanted that book to be censored."

Heidi sighed. "You're right about that. At least the author knew *The Bloudy Tenent of Persecution* would be censored, so some copies were distributed secretly to different people."

"Why do you think Roger Williams knew about the upcoming censorship?"

"His book was secretly published by Gregory Dexter. There weren't a lot of publishers back then, so people were able to figure out who the publisher was. Because of people's reactions to that book, Dexter had to quickly leave England in 1644 with Roger Williams."

Heidi stared at the fire, which was inside its fireplace again. She then looked at the bookcase. "I love how all the books in here are talking to me." Heidi glanced out the window. "I wonder if there are any people or farm animals outside."

The front door opened, and some cows walked into the room. They paused to stare at the fire, which was flaring up again.

Heidi asked one of the cows, "Are you supposed to be in here, rather than outside?"

"We're free to roam wherever we want to roam."

"You're a cow. You can't just go running into someone's house," Heidi said.

"Yes, we can. The grant for Providence and Pawtuxet says that 'if their cattle strayed beyond the town's boundaries it would not be regarded as trespass.'[18]"

"Things have changed since then," Heidi said.

The flaming fire made loud noises, showing its agreement with Heidi.

The same cow asked, "How have things changed?"

"Cows are usually fenced-in somewhere," Heidi said.

"Why can't we be free?"

"You need to be kept safe from things like cars on the roads." Heidi looked at the fireplace and added, "Also, fires can jump out of their fireplaces, so you need to be careful."

"I know to watch out for fires. However, are cars really dangerous?"

"Yes, they're even more dangerous than fires are."

"Are you saying there's less freedom in your century than there was in the seventeenth century?"

"No, I'm saying there are more fences. Even regarding freedom of speech, people in my world are not that free. They are often censored or have to censor themselves."

A horn started blowing from within the fireplace.

The cow looked at the fireplace and then out the window. "Is that noise being made by a fire or a car?"

Heidi said, "It's some kind of strange noise. Maybe a censor is trying to keep us from talking to each other."

The horn kept getting louder until it woke Heidi up. She then realized the blowing horn was her alarm clock, rather than a fire or a car. She also realized that the timing of the alarm had censored her freedom to dream some more about books, fires, censors, and even cows. With a frown on her face, she pressed heavily against the "off" button on her alarm clock, which immediately became silent. Heidi laughed and then said out loud, "I'm censoring my alarm clock. Censorship is a great way to hide things, especially too-noisy alarm clocks."

PRINTING

HEIDI JUMPED OUT OF bed and quickly got ready for work. By seven forty-five, she had driven to her office building, parked, walked inside, and reached the elevators. A man who looked similar to the gray-suited man was standing in the front lobby. His shirt was a different color, and his hair was shorter. Also, he had no beard. He had already pushed the "up" button for the elevator that was closest to the front door.

Heidi walked up next to him and asked, "Were you near the Dexter house in Providence yesterday?"

The man kept staring at the floor and did not even look at her.

Heidi moved forward slightly and took a picture of the side of his face with her glasses. Before she could ask him any other questions, the elevator door opened. The man quickly walked into the elevator. He did not hit any of the elevator's buttons, but instead moved into one of the back corners.

Heidi followed the man into the elevator and hit the "ten" button. Before the doors could close, a lady with a red purse walked into the same elevator. The lady pressed one of the elevator's buttons, but the man still did not do anything. He just stood there quietly staring at the elevator's floor until the elevator started moving upward.

Heidi began typing a text message on her cell phone to Kevin: "One of the Dexter house criminals might be here."

Before she had a chance to finish the message, the man inside the elevator asked her "Is that message going to anyone important?" He moved closer to Heidi and looked down at her cell phone.

Heidi frowned as she turned her phone upside down, so the man could not read the content. She then said, "You shouldn't be reading things on my phone."

"Why can't I?"

"It's my phone; it doesn't belong to you."

"You have your phone turned on in a public place," the man said.

"Even so, some things are still private."

The man moved the left front corner of his jacket outward and tried to touch Heidi's purse. She stepped away as she asked, "Are you trying to steal my whole purse or just some information from my credit cards?"

"I'm just stretching." By the tone of his voice, Heidi knew he was lying.

The elevator doors opened up. With a scared expression on her face, the red-purse lady got off at the seventh floor. The man stayed in the elevator with Heidi.

When Heidi exited on the tenth floor, the man followed her into the corridor. After only walking for about five feet, she turned to face him. "Stop following me, or I'll call the cops."

"I'm not following you."

"Then where are you going?"

He looked down the corridor and pointed his finger at one of the businesses. "I'm going over there to the doughnut shop."

As Heidi watched the man walk toward the doughnut shop, she finished typing her text message and quickly sent it with the photo to Kevin. After the man entered the doughnut shop, Heidi walked over to the printing shop and went inside.

In the front section of the office was a waiting area for customers. Nine chairs were placed around several tables. Pamphlets and small models of printing presses sat in the centers of the tables. In the middle of the room were three desks with laptops. Men were seated at each of the desks. In the back of the room were several doors, bookcases, a bulletin board, and displays of marketing materials, including banners and posters.

Before Heidi had a chance to sit down, she received a message from Kevin: "I received the picture you just sent. I agree with you. He could be the same gray-suited man who followed you to the Dexter house yesterday. I'll have the facial-recognition people compare the two photos we have. The man's shorter hair and missing beard are probably his attempt to hide his identity."

Heidi texted back: "Is there any way I can bring him in for questioning?"

"I wish there were. We first need some kind of positive identification. I'll let you know as soon as the facial-recognition people are done."

"Thanks." Heidi put her cell phone in her purse as she stared at one of the tables in the printing office. In the center of the table was a metal model of a printing press. It had a handle, a roller, a horizontal lever, and a large screw near its top. Heidi picked up the model and looked at the bottom metal section. The printing company's name, "123 Printing 4 All," was engraved into its metal base. Heidi returned the model printing press back to its position on the table.

On the same table was another small model of a printing press. This one was labeled as a reproduction of the Gutenberg printing press. On top of the model was a quote about the importance of printing in conveying knowledge and freedom for people's minds: "Gutenberg's invention of the mechanical printing press made it possible for the accumulated knowledge of the human race to become the common property of every person who knew how to read—an immense forward step in the emancipation of the human mind.[19]"

One of the employees stood up and walked over to where Heidi was standing. Heidi looked at the employee and said, "I love that quotation about printing giving people more knowledge and freedom."

"I like the whole idea of freedom of the press and how it has helped people to better learn, think, and communicate with others," the employee said.

"I'm a descendant of Gregory Dexter and William Brewster, so I love printing in almost any form."

"This is really interesting. My name is Paul, and I'm a descendant of Roger Williams."

"This is really, really, really interesting!" Heidi said.

"Did our ancestors know each other?"

"Yeah, they did." Heidi paused for a few seconds before adding, "My ancestors, Dexter and Brewster, both knew your ancestor, Roger Williams. However, I don't know for sure if my ancestors knew each other."

"Dexter and Brewster both came to New England, right?" Paul asked.

"Yeah, they did, but I don't know if they ever actually met each other."

"Because of the small number of people in Massachusetts and Rhode Island back then, it's logical that they at least knew about each other," Paul said.

"Dexter and Brewster probably knew about each other, but I don't know if they ever actually met." Heidi sighed. "I do love to imagine how my ancestors met each other, and I've had dreams about them printing books together. However, they might not have seen each other in person. Brewster died in Duxbury, Massachusetts, in 1644, which is when Dexter had to flee from England and settle in Rhode Island."

"Before then, back in 1638, Roger Williams gave Dexter some land in Providence," Paul said as he pulled at his tie. An image of the Roger Williams statue in Roger Williams State Park was on his tie. Paul's blue shirt made a great background for his tie. The Roger Williams image appeared to have a blue sky for its background.

Heidi's eyes moved from Paul's blue shirt to his blue eyes. She then said, "I know about that wonderful gift of some land. Dexter was also one of the thirty-eight people who signed an agreement in Rhode Island on July 27, 1640.[20] The agreement was to form a Rhode Island government, so Dexter must have been in Rhode Island in 1640. He probably then went back to England to work at his publishing company."

"Even if the facts show Dexter and Brewster were both in New England in 1640, that doesn't mean they ever really met each other," Paul said.

Heidi sighed. "At least in 1640, Dexter was probably in Rhode Island, and Brewster usually would have been in Plymouth Colony."

"If they did a little bit of travelling, they may have met each other."

"In 1646, Dexter helped some people to set up a printing business in Boston, so he did leave Rhode Island at least that one time," Heidi said.

"It's possible that Dexter and Brewster really did meet each other."

"Yeah, it's possible, but they definitely would have heard some information about each other, especially since they both had experience with the printing industry."

"You're right." Paul shook his head up and down. "Dexter and Brewster also both knew Roger Williams, and all three of them were important religious leaders in New England during the first half of the seventeenth century."

Heidi's cell phone vibrated. She took it out of her purse, checked the caller's identity, and said to Paul, "Please excuse me for a minute."

Paul shook his head and walked over to his desk.

Heidi began talking into her phone: "Yeah, I'm at the printing office." After listening for a few seconds, she looked around the room before saying, "Only employees are here right now, so I should be able to talk to them okay."

Heidi turned off her phone and waved at Paul. He walked over to Heidi and asked, "What do you need to talk to us about?"

"We need a company to do some printing of classified material."

Paul laughed. "We're doing what our ancestors did."

"Are we really?"

"Yeah, I think so. Back in the seventeenth century, our ancestors worked together to write and print things."

"You're right. They did, except the roles today have been switched around. Back then, Gregory Dexter was the printer for the author Roger Williams. Now, in our century, a descendant of Gregory Dexter will be the author, and a descendant of Roger Williams will be the printer."

"Hopefully, the end result will be very positive for whatever material my company will be printing for yours."

"Yeah, it should be." Heidi smiled. "After *A Key into the Language of America* was printed, many people in Old England and New England responded in very positive ways."

"People liked that book by Roger Williams for its translations of some of the native people's language. The information about native culture was also very helpful in making positive political connections in New England."

"If only everything in our century worked out as nicely, our world would be a better place," Heidi said.

"Back in the seventeenth century, the King Phillips War and other problems happened, but at least Roger Williams and his books helped for a little while."

Heidi shook her head in agreement. "After so many people liked his first book, a lot of the same people had very negative reactions to his next book: *The Bloudy Tenent of Persecution for Cause of Conscience.*"

"When Dexter printed that book in 1644, he had to flee from England and go to Providence."

"*The Bloudy Tenent of Persecution* was ordered to be burned in London, and thankfully, Roger Williams also had just left to go back to New England."

Paul said, "I didn't realize that Dexter was also the printer for *The Bloudy Tenent.* I thought the printer was unknown."

"The printers back then were often unknown. Occasionally, even the authors were unknown."

Paul laughed. "They were sometimes unknown on purpose."

"You're right. For some publications, they had to hide their identity. Depending on what they were saying, they could be thrown into prison, have their ears cut off, be killed, or be banished."

"Was Dexter really the printer for *The Bloudy Tenent of Persecution?*" Paul asked.

"Yeah, he was. I just read a book about Dexter's life." Heidi thought for a few seconds and then said, "The author of the book, Bradford Swan, said that, 'after 300 years, we must recognize Gregory Dexter as the printer of this book, one of the landmarks in Anglo-Saxon thought and possibly the most important book by an American prior to the Revolutionary War.'[21]"

"You have a good memory."

"Thanks. I practice memorization a lot," Heidi said.

"So Dexter had to leave England and go to Providence after that book was published?"

"Yeah, he did. That's also when Roger Williams quickly left London and returned to Providence," Heidi said.

"It must have been awful to have to run away after printing something debatable."

"Yeah, things back then were tough." Heidi sighed and then added, "Even today, though, problems with printing happen."

"I know about how the copyright and defamation rules need to be followed. Otherwise, lawsuits, being fired, and other things can happen. Thankfully, I have a clean record," Paul said.

"Yes, you do. My company has already checked you out." Heidi smiled. "When you sent information to the police about a potential counterfeiter, we heard about your report."

"Did you really?"

"Yeah, we were contacted about that person of interest who wanted you to copy counterfeit bills." Heidi frowned. "There are so many strange criminals in our world."

"I know. We had our security system upgraded, just in case a counterfeiter wants to break in some night and print some counterfeit bills while we're closed."

"We were told about the security system improvement, and I think it's really great what you're doing to maintain your company's honesty and reputation."

"I guess it's nice to know that a new customer—someone like you—will trust us," Paul said.

"Since our ancestors, Roger Williams and Gregory Dexter, trusted each other and were great friends for so many years, we'll have to become friends, too," Heidi said.

"Yes, we'll need to do that. I'll send you a friend request on Facebook."

"I'll watch for it." Heidi opened her purse and pulled out some paperwork. "I have some information and forms here. We'll need to discuss the nature of this printing project. Then you'll need to sign some forms."

The noise of an opening door made Heidi turn around. A lady was walking into the room. Her steps were very purposeful and strong; she had complete control over the movements of her feet as they strode forward while inside of her three-inch heels. A hat with gold triangles on its edges was sitting on top of her head; the hat looked almost like a crown. The lady had a brown leather briefcase in her right hand. After taking just a few steps, she paused and set the briefcase on the table that was closest to the front door. One of the employees stood up and walked to the front of the room to help her.

Paul said to Heidi, "Let's go into the conference room and talk about what your company needs."

Heidi followed Paul to the back of the room. He opened the central door and held it open, so Heidi could enter first.

The room was dark, but Paul turned on the lights right away. They were very bright. After Paul noticed the expression on Heidi's face, he moved the light switch, making the lights slightly dimmer.

Heidi said, "Thanks. It would be nice if all light switches were like that one."

"This room is awfully bright, but we sometimes show PowerPoint presentations in here, so we often need to adjust the lights."

The center of the conference room had a round wooden table with eight chairs around it. Some file cabinets and bookcases were set up against all of the room's walls. The walls displayed framed documents with examples of different fonts.

Paul went over to the table and pulled out a chair. He waved his hand, indicating that Heidi could sit there.

Heidi said "thank you" as she placed her purse and documents on the table. She then sat down, and Paul sat in the chair next to hers.

After Heidi explained the security process, Paul signed several forms for her records. She then told him about a printing project: a booklet for new employees. Paul gave her some information about different printing options; each option had its own price.

Heidi pulled out her cell phone and said, "I just need to check with someone in my office about things."

"Since you might need some privacy, I'll leave for a minute."

As soon as Paul had left the room, Heidi sent a text message to Kevin with information about the different costs for a variety of printing options. A minute later, Kevin responded to her message with explanation about what option should be chosen.

While Heidi waited for Paul to come back into the room, she checked her email accounts. She then sent out several messages to family members about an upcoming family reunion. Finally, she began a search for online sale items.

About five minutes later, Paul returned. He gave Heidi a form to fill out. Heidi used her company's credit card to pay for the project and gave Paul a USB flash drive with the electronic text that her company wanted printed.

Before Heidi had the chance to stand up and say "good-bye," someone knocked on the closed door of the conference room. Paul walked over and opened the door. The employee who had been helping the lady with the crown hat and the briefcase glanced at Heidi as he whispered something to Paul.

Heidi walked up to Paul. "Can I help in any way?"

Paul said, "No, thanks. This is something I should handle." He glanced at Heidi and added, "If you don't mind, Heidi, you can just stay here and relax; I'll only be a minute."

Paul and the other employee went into the front office. Heidi took two steps forward and stood in the doorway. She could see the lady with the crown hat and briefcase; this lady was seated at one of the desks and crying.

Paul walked over, sat down, and asked the crown-hat lady, "What's wrong?"

The lady pointed to the other employee who had been helping her. "He's telling me what to say. I'm the customer. It's my right to say what I want to say."

"Do you need our company to print something for you?"

"I want you to put my words into my pamphlet and print it for me."

"Can I see what you need to have printed?"

The lady pulled a notebook out of her briefcase. She then showed the wording that she wanted included in a pamphlet.

Paul said, "The wording here can be clearer."

"I'm the writer and the customer. It's written by me."

"I understand that you're the writer. However, we can help to fix things. For example, we have people here who can do different kinds of editing, including format, content, grammar, and photo editing," Paul said.

"I don't want it to be edited. It's my writing. I already edited it—all of it."

"Our editors will keep your ideas while helping them to be clearer."

"Editors censor it. They delete things. The writing then becomes filled with an editor's ideas," the crown-hat lady said as she pressed her hand against her crown.

"The editors only change the wording. They don't change any of the ideas, unless there's an idea that you might be sued for. Plus, you'll have a chance to look at the editor's suggestions."

"Whatever it is that I want to say it about it should be printed in it."

"What did you just say? I couldn't understand you."

"It's all mine!"

"If you're going to give the pamphlet to other people, then there will be an audience. If this audience can't understand what you're saying, then you're wasting your time and your money."

"It's my writing, and it's my time, and it's my money. You have to do it how I want it done and when I want it done."

"A person who can't understand something usually will just throw it out. Most people won't even try to re-read a pamphlet if it's not well written."

The lady said in a loud voice, "It was also told to me that you won't include anything about this criminal." She pointed her right index finger at a name in her notebook.

"Our company can't just print negative information about people. We'll need some kind of evidence to show that the information is accurate."

"It's my pamphlet. It belongs to me. It's mine. What I'm saying about someone, it's my words. How can your company complain about it?"

"If we print slanderous information about someone, the person could sue not just you, but us also."

"You're just a censor! It's really what you are. You just want to charge me extra money for editors to censor it." The lady stood up, moved her notebook above her head, and slammed it down onto the desk. A paperclip from inside the notebook flew out, bounced off the desk, and landed on the floor near one of Paul's feet.

Paul stood up, glared at the crown-hat lady, and asked, "Are you trying to hurt me or someone else in this office?"

"Because you're not allowing it to be printed, you're hurting my freedom of speech. You hurt me first. It was done to me first." The lady sat down and started crying again.

Paul also sat down before he said, "I think you should leave this office until you've calmed down a little bit. Then, if you want to, you can come back inside again, and we'll talk about your pamphlet."

"What difference does it make to you? Why do you care about how it's worded?"

"I've already explained the problems with the wordings in your notebook. Also, because our company's name will be included on the pamphlet as the publisher, we should only print appropriate things."

"You're just censoring!" The crown-hat lady stood up while grabbing onto her briefcase and notebook. In just a few seconds, she had angrily walked into the hallway and away from the printing office.

Paul turned around and noticed that Heidi was standing in the doorway. He asked, "Did you hear that interesting debate?"

"Yeah, I did. Not only was that lady very upset, but she also couldn't talk too well."

"She used similar structures while talking and writing. For example, when she talked, she used the word 'it' too much; she did the same thing in her writing."

"Talking is often a little more informal, Paul, but there are definite connections between a person's talking and writing styles."

"You're right about those connections."

"With customers like that, printing must sometimes be a tough field to work in," Heidi said.

"Like any job, printing can occasionally be difficult," Paul said.

"Making a customer happy with a printing product is probably not as easy as most people think."

"Most of our customers are really happy. Once a written document is designed and formatted, its appearance is so much nicer than just the written words all by themselves."

Heidi picked up one of the sample booklets. "I like the design of this one."

Paul pointed to the back cover of the booklet and said, "I know your ancestors are seventeenth-century printers, but you should still read this quote about eighteenth-century American newspapers. The quote says that freedom of the press is important for other freedoms and a government that behaves itself."

Heidi looked at the back cover. One of the other employees was watching and listening, so Heidi said out loud, "This quote on the booklet is from James Wiggins's book *The Press & the American Revolution:* 'The small weekly newspapers of the eighteenth-century American colonies did not forever fasten freedom of the press, or any other freedom, upon the institutions of the world; but they demonstrated its efficacy as a revolutionary force, its indispensability as an element in a really free society, and its compatibility with orderly government.'[22]"

Paul said, "I like the idea of how a free press affects government in a positive way."

"I do, too. Back in the sixteenth and seventeenth centuries, governments often censored publications," Heidi said.

"Censors back then were often trying to silence the spread of knowledge about misbehaving governments and governmental officials."

Heidi shook her head. "Even now, some governments in some countries censor publications with the intent of hiding the truth from the public."

"Freedom of the press definitely helps people to live in a freer society."

Heidi's cell phone vibrated, indicating a text message. She said to Paul, "We're definitely freer. Even when we supposedly need to respond back right away to text messages on our cell phones, we can often wait for a few minutes or even a few days."

"Cell phones are nice because we're free to say whatever we want to say," Paul said.

"You're right, as long as we don't hurt other people with our messages," Heidi said with a thoughtful expression on her face.

"Are you thinking about self-censorship or about parents censoring their children?" Paul asked.

"I'm thinking about everyone." Heidi paused and then added, "I really should get going, but I'll be checking back with you."

Paul thanked Heidi and said good-bye.

As soon as Heidi walked out of the printing office, she checked the content of the text message, which had been sent by Kevin: "Agents are looking for the gray-suited man and intend to bring him in for questioning."

Heidi texted back: "That's great!"

Kevin's next message read: "Please meet me in the jewelry store on the thirteenth floor of our building."

Heidi texted: "I'll be there in a few minutes." She then headed toward the elevator.

Gold & Silver

When Heidi arrived on the thirteenth floor, Kevin was already there. He was standing in front of a store and waved at Heidi to join him. Even though she was more than fifty feet away, the brightness from light bouncing off of items in the store's front window was noticeable. The closer she came to the window, the brighter the corridor became. When she was standing next to Kevin, she stared at the items on display. The store's name—Tina's Gold & Silver Sales & Distribution Company—was crafted with multi-color gems that were twinkling on top of gold, silver, copper, and brass letters. Necklaces, earrings, bracelets, rings, and pins were displayed on manikins, racks, and motion stands. Some of the stands were moving along a tiny train track. Others were staying in one place, but the top parts were twirling, waving, or sliding back and forth. One twelve-inch manikin had a moving head that was wearing a golden crown. Another small manikin had waving hands with three rings on each finger.

Kevin nudged Heidi's arm as he said, "We'd better get inside."

"The inside of this store should have some even brighter jewelry."

"These window items will be the best ones," Kevin said.

Heidi's eyebrows moved upward, showing her surprise. "Why do you think that?"

"Store owners always want to attract people to come into their store. A front window display is therefore a marketing device and a way to attract customers."

"With a jewelry store, though, there's a problem with that marketing strategy," Heidi said.

"What's wrong with attracting customers?"

"The most expensive jewelry shouldn't be displayed this openly. Shoplifters can easily steal window items." Heidi's eyes moved back and forth between two rings in the window.

"The most expensive items probably won't be here in the window; they will normally be locked up in a safe. The items on display will be the brightest, most interesting ones," Kevin said.

"That does make sense." Heidi's eyes were bright as they moved between two twirling manikins.

"Also, this store is sure to have enough security devices to keep all these items safe." Kevin touched the window. "For example, this glass is really thick."

"You're right. I didn't even notice how thick it was."

"Plus, there's a thick-glass background for the window display, so people inside the store can't touch the display items," Kevin said.

"Do you think the window and its background are bullet-proof?" Heidi asked.

"These days, they probably are," Kevin said as he took a step toward the door. Before he could open the door, a man inside the store hit a button on a wall panel. The door then opened automatically.

Kevin walked quickly into the store. Heidi was much slower because she kept on pausing to look around at the jewelry, containers, and display methods. All the store's furniture was shiny with polish and bright attachments. The file cabinets had jewelry items attached above their handles. The desks had sparkling pens and gem-covered laptops.

The man who had opened the door extended his hand and said, "Hi, I'm Fred." His hair was short and black. He was wearing a jacket with a white shirt and a black tie. His jacket had gold cufflinks. His tie had multiple animal-shaped pins attached to it. Heidi stared for a few seconds at Fred's gold tiger pin. The eyes were silver, and the black stripes were painted strips on top of the gold background. Heidi's eyes moved away from the tiger pin when Kevin stepped forward.

Kevin introduced himself and Heidi while shaking hands with Fred. Kevin and Heidi showed their badges before following Fred over to his desk.

Heidi said, "You have an interesting mouse for your computer. Can you actually use that mouse okay, or do the bumps from the gems bother your hand after a while?"

Fred picked up the mouse, which was shaped like a star. "These gems are actually just colored-glass insets, and believe it or not, they're really smooth. I love this mouse." He handed it to Heidi, who rubbed a few of the insets. She smiled before handing the mouse back to Fred.

After repositioning the mouse near his laptop, Fred opened the top drawer in his desk and took out a folder. He handed three papers to Kevin and said, "I printed these pages for you guys to have. The first two pages are the written report of what happened, and the third page has information about the person of interest. There's even a picture."

After Kevin and Heidi were done reading the pages, Kevin said, "Thanks for all of this information. It'll be a helpful start for us."

"I also have a video, which was just copied onto a DVD. It shows the guy when he actually took off his sunglasses for a few seconds."

Heidi laughed and then asked, "Why did he do that?"

"He wanted to try on a pair of our sunglasses."

Heidi laughed again. "He should have tried on a pair of regular glasses, so he could have seen the video camera that was recording what he was doing."

Fred smiled as he stared at Heidi's glasses. "Do you need some new glasses for yourself? We have some really nice frames here."

Heidi looked over at an eyeglass display on one of the walls. "I love your company's styles, but I really need something like what I'm wearing. The big heavy frames can sometimes be helpful."

Fred frowned, showing that he disliked Heidi's glasses.

Heidi asked, "What's wrong with big frames?"

"They're not really fashionable anymore." Fred stood up, waved at the eyeglass display, and said, "Designers and manufacturers are using different styles now."

Heidi sighed and moved her eyes from Fred's face to Kevin's. Kevin glanced at Fred and then swirled his eyes up and down in an expression of disrespect for Fred's view. He stepped closer to Heidi and said, "We both know why large glass frames are better than the smaller ones."

Heidi shook her head in agreement. She glanced at Fred, who had begun to walk away. She then looked up at the video camera and blinked at it several times. When she moved her eyes back toward Kevin, she was still blinking. Her lips were also firmly pressed together.

Kevin's eyes were also moving; he was talking with his eyes, just like she was. With his eye motions and expressions, he was saying, "Yes, I'm watching the video camera and keeping my mouth shut."

Fred suddenly said, "Let's go into another room and watch the video together. Then if you don't have any questions, you can take the DVD version away for your records."

Kevin said, "Thanks so much. The video sounds like some great evidence." He and Heidi followed Fred to a door on the right side of the front part of the store. After Fred entered some numbers into a security device, the door opened. They all walked through the doorway. A moment later, the door automatically closed and locked itself.

The new room was set up as a small distribution center. It had conveyor belts, tables, scales, jewelry products, plastic containers, foldable boxes, and cabinets. Fred led the way to the other side of the room. He, Heidi, and Kevin then went through another locked door and entered a different room. This one had security devices, including two screens that were showing live videos of the main store area and the distribution center.

Fred changed the settings on one of the computers, pointed to a large projection screen, and said, "Here's the video." He gestured for Heidi and Kevin to sit down.

The video started to play; it showed a man who was standing outside the front window of Tina's Gold & Silver Sales & Distribution Company. He was wearing sunglasses and seemed to be just staring at the products on display. He then touched the window, pressed on it with both hands, and finally placed the left side of his face up against the thick glass. He appeared to be trying to analyze the depth and strength of the glass window. He then pulled out his cell phone and started taking some pictures. Before he was finished, an employee in the store stood up, walked out the front door, and moved close to him. The employee was wearing a lot of jewelry. The sunglass man stopped taking pictures.

The employee asked, "What are you doing?"

"I want a little bit of information about your company, so I can share it with my business partner."

"I'm Tina." The lady moved her hand forward. Her wrist had at least five bracelets on it, and every one of her fingers was wearing at least one ring. The man did not shake hands with Tina. Instead, he put his cell phone into his pocket and stepped to the front door of the store.

Tina followed the sunglass man through the door. He walked over to the opposite side of the room, took his cell phone out, and started taking pictures of the inside of the store.

"You can't do that," Tina said as she walked up to him and put her hand in front of his phone.

"Why can't I? Is there a law against taking pictures in a public place?"

"You're not in a public place. You're in a private store."

The man looked to the right of Tina's hand and turned his head toward the sunglass display. After staring for a few seconds at the sunglasses, he said, "If you want business collaboration between our companies, then I first need to convince my partner that your security devices are good enough."

"What's your name?" Tina asked.

The man ignored Tina's question and walked over to the sunglass display. He grabbed a pair of sunglasses with black gemstones on each corner. Scrunching his head forward and hiding his face from Tina, the man removed his sunglasses and placed the gemstone ones on his face. He then turned around, taking multiple selfies of himself with different parts of the store in the background of each photo. When Tina started walking toward him, he moved his head forward, trying to hide again. He then took off the store's sunglasses and put his own pair onto his face. He waved the gemstone glasses at Tina. "I like these. Are the gems black diamonds or something else?"

"Do you really care if those gems are real diamonds or just fake ones?"

"Yeah, I care." The man paused before adding, "Real diamonds will make me look better."

"That's true. If you can tell me your real name, I'll tell you if those gems are real or not," Tina said.

"I'm Joe Smith."

Tina laughed. "I asked for your real name, not for a fake one."

"Joe Smith is my real name."

Tina stared at his face, but he was still wearing the sunglasses, so it was tough for her to see his facial expressions. "Can you prove what your name is by showing me your driver's license?"

"I left my license in my car." The tone of his voice was a little higher than in his previous statements.

Kevin asked Fred to pause the video for a moment and then asked Heidi, "Did you notice the change in the tone of Joe's voice?"

"Yeah, I did. I'm guessing he was lying."

"You're right. He really was lying," Kevin said.

"It's strange that the sunglass man said 'Joe Smith' without sounding like he was lying," Heidi said.

"He's probably been calling himself 'Joe Smith' a lot, so he almost feels like it's his nickname or something similar." Kevin gestured toward Fred to start up the paused video.

The video images began moving again on the screen. Joe was still wearing his own sunglasses while handing the gemstone sunglasses back to Tina. When she turned to put the glasses on the display, Joe started walking toward the door.

"Don't you need to buy anything?" Tina asked him.

"No, thanks, I'm okay for right now," Joe said as he exited the store.

Tina ran over to the front door and looked out into the corridor, but Joe had already gotten away from the store's video cameras. She went back into the store and made several phone calls about Joe being a suspicious customer. Then the video ended.

Fred said, "I have more video files of Tina at work that day, but

I doubt if there's anything else that would help you to catch this 'Joe Smith' guy."

Kevin stood up, shook Fred's hand, and said, "Thanks. Is it possible for us to talk to Tina?"

"She's probably out in the front part of the store by now." Fred retrieved a DVD tape and handed it to Kevin. He then led the way out of the video room, into the distribution center, and back to the front section of the store. Tina was sitting at the desk nearest the sunglasses. Fred introduced Tina, Kevin, and Heidi before going back into the distribution room.

Kevin said, "We saw the video of you with Joe Smith, Tina. Is there anything you would like to tell us?"

Tina shook her head "no." Kevin asked her some additional questions about Joe Smith, but she was unable to supply any added information. He then asked her some questions about the store's security systems. After answering as many of his questions as she could, Tina asked, "Do you think Joe Smith will try to break into this store and steal things?"

"It's possible," Kevin said.

Tina frowned, thought for a few seconds, and then said, "When Joe Smith was checking out this place, he would have noticed the large number of security devices. Hopefully, he won't come back here again."

Heidi said, "He did seem interested in your store. Plus, you have a lot of expensive jewelry items in here. Even standing out in the corridor, people notice the brightness of the products that you're displaying."

"Is there anything you want to buy? I'd be happy to give you a special price."

"Why would I get a special price?" Heidi asked.

"With your job in law enforcement, you're really helping a lot of people in this world of ours," Tina said.

"Thanks so much for being supportive." Heidi looked at a golden necklace with a diamond-covered heart pendant before sighing. "I actually just like to look at expensive jewelry. I can't really buy it, and I don't normally wear it."

"Expensive jewelry is a way of saying something to other people. For example, the diamond-heart pendant that you're looking at will be very noticeable. Other people will look at it, think about love, and be happy."

Heidi's eyes moved to a silver necklace with a cross pendant. "While this cross necklace only has one small diamond on it, I actually like it a lot more."

"I also like that necklace," Tina said.

"It's saying something wonderful, too. It reminds people about how Christ gave up his life in order to save many other people," Heidi said.

Tina put the heart and the cross necklaces next to each other. "These actually can say something together."

"Yes, they can." Heidi stared at the necklaces for a few seconds before adding, "My favorite Bible verse tells us about love and Christ's sacrifice: 'For God so loved the world that he gave his only Son, so that everyone who believes in him may not perish but may have eternal life' (John 3:16 NRSV)."

Tina looked at the prices and then said, "If you want to buy both of these necklaces, I'll let you have them for half of the listed price."

Heidi opened her mouth to say something, but before she could agree or disagree, Kevin said, "I'm sure Heidi would love both of those necklaces, but she can't buy anything right now from your store."

"Why can't she?" Tina asked.

"We're working now. We're also investigating a possible criminal act, so it's wrong for Heidi to buy anything from people who potentially could be court witnesses."

Tina said, "The necklaces, though, are ways of communicating to other people. We have freedom of speech in this country."

"I know we do." Kevin gazed at the two necklaces while adding, "It's really amazing that jewelry can show freedom of speech with no words and with only their symbolic meanings."

Tina picked up three more necklaces. "These have actual words on them." She pointed to the words on the necklaces: "faith," "love," and "faith is love."

Kevin touched the necklace that said "love," looked at Heidi, and smiled.

Heidi returned his statement of love by pointing to the necklace with the heart shape on it, staring at him, and smiling.

After a moment of sharing their love with each other through their eyes, Kevin said, "Free speech takes many forms."

Heidi shook her head in agreement. She and Kevin then looked at Tina.

Necklaces were still hanging from Tina's hands as she said, "Free speech is interesting, especially when the freeness is paid for by money."

Kevin smirked while asking, "What are you saying? Doesn't 'free' mean 'free'?"

Tina laughed. "These necklaces aren't free."

Kevin said, "I know. I was just kidding. The reality of free speech is that it often means spending money, especially if someone wants to say something to other people."

"Companies, organizations, and politicians spend quite a bit of money, so they can talk to others about their ideas," Tina said.

"Some people say that politicians are spending too much money on their ads," Kevin said.

"You're right. However, other people claim that politicians should have free speech, no matter how much money they spend. There's the issue of financial reform for political campaigns; 'in politics, money is speech, in essence, and that putting limits on contributions can thus run afoul of First Amendment protections.'[23]"

"I actually love the first amendment. Politicians should be able to spend as much money on advertising as they want to," Kevin said.

Tina said, "I agree with you. I've also read in an article that people in our country have 'greater freedom against governmental interference in the realms of the spirit, intellect, and political activity than exists in any other country.'[24]"

"Politicians in our country really do have a lot of freedom," Kevin said.

"Not just politicians, but other people—like us—have freedom of speech. We should be able to say whatever we want to say," Tina said.

Kevin frowned. "There are limits to free speech. For example, we can't yell 'fire' in a crowded theater. We also can't hurt others by saying untrue things about them."

"Even so, we have freedom of speech in this country. Just like what we're doing today, we can stand here and debate about politicians, ads, and all kinds of things." Tina looked at Heidi and smiled before adding, "Even though Heidi's being quiet right now, she has freedom of speech, too."

Heidi cleared her throat, sounding as if she wanted to say something, but her eyes were blinking slightly; she looked uncertain about whether or not she should speak up. She then asked, "Doesn't freedom of speech mean I can also be quiet?"

Kevin said, "In some situations, you can be quiet. However, in our field, we see too many people who are quiet about their knowledge of crimes."

Heidi stared at Kevin, blinked her eyes in a strong way, and asked, "Would it be a crime to withhold information about two colleagues who are dating each other?"

Kevin blinked his eyes to show Heidi that he understood what she was asking. "Sometimes, it's tough to decide about silence." After pausing for a few seconds, he added, "Your possible action of spending money on jewelry in this store is what we're debating anyway."

Heidi swallowed and then said, "Okay. I like the gorgeous necklaces that you're showing me, Tina, but I really can't afford them."

"You haven't even looked at the prices," Tina said.

Heidi's face flushed slightly. "If those are real diamonds on the necklaces, I know they'll be too much money."

Tina sighed. "Okay, I understand. You're just trying to follow the rules about potential witnesses for crimes, so you're planning on not buying anything right now."

Kevin looked at his watch. "We really need to leave anyway, but thanks so much for your help, Tina. Here's my card. If something else happens, please give me a call or send me an email."

Tina shook Kevin's hands, waved to Heidi, and held open the front door for them to leave.

Once Kevin and Heidi had walked part-way up the corridor, Kevin stopped moving forward and turned to face Heidi. "Once we actually go out on our first date, we'll have to decide how to be silent about—or noisy about—our love for each other."

"I know. We probably should be following the policies of our workplace." Heidi stared at Kevin while partially opening her mouth.

"The policy doesn't clearly define what an actual date is."

Heidi laughed. "You're right about that."

Kevin said, "The guidelines about buying products from potential witnesses are a little bit clearer."

"I'm really thankful for your help in that situation. I also can't afford to buy diamond necklaces right now. I love to look at beautiful, expensive jewelry, but I'll need to make a lot more money before I can even think about buying something like that."

"As you know, you've just switched to a permanent field position. You might now be able to buy some of those necklaces," Kevin said.

"I need my next paycheck before I have any of the extra money. Even then, there won't be enough for multiple diamond necklaces."

Kevin's cell phone rang. He listened for a few seconds before saying, "Okay, we're leaving now."

"Are we supposed to get back to the office right away?"

"We need to get back there just to write up a report." Kevin paused and then added, "Actually, Heidi, I'll write the report about the jewelry store interview. One of us needs to go to the 'Trips and More' store and set up a possible meeting about transportation costs." Kevin took out his cell phone and forwarded a file to Heidi. "After you've read the file that I've just sent you, can you please run over to the store and talk to them?"

"Yeah, I'd love to," Heidi said as she took out her phone and started to read the file.

"I'll see you in a little while back at the office."

"That sounds great, Kevin. My trip to 'Trips and More' won't include being on a plane or on a cruise ship, so I should just be fifteen or twenty minutes."

Kevin waved before walking over to the elevator. In just a few seconds, he was on the elevator, and the doors closed.

Heidi continued to read the file on her cell phone. About ten minutes later, she entered the elevator and got off on the fifth floor. According to the building map on her cell phone, the store that she needed to visit was near the end of the corridor. After Heidi placed her cell phone back into her purse, she rubbed the top of her nose and pushed her glasses up onto the top of her head. The glasses she was wearing were heavy because they had a built-in camera, a text-messaging system, and other technological elements. With a sigh, Heidi traded the heavy glasses for a lighter pair that was inside her purse. She then moved forward along the corridor toward the Trips and More Office.

Tripping

After just a minute of walking quickly past several other stores, Heidi reached "Trips and More." The sign on the glass door had the company's name and website information. To the right and left of the door were windows that were covered with pictures of tourist destinations. Heidi stared at a *Mayflower II* photo before looking through the glass window into the interior of the store. Closest to the windows and door was a desk with tiny Disney figures on its corners. The desk's front section had a large banner depicting several Disney World rides. The other desks had decorations from different countries.

The lady who was seated at the Disney World desk stood up and opened the door. Her black hair was topped with a red bow with white polka dots on it. She was wearing a red skirt and a white blouse. Her bow and other clothing made her look like Minnie Mouse.

Heidi entered through the store's front door and said, "It's warm and bright in here."

"You're right. The thermostat is always turned up, and the lighting is really great. Whenever I'm at work, I feel like I'm out on a beach and need my sunglasses." The Minnie Mouse lady extended her right hand and said, "My name's Tasha."

Heidi told the lady her own name while they shook hands and walked over to the Disney World desk.

Tasha asked, "Are you thinking of going on a trip somewhere? We can help with air fare, hotel rates, and a lot more."

Heidi moved toward a chair on the right side of Tasha's desk. Her foot tripped over the outer edge of a rug. As she fell to the ground, her glasses slipped off her face. Her purse and then her elbow landed on top of the glasses. A scraping noise was heard.

"Are you okay?" Tasha asked.

"I'm fine." Heidi rubbed her elbow for a few seconds, stretched it out, and smiled. "I think I'm okay." She moved her purse and picked up her glasses. One of the lenses had a crack in it and had fallen out of its frame. "These are broken, though."

"That's too bad," Tasha said.

"It's okay. I have another pair." Heidi stood up, opened her purse, and pulled out her security glasses. "These will work okay." Heidi pushed one of the buttons on the right side of the frame. The lenses became darker, so they looked almost like sunglasses.

"Those glasses are even better than your other ones," Tasha said.

"Thanks."

"I'd love to buy a pair. Where'd you get them from?"

Heidi thought for a few seconds before saying, "I don't know."

"You don't know where you bought those glasses?"

"I didn't buy them. Someone else gave them to me," Heidi said.

"Oh, can I see them? The frame will have the company's name on it."

Heidi took off her glasses and closely examined different parts of the frame. The name "Multi-zooming Glasses" was inside the frame's left corner. Heidi moved her index finger to hide the company's name. "I don't see anything here."

"That's really interesting." Tasha frowned before adding, "Maybe there's some reason for the company to hide its identity. Perhaps it's trying to avoid paying taxes."

"It's probably just a manufacturing error."

Tasha rubbed one of her fingernails. "You're probably right. Companies in our time and in our country don't hide their identities. For economic reasons, they want their names known, so they can market their products and services."

"Back in earlier centuries, there was a lot more censorship. Printers and authors would sometimes remain anonymous on purpose," Heidi said.

"Are you a history teacher?"

"No, I'm not, but I do know a lot about some of our country's history because I'm a descendant of two of our great ancestors: William Brewster and Gregory Dexter."

"Their names sound familiar," Tasha said.

"They both did some printing in England and then had to leave to avoid being punished for the items they printed."

"What did they print?" Tasha asked.

"Gregory Dexter printed some books for Roger Williams."

"What about your other ancestor?"

"Brewster printed multiple items, including *Perth Assembly.* He had to hide from authorities in Holland and England. He then left on the *Mayflower.*" Heidi paused and then added, "He was a Baptist minister and became Elder William Brewster. He has actually been called the 'Father of New England.'[25]"

"So, you're the great, great, great, great, great granddaughter of New England's father. I'm obviously guessing at the number of 'great's' that should be included, but you seem to be a person who should have a lot of 'great's' connected to your name."

"Thanks so much. You're really great, too." Heidi smiled. "I really like your accent. Can you speak Spanish?"

"Yes, I can. I also can speak French and Swahili."

"Because you can speak four languages, you're even greater than I am," Heidi said.

"No, you're the greatest!"

Heidi smiled. "Whenever two people are complimenting each other like we are, they're both the greatest!"

"I so agree with that." Tasha extended her right hand forward. After she and Heidi shook hands, Tasha asked, "So, how can I help you today?"

"My boss wants to have a private meeting with the owner of Trips and More."

"What will the meeting be about?"

"He wants to talk about transportation costs." Heidi took a business card out of her purse. "Here's his contact information. Can you contact him about a meeting date and a time?"

"I definitely can." Tasha looked at the card and then asked, "Are you some kind of a police officer?"

"Yes, I am. I work for the same H.I.D.E. company." Heidi stood up. "Meeting you has been fun, but I really should get going back to my office."

Loud noises in the hallway outside of Trips and More made Heidi and Tasha both look at the entry door.

Tasha asked, "Are those noises some kind of fireworks or something?"

Heidi tried to talk, but no noises came out of her open mouth. She inhaled and then managed to say, "I don't know." Heidi's facial expression suggested that the noises were something fearful. She placed her right hand into her pocket, withdrew a small gun, walked over to the door, opened it up, and peeked out into the hallway. No one was visible.

While Heidi was standing in the front doorway of Trips and More, a slight vibration in the frame of her security glasses told her that a message had just been sent to her. With shaking hands, she pressed one of the buttons and saw a message: "Shooters are in the building."

She typed in a response on the frame of her glasses: "At Trips and More, I heard gunshots."

Tasha's line phone rang. She picked it up, listened for a few seconds, and then started to shake. She tried to hang up the phone, but it fell from her shaking hand onto the floor. Tears were forming in her eyes, so she could not see where the phone had fallen.

Heidi looked at Tasha's nervous hands and then looked down at her own hands, which were also twittering with anxiety. She then said, "I think the phone slid under your desk. I'll get it." She fell to her knees, found the phone, and used her anxious hands to place it into Tasha's nervous hands. The phone was making a humming sound.

"Thanks."

"It's tough for a phone to hide, especially when it's making noises."

With a wild, frightened look in her eyes, Tasha was staring at the phone. She did not seem to be listening as Heidi asked her, "What did you hear on your phone?"

Tasha stood up, ignored Heidi, turned around to face her colleagues at their desks, and yelled out, "There's a shooter in the building. We're supposed to hide."

A man in a blue shirt was seated at the desk next to Tasha's. He stood up and angrily shouted, "Why should we hide? Can't we just run away?"

Tasha said, "I was told the shooter might be too close for us to run. We should hide and be ready to fight."

While no one was looking at her, Heidi sent a text message to Kevin on her glasses: "Trips and More employees heard about the shooter on their line phone. They were told to hide."

Two loud noises sounded from the hallway. Heidi's eyes widened. She sent another message to Kevin: "More shots were just fired. They sounded close by, possibly right outside in the corridor."

A message from Kevin appeared immediately on Heidi's phone: "Hide and be ready to fight."

Heidi responded by hitting the "yes" button on her glasses. She looked at the other people in the room. Tasha was still standing next to her desk with a shocked expression on her face. Some other people in the room were sending text messages on their cell phones.

The blue-shirt man stood up straight and yelled, "We should run!" He started walking quickly toward the front door. Several other people stood up from behind their desks and began to follow the blue-shirt man toward the door.

Tasha raised a nervously shaking hand up high and said, "No, please don't run. I was told we need to hide."

The blue-shirt man said, "In case of a shooter, we're supposed to run first. Then if we need to, we hide. Finally, if there are no other options, we fight."

Tasha leaned sideways against her desk while pressing her hands onto her forehead. She looked like she had a headache or was feeling faint. Heidi said a silent prayer and then looked down at her own hands. They were now less nervous and appeared steady. She stepped close to Tasha and said loudly to the blue-shirt man: "That rule about 'run, hide, and fight' is not a sequence. We're supposed to do whatever is the most logical thing. Like Tasha did, I also received a text message about needing to hide, so we should hide."

The blue-shirt man stopped walking forward. He hesitated and then walked backward to his desk. Other people in the room also went back to their desks. Most of them immediately hid under their desks.

Heidi walked over to the front door and locked it. She looked at the wall, found the light switches, and turned off all the lights.

A new voice yelled out, "I can't see anything, and I still need to send a text message to my wife. Please turn those lights back on."

Heidi remained silent.

The blue-shirt man's voice asked, "Will having those lights off really help anything? Won't the shooter still know that we're in here?"

Heidi hesitated for a few seconds before saying, "If we're quiet and have the lights out, the shooter might think we're somewhere else, like hiding in a different office."

The blue-shirt man said, "No, I doubt we can fool someone that way. Besides, with the lights out, we won't be able to see him."

In a stammering voice, Tasha said, "With no lights, we won't be able to see him or her—the shooter could be a man or a woman."

"There also could be more than one shooter," Heidi said. She took a small flashlight out of her purse and turned it on. Pointing it at the back of the room, she said, "Here's a little bit of light."

"Thanks," Tasha said as she took out her cell phone and turned on its flashlight. Then several other flashlights were turned on in different sections of the room.

Heidi said, "Having less light in here will mean someone will be less likely to shoot us. Is there too much light in here now?"

At the same time, two voices said, "No."

Heidi said, "With less light, we'll all be less noticeable. Plus, with no lights, the shooter can't start shooting at the places where the lights are."

Tasha shook her head and then turned off the light on her cell phone. All of the other lights, except for Heidi's, were also quickly turned off.

Heidi moved her flashlight around the room, trying to see the doors and windows.

An angry voice yelled, "Don't point that light at me!"

"I'm sorry. I'll turn it off." Heidi turned off her flashlight and then asked, "Are there any windows or vents—things that might open up to the outside of this building?"

"There are no windows that connect to the outside, but I don't know about the vents," Tasha said.

The blue-shirt said, "We have some vents in here, but they only open up into the corridor. They're also too small for anyone to fit into."

A slight vibration in the frame of Heidi's glasses indicated that a text message had been sent to her through her glasses. Heidi pressed a button on the frame and then put her hand in front of the lenses. She was trying to hide the incoming message, so the other people in the room wouldn't see it. The message from Kevin across her glasses said: "There's no safe exit. Hide with weapons."

Heidi said loudly, "We all need to hide somewhere. Does this room have some closets?"

"A small walk-in closet is over there in the corner." Tasha turned her phone's light on and pointed it toward the right rear corner of the room.

"Is there a restroom?"

"There are two restrooms, and they're both bigger than the closet."

"Are there any other rooms?"

"The kitchen is small, but it's definitely bigger than the closet."

Heidi turned on her flashlight and asked, "Can you all stand up and raise your hands, so I can count how many people are in here?"

Tasha quickly said, "No, don't you all stand up. I already know how many of us are in here. Heidi, there are twelve people, including both of us."

Heidi said, "We need to split up and hide in the kitchen, restrooms, and maybe the closet."

Tasha said, "I don't think anyone wants the closet."

Heidi asked, "Are there any volunteers for the closet?"

Everyone was silent; there were no volunteers.

"Does anyone want the men's room?" Heidi asked as she moved her flashlight to light up its door.

Four men stood up and walked toward the men's room.

Heidi said, "Before we go into different rooms, we should try to find some weapons."

"I know you have a gun, Heidi, but does anyone else have one?" Tasha asked.

Everyone in the room was now standing up, and multiple flashlights were turned on.

People looked around at each other, but no one admitted to having a gun.

Heidi asked, "Does anyone have a knife or some mace?"

Tasha jumped upward. "The kitchen has some sharp knives. I'll run and get them."

"Forks also would be nice. Anything sharp that we could throw at a shooter would be helpful." After pausing, Heidi added, "Spoons—or anything we could throw at a shooter—would be nice, too. The items don't all have to be sharp ones."

Tasha went into the left rear corner of the main store and walked into the kitchen. A minute later, she returned with some silverware. The blue-shirt man passed them out to everyone while Heidi asked Tasha, "Do you have any glasses or coffee mugs?"

Tasha said, "We do. I'll also look around for some other items that we could throw. I know we have some salt and pepper shakers."

The blue-shirt man followed Tasha back into the kitchen. Heidi picked up pens, pencils, and a stapler from Tasha's desk. She raised them above her head, smiled, and waved the items at the other people still in the room. Everyone started looking on top of desks, as well as in desk drawers, for more objects that could be thrown at a shooter.

Tasha and the blue-shirt man returned with cups, glasses, several more knives, spatulas, and other kitchen utensils. They started to pass them out to their colleagues. Tasha's hands kept on shaking. As she handed a large knife to a man, it fell and hit one of his feet.

"Oh, no! I'm so sorry," Tasha said with tears forming in her eyes.

The man looked down at the top section of his leather shoe. "I'm fine. There's just a little scratch on one of my shoes. No one will even notice it."

"Are you really fine?" Heidi asked.

"Yeah, my foot's okay. It doesn't hurt or anything." He bent over and picked up the knife.

Heidi said, "Just to be sure, maybe you should take off your shoe and sock, so we can check out your bare foot."

The man looked over at the front door of the store. "I'll check it out in a minute. I think we should all go and hide in other rooms first."

Tasha said, "You're right. I'm actually surprised the shooter—or shooters—aren't in our office yet."

Heidi said, "The shooter is probably busy in another store or office, but we should still try to be fast."

Tasha finished passing out the silverware, mugs, and other items, so everyone had at least seven weapons. The four men then began walking quickly toward the men's room again.

One of the women asked, "Should everyone also get some food and water items?"

Heidi said, "I'm guessing the restrooms and kitchen all have some running water, but food might be nice, especially since I'm already hungry."

Tasha said, "We can be really fast if we all just run into the kitchen and grab a few things." She turned around, ran to the kitchen, opened several cupboards, and waved her hands at people. Everyone took turns grabbing items from the open cupboards.

The four men ran toward the men's room again. The man with the new scrape on his shoe tripped. Two of the other men helped him to get up; they then went into the restroom. As they stepped inside, they each waved at the women who had returned to the front area.

One of the women said, "I think we can all fit into the ladies' room."

Heidi said, "It's probably safer if we split up."

Tasha said, "The ladies' room is closer to the front door, and the kitchen is further away, so the kitchen might be safer."

After thinking for a few seconds, Heidi said, "Because the shooter will probably be a male, he's more likely to walk into a kitchen than into a ladies' room. I'll still volunteer to go into the kitchen." She started moving in that direction. Tasha followed Heidi into the kitchen as the other women walked quickly toward the ladies' room.

After Tasha moved over to the back wall of the kitchen, she noticed the coffee pot was empty and turned off. She put water into the pot. Before she added some coffee, Heidi said, "It's probably not a good idea to brew coffee."

Tasha frowned. "Coffee was one of the big reasons why I wanted to be in here, instead of in the ladies' room."

"The smell of the coffee will draw attention to this whole store, as well as to this kitchen," Heidi said.

"Oh, do you really think the shooter will notice if there's coffee in here? The front door is closed, and we're going to close this door, too, right?"

"A shooter might still smell newly-brewed coffee," Heidi said.

"You may be right about that." Tasha sighed. She grabbed two cereal bars and gave one to Heidi. Tasha then looked at her phone's light, which was still turned on. She turned it off.

Heidi glanced at the kitchen's door, which was open. She closed it. Even though she had turned her flashlight on, the room was still fairly dark; she could barely see any of the room's objects. She clicked a button on her glasses, which changed them into night-vision glasses. She was then able to see everything much better. She tore the paper off her cereal bar and began to eat the bar. Her eyes moved to the door's handle before moving up to the door's top right corner. "Is there any way to lock this door?"

Tasha stammered as she said, "No, I don't think so." She turned on her cell phone's flashlight.

Heidi pointed just above the door. "A nice coat hook is up there, and it's on the wall, rather than on the door."

"That's where we sometimes hang our clothes," Tasha said.

"That hook might help us to hang other things right now. Do you have any duct tape?"

"I can look, but I think we just have regular tape." Tasha walked over to one of the drawers, pulled it open, found some invisible tape, and handed it to Heidi.

"Right now, I wish we were as invisible as this tape," Heidi said.

Tasha laughed in a jittery, nervous way before saying, "So do I."

Heidi wound the beginning part of the tape onto the hook above the top of the door. She then stretched out one long strip of the tape toward the door handle. Finally, she wound the tape multiple times in large circles, stretching from the coat hook to the door handle. Stepping backward, she said, "It's interesting that we can sometimes see invisible tape, but the tape really is invisible now. Even with our flashlights on, there isn't too much light in here."

"I hope we'll also be invisible to the shooter." Tasha inhaled, exhaled, and then asked, "Should I turn off the light on my phone now?"

"Yeah, we both should." Heidi and Tasha both turned off their lights.

"Now we're probably invisible, but not if someone pushes open that door," Tasha said.

"You're right. If someone just tries to turn the handle, the tape probably won't be good enough." After pausing for a few seconds, Heidi added, "I need to pray." She bowed her head, closed her eyes, folded her hands together, and said a silent prayer.

Tasha asked, "Can I interrupt your prayer and ask you to pray out loud? I want to pray with you."

"Yes, I'd love to pray with you." Heidi closed her eyes again and said, "Dear Lord, please keep us safe from the shooter. Please also help to keep other people safe today. One of my favorite Bible verses says, 'Even though I walk through the darkest valley, I fear no evil; for you are with me; your rod and your staff—they comfort me' (Ps. 23:4 NRSV). I know that your love and your strength are here with us. I thank you for your help. In Jesus's name we pray, Amen."

Tasha also said, "Amen." After a few seconds of silence, Tasha added, "That was a nice prayer."

"Thanks. I love to pray," Heidi said.

"Do you pray often, or do you pray more like I do?"

"How do you pray, Tasha?"

"Sometimes, when I'm having a really big problem, that's when I pray."

"I've recently been very thankful, so I've been praying at least twice a day," Heidi said.

"Why are you so thankful?"

"I was trapped in an elevator a couple of years ago. Ever since then, I'm just thankful to be alive and free," Heidi said.

The noise of breaking glass came from the next room. Heidi said softly, "I think someone has broken a window."

Tasha's hand was shaking, but she still managed to turn on her cell phone's flashlight. She pointed the light beam toward the door.

Heidi stepped forward, stood in front of the light, and tried to talk. After a couple of seconds, she managed to say softly, "Please, Tasha, turn that light off." Her voice was rising and falling in its tone, which showed her anxiety.

Tasha's hand was still shaking as she said, "I need to see what's happening."

"If you just leave the light off for a minute, your eyes will adjust, and you'll be able to see a little bit."

With both hands shaking, Tasha turned off her cell phone. She then slowly stepped backward. When she got to the wastepaper basket, she tripped, fell sideways, and landed noisily on the floor.

Someone in the next room yelled, "Come on out! I know you're in there!"

After a few seconds of silence, a shot was fired. It sounded like the bullet landed in the kitchen door. Heidi was unable to talk. She raised her right hand up to her throat and rubbed it. She then cleared her throat and said in a jittery voice, "Okay, I'm coming out. Please don't shoot me." She turned on her flashlight and put her finger in front of her lips, telling Tasha to be quiet.

After Heidi had torn off a few pieces of the tape, the man's voice on the other side of the door said, "What's taking you so long?"

"There's tape on the door. I'm removing it as quickly as possible."

"Be faster. In ten more seconds, I'll be firing my gun again."

Heidi's hands started shaking, and she could no longer pull the tape off. She instead grabbed onto the door's handle and leaned backward, pulling at the door with her body's weight. After just a few noises from the tape being pulled and broken, the door opened.

In the main room, the lights were on. One of the shooters was visible. He was the gray-suited man who had followed her to the Dexter house. Now, he was wearing jeans and a black cap. His tee shirt had a picture of a snake on it. The man's right hand moved upward. The back end of a machine gun was resting on his right shoulder. He moved his index finger onto the trigger. He then opened his mouth, but before any words came out, the store's front door opened.

Another man walked quickly into the main room of the store. He also was carrying a machine gun. On top of his head was a pair of sunglasses. On the left side of his face, in front of his ear, was a tattoo of a hundred-dollar bill. He immediately moved the glasses onto the front of his face. This man now looked like the one who had taken pictures yesterday at the Drive-through Technology office. He said to the other man, "Hi, Moe."

Moe said, "Hi, Joe."

The two men both looked at Heidi, who tried to say something, but only her mouth moved. No words came out.

Moe laughed. "Are you unable to speak?"

Heidi tried to say something again, but she was still unable to even make any noises.

Joe said, "Oh, maybe we don't need to shoot her. She'll just keep her mouth shut and not say anything to anyone." He and Moe both laughed.

Heidi kept her mouth closed and did not even try to say anything. Her shoulders went slightly downward, so she looked shorter. She then moved her hands to the center of her stomach and folded them. Before she had a chance to pray more than a few words, a squeaking noise came from the men's restroom. Heidi turned around to see the door being opened.

All at the same time, four knives flew out of the restroom toward Moe and Joe. Moe stepped sideways and pushed his machine gun outward like a shield. Joe ducked down as he used his left arm and elbow to partially cover his face.

One of the knives scraped Moe's left forearm. Moe looked at his arm, which only had a minor scrape on it. He then moved the machine gun up and rested its back section on his shoulder. He stared at the still-open door of the restroom and took several steps forward. The four men inside the room must have stepped backward, for not a single one of them was visible.

"Now it's my turn," Moe said. His index finger had the angry strength of steel even before he moved it onto the machine gun's trigger.

Heidi stared briefly at the blood residue on Moe's forearm. She then ran out of the store while yelling, "You should catch me first. I'm the one who gave those men their weapons."

Moe looked toward the door, trying to find Heidi. She had vanished into the corridor. Her voice screamed, "I know where more guns are hidden."

Joe laughed before saying loudly, "I don't believe you."

Heidi had already run down the corridor and into the stairwell. She stood up against the wall, so no one in the corridor could see her. She took out her cell phone. Another warning about a shooter in the building was on her cell. She ignored the warning and opened a secure link to the building's security cameras. Within just a few seconds, she was watching and hearing what was happening inside the Trips and More store.

Moe was standing next to the front door. He said to Joe, "I think she's one of the spies in this building. Perhaps we should catch her."

"Why?"

"If she gets more weapons, she'll give them to a bunch of people in this building," Moe said.

"That wouldn't be good, but does it really matter? First responders are now outside of this building, and they have more than enough weapons to keep us busy."

"That spy lady also knows what we look like, and she probably can shoot guns really well."

Joe sighed and then followed Moe out the front door and down the corridor toward the stairs. They were moving away from the elevator. Joe asked, "Are we going in the right direction?"

"Yeah, I saw her moving this way. I'm also guessing she'll be running up or down the stairs, rather than being stuck inside an elevator."

Heidi turned off her cell phone before moving away from the wall and into the center of the stairwell. She quickly started climbing up the stairs. After a minute, she looked at her cell phone again. The link to a different security camera showed Moe opening the door from the corridor into the stairwell. He held open the door, so Joe could go into the stairwell first. Joe looked up and down the stairs, but he couldn't see Heidi or anyone else. When he turned to talk to Moe, Heidi shut off her cell phone and quickly sprinted up several more flights of stairs. On the eleventh floor, she paused in the stairway and turned on her cell phone again. She lowered the volume slightly, so she could still hear Joe and Moe while not making a lot of noise.

Moe was standing close to Joe. They were still on the fifth floor. Moe asked, "Which way should we go?"

"If she's trying to get away, she would have gone downstairs."

"I think you're right," Moe said as he took a step downward.

Joe put a hand on Moe's shoulder and said, "Wait a minute. She's probably trying to get some weapons."

"Where would she go for the weapons?"

"It'll be the eighth floor or higher," Joe said.

"Okay, I've been exercising a lot lately, so I can climb up a few stairs," Moe said.

Joe smiled. "We'll be going up more than two flights of stairs."

"I'm up to that."

"Whether we're up to climbing up the stairs or not, the exercise will help us to get up to being able to climb up more stairs. I think we should go up, up, and up."

Moe laughed as he and Joe began to climb up the stairs. At the sixth floor, they paused for a few seconds. Joe walked over to the door that led into the corridor and opened it slightly. A small piece of paper fell out of the doorway. Joe said, "She didn't go through this door."

"Did the piece of paper tell you that information?" Moe said with a smirk on his face.

"Yes, it really did."

"I didn't even see you read anything on that paper." Moe frowned and reached out his hand; Joe gave him the paper. After looking at the front and back of it, Moe said, "This paper has nothing written on it. Did you use invisible ink?"

"No, I didn't. The paper is telling me something just by its location," Joe said.

"How can that be?"

"I placed pieces of paper in all of this staircase's doorways. I put the papers between the top of the doors and their frames. Then if anyone opens a door, the paper will fall down, rather than staying between the door and its frame."

Moe handed the paper back to Joe, who placed the paper on top of the door as he slowly closed it. The paper remained there as Joe and Moe climbed up another flight of stairs.

After Joe again checked on the position of a piece of paper between a door and its frame, he said, "We need to move faster, Moe, or we might get too far behind Heidi."

"Yeah, we need to catch her."

Cubicles

Heidi turned off her cell phone and stepped out of the stairwell into a corridor on the eleventh floor. She immediately turned off the lights in the corridor. Even with her security glasses set to "night vision," she could not see too well, so she switched the corridor's lights back on. After finding her small flashlight, she again turned the corridor's lights off. With a slightly shaking hand, she moved the beam of her flashlight along the corridor's walls as she walked over to the first set of windows and doors. On the glass doors of the first office was a sign: "My T Marketing." Flyers, posters, and other marketing materials were displayed in the large windows next to the front door.

Inside the office area, the lights had not yet been turned off; some sections of the large office were visible from the corridor. Three large wooden tables with chairs were set up near the door. Pens, forms, and pamphlets were on the tables. Behind the tables was the largest section of the office, which had more than forty cubicles. The visible cubicle areas each had a desk, a chair, and at least one filing cabinet.

The bottom halves of the cubicles were wooden; the top halves looked like glass. The glass sections were not very transparent because they all displayed a large number of taped items: photos, drawings, calendars, print-outs, and posters.

Heidi tried to open the door; it was unlocked. As she stepped inside, her right hand went up to the light switch on the wall. She hesitated for a few seconds and then moved her hand away from the switch, leaving the lights in the room on. She asked loudly, "Is anyone in here?"

No one responded. Heidi took a few steps into the room and said, "I'm Heidi. I'm just here to hide from the shooters."

No noises were heard, and no people were visible. Heidi walked past the wooden tables and moved into the cubicle section of the room.

The first cubicle area was cluttered with too many items. A computer keyboard was placed on top of two stacks of books. Covering the desk's top were speakers, stacks of papers, some folders, photos, a line phone, a lamp, a desk calendar, a metal box, pens, pencils, a stapler, tissues, a coffee mug, a lunch tote bag, and a small fan. The glass top panels were completely covered with posters and photos. Some of the photos were even covering parts of the posters.

Heidi walked up to the next cubicle. This area was showing the worker's love for cats. A cat calendar and cat photos were taped to the glass windows. More photos were displayed in frames on top of the desk. Two cat statues sat on top of the computer.

The third area belonged to a reader. The desk had a stack of books, several newspapers, and a pile of magazines. A dictionary was sitting on top of the computer. Posted on the glass window sections were photos of authors, children reading books, and famous quotations. One of the quotes was from President Barack Obama: "We, the People, recognize that we have responsibilities as well as rights; that our destinies are bound together; that a freedom which only asks what's in it for me, a freedom without a commitment to others, a freedom without love or charity or duty or patriotism, is unworthy of our founding ideals, and those who died in their defense."[26]

Heidi shifted her purse, which had been hanging from just her forearm, up to a higher position on the top of her shoulder. The strap was now near her neck, and the purse was pressing against her shoulder, arm, and back. She softly said, "Being a new field agent means so many more responsibilities, but I love being able to help others." She looked around the room; no one was visible. If any people were present and had heard her, they were staying in their hiding places.

Heidi moved forward to the fourth cubicle area. A moving arm was under the desk. Heidi said to the arm, "Hi, I'm Heidi."

The arm under the desk stopped moving, and the person remained silent.

Heidi bent downward slightly and said softly, "I'm just here to find a place to hide. Is there somewhere I can stay without people getting mad at me?"

A pair of scissors flew out from under the desk. Heidi stepped sideways, but the scissors still hit her purse. The scissors were small with curved ends, instead of sharp ones, so no damage happened to her purse. "Are those your scissors, or do they belong to a child?"

The person under the desk said, "They're mine. I used to prefer the safe kind, but after today, I'll be buying the sharpest scissors possible."

"Can you please help me? I just need somewhere to hide."

"I don't know where a safe spot is. Plus, you're claiming your name is Heidi, and you want to hide. How do I know your name is really Heidi?"

"I can show you my identification badge."

"I don't want to see your identification. I'm worried that you're the shooter."

"If I was the shooter, wouldn't I have shot you by now?" Heidi asked.

After a few seconds of silence, the person under the desk said, "You're right. I'm still alive, so you're probably not the shooter."

"Thanks for trusting me," Heidi said.

"I'm really sorry about throwing those scissors at you. Are you okay?"

"I'm fine. The scissors didn't even hit me."

"I'm glad about that."

Heidi knelt down on her knees and looked under the desk. A man's head was resting against the back-corner area. He was wearing a suit with a red, white, and blue tie. After gazing at Heidi for a few seconds, he said, "I'm Tom." He extended his hand out from under the desk. Heidi shook his hand and then gave him back his scissors.

"Is there any place I can hide in here?" Heidi asked.

"Some desks near the door have no one hiding under them yet."

"I'd love to choose any one of those desks," Heidi said.

"Aren't you afraid of being near the door?"

Heidi showed Tom her badge and her Taser weapon. She then touched her pocket which contained her small pistol. After looking at Tom's nervous face, she decided to keep her pistol hidden and to just show her Taser to him and other people.

Tom asked, "Is that a gun?"

"It's a Taser, which is a nice weapon because it uses electricity to stun someone. I can incapacitate criminals without having to kill them."

"Do you have to be close to stun someone?"

"With a Taser, I can stun someone up close or at a distance," Heidi said.

"So, you don't have to be near the door to stun the shooters."

"I should still be the person who's the closest to the door, Tom. I need to do my job, and a big part of my job is to protect people," Heidi said.

"For you, being near the door makes sense."

"I just don't want to get under someone's desk without checking with the person first."

"I'm the office manager here, so if I say you can hide somewhere in this room, then you can," Tom said.

"That's very nice of you. Thanks." Heidi went back to the front part of the office; after looking at several desks, she placed her purse on the one that was holding a Bible. On the glass section of the cubicle divider were multiple pictures of family members. In the photos, all the people were smiling joyfully, as well as holding hands or hugging each other. On top of the computer was a metal cross. Taped to the front drawer of the small file cabinet was a drawing of Jesus.

Heidi said, "I love this desk."

"I like that desk, too." Tom was now standing next to Heidi.

"I love having freedom of religion in this country." Heidi looked at the drawing of Jesus and then added, "The First Amendment to our constitution has freedom of religion and freedom of speech in the same amendment. We're free to speak about religion in our country."

Tom pointed to a highlighted quote on a page that was taped to the glass of the cubicle area. "Here's a quote from an article by Murray Dry. I'll read it to you." Tom read the quote out loud: "The first amendment freedoms of speech and religion are particularly interesting and important because of their connection to the liberal principle of toleration, and through that principle to philosophy, or the quest for truth."[27]

"Toleration is definitely connected to freedom." Heidi paused and then added, "Freedom of speech can include setting up a desk to say something about one's religion."

"The people working in this office have a lot of freedom about what to include in their cubicles. I know at least one of the employees is Jewish because of the candles on his desk." Tom pointed to one of the cubicle areas and smiled.

"The desk items must help employees to discuss ideas with each other, as well as to connect together in a variety of ways."

"They do." Tom took a few steps backward and waved at two cubicle areas that were off to his right. "It's interesting that a democrat and a republican have desks right next to each other."

Heidi laughed. "Does anyone in your office have political items from both parties?"

Tom moved back to his desk and pointed to four stickers on his cubicle window area. "I have some stickers from different parties. I'm trying to show everyone that I support some of the ideas of both parties."

Heidi looked at the top of the desk where she had placed her purse; the desktop had a calendar with a Bible verse present on its current page.

Heidi said, "I love that Bible verse, and we really need to think about it today."

Tom asked, "What's the verse?"

Heidi read the Bible verse out loud: "God is our refuge and strength, a very present help in trouble" (Ps. 46:1 NRSV).

Tom said, "That's a nice verse to think about right now."

"It is, but even when I'm not in trouble, the Lord is still my strength, and he always helps me to overcome my fears."

"Have you ever had any miracles happen?" Tom asked.

"Yeah, I've experienced so many miracles that the large number of miracles is a miracle all by itself." Heidi paused and then added, "When I was only ten years old, I was in a car accident. Our car was pushed into a ditch, turned upside down, and completely ruined. Firefighters and police officers had to come and extract me and my family from the car. We were so thankful that no one in our family was injured. None of us had even a tiny bruise, sprain, or scratch."

"That must have been so nice to have a miracle for your whole family while you were all together," Tom said.

"It was. Even now, just remembering what happened back then, makes me feel so much stronger and less scared."

"I'm still scared, but less scared than I was a few minutes ago," Tom said.

"So am I. While I'm still afraid right now, I'm better able to walk around and do things that might help with this horrible situation." Heidi looked around the room and asked, "Can I lock the front door?"

"Is it unlocked right now? It should be locked."

"It was unlocked when I came in, so I didn't want to lock it without checking with someone like you."

"Yes, please lock the door. Here are my keys. You'll need to use the large brass one."

"After I lock the door, can I turn off the lights in here?"

"No, please don't do that."

"We'll be safer with the lights out," Heidi said.

"I'm the manager, and I've already decided that darkness will scare everyone too much. It's more important to keep people less stressed out, especially since the shooter probably isn't even near our office right now."

"With the lights out, the shooter might just walk past this office, rather than coming inside, looking around, and shooting," Heidi said.

"That's not true! Many people in here are using their cell phones right now. With the ceiling lights out, a shooter will be able to see some moving cell phone lights."

"People could also turn off their cell phones."

Two employees came out from under their desks and raised their cell phones up high enough for Heidi to see them. One of them said, "I need to keep my cell phone on."

The other employee said, "I need my cell phone to stay on, too. I'll be able to take pictures and videos. This will help to prove the shooters guilty."

"Are you both sending out text messages to family members?"

The two employees shook their heads up and down.

Heidi said, "It's so nice that you can contact your loved ones during a time like this. I understand how communicating with family and friends can help people to feel less stressed."

Tom said, "If the lights are out, all of us will have to turn our cell phones off. Otherwise, each area with a little bit of light from a cell phone will show the shooter where people are hiding."

Heidi looked around the room before asking, "Can I turn the lights out for a few seconds, just so I can see if this is really true for all parts of the room? It's possible that cell phones in one or more sections might not be too noticeable."

Tom sighed. "Okay, but let me tell everyone what you're going to do first." He stood up and said in a loud voice, "Heidi will be turning the lights out for five or ten seconds. She'll then be turning them on again. Please stay under your desks with your cell phones on, so we can see if they're visible or not. We're just trying to see what the safest light option is."

Heidi walked over to the switch and turned out the lights. After her eyes adjusted to the darkness, she noticed several spots where a small amount of cell phone light was visible. She could also see reflections from the glass windows in the top parts of some of the cubicles.

Heidi's glasses suddenly vibrated. She read a text message from Kevin: "There's a third shooter who is not in this building. He has a bomb in a mall and is threatening to set it off. For this reason, we should try to not kill the shooters, but we instead need to capture them and make them talk. It's really important to not let them escape."

Heidi sent to Kevin a "yes" message on her glasses by pressing one of the buttons a single time. She then turned the lights back on and said loudly, "Tom's right. We're probably safer with the lights on inside this office."

Several people stood up and shook their heads in agreement. One of them said, "I also get really nervous if things are too dark."

Heidi said, "I understand that. A lot of people have the same fear." After pausing she added, "I'm guessing you all prefer the lights in the corridor outside your office to be turned off, like they are now."

Tom said, "It's a good idea to keep those lights off. Then if one or more shooters suddenly appear, they will probably turn the corridor's lights on, and we'll have a little bit of advanced warning."

Heidi said, "That's a great idea."

A lady near the back of the cubicle area asked, "Do you know how many shooters there are?"

"I'm not completely sure," Heidi said. After pausing for a few seconds, she added, "There could be three or more shooters, but I only saw two men with machine guns. They're working together. The shooters also may be just a couple of thieves. They already had a chance to shoot people, and they didn't. They might or might not shoot anyone."

One of the people who were still standing up near the back of the room said very loudly, "Tom told us all to hide, but I've been wondering if we're better off running, hiding, or fighting."

Tom said, "Denise, I know you're nervous, but let's keep our voices down."

She frowned and then said in a softer voice, "Can you still hear me okay?"

Tom and Heidi both shook their heads "yes."

Denise asked, "Should we run, hide, or fight?"

Heidi sighed before replying, "Right now, the shooters might be too close for us to try to run away. Your office doesn't seem to have any expensive items in it, so if the shooters walk down the corridor, they're likely to just keep on walking right past us."

Denise asked, "Even if the shooters are close by, shouldn't we run away?"

Tom said, "I was told in a text message to hide, so I think Heidi's right about what we should be doing. Also, the only one of us who has a weapon is Heidi."

"Does she have a gun?"

"She has a Taser."

"Because the rest of us don't have any guns or weapons, hiding might not be safer than running," Denise said.

Heidi said, "You actually do have some items in here that could be used as weapons."

"Where are they?" Tom asked.

Heidi gave Tom back his keys and said, "Many of us have keychain attachments, like knives, that can be used as weapons."

About half of the employees raised their key chains up high and clapped their hands softly together. They were trying to be cheerful without making a lot of noise.

Heidi picked up her purse. "Many items in a purse or in people's pockets can also be used as weapons." From her purse, she pulled out her own keys, some make-up, a small mirror, and her billfold. After waving the items in front of her face, she said, "These can all be thrown at the shooters. If multiple people throw things at the same time, the chance of hurting the shooters will increase."

Denise said, "For the first time in my life, I'm so thankful to have so many items in my purse."

Heidi opened up her billfold and took out some twenty-dollar bills. She waved them around, and everyone's eyes stayed focused on the bills. "How many of you are still staring at this money?"

All of the people in the room raised their hands. Tom said, "Oh, so money can be a distraction for the thieves."

"Money is usually their number-one desire in life, so they will stare at the money even more than you all are doing right now." Heidi moved her right hand and almost dropped the twenty-dollar bills out of her hand. She then said, "I don't really want to throw my money around right now, but during an emergency, if I toss money into different places on the floor, the thieves might think about picking up the money, rather than shooting people."

"We'll all plan on keeping our money available, so we can throw it around the room at the same time," Tom said.

"Coins will be helpful, too, as weapons and distractions," Heidi said.

"When will be the right time to toss our money around?" Tom asked.

"I think we should wait until the thieves are actually in this room and are looking at people," Heidi said.

"Why can't we leave money around the room right now?" Denise asked.

"The shooters might see the money from the corridor and decide to come into this room just because of the money. We really want the crooks to think there's nothing expensive in here and to just walk right past us," Heidi said.

Denise took about twenty dollars in fives and ones out of her purse. She then asked, "If the lights are turned on in the corridor outside of our office, is that when we should start throwing our money around?"

Heidi said, "We should wait until the shooters are actually inside this office. I can give a signal when it's time to throw the money around."

"What kind of a signal will you give?" Denise asked.

Heidi thought for a few seconds and then said, "I'll just yell the word 'money.'"

"If you yell, the shooters will hear you and go after you." Denise turned on the flashlight in her cell phone. "A different signal would be to shine a light. If you just shine your flashlight upward, the shooters might not notice it, so you'll be safer."

Heidi said, "I really need to do something that people can hear. Because we'll all be hiding under desks, we won't see light from a flashlight, but we'll be able to hear a yell."

Tom shook his head in agreement. "Okay, if you yell 'money,' we all should throw our money up into the air and out beyond our desks."

Heidi pointed to the top of the desk next to where she was standing. "Besides money, there are a lot of other items that can be used as distractions and weapons."

Denise asked, "What are you suggesting?"

Heidi pointed to items on top of the desk: a stapler, some pens, a book, and a picture in a wooden frame. "We can also disconnect the keyboard and mouse from the computer, so we'll have some additional items to use as weapons and distractions."

Denise asked, "I understand how throwing things at people means the things are weapons, but can we also make those things into real distractions, like money is?"

Heidi pointed to the back of the room. "If someone throws an item into the back of the room, it'll make a noise. The shooters may then go over to see what the noise is."

"Should you also give us a signal for a noise distraction?" Denise asked.

Heidi said, "People should just determine by themselves if and when a noise distraction is needed in their section of the room. If I yell to try and tell people to make noise, then the shooters will be focused on me, so I will be the actual noise distraction. This distraction might or might not be helpful."

Tom asked, "Can you think of any other noise distractions?"

Heidi replied, "We could argue with each other. As long as we don't debate something directly with the shooters, they might pause and listen to two people with different views. Arguments are sometimes fun to listen to."

Tom asked, "Do you know what topic might work?"

Heidi said, "People like to talk about animals. Punishment for animal cruelty could be debated. Another topic could be whether animals should be caged up or set free."

Tom said, "Those topics probably would be interesting for criminals worried about possible jail time."

Heidi said, "An argument like that might distract the criminals, so other people might be able to sneak out of this room and run away."

Tom looked at his desk top and then said, "We should also look inside of our desk drawers for weapons and distractions." He opened the top drawer of his desk and pulled out a dictionary. "I think all of us will have at least one book. These can be thrown around and might physically hurt a shooter."

"Books can also be used for more positive things. Instead of just waiting for shooters, you might want to read a book right now."

Denise said, "That's a good idea. Reading will probably make me less anxious."

"Books can also be read by people who are trying to learn something." Heidi paused and then added, "I'm reading some texts at work; these are helping me to learn more about how to do my job well."

Denise smiled. "My oldest son is now in college. He does a lot of reading in order to learn things, but he also just enjoys being able to read."

"I often give books to my loved ones as presents. Books can show our love for someone," Heidi said.

Tom pointed to the back-left corner of the room, where several bookcases were situated. "We often think of books as sitting on shelves in bookcases, but they're not just sitting there and doing nothing. Books can look very nice in such a setting, and even their cover designs say something to people."

Denise said, "People often say 'Don't judge a book by its cover,' but the cover design conveys a part of the book's meaning."

Tom said, "You're right. I think I'm going to be reading a book with a nice cover design in a few minutes."

Denise opened up the top drawer of her desk. "I have at least six books in my desk drawers. I also have some push pins. I can share the books and pins with anyone who wants them."

Heidi smiled. "Push pins can be a distraction, but they aren't really heavy enough to do too much harm to the shooters, unless multiple people throw them really hard and can hit the shooters' eyes."

Tom opened up one of his desk drawers and pulled out some items. He put two ink cartridges for the office's printer next to the pens on his desktop. "It would be so nice if we could write something on the shooters' faces with these ink cartridges and pens."

Heidi said, "Just by throwing ink items at people, you're telling them that you want to be left alone."

Tom said, "If we throw ink cartridges at them, maybe exclamation points will wind up on their faces."

Heidi laughed. "That could really happen. Something as simple as an 'x' could also wind up on their faces."

Denise said, "I could first throw my push pins at their faces. Then Tom could throw partially-open ink cartridges. We might be able to imprint tattoos on their faces."

Tom laughed. "That actually might work."

Heidi scratched her left ear. "One of the thieves already has a tattoo on his face."

Tom asked, "What kind of a tattoo?"

"I think it's a hundred-dollar bill."

The lights in the corridor suddenly were turned on by someone outside of the office. Tom gestured with his hands for people to get under their desks. Heidi stepped back to the desk where her purse was. She moved the chair out of the way and went under the desk. She finally moved the chair in front of her body, so it would be tougher for people to see her.

Loud noises from bullets and breaking glass were heard. Joe's voice said loudly, "Come on out! We know you're in here."

After a few seconds, more sounds of bullets and breaking glass were heard. The sounds were initially near the front door, but they quickly moved through some of the cubicles up to the one where Heidi was hiding. Several pieces of glass were kicked forward by the shooters and flew across the floor. Then the noise of bullets was followed by more broken glass. One of the glass dividers next to Heidi's desk was shattered. A piece of glass bounced under the desk and hit her purse. She pulled her purse up against her chest and hugged it. She then bowed her head and prayed silently for God's help. As she separated her clasped-together hands, Joe's voice said, "I know you're in here, Heidi. We've been following you."

Heidi inhaled and exhaled slowly. She tried to talk, but no noises came out of her throat. Her lips silently formed some words: "Okay, I'm in here." She then pushed the chair outward, crawled forward from under the desk, and stood up.

Joe was standing just a few feet away. His machine gun was partially resting on his right shoulder. He took his right index finger off of the trigger, placed his gun on the desk where Heidi had been hiding, and said sarcastically, "We meet again."

Heidi's eyes were blinking, and her hands were shaking. Her right hand moved to the pocket on the right side of her pants. Before she could pull out her Taser or small pistol, Joe grabbed her right hand. While firmly gripping Heidi's hand, Joe removed her Taser and small pistol. Joe then walked over and stood behind Moe. He put Heidi's weapons into the backpack that was strapped to Moe's back. With a frown on his face, Joe walked back to stand near Heidi.

She tried to talk, but her lips were wobbling, and no sounds came out. She then cleared her throat a couple of times, making noises each time, and closed her mouth.

Moe, who was standing five feet behind Joe, kept his index finger on the trigger of his machine gun. He moved the barrel, so Heidi's head was in line with the front and rear sights of his gun. Moe then asked, "Is it my turn, Joe, to shoot someone?"

"I think it is your turn, but we should wait to see if there are more people in this office." Joe looked around at some of the other cubicles. "We might both need to be shooting people at the same time."

Heidi's eyes looked down at the floor as she clasped her hands together. She closed her eyes and was silent.

Joe laughed. "Are you praying?"

After a few seconds of silence, Heidi looked up at Joe and said in a strong voice, "Yes, I am."

"Do you really think God can help you?" Joe asked.

"He definitely can," Heidi said. "He already has helped me to get my voice back again."

Joe looked at Heidi's throat, took two steps forward, and stood right in front of her. He then reached his right hand up and touched her throat. "Let's see if he gives you back your voice if I take your throat away."

Heidi took a step sideways; Joe took a step in the same direction. He then grabbed onto her throat with both of his hands. "How does this feel?" he asked.

As Joe began to squeeze her throat, Heidi inhaled and then coughed several times. Phlegm flew out of her mouth onto Joe's neck.

Joe squeezed her neck tighter as he said, "You won't be spitting at me if I close up your throat a little more."

Moe said, "Even if you strangle her, that won't get rid of her throat."

Joe loosened his grip slightly and stared through Heidi's glasses into her eyes. The tears forming in her eyes were making the lenses of her glasses foggy.

Joe raised the corners of his mouth in a smirking gesture. "We could just hide her under that desk again."

"We could also just leave her on the floor," Moe said.

"Do you want to shoot her in the throat, Moe?"

"Yeah, I'd love to do that. I've never shot a woman before."

"We could check and see how long it takes to quiet someone's voice by shooting a throat," Joe said.

"Shouldn't we make her scream before we try to make her quiet?" Moe asked.

Joe let go of Heidi's throat, stepped backward, and removed a knife from one of his pockets. "If I cut off one of her fingers, she'll be in a lot of pain and start screaming."

"Then I can shoot her throat."

"That sounds like a plan." Joe smiled as he reached to grab onto Heidi's left hand.

Heidi jumped sideways and said, "I have a better plan for you."

Joe stared at her. "It's interesting that your voice is still strong even though your hands are shaking and your eyes are crying."

"Thanks." Heidi removed her glasses, rubbed her eyes, touched the frames in several spots, and then put her glasses back on again. "If I help you, will you wait a little while before injuring or killing me?"

"I don't think someone like you can really help us," Joe said sarcastically.

"I actually can help you," Heidi said as she looked down at the floor. "I know a little bit about some of the security devices in this building."

Joe turned to Moe and asked him, "What do you think about letting her live for a little while?"

"I don't think she'll really help us." Moe moved his machine gun slightly. "She'll just wait until a good moment to run and then run away again."

Heidi said, "I have some rope in my purse. You could tie me to one of you, and then I won't be able to just run away."

Joe made a face, "I don't see a purse anywhere. Where's your purse?"

"It's under the desk where I was hiding when you first came into this office." Heidi pointed to the desk and asked, "Should I get it for you?"

Joe said, "Okay, you can get your purse, but I'll be the one to pull out the rope."

Moe laughed. "Do you really think there's a rope in her purse?"

"I don't know. I haven't looked inside of it yet," Joe said.

"Why would a woman carry a rope around in her purse?" Moe asked.

Joe turned to Heidi and asked, "Why do you supposedly have a rope in your purse?"

"I just bought one a few days ago. I needed a new clothesline for when I hang up my clothes in my backyard."

"Why is it still in your purse?" Joe asked.

"I just forgot about it."

Joe waved his hand sideways, indicating that he wanted Heidi to move away from the desk. He then looked under the desk, bent over, pulled out Heidi's purse, and opened it up. "Look at this. There really is a rope in here."

Moe lowered his machine gun and said, "The rope's in a plastic bag with a price tag on it, so she really did just buy it."

Heidi said, "There are some scissors attached to my keychain, so you can even cut the plastic away and open up the rope."

Moe sighed and moved his machine gun upward. "Well, that explains why you wanted to get into your purse."

Heidi frowned. "What do you think I wanted in my purse? You already have my Taser and my gun."

"You obviously wanted to get the scissors and attack us," Moe said.

"Those scissors are really small. I wasn't planning on using them to attack two men with machine guns."

Joe looked in Heidi's purse again. He then took out the keychain and showed the scissors to Moe. "She's right. These scissors are really too small to be a good weapon, Moe."

As Moe kept his machine gun aimed at Heidi, Joe cut the plastic covering away from the rope. He then cut off a nine-foot long section. He put the scissors and the rest of the rope into Moe's backpack. Finally, Joe tied one end of the nine-foot long section of the rope around Heidi's waist and the other end around his own waist.

Moe said, "Now, we're all set and can shoot the other people in this office."

Heidi gasped. "Why do you think more people are in here?"

Joe said, "Moe's right. With the large number of desks in this cubicle office, there have to be more people than just you."

"They all ran away."

Joe waved at the front door. "I don't think so. I doubt if you would have gotten into this office all by yourself. Someone must have had a key, let you come in here, and then locked the door to keep us out."

Heidi said, "This is only a marketing and advertising office anyway. I don't think there would be anything here worth stealing."

A noise was made from under the next desk. Tom pushed the chair, crawled out from under the desk, and stood up. With an angry expression on his face, he asked Heidi, "Are you trying to say that My T Marketing is unworthy?"

"No, I wouldn't say something negative like that. My T Marketing just doesn't have any jewelry, electronic equipment, or other really expensive things that people could sell."

Moe said, "There actually are computers and printers in here. There also might be some money from customers, information worth stealing, and other neat items here."

Joe shook his head. "While there may be some money and customer information here, Moe, there are other places in this building with better items."

"Should we just shoot everyone here?" Moe pointed his gun toward Tom. "I can get us started."

"No, that guy's mine. I want to shoot him." Joe picked up his gun and swung the barrel upward. In just a couple of seconds, his fingers were on the handle, and his eyes were focused on the gun's front and rear sights.

Heidi shrieked.

Joe turned and pointed his gun at Heidi. "What are you screaming for?"

"I'm just trying to help. It's really a waste of time and ammunition to shoot people in an office where nothing will be stolen anyway." After pausing, Heidi added, "It'll also take a while to look under these desks and inside the other rooms to find all of the people in here."

"As long as we don't shoot you, why should you care?" Joe asked.

"I really don't want to see people killed. If you let the people in this office live, I promise to be good and to follow you around to any other offices where you want to go."

Joe stared at Heidi and then asked, "Will you also help us with the security mechanisms, so we can get into all of the other offices?"

"I promise to try. I can't get you into most of the locked offices, but I can probably help with a few of them."

Joe lowered his gun. He then said, "We can possibly use the security help. Let's go." Joe started walking toward the front door. Heidi was attached to Joe with the rope, so she also moved toward the front door. Moe put his gun into its holder before following Joe and Heidi out of the office. When they were all standing in the corridor, Joe began to check the rope connecting his waist to Heidi's.

Moe took off his backpack and took out Heidi's Taser weapon. He then shot Heidi with the Taser. She stumbled in pain and hit her head against the corridor's wall. As she fell to the floor, Joe asked, "Why did you do that, Moe?"

"I really don't believe she'll help us. We're better off without her."

Before Joe had a chance to respond, Heidi's eyes were closed. She seemed to be unconsciousness, but she was still able to hear what they were saying.

Joe said, "When we go outside, we'll have to get past the police officers. A kidnapped victim will be helpful then."

"Why should we use her? Shouldn't we kidnap someone right before we leave?" Moe asked.

"Some of the people in this building will have run away, so we might not find a possible victim when we need one. Also, since Heidi volunteered, she's less likely to fight us. We're better off using her as the victim," Joe said.

"Okay, Joe, your reasoning makes sense."

"When we no longer need a victim, then we can get rid of her."

For a few seconds, Heidi felt her body being pulled along the floor. She then lost consciousness and was unable to see, hear, or feel anything.

The Strength of Faith

While unconscious, Heidi began to dream. A large granite statue appeared before her. The top section of the statue was a lady with her right hand raised up and pointing toward the sky. Her left hand was holding a Bible. The name of 'Faith' was carved into the stone below the granite lady's feet.

Heidi put her arms over her head, scrunched downward, and tried to hide her face.

"Why are you trying to hide from me?" Faith asked her.

Heidi separated her hands slightly. She then peeked through her hands at Faith before asking, "Aren't you the one who hurt me with electricity from my Taser?"

"No, I would never do anything at all to hurt you."

"My hands are partially covering my eyes, so I don't even know if I'm really seeing you."

"You must be seeing me. Otherwise, why would you be trying to hide from me?"

With her fingers still covering most of her face, Heidi peeked upward between her middle and index fingers. "I guess I can see you." Heidi breathed heavily for a few times and then asked, "If you didn't hurt me, then why is your right hand raised up so high above me?"

"I'm pointing to heaven, which is where our faith will take us."

"Am I dying and about to go to heaven?" Heidi asked.

"No, you're alive and will stay alive for years." Faith smiled at Heidi.

"Do you know what happened to me?"

"Someone used a Taser. You fell down and lost consciousness," Faith said.

"Was it one of those thieves?"

"Yes, it was the one called 'Moe.'"

"Why did he try to hurt me?" Heidi asked.

"He and Joe are evil."

Heidi heard some hissing and looked down at the ground. Two snakes were circling around her feet. One of them had Joe's face; the other one had Moe's face. They glared angrily at Heidi, hissed, and started to bite her toes. Heidi kicked her feet, but she was unable to make the snakes stop. "Why is God letting such evilness hurt me?"

"God is not evil. Satan is the evil one."

Heidi's eyes were tearful as she kept on staring at the snakes. She then said, "I can only see these evil snakes that are biting me. I even want to do evil things back at them, like biting and stabbing them. I can't see you anymore, Faith."

"You're letting yourself look at and stay focused on something evil. The Bible tells us, 'Do not be overcome by evil, but overcome evil with good' (Romans 12:21)."

Heidi glanced up at Faith, back down at the snakes, and then up above Faith into the sky. "You're right. I need to think about the goodness of God, not about the evil of Satan."

"Goodness can overcome evil."

The snakes made a hissing noise at Heidi's feet, but she refused to look at them anymore. She instead focused her now-happy, tear-free eyes on the statue's face. "Who are you?"

"My name is Faith. I'm a part of the National Monument to the Forefathers."

"I remember visiting you a few weeks ago." Heidi paused before asking, "Is there some way I can see my real faith, rather than just a statue of faith?"

"Why do you have to see your faith?"

"I want some physical evidence of my faith."

Faith asked, "Have you ever been in love?"

"Yes, I'm in love right now," Heidi said.

"Do you need to see your love coming out of your heart and moving through the air to your loved one?"

Heidi hesitated before she said, "I guess abstract things don't need to be seen, but I love to see the person whom I love, as well as the items that remind me of my love."

"Everyone loves pictures of their loved ones."

"Wedding rings and other kinds of jewelry are also nice."

"Faith is visible through your mind, heart, and soul. You can also see me as a real statue that's a symbol of your faith."

Soft music from the Afters' song, "Lift Me Up," began to play. Heidi blinked her eyes when she heard the line, "You lift me up when I can't see."[28]

After listening to the song, Heidi said, "I guess I don't have to see my faith in a physical way. My faith in God will still help me with everything."

"You don't need to see to have strong faith in God." Faith raised her Bible upward and opened it while saying, "The Bible tells us a lot about faith. One of my favorite verses says, 'Now faith is the assurance of things hoped for, the conviction of things not seen' (Heb. 11:1 NRSV)."

Heidi thought for a few seconds and then said, "I like that definition of faith."

"Are you convinced there's a God?"

"Yes, I am. I know there's a God," Heidi said.

"How do you know?"

"Even though I've never seen him, I've seen a lot of his miracles." Heidi thought briefly before adding, "I've also seen evidence of his presence in the Bible, in the wonders of our world, and in the many good deeds that some people do."

"People often get upset about the evil in our world, but there's so much goodness that can overcome the evil," Faith said.

"I know. Just thinking about goodness can help. Instead of hissing snakes biting at my feet, there are now two fluffy, purring cats." Heidi glanced down at her feet. The cats were there. She then looked back up at the Faith statue. "You're a nice symbol of faith."

"Thanks. I like being a statue in Plymouth, Massachusetts. I was created in the nineteenth century. When people in the twenty-first century see me, they also see my name: Faith. I'm therefore thought of as a symbol of faith."

"You're very strong. Your physical form is granite, so you're showing people the strength of faith."

Faith moved her hand higher toward heaven. "Because I'm in your dream, in reality, you're communicating right now with yourself. You're actually telling yourself something about your own faith."

"You're a symbol of my faith in God, just like you're a symbol of the Pilgrim's faith in God," Heidi said.

"I really am. Both of my hands show my own faith. The index finger of my right hand is pointing up toward heaven, and there's a Bible in my left hand."

Heidi stood up and began to walk around the statue. Her eyes moved from Faith to other parts of the National Monument to the Forefathers. "The bottom part of your statue has some really neat parts. I love the pictures, which show some of the important activities of the Pilgrims."

"The four smaller statues seated on the corners of my granite structure are really neat, too."

"I love all four of the small statues: Liberty, Education, Law, and Morality," Heidi said.

"Carved into one of the panels of my granite form is a quote from William Bradford's book."

Heidi paused in front of the granite panel with the Bradford quote on it. She said, "*Of Plymouth Plantation,* the book by Bradford, is the best source of information about the Pilgrims."

"It is. Bradford was one of the Pilgrims who came over on the *Mayflower.*"

"Starting in 1621, he was the governor of Plymouth for over thirty years. He really did a lot to help the Pilgrims." After staring at the Bradford quote, Heidi read it out loud:

> Thus out of small beginnings greater things have been produced by His hand that made all things of nothing and gives being to all things that are; and as one small candle may light a thousand, so the light here kindled hath shone unto many, yea in some sort to our whole nation; let the glorious name of Jehovah have all praise.[29]

Faith said, "Bradford is thanking God for His production of great things and His light that has shown on our nation."

"He also was talking about how one small candle could light a thousand other candles." Heidi smiled and then added, "One good action can result in a thousand other good actions."

"You're really great at interpretation, Heidi."

"Thanks, Faith. You're really great at knowing when important quotations are needed." Heidi walked around and looked at the other three panels. One of them had the monument's name and other information on it. Two of the panels had listings of the Pilgrims who came over on the *Mayflower*. "One of my ancestors, William Brewster, is listed on this same panel as William Bradford is."

"John Carver, the first governor of Plymouth, is the first of the Pilgrims listed on that panel over there."

"You're right." Heidi was still looking at the listing of names. "I'm familiar with all of these names."

"That's so great. As a descendant of one of the Pilgrims, you must have a lot of faith and courage."

Heidi said, "Even though I have faith in God, I don't have a lot of courage. I'm really scared about what's happening right now."

"What's happening?"

"Shooters are in the building and threatening to kill people."

"Are they really going to kill people, or are they just trying to scare everyone?"

"I don't know." Heidi's facial expression showed her fear. "Either way, I'm really fearful about me and other people dying."

"So many things are really scary, but the strength of God can help with our fears. He even tells us how to dress ourselves in his armor." Faith moved her Bible up, turned a page, and read:

> Therefore take up the whole armor of God, so that you may be able to withstand on that evil day, and having done everything, to stand firm. Stand therefore, and fasten the belt of truth around your waist, and put on the breastplate of righteousness. As shoes for your feet put on whatever will make you ready to proclaim the gospel of peace. With all of these, take the shield of faith, with which you will be able to quench all the flaming arrows of the evil one. Take the helmet of salvation, and the sword of the Spirit, which is the word of God. (Eph. 6:13 – 17 NRSV)

Heidi said, "I pray that I'm good enough to be wearing God's armor."

"You're already wearing a lot of belts. Is one of them the belt of truth that was mentioned in that quote from the Bible?"

Heidi looked at her waist before saying, "You're right. I am wearing three belts: a clothing belt, a belt with the word 'truth' on it, and an ugly belt that I want removed."

"What's wrong with the ugly belt?"

"It's actually a rope tied around my waist and connecting me to one of the shooters."

"I can see why you want that one removed."

Heidi tried to pull the rope off her waist, but it wouldn't move. She then moved her hand to different positions and kept on rubbing her soft gray sweater. Nothing happened. She then prayed to God about needing his armor. As soon as she said "Amen," her sweater's softness became hard and shiny. "This gray sweater has turned into a silver-colored breastplate. Maybe it's now a bullet-proof vest."

"With God's help, it could be your breastplate of righteousness."

"That would be even better than a bullet-proof vest." Heidi's eyes moved down to rest on her feet. She was wearing a pair of metal boots. After taking a couple of steps forward, she said, "These tough-looking boots are unbelievably comfortable. I could walk around for days in them."

"They look strong enough to protect your feet from bullets and knives."

"They might even protect my feet from hissing, biting snakes." Heidi stared at her boots for a few seconds and then added, "With two shooters and a lot of innocent people around me, I don't know if these boots can help to make things peaceful."

"You may be able to talk to the shooters," Faith said.

"I've already talked to them a little bit. It's really hard to be courteous to them and not to yell out bad things."

"If you say words from the Bible, you might help the shooters to change and become peaceful."

Heidi smiled. "With God's help, anything is possible."

Faith knelt down on her knees, reached out, and placed a Bible in Heidi's hands. "Here's some help."

Heidi said, "I can't take your Bible."

Faith smiled. "That's not my Bible. It's yours."

"You're supposed to have a Bible in your left hand."

"I'm still holding onto my own Bible. Can you see it here?" Faith stood up and reached her left hand forward. Her Bible was still in her hand.

"Thank you so much." Heidi moved the extra Bible up to her chest and placed it over her heart. "I'm so glad to have the word of God to help me with this tough shooter situation."

Faith's right hand, which was pointing up to heaven, moved down and pointed at the ground in front of Heidi's feet. A tiny shield, helmet, and sword flew out of Faith's hand and landed on the ground just a few feet in front of Heidi. The pieces of armor grew large enough to perfectly fit her. The shield covered most of her body. The helmet covered her entire head. Her glasses merged into the helmet's metal and became thick bullet-proof glass. Her eyes could now safely look out at the world around her. Her left hand held onto the Bible while her right hand held onto the sword.

Faith and Heidi both bowed their heads in prayer. Heidi said, "Dear Lord, I'm so thankful to you for your support and guidance. You have helped me, my ancestors, and so many other people in our world. Even when I'm trapped in a scary, horrible, evil situation, my faith in you is strong and never-ending. When it's my time to die, I know you will be with me, love me, and protect me for all eternity. Please continue to stay with me and to help me to do your will. In Jesus's name I pray, Amen."

Faith added, "Please be with her, Lord, and help her to help others. In Jesus's name I pray, Amen."

Heidi and Faith both raised their heads up. Heidi's head was heavy because of the weight of the helmet; Faith's head was heavy because of its granite structure. Despite the heaviness, Heidi and Faith were able to easily raise their heads up high into the brightness of the sky. They then shook hands and waved good-bye to each other. Heidi marched forward joyfully, easily, and quickly while wearing the armor of God.

Below Low

Heidi opened her eyes. Her glasses were on correctly, but her nose felt as if her glasses had been pressed too tightly against it. Heidi moved her glasses up onto her forehead. She then noticed that the top of her head hurt. She reached her right hand up further to the sore spot on her head. The helmet from her dream was no longer on top of her head; a small bump was there instead. Her hair, though, seemed messed up, as if she had been wearing a hat or a helmet.

Heidi blinked her eyes in the brightness of the light and then moved her glasses back into place. She could see the ceiling; it needed to be repainted.

"Are you awake?" a voice asked.

Heidi's eyes shifted toward the voice. Someone who looked familiar was standing right in front of her. After a few seconds, she said, "Oh, you're Joe."

"I am." Joe frowned and then asked, "Do you know your own name?"

"Yeah, I do."

"What's your name?" Joe asked.

"Heidi."

"What's your last name?" Joe asked.

"Dexter." Heidi rubbed her knees and ankles while asking, "Did I get hurt?"

"You fell down, so you might have a few bumps and bruises," Joe said.

"Where am I?" Heidi asked.

"You're here with me and Moe." Joe swept his hands sideways, indicating to Heidi that she should look at their surroundings.

Heidi turned her head sideways. She was lying on a floor in a hallway near a stairwell. A rope was tied around her waist and connected to Joe's waist. Heidi slowly stood up.

Joe said, "I see you're awake now. Do you remember what happened?"

Heidi gasped. "Yeah, I do." She looked down at the floor. It was cement. "I remember what happened in that store when someone used my Taser on me, but I don't know how I got here."

"Why do you think you're in a different place?" Joe asked.

"The floor is different," Heidi said.

Joe glanced at the floor. "You're right. With this cement floor, you can probably guess where we are right now."

"Are we in the basement?"

"Yes, we're in a hallway in the basement. Moe and I carried you here."

Heidi looked down at her knees and ankles.

"Okay, we sometimes had to drag you, rather than carry you," Joe said.

Heidi sighed. "At least I'm still alive."

Joe pulled at the rope connecting himself to Heidi; she was forced to take a step forward. He then said, "It's good that you can walk. You'll be able to stay alive for a little while longer."

Heidi moved her arms up and down while saying, "I can move okay." After pausing for a few seconds, she added, "I just feel a little bit strange, like I've just woken up and need to stretch."

Joe said, "Go ahead and stretch. We'll wait for a few seconds."

Heidi stretched her arms and legs into different positions. "I feel better now. Thanks for letting me do that."

Joe asked, "Are you hungry or thirsty?"

"Yeah, I actually am."

Joe reached into the backpack; he quickly pulled out a cereal bar and a bottle of water. He then said, "As long as you can eat these while walking as fast as I can, you can go ahead and have them."

"Thanks." Heidi took a bite out of the cereal bar before asking Joe, "Do you also need some food?"

"Moe and I are fine. We already had some lunch while you were unconscious."

"Thanks again for this food and water."

"Okay, let's get going." Joe turned around, pulled on the rope connecting himself to Heidi, and walked away from the stairwell.

While walking, Heidi asked, "How did we get here? Did we take the stairs?"

"Why should you care?" Joe asked.

"I'm just curious about whether the elevators are working or not."

"Why do you want to know?" Joe asked.

Heidi looked at the door leading into the stairwell. "A couple of years ago, I was stuck in an elevator. I'm just worried about people being stuck in elevators again."

"I don't think anyone's in the elevators right now." Joe yanked on the rope, pulling Heidi away from the stairwell. Moe followed them.

After a few steps, Heidi cleared her throat before saying, "I'm curious about something. Is it okay if I ask you a question?"

Joe stopped walking, turned around, and said to Heidi, "You just did ask me a question."

Heidi blushed. "Oh, I'm sorry. My head just hurts a little bit, so I'm not thinking too well."

"Okay, what do you want to know?" Joe asked.

"What happened to the people in the marketing store?"

Joe and Moe looked at each other. They both shook their heads; they were telling each other that it was okay to talk to Heidi about what had happened.

Joe said, "The people in that store are okay. We just took away their cell phones and tied them up, so they wouldn't call the cops."

Moe started moving forward; Joe and Heidi followed him. Heidi was a couple of feet behind Joe, so he wasn't watching her. She reached up to her glasses, pressed a button, and read the following message from Kevin: "Are you okay?"

She sent a text response back through her glasses: "I'm okay, but I'm tied on a rope to Joe."

Her glasses vibrated with an incoming message. She moved her hand up and again pressed the button to read the incoming message from Kevin: "I love you."

"I love you, too, Kevin."

Another vibration happened in Heidi' glasses, but she did not hit the incoming-message button on her glasses because the hallway was becoming dark. She was unable to clearly see if Joe and Moe were watching her or not.

Suddenly, a beam of light from Moe's flashlight lit up the wall; Moe found a light switch, turned on the lights, and waved his gun outward. He was telling Heidi and Joe to walk forward. After passing Moe, Heidi kept on walking behind Joe. About twenty feet later, the corridor broke off into two smaller hallways.

Everyone stopped moving. Heidi glanced quickly to the right with a blank look on her face. The corridor was empty, and she sighed slightly, showing her relief. She looked into the hallway on the left. She purposefully stared more directly and longer at different parts of that corridor; she obviously wanted Joe to move in that direction, rather than to the right.

Joe asked, "Do you know what companies are down here?"

"I know the heating system and some appliances are down here somewhere, but I don't know about any of the companies," Heidi said.

"What kind of appliances would be in the basement of an office building?"

"I thought there were washers, dryers, and maybe a couple of microwave ovens. However, I never actually saw any of them."

"How can you know about appliances if you never saw them?" Joe asked.

"Someone told me about kitchen and laundry things being down in the basement."

"If you were told about the appliances, weren't you also told about the companies down here?" Joe asked.

"No, I wasn't." Heidi stared at Joe and tried to look like she was telling the truth.

"You're a spy, right?" Joe asked.

"I do some work with federal agents, but I'm only an administrative assistant."

Joe laughed. "Do you really expect me to think of you as just a secretary, especially since you have a Taser and a pistol?"

"That's what I am."

Joe and Moe both laughed. Joe then said, "Neither one of us believes you."

Heidi frowned, opened her mouth, and quickly closed it again without saying anything.

Joe took a step closer to Heidi, placed his hands on his hips, and said, "Tell us about the Below Low store."

Heidi's eyes opened wide. After thinking for a few seconds, she said, "This is a new building with over fifty companies and organizations. I don't think anyone knows everything about every business."

Joe looked at some information on his cell phone before he grabbed Heidi's arm and turned to the right.

For the first fifty feet, only cement walls, vents, pipes, and electrical outlets were visible. Then the corridor turned ninety degrees to the right; a large set of closed steel doors was up ahead. Joe opened one of the doors and seemed very interested in the cement room's interior. The inside of the room had pipes and machinery for heating, air conditioning, water, and venting. Up against the furthest wall were some storage bins.

Moe asked, "Is there anything in this room really worth our time?"

Joe glanced at Heidi, but she was just looking down at the floor and trying not to show any facial expressions. Joe pulled at the rope, but Heidi still kept her eyes turned down toward the floor.

Joe said to Moe, "Even if Heidi doesn't want to tell us about it, there's probably something nice down here."

"The people in the Below Low store have been using this room as a storage area, right?" Moe asked.

"I think so." Joe stepped into the cement room. Heidi was forced to follow him because of the rope connecting them together.

Moe watched Joe and Heidi as they checked out the first of the bins. Inside were some tools. Joe picked up one of the large wrenches, showed it to Moe, and laughed. "If this weren't so heavy, Moe, I'd ask you to carry it around for me in that backpack of yours."

Moe said, "If we find anything nice that's light enough to carry around, I'll be happy to put it into my backpack."

Joe and Moe began looking inside some other storage bins. Heidi felt her glasses vibrate again. Because Joe and Moe were not watching her, Heidi pressed the button on her glasses and read two text messages from Kevin. The first message told her more details about the person in the mall who was threatening to set off a bomb. The second message said, "Make Joe and Moe go slower. If they enter fewer offices, fewer people will be endangered. You can also try to talk to them and get some information that might help the investigation."

Heidi responded "yes" to both of the messages. She then watched as Joe and Moe kept on looking inside the rest of the storage bins. The thieves only found items they did not want to steal, including some heavy tools, pipes, wires, and spare parts for the heating, air conditioning, water, and venting systems.

After ten storage bins had been examined, Joe, Heidi, and Moe left the cement room and moved forward along the corridor. They walked through another ninety-degree turn of the corridor; they then stopped in front of a set of glass windows. The store's name, "Below Low," was on the lowest section of one of the windows. Some of the store's products were in its window displays.

While standing in the corridor, Heidi, Joe, and Moe could see through the big front windows into the front section of the store's interior. Different manikins were wearing inexpensive clothing and jewelry. One of the manikins was too close to a jewelry display. Heidi stared at this manikin as it shook its right hand slightly.

Even though both Moe and Joe were near the front door of the store, they did not see the manikin's motions. However, Joe noticed Heidi was not walking forward. He pulled the rope, glared at her, and waved his hand.

Heidi stepped forward quickly and stood behind Joe while he tried to open the store's front door. It was locked, so Joe shot at the door's handle. With just a few bullet holes in it, the door's lock broke apart.

Joe pushed open the door. He and Moe walked over to the two cash registers. With their guns, they broke into the cash drawers.

Joe started to laugh.

"What's so funny?" Moe asked.

"There isn't a lot of money in this drawer."

"How much is there?" Moe asked while staring at the cash drawer in front of Joe.

Joe picked up four bills from the drawer. "I'm wondering if I'm seeing everything. There are only four one-dollar bills and some change."

Heidi walked closer to the cash drawer. "Sometimes people hide the money in different places. Did you check below the money tray and above the top cover section?"

Joe waved his hand at the cash register, inviting Heidi to check it out. "Have fun with it. If you happen to find some extra money, I might let you keep a penny or two."

Moe snickered and then asked, "Why can't I have some of the pennies?"

Joe replied, "We've already planned to share everything anyway, so you will be getting half of the pennies."

Heidi removed several metal sections of the cash drawer, but she was unable to find anything. "This drawer actually does only contain four dollars and seventy-two cents."

Joe said, "Yeah, that's really crazy. I'm guessing the employees stole the cash. They will probably claim that thieves broke into the store and stole it."

Moe laughed as he took some money out of the other cash register. "This one has over five hundred dollars in it. Should we take it or let the employees steal it?"

"Five hundred is still not as much as I expected, but we should take it," Joe said.

"I'll put the cash into my backpack."

Heidi said, "This is a small, cheap store all by itself in the basement. Most of the time, there probably wouldn't be a lot of customers or a lot of money in here." After hesitating, she asked, "Isn't five hundred dollars logical for such a place?"

Joe and Moe both stared at Heidi. Joe then said, "I guess you really don't know much about this store."

"What do you know about it?" Heidi asked.

Joe and Moe completely ignored her question. Joe's eyes were gazing intently at different sections of the store. At the same time, Moe's eyes stayed focused on the cash register as he concentrated on pulling the money out of the register and stuffing it into his backpack.

Joe said, "Don't bother with those coins. I don't think you want to carry around a bunch of heavy, noisy metal objects."

Moe walked over to one of the counters and lifted up two of the necklaces. "Can I grab some of these noisy, heavy necklaces? They're worth a little more than the coins are."

"Sure, I think jewelry will make a great gift." Joe paused and then added, "You can wrap those necklaces in something and then place them into your backpack. They'll be quieter that way."

Moe picked up four more necklaces. "How many of these do you think we can carry around?"

"How many do you want to carry?" Joe asked.

"I don't know." Moe thought for a few seconds and then added, "I'll need at least ten of them. How many do you want?"

"I think another ten would be good for me, especially if you want to carry them all."

"We should make Heidi carry things for us," Moe said.

"Oh, Moe, that's a great idea." Joe looked at Heidi, who sighed and then smiled hesitantly.

Heidi took a step closer to one of the jewelry counters and picked up a necklace with a cross on it. "Will I be able to wear some of the jewelry, rather than just carrying it for you?"

"Of course, you definitely can. If you like that necklace, take it," Joe said. After pausing for a few seconds, he added, "We might even let you keep it. We'll just need to check out the price tag. Moe and I obviously need the expensive stuff."

Heidi slowly inhaled and exhaled. "I don't want to steal anything, but I might be able to carry some things for you."

Joe took the necklace that Heidi was holding onto and put it with the jewelry that was being collected.

The pile of jewelry became larger when Moe added a few more items. He then examined some jewelry for pet owners. He picked up a necklace with paw prints on it. "Would this one be for the owner or for the pet to wear?"

Heidi said, "Perhaps they could both wear one."

Moe shook his head before picking up four of the paw-print necklaces. "I don't know, Joe, if there's anything really expensive here. I think it's all cheap stuff without any real gold, silver, pearls, or gems."

Heidi asked, "How do you know if it's cheap jewelry?"

Moe lifted up a necklace and waved the price tag in Heidi's direction. "The price for this necklace is only two dollars. Is that cheap enough to be called cheap?"

Heidi sighed. "I guess you're right."

Moe said, "If the employees are going to steal things anyway, it's better for the store's owners to just have cheap products for sale."

As Moe continued to look at some jewelry, Joe pulled Heidi over to a door on the right side of the store. It was unlocked. He and Heidi went inside.

"This must be the supervisor's office area," Heidi said.

"How do you know that?" Joe asked.

"There's a cheap desk for an administrative assistant and then a much better desk for the supervisor."

Joe pulled Heidi over to the supervisor's desk. He then sat down, leaned backward, and put his feet on top of the desk. He picked up a piece of paper on the edge of the desk and laughed. "Here's an interesting note. Apparently, this one employee named Skipper keeps on calling in sick. He's really a 'skipper' who keeps on skipping work."

A noise was heard from under the desk. Joe stood up, pulled out his gun, moved the barrel forward, and said, "Get out of there."

Nothing happened. After a few seconds of waiting, Joe moved the chair away from the desk. He then put the barrel of his gun under the desk before yelling. "I know you're under this desk. Get out right now, or your life will be over."

A young man crawled out from under the desk. His face and hands were quivering as he tried to stand. After pulling himself up by gripping the desk, he quivered while trying to stand.

Joe put his gun into its holder, placed his hands on his hips, and asked, "Are you the boss here?"

"No, I'm just a minimum-wage employee."

"Why are you hiding under the boss's desk?" Joe asked.

"I thought I'd be safest over here." The employee moved his body weight onto his left foot and then hopped sideways onto his right foot. He looked like he was skipping sideways.

"Who are you?" Joe asked. "Is your name Skipper, by any chance?"

The young man's face turned red as he said, "Yeah, I'm Skipper, but as you can see, I'm at work today."

"Why do you always call in sick?" Joe asked.

"Sometimes I'm really sick, but at other times, I need to take care of my son. He's less than a year old."

"Are you the one who stole the money from the cash register?" Joe asked.

"What cash register are you talking about?" Skipper asked.

"One of the registers in your store has less than five dollars in it," Joe said.

"I don't know anything about the cash registers. If I had to guess, though, I think Max might be stealing things."

"Why do you think Max is the thief?" Joe asked.

"About a month ago, someone stole some of the customers' credit card information. The boss thought the thief was Max." Skipper took a step forward and then a step backward. He repeated the forward and backward steps several times. He began to move faster, so he looked like he was skipping.

Joe said, "Stop that! You're driving me crazy."

Skipper stopped jumping, but instead quivered while he said, "Skipping helps me when I'm anxious. It's a physical activity."

Joe's hand went to the side of his gun. "You don't want to upset me when I'm carrying this weapon, do you?"

Skipper cleared his throat and swallowed. "No, I really don't want to make you mad. I'm sorry. I'll try to stand still." His body became tense; his face and hands kept on twitching.

Joe pointed his gun toward the door. "Let's go into the main part of this store." He, Skipper, and Heidi walked out to where Moe was still looking at jewelry. Joe said to Moe, "Can you tie this person up?"

"Yeah, I can do that."

Skipper jumped backward. Joe pulled Skipper's arm and made him move forward, so he was closer to Moe.

Joe said to Moe, "This guy's name is Skipper. He likes to skip around. If he jumps or twitches too much, just shoot him."

Moe took Heidi's rope and scissors out of his backpack. He then cut two pieces off of the rope, tied Skipper's hands together, and tied his feet to one of the legs of a heavy desk. Even after Moe was finished putting knots in the ropes, Skipper's hands and feet were still twitching.

Joe asked Skipper, "Okay, where are the other people who were working in your store? Are they still here?"

Five times, Skipper shook his head sideways. He was trying to say "no." He then talked by putting some words into the wrong places: "Don't here if know. Hiding was I. Heard people leaving desk under. Hiding some people."

Joe frowned. "You're skipping while you're talking. What do you mean? Do you know if some other people are in here right now?"

Skipper shook his head sideways multiple times.

Joe sat down and watched as Moe walked around the store, looking behind counters and under the tablecloths on several tables. Beneath one of the tables, he found a man seated up against one of the tables' legs and hidden under the tablecloth.

Moe said, "Come out of there."

The man crawled out from under the table and stood up with his arms and legs tensed in a strong fashion. His right hand was in his pocket. He then looked over at Skipper and frowned.

Skipper shook his fingers slightly; the shaking helped him to be less anxious. In normal—rather than in skipping—language, he said, "Hey, Judas. Are you okay?"

"Yeah, I am, especially since I have my gun." Judas pulled his right hand out of his pocket and pointed a small gun directly at Moe.

"I think that gun's only a toy," Moe said.

Judas moved the gun closer to Moe and said, "No, it's the real thing."

Moe looked over at Joe and asked him, "Do you know if any manufacturers really make such small guns?"

Joe said, "That might be a real gun. Some guns are made small on purpose, so people can easily hide them in their pockets and purses."

Judas glanced over at Joe and noticed that Joe was holding onto a larger gun. Judas waved his gun at Moe and said, "Even my small gun can kill this guy."

Joe said, "Stop kidding around, Judas. You know what I'll do with my gun if you shoot Moe." Joe stretched out his arm, so his gun was closer to Judas's head.

Judas glared at Joe and said, "If you guys want to just leave my store, then everyone will be safe."

Joe frowned. "No, if we leave your store, then you still won't be safe. We'll be coming back again when you least expect us."

Judas turned his gun toward Joe. "I think I'll shoot you first."

Joe moved his gun in a circular motion. He was trying to distract Judas as Moe silently took his own gun out of its holster.

Before Judas noticed what was happening, Moe had shot his gun. One bullet scraped Judas's arm. Another one hit his gun, knocking it to the floor. Joe walked over to Judas, picked up the gun, and made him sit down on the floor. Joe then said to Moe, "Can you look for some more people in here?"

Moe checked out the restrooms and found a lady with the nametag of "Diva" in the ladies' room. He brought Diva over to where Skipper was tied to the desk.

Joe told Judas to sit next to the desk where Skipper was tied up. While seated on the floor with his feet being tied by Moe to one of the legs of the desk, Judas was tightly clasping his left hand onto his right arm. While there was a small amount of blood on the right sleeve of his shirt, the bleeding seemed to have already stopped.

After a few seconds, Diva said, "It's too bad about your arm."

Judas looked at his arm and said, "It's really just a deep scratch. I should be okay, but to make you feel better, maybe this guy can put some kind of clothing item under a rope and tie the item tightly over my scratched arm. Then if I bump it again or something, it'll still be okay."

Moe laughed. "Why would I want to stop some minor bleeding in your arm?"

Judas asked, "What do you think will happen if you're caught? If you hurt me and then try to make things better, you'll get into a lot less trouble."

Moe glanced over at Joe, who shook his head in agreement. Moe then looked around at several of the clothing displays, picked up a pair of gloves, and said, "Okay, I'll tie these gloves to your scratched arm." After tying gloves around the scratch, Moe tied Judas's hands together. He then tied Diva to a different leg on the same desk.

Joe asked, "Is one of you the boss?"

Judas shook his head "no" and then pointed his finger at Diva. She angrily said, "You're the boss, Judas! Like usual, you're just trying to make yourself happy while you hurt other people!"

"Do I really look happy tied up here in front of two gunmen?"

"You look less scared than I do." Diva tried to shrug her shoulders, but she was unable to move them for more than an inch. She then added, "Every time employees ask for a raise, you say 'no.'"

Skipper was shaking his head in agreement with Diva. He then looked across the room at a broom and a mop that were standing against the wall. "Then you add extra duties for all of us to do, and you let yourself do fewer things."

Diva said, "I saw online that you got a raise last month. It's not fair for you to get some extra money because you're hurting low-income, poverty-level employees with children!"

Skipper said, "You even spend less time here at work than the part-time employees do."

Judas said, "That's because I often have to go to meetings."

Diva and Skipper glared at Judas. Skipper then said, "Your meetings are just an excuse to leave work whenever you feel like it."

Judas looked down at his feet. He seemed to be zoning out and trying to avoid eye contact. After a few seconds, he inhaled and said in a high-toned voice to Joe, "Diva and Skipper are just lying. They're trying to save themselves by hurting me."

Heidi looked at Judas with a blank expression on her face; Joe and Moe frowned. None of them seemed to believe what Judas had just said.

Joe glared at Judas, moved his gun forward, and said, "It doesn't matter who's the boss. What does matter is if all three of you live or die."

Skipper's nose and hands started twitching. "What do you want us to do?"

"Moe and I want the money that was stolen from that cash register. We also want some real gold jewelry. If you three can give us at least ten thousand dollars in cash and gold, we'll let you live."

Skipper looked at Diva. "Do you know where the money is?"

"No, I don't. Judas, though, knows where everything is."

They both looked at Judas. He was staring off into space.

Diva said, "You can at least look at us, Judas."

Silently, Judas was still staring at nothing. He then rubbed his right ear against his right shoulder.

Joe yelled, "Look at me!"

Judas was still staring off into nothing.

Skipper said, "This is how Judas usually acts. He never respects people enough to even look at them."

Joe pointed his gun at Judas, put his index finger on the trigger, and said, "Judas, tell me where the money is, or I'll shoot you right now."

Judas did not even look at Joe, but rather kept on staring at nothing.

Joe stepped up to Judas and placed the barrel of his gun against Judas's right foot. "Say something."

Judas looked at the gun barrel and frowned. "What do you want me to say?"

"Tell me where the money is, or I'll shoot you right now." Joe slid his index finger up and down on his gun's trigger.

Judas turned his face to the right, looked at one of the walls, and zoned out again.

Joe said sarcastically, "Okay, you're the boss; we'll do it your way." His hand tightened around the handle of his gun. He then pulled the trigger and shot at the center of Judas's right foot. Judas screamed and said some negative words. He tried to move his foot, but it would not move. He then tensed up his leg and ankle muscles.

Joe asked, "Do you want the same thing to happen to your other foot?"

With a facial expression of extreme pain, Judas looked at Joe for a few seconds before saying, "I'll tell you, but can I first have a bandage for my foot?"

Moe grabbed a belt and a sweater from two of the clothing racks. He handed the items to Heidi and gestured toward Judas's foot. Heidi looked at Joe, who shook his head affirmatively. Joe then stepped forward, so Heidi could reach Judas.

Heidi knelt down on her knees. As she put the sweater onto Judas's foot and tied the belt tightly around his ankle, he kept on murmuring.

"Are you okay?" Heidi asked.

Judas said, "The belt and sweater are making my foot hurt even more. Did you put them on correctly?"

"Yeah, I think so," Heidi said.

"Maybe the problem is my foot. My second toe is bigger than my big toe, and the veins are a little big in my feet."

Joe laughed. "Even with your shoe on, your foot appears to have more problems than just those two things."

Moe said, "Yeah, your shoes are both bumpy in a few places; your feet have made bumps in the shoes' leather."

Judas said, "Okay, both of my feet are bumpy. For my foot that's been shot, though, can you please take off my shoe? You can then put the sweater and belt back on, and my foot will probably feel a little better."

Heidi looked at Judas's shoe. "It's probably better if we leave the shoe on your foot, so it can help to compress your foot."

Judas said, "I don't even think my foot is bleeding, but it really hurts. Can you just loosen up the belt a little bit?"

"I could, but I've had a little bit of training with injuries. You'll be safer if I leave things the way they are." Heidi sighed.

Judas said angrily, "Okay, I'll just have to deal with this pain somehow."

Heidi stood up and stepped away from Judas.

Joe said, "Now that your foot's not bleeding, tell me the truth: Where did you hide the money?"

"It's in the middle one of the three drawers in my desk."

"I looked there already. I didn't see anything," Joe said.

"You have to remove the folder and the piece of wood at the bottom of the drawer."

Moe went into the room with the supervisor's desk and returned a few minutes later with a stack of money. He said, "Knowing what a liar this Judas is, we should ask him for the rest of his money. He probably has more in a different place, like in a safe."

Judas said, "No, I don't have a safe."

Skipper looked at Diva. They shook their heads "yes" at each other. Skipper then said, "Judas does have an office safe. I don't know what's inside of it, but I know its location."

Joe asked, "Where is it, Skipper?"

"It's beneath Judas's desk. You need to slide the desk about a foot to the right, and then you'll see where the safe is located."

Joe moved his gun close to Judas's left foot. "How can I unlock that safe?"

Judas sighed before saying, "The numbers are six, six, and six."

Moe went into the back-office area. The sound of a sliding desk was followed by a cracking noise. A few minutes later, Moe came back into the main part of the store. He was carrying pieces of gold jewelry, paperwork, and some money.

"What are those papers for?" Joe asked.

"I didn't have a chance to read them much, but they seem to have something to do with stock market options," Moe said.

"That's interesting. We might have over ten thousand dollars in items right here." Joe moved his gun close to Judas's head. He then asked Diva and Skipper, "What should I do to Judas?"

Diva said, "While he's perhaps the worse boss I've ever had, I don't want to see him die."

Skipper shook his head in agreement. "Even though he's a lying, back-stabbing person, I'm not the one to decide if he should die or not. That's God's job."

Judas tried to smile, but it looked like a frozen, fake one. He then looked up at Joe and said, "Please let me live. I promise I'll be a better person."

Joe stared at Judas in disbelief. "Do you really expect me to believe that?"

Turning his head away from Joe, Judas looked at Diva and Skipper. After a few seconds, he asked them, "You two believe me, right?"

Diva hesitated and then said, "I don't know."

Skipper looked over at Judas's injured foot. Skipper's eyes then started to blink. He inhaled and exhaled while his eyelids flickered at an increasingly faster rate.

Judas asked, "What do you think, Skipper?"

"I believe you." Skipper's eyes were blinking so fast that everyone knew he was lying.

Joe shifted his weight slightly and lifted up his gun. "Is there any reason why we should let you live?"

Judas turned his injured foot slightly inward and said, "I'll tell you where there's another employee in this store. She's even wearing expensive rings, and she has thirty silver earrings in her purse."

"Where is she?" Joe asked.

Judas pointed toward the manikins. "She's over there. She's the manikin in the blue dress."

Moe went up to the blue-dressed manikin. The manikin was tensed up and trying to stay still, but her right arm, which was holding onto a purse, started shaking. Moe grabbed her purse and then pulled her over to where the other employees were. After he tied her to the table, he grabbed a bag from under one of the counters. He then pulled the living manikin's wedding, engagement, and other rings off of her fingers. Reaching into her purse, he found thirty silver earrings. He put all of the jewelry back into the purse and then put the purse into his backpack.

The living manikin was crying. With tears in her eyes, she said to Judas, "I just bought those silver earrings an hour ago because of the great deal you offered to me. Can I have my money back?"

"No, I can't refund your money because you don't have the earrings anymore. I could only refund your money if you were able to give me back the earrings."

"You offered such a low price for those earrings because you were worried they would be stolen," the manikin said.

"I was right about that. The earrings have been stolen."

"They were only stolen because you told Moe and Joe about them. If you had just been quiet about a manikin having earrings, I'd still be free, and I'd still have those earrings in my purse."

"When the earrings were stolen, they were in your purse. They were legally yours," Judas said.

"I didn't pay cash for the earrings." The living manikin raised her chin upward and her eyebrows even higher. Her eyes were no longer filled with tears. "I charged them on one of my credit cards."

Judas opened his mouth, closed it, and then frowned. "Oh, did you really charge them?"

"Yes, I did. I'll have the credit card company put the money back onto my card. Then you'll be refunding me my money, whether you want to or not."

Judas stared angrily at the living manikin. "If you dare do that, you'll have to find yourself a new job."

The living manikin inhaled quickly. Tears formed in her eyes again.

Even though Judas's hands were tied together at the wrists, he raised his hands upward a few inches, closed his fists, and shook them. He turned his head to look at Moe, who had just cleared his throat.

Moe moved his gun upward and said, "Hey, Judas, you can't fire anyone. You're not the boss right now. You're tied up."

"I know that, but I won't always be tied up here. When I'm free, I'll be able to do whatever is appropriate for me to do as the person in charge."

Moe said, "You just promised to be a better person."

"I really am being a good person. A good boss doesn't let employees steal things."

The living manikin still had tears in her eyes as she said, "I'm not stealing anything. You're the one who's stealing things."

Judas said, "No, I'm not the thief here. Max is."

"Max isn't here now. Plus, he's not trying to steal anything from me, like you are."

"He's stolen credit card data from customers."

The living manikin said, "If Max really was guilty, then why didn't you fire him?"

Judas stared silently at his feet.

The manikin said, "So, you're hiding something from us. Did Max pay you to keep his job and to keep you quiet?"

Judas remained silent as he gazed off into the empty space above his feet.

Moe frowned at Judas and then turned to face Joe. "I really think we should shoot this guy. He's the worst boss I've ever met."

Joe shook his head in agreement and turned his gun toward Judas's head. "It might be even more fun if we both shoot him at the same time."

"You can shoot his head, and I'll shoot his heart," Moe said as he aimed at the center of Judas's chest.

Joe said, "That's a good idea. If we watch his breathing, we might even be able to figure out which bullet makes him die first."

Judas began to breathe really quickly. He then said in a low voice, "I'll tell you where the drugs are."

Joe and Moe looked at each other and then shifted their guns downward.

Heidi took a step backward, so no one would notice what she was doing. She then sent a message through her glasses to Kevin: "Judas knows about some drugs. I'll try to videotape what's happening."

Kevin responded back, and the word "yes" appeared to Heidi on her glasses.

Heidi showed her agreement by pressing one of the buttons on her glasses a single time. As she turned to watch Judas, some barely noticeable flashes of light moved along the front of her lenses.

Judas raised his chin toward one of the walls and said, "A closet door's over there."

Joe stared at the wall. Some shelves and a bookcase were all that was visible. "I don't see any doors." He looked at Judas, who was again staring off into space. Joe then turned to the employees and asked, "Do any of you know about the closet?"

Skipper's eyes skipped back and forth while looking at Diva and the manikin. He then said, "I didn't realize Judas was into drugs. Did either one of you know about this?"

The other employees shook their heads "no" before turning to stare at Judas.

With a strong voice, Judas said. "I'll tell Joe and Moe about how to find the hidden closet if they promise not to shoot any of us."

Joe said, "I promise." His facial expression and high-toned voice showed that he was lying.

Moe glanced at Joe, smiled, and said in a similar high-toned voice, "I also promise."

After hesitating for a few seconds, Judas said, "Okay, I'll tell you. It's behind the bookcase."

Joe asked, "Do we need to move that bookcase?"

"Yeah, you do. The bookcase has wheels, so you just need to push it to the side."

Moe went up to the bookcase and pushed it away from the wall. A six-foot high door was now visible. Moe pulled at the handle, and the door immediately opened. He went into the closet. The beam of his flashlight could be seen moving around inside the closet. After a minute, he came back out with a bag in his right hand. He put the bag into his backpack and then said, "I brought out just a few items, but more than fifty boxes are in there."

Joe said, "I guess that's too much for us to carry right now."

"Do you think we'll be able to come back again in a week or two?"

"I doubt it. After we leave this building, we'll need to hide out for a few years." Joe looked at Judas, who was staring down at the floor, and then added, "I also doubt Judas will keep his drugs in that closet anymore. Too many people will know about it."

Judas was still looking at the floor and trying to avoid eye contact with anyone.

Joe said, "Okay, I think it's time for us to shoot him."

Judas looked up at Joe. "I told you about the drugs. You also promised not to shoot anyone in here."

Joe and Moe both moved their guns upward and pointed them at Judas. Joe said, "You're still a really bad boss, especially if you hide drugs in a secret closet at work."

Scrunching his head down onto his chest, Judas tried to move his hands up onto the top of his head, but the rope around his wrists was too tight. With the fingers on his hands clasped together, he started to cry. With tears falling onto his hands, he looked up at Joe. "Please let me live. I promise to be a better boss."

Joe smirked as his finger moved onto the trigger of his gun. He then said, "Okay, Moe, I'll be the one who counts to three."

Before either gun was fired, Heidi stopped recording the action through her glasses, so her glasses looked normal again. She then was able to draw attention to herself by talking; she said, "Please don't kill him."

Joe swirled his gun toward Heidi. "Why are you saying that? Why should someone like him be allowed to live?"

"He's only trying to do his job," Heidi said.

Joe frowned. "He hasn't been doing it too well. Everyone hates him. Plus, he's been hiding the actions of a thief stealing credit-card information."

"Well, he's been trying. Plus, right now, he's probably too scared to be acting rationally."

"If we let Judas live, what will you do to thank us?" Joe smiled in a leering way.

Heidi looked down at her feet and over to the backpack that she had been carrying. "I promise to not complain about carrying the backpack for you."

"What about when we go up the stairs?" Joe laughed.

"I might have to walk a little bit slower, but I'll be good. I won't complain." Heidi smiled. "Don't you want me to be more of a helper and less of a complainer?"

Joe and Moe looked at each other. They were reading each other's eye language. Joe's eyes swirled around slightly, showing a possible positive response to Heidi's request. Joe then said out loud, "Okay, he lives, but he'll live in more pain." He turned his gun downward and shot Judas's other foot. Judas yelled some negative words and tried to move his feet forward and backward. With his ankles tied onto the leg of a table, he was only capable of moving his feet a few inches.

Heidi said, "Thanks, Joe, for not killing him."

"You're welcome."

"Can I put some clothing around his left foot to possibly stop any bleeding?" Heidi asked.

"Yeah, that's a good idea, especially since tight clothing on both of his feet will make his pain even worse," Joe said.

While Heidi wrapped a belt and a sweater tightly around Judas's left foot, Judas kept on inhaling and making noises that showed his pain.

Moe put the stock-market paperwork and some money into a new purse. He then pushed the purse into the backpack.

Joe pointed to the pile of jewelry that they had created earlier. "Should we bring these, too?"

"Yeah, I think we should. Even though they all are inexpensive, I like some of them." Moe grabbed three of the necklaces from the large pile of jewelry, put each one into a sock, and placed the socks into the backpack. One of the necklaces was the one with the cross on it.

Heidi said, "I like that necklace, but I don't want to steal it. Can you at least take some money out of my purse and leave it in the cash register?"

Moe said, "Give me your purse."

Heidi handed her purse to Moe, who opened it up and took out all the cash from her billfold. He then put her money into his backpack.

Heidi opened her mouth to say something. When she saw Moe's expression, she closed her mouth without saying anything. After a few seconds of silence, she looked at Judas and said, "Okay, I'll just have to pay for the necklace at a later time."

Judas stared at her with a surprised look on his face. He then said, "Thanks."

"You're welcome." Heidi looked at Judas's arm and feet as she added, "I also hope you recover quickly from your injuries. You'll be in my prayers."

Before Judas could say anything else, Joe pulled at the rope that was attached to Heidi's waist. He gestured for her to stand up and for Moe to attach the backpack to her back.

Heidi moved her shoulders backward, sighed, and stood up. "That backpack is probably super heavy."

Joe said, "I thought you were not going to complain about the backpack."

Heidi put her right hand in front of her mouth. "Oops, I'm sorry. I'm just tired."

Moe attached the backpack to Heidi. He then left the Below Low store and began walking through the corridor leading over to the stairwell. Joe followed Moe; Heidi was several feet behind Joe. After they had moved about twenty feet away from the store, Heidi reached up to her glasses and sent a text message to Kevin: "Judas in Below Low was shot in both feet. He's okay for now, but he needs medical help."

An immediate response to her message said, "Yes."

A minute later, Moe, Joe, and Heidi arrived at the stairwell. Heidi glanced at the stairs and sighed.

Moe looked at the backpack attached to Heidi and asked, "Do we really have to take the stairs again?"

Joe replied, "The elevators can't be working. The security people would have shut them down."

"What store are we going to?" Moe asked. "Hopefully, it's only one or two floors above us."

"We really need to go to that jewelry store on the thirteenth floor," Joe said.

"Is that the one you told me about—the one with the neat sunglasses?"

Joe smiled as he said, "Yeah, it is. It's called Tina's Gold & Silver Sales and Distribution Company. It has all kinds of neat items. I want some of the sunglasses, and much of the jewelry is made from real gems."

"The gold and silver are probably real, too," Moe said.

"Yeah, I think they are."

"That store does sound really nice." Moe paused before adding, "Maybe we should stop at the fourth or fifth floor first. I don't really want to climb up thirteen flights of stairs, at least not all at the same time."

Heidi looked at the stairwell with a frown on her face. "With this backpack, I'll have to pause to relax a few times."

Joe's face showed his resolution. "We really do need to go up to the thirteenth floor as soon as possible. Just in case we have to suddenly leave this building, I want to make certain we've been to all of the companies at the top of my list."

Moe shook his head in agreement. "We should definitely go to that store, and an elevator would be faster than the stairs."

"Running back and forth between the elevators and the stairs will take up more time," Joe said.

"If the elevators aren't working, then we'll be wasting some time. However, if the elevators are working, we'll be saving time." Moe looked at his watch and smiled.

Joe sighed. "It doesn't make sense that the elevators will still be working."

"Even if the elevators were shut off earlier, it's possible they're working again," Moe said.

Joe thought for a few seconds before saying, "I guess anything's possible."

"We could just check out one of the elevators now. If it's not working, then we'll know for sure to keep on taking the stairs."

"Okay, Moe, let's try an elevator, just to make you happy."

They walked over to the closest elevator. Moe pressed the "up" button, but nothing happened. The button remained unlit. "You were right, Joe. The elevators are not working."

"I think we all really knew the elevators wouldn't work. We'll just have to keep on taking the stairs." Joe turned away from the elevator and pulled at the rope that was attached to Heidi. She followed him down the hallway over to the stairwell.

Joe walked to the stairs and started to climb up. Heidi followed him, and Moe followed Heidi. At the first-floor level, Joe paused and glanced back at Heidi.

Heidi was hesitating, rather than taking another step. "Can we pause for just a minute?"

Joe looked closely at Heidi. "Are you kidding?"

"No, climbing up these stairs with a backpack is not easy."

"You're not even tired yet. You're breathing okay." Joe put his right hand on his gun and asked, "Are you trying to slow us down?"

The surprised look on Heidi's face showed that she really was trying to slow them down. In a high-tone voice, she said, "I'm just trying to rest now, rather than having to rest in the middle of a stairway."

Joe frowned. "You really are trying to be slow, possibly to give the first responders some extra time to set things up. When you're actually out of breath, then we'll pause." Joe moved onto one of the stairs. He pulled at the rope, and Heidi followed him. Moe stayed behind for a few seconds and then followed Joe and Heidi as they climbed up the stairs.

By the time Joe reached the third floor, he, Heidi, and Moe were all slightly out of breath. They paused in the stairwell for a minute. Moe pulled out his cell phone and tried to check his Facebook page. However, there was no internet connection.

Joe said, "You shouldn't do that anymore."

"Why can't I check Facebook? I could possibly find things that people are saying about us. My friends might be talking about the shooters in this building."

"It's better if you check one of the online newspapers, rather than Facebook," Joe said.

"People are freer to say what they want to on social media," Moe said.

"You're right. I never thought of that." Joe paused and then added, "The regular news media reporters have to be more careful about what they say."

Moe shook his head in agreement. "The reporters say 'person of interest,' but people on Facebook might say 'thieves' or 'killers.'" He stepped forward a few paces, but he still could not get internet access. He stared at Joe and said, "I wonder if the police turned off cell phone connections in this building."

Heidi said, "I doubt if that would happen right now. People stuck in the building would want to talk to their family members." After staring at Moe's phone, she asked, "Could there just be a problem with your phone?"

"I don't think so." Moe turned on his cell phone's flashlight. "My phone's working fine. It's the internet that isn't working."

Joe said, "Let's just get going again." When he started climbing up the stairs, Heidi and Moe followed him.

Gold & Silver Again

Joe, Heidi, and Moe kept climbing up the stairs until they reached the thirteenth floor. They headed down the corridor and walked past a small window and a door. When they arrived in front of a large window, Joe said, "The jewelry store's right here."

Moe asked, "Are you sure this is Tina's Gold & Silver Sales & Distribution?"

"Yeah, it is. I remember its location. Plus, this window is the one with lots of neat jewelry items in it."

"Where's the jewelry? I don't see anything but that curtain."

Joe said, "Someone must have put that curtain up there to block people from seeing things."

Moe moved his flashlight's beam around to different sections of the big window.

The large curtain was possibly hiding the company's name and jewelry items. The curtain had the following words written on it: "Theft from companies and hard-working people hurts our whole economy, which will hurt everyone, including the thieves."

Joe laughed. "When we get inside, we'll have to add our words onto that curtain."

Heidi asked, "What words are you thinking about?"

Joe and Moe exchanged glances. Their heads and eyes moved up and down in circular motions. They were saying to each other, as well as to Heidi, that she was being silly.

Moe asked Joe, "Should we tell her anything?"

Heidi said, "It seems like you did just tell me something."

Moe said, "No, we didn't."

"Yes, you did." Heidi paused and then added, "You told me what you were thinking with your eyes and your faces. You just didn't say your thoughts in words because you were trying to be nice."

Joe said, "Okay, we're only partially hiding our thoughts. At least we're not as bad as the owners of this jewelry store. They're hiding everything, even their company's name."

Moe shook his head in agreement. He then flashed his light around the top of the big window's curtain. Nothing was visible. Joe also turned on his flashlight. The two beams of light moved up and down on the side edges of the curtain. The curtain was several inches too narrow to fill the entire window area, so the extreme left and right sections of the big window area were not blocked.

Joe was pointing his flashlight around the left edge of the window's curtain. Heidi stood behind and slightly to the left of Joe; she could partially see the store's interior. Some furniture was visible. However, none of the gem-decorated jewelry items could be seen.

Joe was intently staring through the window's small open section on the left and looking inside the store. "I can't see if the sunglasses are still here, but we should be able to break in and find out." He took a step backward, moved his gun up, and shot at the window. Loud bullet and crackling noises were heard, but the glass did not break.

Moe said, "It must be bullet-proof."

"Yeah, I thought it was." Joe moved his gun to the right. He shot multiple bullets at the front door's handle and lock. Splinters of wood and metal flew outward toward Joe, Moe, and Heidi.

While all of the splinters landed on the floor without hitting anyone, Moe still asked, "Can you wait a minute, Joe, until I get out of the way?"

"Okay." Joe stopped shooting. Moe walked several feet to the left, and Heidi stepped backward. Joe fired his gun a few more times, but the door remained locked. He tried to twist the handle off of the door, but the handle was firmly attached. He walked up closer and looked at the door's hinges. "There's something wrong here. I'll try these." He stepped backward, lifted his gun again, and sent multiple bullets toward the door's hinges. He then took a small chisel out of the backpack on Heidi's back and pulled the right side of the door off of its hinges.

Moe clapped his hands while yelling, "Yahoo!"

Heidi scrunched her eyebrows together and asked, "How did you make that happen? Aren't the hinges made of metal? They should be tough enough to resist bullets."

"Hinges are tough, but the areas where the hinges are connected to the door are sometimes a bit too weak." Joe laughed. "Plus, in this case, the hinges were attached wrong."

As Joe pulled Heidi through the partially-opened door, she stared at the hinges. She then said, "Maybe someone did this on purpose, just to make it easier to break into the store."

"Anything's possible these days," Joe said as he marched quickly over to the curtain hanging in the front window. After pulling the curtain down onto the floor, he took out a pen and wrote, "When thieves sell things, they're helping the economy."

Moe watched what Joe was writing and then added his own idea onto the curtain: "Thieves help security people and police officers to keep their jobs, instead of being laid off."

Joe smiled at Moe's added commentary and then asked Heidi, "Do you want to write anything?"

Heidi slowly inhaled and exhaled. She then shook her head in a negative way. When Joe turned his face away from her, she said softly, "Dear Lord, please help me to know how to interact properly with these thieves. I don't want them to kill me or other people, but I also hate what they're doing and saying. In Jesus's name I pray, Amen."

Joe asked, "What were you just saying?"

Heidi gripped her hands together. She looked up at the ceiling, sighed, and said, "I was just praying."

Joe shrugged his shoulders and then walked over to the left side of the room, where the sunglass display was. About half of the glasses had been removed. The one pair that Joe wanted, though, was still there.

He picked up the glasses, waved them in the air, and asked Moe, "Do you like these?"

"Yeah, I do."

"Do you think these gems on the glasses are real black diamonds?" Joe asked.

Moe stared at the glasses before saying, "I doubt it. If those glasses had real diamonds, they wouldn't have been left out on a shelf like that. The people who were working here would have hidden them away or locked them up somewhere."

"You're right. Many of the glasses actually were removed from this display and hidden away somewhere."

Moe nodded. "The hidden ones must be the ones with the real gems."

Joe smiled at the sunglasses in his hand and then placed them on his face. As soon as the bridge between the two lenses landed on his nose, he said, "Oh, no!" He quickly removed the sunglasses from his face and stared at the bridge section.

Heidi asked, "Are you okay?"

"Yeah, I think there's a needle or something here." With his fingers, Joe pulled a half-inch-long thin piece of metal out of the bridge area of the sunglasses. After throwing the piece of metal onto the floor, he rubbed the top section of his nose. A small scratch was there, but no blood was flowing out. Joe put the sunglasses back onto his face.

Moe asked, "Did anyone in this store know about you liking those sunglasses?"

"Yeah, at least one lady did," Joe said.

"Then she probably put that needle into the sunglasses on purpose," Moe said.

"She probably did, but she also may have told other people about me liking these sunglasses."

Heidi said, "Some bacteria, drugs, or something else might have been placed on that little metal needle."

Joe swallowed, removed the sunglasses from his face, and placed them in the backpack that Heidi was carrying. Then with Heidi following him, he moved around the room and knocked on different sections of the walls. Everything sounded the same. While Joe was knocking on the walls, Moe began to look into the drawers of the room's desks and file cabinets. No expensive jewelry was found anywhere.

Joc asked Heidi, "Why aren't there any computers in here?"

Heidi stared at the desks. The gem-covered laptops were no longer on the desktops. "I don't know. Maybe people hid the computers somewhere to make certain their customer information was kept secure."

"Why are you lying?" Joe asked.

"I'm not lying," Heidi said.

"Then why are you blinking your eyes so much?" Joe asked.

"The light in here is affecting my eyes. They're very light sensitive." Heidi swallowed and then pointed to the door on the right side of the room. "The computers were probably put in there."

"Is that some kind of a vault?" Joe asked.

"I know the door's metal, but someone once told me that this store also has a distribution center," Heidi said.

Joe laughed. "I already know that. The word 'distribution' is in the company's name."

"Oh, you're right." Heidi smiled. "That other room is probably where items are made ready for distribution to different stores and people."

"There should be some interesting and expensive jewelry items in that room." Joe walked over to the door and tried to open it, but the door was locked. After moving his rifle upward, he shot multiple times at the door's handle and hinges. The door remained closed and locked.

Joe then shot at the control panel that was next to the door. One of the numbered buttons fell off and landed on the floor. Joe walked up to the panel. Nothing else was damaged. Joe looked at Moe while saying, "I guess we're not going to get any expensive things in here."

Moe asked, "Should we use one of our bombs? If it's placed up against that metal door, we might be able to get into the room."

Heidi inhaled and coughed. Joe looked at her and asked, "What's wrong?"

"I didn't know you had bombs."

Joe said, "We do."

Moe scratched his head. "For expensive jewelry, it makes sense for us to use one of our bombs."

Joe rubbed his chin. "I don't know if that room contains anything worthwhile. What if we use one of our bombs, and the distribution area only has packing supplies and cheap glass jewelry?"

Moe frowned. "Yeah, that could happen, but I think we should try for something that could really be possible, rather than running around to other stores and maybe finding nothing."

"Okay, let's use one of our bombs. However, we should first help ourselves to some of the items in this room." Joe walked over to the sunglass display again, picked up two more pairs of sunglasses, stared intently at the bridge sections of each one, and finally put them into the backpack that Heidi was still wearing.

Moe moved close to one of the desks. It had some sparkling pens, some interesting notepads, a paperclip holder, a stapler, and a mouse with glass inserts. After he picked up a few of the items and put them into the backpack, he asked Joe, "Should we take anything else for other people?"

"No, let's not bother, at least not from this room. We need to get some more expensive items for our friends and family." Joe turned around and stepped close to the backpack that Heidi was wearing. He opened up one section and began to remove some items.

Heidi shivered as she asked, "Do you really have bombs in this backpack that I've been carrying for you?"

"Yeah, we do, but as long as you behave yourself, you'll be safe."

"What if I fall down?"

"You'll be fine."

"Will I still be okay if I fall down a staircase?" Heidi turned her head to try and see Joe's face, but he was standing behind her.

"Of course, you'll be okay. Bombs won't go off until they're set up to do so." The tone of Joe's voice was slightly higher than usual; he sounded like he was lying.

Moe asked Joe, "Are you sure the other bomb won't go off if she falls down five or ten stairs?" He paused before continuing, "I really don't want to be standing that close to an exploding bomb."

Heidi asked, "Is there just one other bomb left in the backpack, or is there more than one?"

Joe frowned at Moe. "Why did you tell her how many bombs we have?"

"I'm sorry. I should have kept my mouth closed. I didn't mean to tell Heidi that we only have two bombs: the one we're building and the one left in the backpack."

Joe sighed. "Let's just get moving and open up that door."

Heidi turned around and watched as Joe and Moe carried a four-inch square box and a timer over to the door. Moe began to attach the items to the door's handle. "Is this the best spot?"

Joe stared at different sections of the door and then glanced at the control panel on the wall next to the door. "The control panel is probably the best place for the bomb."

Moe detached the bomb from the door's handle and gave it to Joe, who set it up on top of the control panel. Heidi and Moe then followed Joe as he left the jewelry store. They all walked through the corridor and about fifteen feet away from the store. While standing behind Joe and Moe, Heidi sent a text to Kevin on her glasses: "A bomb soon will explode in Tina's Gold & Silver. Only a locked door should be hurt."

A response message was sent by Kevin: "Do they have more bombs?"

"After the explosion, they'll only have one more left."

Heidi noticed Joe kneeling down on the floor and entering some numbers into his cell phone. She covered her ears. Just a few seconds later, the explosion happened. Heidi was immediately pulled into the jewelry store by Joe tugging on the rope. He ran over to the right side of the room and paused to look at the bomb's damage.

Next to the door leading into the distribution center, the control panel was partially demolished. Pieces of metal, a torn wire, and plastic buttons had fallen to the floor. Joe moved closer to the control panel, pulled at the wires that were still there, and used his knife to cut several of the wires. He then turned away from the control panel and pushed on the door, which immediately opened with only a single squeaking noise.

Joe turned on the lights. Conveyor belts were present but were not moving, and no jewelry products were visible. While Moe looked inside some boxes and plastic containers, Joe opened up all of the file cabinets' doors. One of the cabinets contained paperwork arranged in different files. The other cabinets had office and shipping supplies.

Joe asked, "Moe, have you found anything?"

"Some of these boxes have packing lists and jewelry." Moe held up a piece of paper and a necklace. "However, I haven't yet found any expensive items."

Heidi asked, "Are you again using the price tags to tell the difference between the expensive jewels and the cheap glass ones?"

"The packing lists have the costs of the items being shipped," Moe said. After silently reading some of the information on the list that he was holding, he added, "I've always thought the tracking numbers are very interesting. I can actually decode some of them. This box, for example, will be going to Connecticut."

Heidi said, "You know a lot about packing lists. Do you work for a company that uses them?"

Before Moe had a chance to say anything, Joe pulled on the rope, grabbed Heidi's elbow, and asked, "Why are you asking Moe a question like that?"

"I was just curious."

Joe's eyebrows showed his anger. "Are you trying to find out our identities?"

Heidi glanced over at Moe, who was frowning at her. "I already know your names. You're Joe and Moe."

Joe slapped Heidi's face and then said, "You'd better behave yourself."

Heidi pushed her glasses up and wiped tears from her eyes. "I'll try to be better. I'm just not used to being kidnapped and tied to a rope."

Joe glared at Heidi. "Okay, from now on, don't try to find out information about us. We want our identities to stay hidden."

Heidi shook her head affirmatively. She then followed Joe as he moved beyond the file cabinets to the opposite end of the room. Joe stopping walking and stood in front of a door. He asked Heidi, "Do you know what's beyond this door?"

Heidi sighed. With inner strength, she stared purposefully at Joe's face. She was obviously trying to show that she wasn't lying, but the high tone of her voice made her sound untruthful as she said, "I don't know."

Joe laughed. "I know that you know."

"No, I really don't."

"Everyone knows what's behind this door. It's expensive jewelry," Joe said.

Heidi's voice stuttered slightly as she said, "You're probably right."

Joe stared at Heidi before looking at different sections of the door. He then knocked on it.

Moe stepped up next to Joe and asked, "Why are you even bothering to knock on that door?"

"If any people are inside, one of them might automatically say something or even open up the door," Joe said.

Moe smirked. "I guess anything's possible."

Joe asked, "What do you think, Heidi?"

She was looking down at the floor, but her eyes moved upward to fasten onto Joe's face. "Knocking on a door might work, but I'm guessing someone should have said something or opened the door by now."

"You're possibly right, but I think all the people inside this place are just trying to hide from us." Joe looked over at the security panel next to the door.

Moe said, "Maybe everyone went home."

Joe pressed some of the numbers on the security panel. "I don't think people have had enough time to move all of the jewelry and then to run away and escape from this building."

Moe asked, "Should we use the other bomb to open this door?"

"We only have one more bomb. I don't think we should use it to open a door that might or might not have something good behind it." Joe pointed to his left as he said, "Besides, another door is over there."

Moe and Heidi both turned to the left. Moe said, "I didn't see that door."

Heidi frowned. "I also didn't notice that one. The file cabinets were blocking our view, so we couldn't see it from the front part of this room."

Joe looked back at the door in front of them. "Since we're here anyway, we should just try this door first."

"Should we try to open the door with our guns?" Moe asked.

"Shooting at that other door didn't work, and this door looks exactly the same," Joe said.

"Shooting at the first door connecting the front room with the corridor actually did work," Moe said.

Joe stared at the door in front of them. "Even so, this door here looks just like the second one, rather than that first one. We'll probably need to bomb it." Joe stepped forward and hit the control panel with the back of his gun. One of the numbers flew off, and a dent was visible.

Moe said, "Maybe shooting the control panel will work."

Joe stepped up close to the panel and stared at the dent. "This panel seems a little bit different from the other panel. Possibly shooting it might work."

After Joe, Heidi, and Moe stepped backward a few feet, Joe shot at the control panel. A large chunk of metal flew off of the panel and landed on the floor. Joe pulled a wrench and some scissors out of the backpack that Heidi was wearing. He then twisted some of the control panel's metal, cut the wires inside the panel, and pushed at the door.

When the door was only open for a half an inch, a voice inside the room began to scream. Joe pushed at the door with his left hand while his right hand extended his gun forward. When the door was wide open, Joe stepped into the room with Heidi and Moe following him.

The owner of the store, Tina, was standing up against the furthest wall with a big screen behind her. The computers had been turned off, so no security videos were visible on the screens or anywhere else.

Tina was no longer screaming, but her lips were jittering against each other. Her left hand was stretched downward and grabbing onto the bottom edge of her blouse. Her right hand was grasping onto a cell phone.

Joe pointed his gun at Tina's phone and said loudly, "Drop your cell phone."

Tina hesitated, hugged her phone with her fingers, and then dropped it. When it hit the floor, its screen cracked in several places. Tina looked down at her phone as tears appeared in her eyes.

"Are you the one who put that little needle in my sunglasses?" Joe asked.

Tina started breathing more quickly.

"Look at me!" Joe yelled.

Tina glanced up at Joe and then shifted her eyes back to the wooden floor.

"Were you just trying to hurt me, or do you try to hurt all of the customers who come into your store?" Joe asked.

Tina remained silent.

"Look at me right now, or I'll shoot at your nose! The hole will be a little bit bigger than the one your needle made in my nose."

Tina swallowed and then looked at Joe. Her lips moved, but she only made some soft humming noises.

"Why did you put that needle in the glasses?" Joe asked.

Tina opened her mouth and tried to talk. After a few quivers with her lips, she was able to say, "I'm really sorry. I didn't mean to hurt you." Tina bowed down on her knees and added, "Please forgive me, and I'll give you some money for your injury. I thought the needle would be just a little scratch, rather than something that would really hurt you."

Joe stared at Tina's posture, lowered his gun, placed it back into its holster, and said, "As long as you have enough cash, I'll forgive you. Stand up."

"Thanks." Tina slowly stood up.

Joe said, "The name 'Tina' is on your nametag. Is that your name?"

Tina shook her head. After a few seconds, her lips stopped quivering. She said, "Yeah, my name is Tina."

"Where's the cash?" Joe asked.

Tina went over to one of the drawers of a file cabinet, pulled out a folder, and withdrew four hundred dollars for Joe.

"This isn't really a lot. Where's the rest of the cash?" Joe asked.

Tina shook her head sideways. She was saying "no."

Joe and Moe started looking around the room. Nothing was under the table and chairs in the center of the room. Moe opened up the other three drawers of the file cabinet, but only paperwork and file folders were visible. While Moe was looking in the cabinet's folders, Joe walked over to the big screen on the right side of the room. He moved the center of the screen slightly outward and looked behind it. Nothing was there. He then stared at Tina, whose hands were shaking while her lips were quivering again. Joe asked, "What are you scared about?"

Tina was unable to say anything. Tears from her eyes moved down her cheeks. She clenched her hands together tightly and began breathing heavily. She then moved up to the left side of the screen and touched it.

Joe placed his right hand on his gun's holster and said, "Move away from that screen."

Tina took a step backward and then moved sideways away from the screen. Joe pulled the right edge of the screen outward and said, "Oh, I love this hidden pocket back here. It's large enough to be holding a lot of jewelry." He stepped behind the screen, reached his hand into a two-foot-square pocket, and pulled out a small purse.

Frowning, he looked inside the screen's pocket again. No other objects were there. He then opened up the purse, but only twenty dollars was inside. He glared at Tina. "Why were you even bothering to hide something like this?"

Tina was inhaling and exhaling quickly as she said, "I don't know why I hid my purse in that screen's pocket. I was just scared and trying to hide my money and credit cards."

Joe took out a few credit cards. "You only have three credit cards in here. Is that all you have?"

"Yeah, it is."

"You must be broke."

Tina hesitated for a few seconds before saying, "I have enough money for food and rent, but my credit isn't too great." More tears began to form in her eyes.

Joe put Tina's purse on the table and then asked, "Where did you put the jewelry?"

Tina looked at the door leading out of the room. Moe was standing there, so she was unable to even try to run away. She said, "I don't know where it is."

"Don't you work here?"

Tina inhaled deeply, exhaled quickly, and said nothing.

Joe put his hand on the top part of his gun. "You have a nametag on. You have to be one of the employees."

Tina remained silent. Her eyes appeared slightly dazed, as if she did not understand where she was or what was happening.

Joe picked up Tina's purse again. He pulled out her keychain. "One of these might open up that other locked office." Joe looked at Moe, handed him the keys, and asked him, "How about if you try to make one of these keys work?"

Moe smiled, took the keys, and left the room. Joe then opened up one of the file cabinet's drawers and flipped through the folders and paperwork. After finding nothing, he examined the contents of the other drawers. When he was nearly finished with the cabinet's folders, Moe came back into the room.

Joe asked, "Did any of the keys work?"

"No, not a single one opened up that door." Moe threw the keys on top of Tina's purse, which was still lying on the table. He then noticed that Joe was replacing some paperwork into the lowest drawer of the file cabinet. Moe asked, "Did you find anything at all in that file cabinet?"

"No, nothing that I want to bother with is in those files," Joe said.

"That's what I figured. When I looked, only some paperwork with no helpful personal information was in there," Moe said.

"I couldn't find any social security or credit card numbers." Joe stared at Tina, who had stepped back up against the screen, and then added, "Perhaps there's another hidden pocket somewhere behind that screen."

Joe waved his hand, indicating that he wanted Tina to move further away. He then pushed the screen away from the wall. Only the same pocket was visible.

Moe walked over, stood next to Joe, looked around, and pointed at the top of the wall where the screen was attached. Immediately below the attachment area was a line in the wooden wall. Moe asked, "Is that a door, a little vault, or something else up there?"

Joe pulled over one of the chairs. He held the screen outward and away from the wall as Moe climbed up onto the chair. Moe opened up a door in the top section of the wall. Shining his flashlight with his left hand, he pulled out a gold necklace with a heart-shaped pendant that said, "Love loves."

Moe said, "I love to love real gold, and this looks like the real thing." He pulled out other pieces of jewelry and handed everything to Joe, who put them all into the backpack on Heidi's back. Joe then turned around to say something to Tina, but she was no longer in the room.

Moe looked around and said, "Maybe Tina went into that locked office."

"We also only have a little bit of this store's jewelry. That locked room might have some more stuff in it," Joe said.

Joe, Moe, and Heidi went back into the distribution room and over to the door behind the filing cabinets. Joe sighed. "Whether Tina's in here or not, this panel looks to be the same as the panel for the door that we had to bomb."

"You're right," Moe said.

"I sort of still want to shoot Tina. I was just waiting to try to get some information out of her about where all the jewelry is." Joe moved close to the control panel. He then stepped backward and fired his gun at it. Nothing happened; no dents appeared in the panel. "You're right, Moe. We won't be able to shoot our way into this room."

"Should we use our last bomb on it?" Moe asked.

"Let's go to a few more stores. If we don't need our bomb somewhere else, we can always bring it back here and try it on that door," Joe said.

"That sounds like a plan," Moe said.

Joe, Heidi, and Moe went back through the distribution center and into the front room. Joe grabbed another pair of sunglasses and looked closely at the frames. "These are safe," he said as he walked out the front door and into the corridor.

"Where are we going next?" Moe asked.

Joe placed the sunglasses into the backpack. "That's a good question."

"I thought you had this all planned out."

Joe frowned. "My plan was to get some money and jewelry from just a few stores." After pausing for a few seconds, he added, "The other day, I just didn't have the chance to check out all of the stores in this giant building."

"You did draw a really nice map of the building. I thought you went to all of the stores on that map."

"I walked past all of the stores, but I could only get inside a few of them. There wasn't enough time for me to actually go into all of them."

Moe sighed. "You're right about time. There's never enough time for anything these days."

Heidi giggled. When Joe and Moe both stared at her, she covered her mouth with her hand and was quiet.

"What's so funny?" Joe asked.

Heidi moved her hand away from her face. After thinking for a few seconds, she said, "I also never have enough time for everything, which is why I multi-task so much."

"Why is that funny?" Joe asked.

"I was just thinking about one day a couple of weeks ago. Right after I got to work, five different people sent me emails and used the 'important' option. They all needed me to immediately find some information and send it to them."

"What did you do?" Joe asked.

"I had to respond to the emails in a correct order."

"Did you respond to the earliest email first?" Joe asked.

"No, the emails had all been sent even before I got to work. I had to respond to the most important one first." Heidi paused, sighed, and then said, "Four upset people came into my office and demanded my immediate help."

Joe laughed. "Talking to these four upset people meant you had less time available to do your other work, right?"

"Yes and no."

"What do you mean by yes and no? Either you had some time or you didn't," Joe said.

"Well, two of the upset people listened to my explanation. They then understood what was going on and apologized before leaving."

"Those two people still took away some of your time," Joe said.

"They did, but only a few minutes. They also were really busy and had some important tasks they were trying to do."

"What about the other two people?" Joe asked.

"After I told them about what was happening, one of them sat down at my desk and helped me with things. The other person went back to his desk and found some of the information for me on his computer."

"So two people helped you with your work, which saved you some time," Joe said.

"Yes, they really did help." Heidi thought for a few seconds before adding, "The extra time was nice, but what really made me happy was having such great friends at work. By being nice and understanding, they made me feel better during a stressful time."

Moe said to Joe, "We need to stop talking. We're going to run out of time if we don't get moving, and I don't think Heidi will give us back our lost time."

Joe sighed. "Okay, let's get going. I'm actually curious about what's on the floor right below us."

Moe said, "At least that should be a close-by store."

"Actually, we'll be walking for a few minutes through a long corridor," Joe said.

Moe frowned as he followed Joe and Heidi to the stairwell. They went down one level to the twelfth floor.

Robots

When Joe opened up the door leading from the stairwell into the corridor, a small piece of blank paper fell down onto the floor. He said, "No one's been through this door for a while."

"Why do you think that?" Heidi asked. "Someone left behind that piece of paper."

"The paper's telling me that no one opened the door."

"I don't see any words on the paper."

"This morning, I put pieces of paper between the doors and their frames. Now, if the paper is still between a door and its frame, rather than on the floor, I will know that no one has gone through the door." Joe smiled. "Even paper with an invisible message can say something."

"You're right about that." Heidi immediately realized that she should have been quiet about invisible messages. Her eyes glanced sideways; she was trying to avoid looking at where text messages came through on the lenses of her glasses. She then gazed down at the ground, so Joe and Moe would not see the expression on her face.

"Are you hiding something, Heidi?" Joe asked.

"No, I'm just thinking about invisible messages. Sometimes people try to be invisible by changing their names."

Joe looked at Moe and said, "She's making fun of our names." The two men stared angrily at Heidi.

After swallowing twice, Heidi glanced at Joe and said in an anxious voice, "I was actually thinking about authors hiding their identities. Authors sometimes use fake names."

"Was Mark Twain one of those authors using a fake name?" Joe asked.

"Yeah, Samuel Clemens used the pen name of Mark Twain when he wrote *The Adventures of Tom Sawyer,*" Heidi said.

"Is a pen name a fake name?" Joe asked.

"In a way, it is. Some authors are trying to hide their real identities; other authors like to have fictional names that work with the content of their fictional stories," Heidi said.

Joe laughed. "Fake names should work well with fake stories."

"Historically, some publishers, as well as some authors, have tried to hide their identities by using fake names or no names. That way, they could hide their crimes." Heidi again looked at the ground and tried to hide her facial expression.

"What crimes were they doing?" Joe asked.

"They were often writing and publishing things that the government didn't like," Heidi said.

"Was it some kind of rebellion?" Joe asked.

"It was. People could argue about a lot of issues by writing and publishing their thoughts. They could even argue indirectly with their government by hiding their identities." After pausing for a few seconds, Heidi added, "If a government official read a book with no author's name and no publication information, then the author would be saying something to the government while trying to remain anonymous."

"Even today, whistle blowers might want to hide their identities."

"You're right, Joe." Heidi stared at the rope tying her waist to Joe's. "At least in our country today, people have freedom of speech, so if they want to talk, they can say, write, and even publish their own ideas."

"I guess they can." Joe rubbed his forehead and then asked, "In the past, could people really hide their identities? Weren't the cities a lot smaller?"

"Centuries ago, people did live together in smaller communities. There also weren't too many printing presses, so even if a publisher's name was not on a book, people could often figure things out," Heidi said.

"What process did they use? Did the cops question everyone?" Joe asked.

"Design elements, like fonts, were often unique for different publishers. The publication city and date could also suggest who had published something," Heidi said.

"That's interesting," Joe said.

"Back in the seventeenth century, not only authors, but also publishers, sometimes had to hide their identity to keep themselves safe." Heidi looked at the rope attaching herself to Joe and sighed.

"Did this kind of hiding happen just in the seventeenth century?" Joe asked.

Heidi looked at Joe and said, "No, hiding also happened in other centuries. In the fifteenth century, Gutenberg, who was the inventor of the movable-type printing press, used 'secrecy in some projects.'[30]"

"Secrecy can sometimes be necessary," Joe said as started walking down the corridor.

Heidi frowned as she was pulled by the rope and forced to follow Joe. They passed by two locked doors with no windows for people to look inside.

Heidi said, "With no windows, I guess these places need to keep some things hidden from the public."

Joe said, "Those doors must be the back doors or side doors for some offices. Possibly the offices belong to bosses, accountants, or payroll employees; the companies might need to keep some things invisible from people like us who are walking down the corridor."

Heidi shook her head in agreement. "Also, some offices have no windows on the outside of the building; they will need multiple doorways."

"You're so right. Offices always need more than one exit, just in case of an emergency, like people running around with guns." Joe paused, rubbed the handle of his gun, and then started walking again.

The end of the corridor was dark. Joe and Moe pulled out flashlights. They slowly moved forward while shining their lights around the ceiling, walls, and floor. When they arrived at a light switch on the wall, Joe tried to turn it on, but the switch did not work. Joe said, "Someone must have loosened the light bulbs or done something to the circuit box."

Moe was walking behind Heidi and asked in a slightly angry voice, "Joe, aren't you upset about these lights being off? In the next office, do you think it will be the right time for us to shoot a few people? I really hate having to shine my flashlight around in a dark corridor."

Joe and Heidi both turned around to face Moe. Joe said, "Perhaps it's a good time for that, Moe. Shooting one or two people might scare someone into turning the lights on for us."

Heidi's voice was anxious as she asked, "What if the people in the next office want to give you some money, instead of lights? Shouldn't they be allowed to stay alive?"

Joe's face looked thoughtful. "If the people are well-behaved and give us some money, we'll probably just wait until some other office to kill someone."

Heidi said, "If you're caught, things will be much better if you haven't killed anyone."

Joe and Moe both glared at Heidi. Joe then pulled on Heidi's rope and said, "I'm in charge here."

Heidi cleared her throat, shook her head nervously, and looked down at the floor.

Joe said to Moe, "We probably should kill someone pretty soon. If the people in this building hear gunshots or see information on their cell phones, they're more likely to do what we tell them to do."

Heidi opened her mouth to say something and then closed it.

Joe asked her, "Are you again hiding something from us?"

Heidi's chin shook slightly sideways. Her right hand shivered, showing her anxiety. "No, I'm just trying to be nice by censoring myself."

Moe laughed. "That's something I do a lot."

Joe said, "You need to censor yourself more often, Moe."

Moe laughed again. "Yeah, I've often said things that I've regretted." After a brief pause, he added, "Once, I was pulled over by a police officer for driving through a red light. While talking to the officer, I said something bad about his nose. I so regretted that mistake."

Heidi touched her nose. Joe and Moe both stared at her nose, glanced at each other, laughed, and then began to quickly walk forward. When they neared the end of the corridor, Joe and Moe moved their lights around.

Joe said, "I was wondering if this corridor was leading into a dead end, but I guess not."

At the end of the corridor was a large wooden door with a window section in its top half. Heidi followed Joe as he went up to the window. The name "Office Connections" was positioned in the top part of the door's window. As Joe shined his light into the dark office, Heidi walked up close to the window and looked inside. Only a single desk and several chairs could be seen. Joe tried to open the door. It was locked. When he stepped backward a few feet, Heidi also moved back until she was at the end of the rope's extension. Joe raised his gun and fired at the door and its window. Only a single bullet was needed to break the glass, but Joe fired six times.

"You know you're wasting our ammo, right?" Moe asked.

"No, I'm not wasting our ammo." Joe glared at Moe before adding, "I'm trying to fire on anyone who might be somewhere near the door. Also, I need to take out that door's lock, as well as the window."

With a sheepish look on his face, Moe said, "That does make sense. I should have censored myself again."

Moe turned his flashlight off and on several times before walking up to the door. He only had to push softly for it to open. He stepped inside, waved his light around, and held open the door for Joe and Heidi. He then tried to turn on the lights, but the light switch was not working.

Moe shined his light on the ceiling and then back at the light switch. "Maybe one of your bullets did something to the lights in here."

Joe moved his light around. "The switch looks fine. It wasn't damaged."

From the left side of the room's darkness, a five-foot tall robot suddenly appeared. Its arms and legs were shining with the brightness of stainless steel. Its head was inside of a helmet with red, white, and blue colors painted on the topmost section. He walked up and shook hands with Heidi, Joe, and Moe.

"What's your name?" Joe asked.

"People call me Rob, but I would prefer to be called something else."

Joe glanced over at Moe. "A lot of us like to use different names." He then asked the robot, "What would you like us to call you, Rob?"

"Any other name would be good."

"Why is that?" Joe asked with a frown on his face.

"The name of 'Rob' means I've stolen something. It also belongs to a human who works here. I want my own name."

Joe moved his flashlight past the robot while saying, "For right now, we'll call you 'Rob,' but if I can think of something better, I'll tell you."

Joe walked a few feet past the robot. He then pulled Heidi forward until she was standing next to the robot. She looked at the robot's eyes, which appeared to be blue lights.

When the robot looked back at her, Heidi asked, "Has someone programmed you to say what you're saying, Rob?"

"I can't tell you that."

Heidi smiled. "By saying you can't tell me, you actually are telling me. I now know for sure that I'm right. You've been programmed to talk about your name with strangers."

Rob stared silently at the front door of the office.

Joe pulled on the rope, so Heidi walked forward past Rob. Joe then turned around and asked Rob, "Can you turn the lights on?"

"No, I can't. Plus, I don't need the lights to see things."

A loud noise came from the darkness in the left rear corner of the office. Joe and Moe both moved their flashlights, trying to find the source of the noise. Their lights quickly fell onto a flat, circular device that was crawling on the floor and moving toward them.

Joe fired his gun at the round device. The first shot broke it into several pieces. One of the pieces kept on moving forward. Joe fired at the moving section three times before it was broken up enough to stop moving.

Rob asked, "Why did you kill Vack?"

Joe moved his gun toward Rob. "Why did you have Vack come after us?"

"Vack wasn't attacking you. He was just vacuuming the floor."

"It doesn't make sense that a vacuum cleaner would be vacuuming the floor now," Joe said.

"Vack always vacuums in the evening. That's his job."

"Who activated Vack? Is there someone in the office right now?" Joe asked.

"Vack is automatically activated every day. No one ever turns anything on."

Joe walked up to the pieces of the robotic cleaner and picked one of them up. "This does look like a part for an automatic vacuum cleaner."

Another piece of the vacuum's plastic structure had landed near Moe. He picked it up and carefully examined it. "You know, someone could make a bomb with some of these parts. Is that why you shot it, Joe?"

"No, if Vack had been a bomb, we would have been blown up. I was thinking about Vack being a video-taping device."

"That makes sense, especially considering how Vack was moving toward us. We really don't want people to have evidence of our identities."

From the back-left corner of the room, another robot appeared. "Hi, I'm Beth," she said as she moved toward Joe with her right hand extended. Beth had red eyes, as well as red hair partially hidden underneath a helmet. She was wearing high heels and a dress that matched the red, white, and blue colors in Rob's shirt and helmet.

Joe looked at Beth's extended hand. He then moved his own right hand forward and shook her hand. Before he could withdraw his hand, Beth had squeezed it, stretched out her free hand, and was reaching for his gun.

Moe, who was standing several feet behind and to the right of Joe, moved his gun upward and fired at Beth's head. The first bullet hit her helmet and bounced off without any damage. Moe then moved his gun downward slightly and sent a couple of bullets straight into Beth's right eye. Bits of glass and metal exploded from her eye socket.

A piece of metal with an attached glass circle flew past Joe and landed in front of Moe's feet. Moe stared at the metal and glass item while saying, "This looks a little bit different."

Joe asked, "What do you mean by 'different'?"

"It's shinier than the rest of the metal and glass on Beth's face." Moe pointed down near his feet.

Joe stared at the shiny item. "It looks more like a camera lens than a robot's eye."

Moe shook his head in agreement before yelling, "Look out!"

Beth had stepped forward. She took another step and grabbed onto the end of Joe's gun barrel. Joe frowned before pulling the trigger multiple times. The shooting sounds from Joe's gun were quickly joined by ones from Moe's gun.

For a few seconds, Beth's metal stomach and chest bounced all of the bullets back toward the shooters. One of the bullets scraped the barrel of Joe's gun. Another one nearly hit Joe's left ear. Then a bullet hole appeared in Beth's stomach. Smoke emerged from the hole. Beth looked down at the smoke leaving her stomach as she placed both of her hands over the hole. She was acting like she was trying to stop herself from bleeding.

Joe asked, "Beth, why did you attack me?"

Beth swayed sideways slightly before saying, "You're the one doing the shooting. I'm a security robot, so I was just doing my job." She then fell sideways, landed on the floor, and lay quietly without moving.

Rob said, "You killed Beth."

Joe said, "No, Beth killed herself. She was the one who grabbed onto and tried to steal my gun."

"You're the thief. You broke into this office," Rob said.

"We're not thieves," Joe said.

"Yes, you are thieves," Rob said. "I even looked up your information online by using facial recognition software."

"Even so, how can you really claim we're thieves? We haven't yet stolen anything from this office." Joe smirked as he walked over to examine Beth's body. No more smoke was visible. He looked into one of Beth's eye sockets. "I think there's some kind of photo or video camera here."

Moe glanced at Beth's eye socket and shook his head in agreement.

Joe asked Rob, "Where are the photos or video files being kept?"

"They're on a server in another state."

"We need you to delete those files," Joe said.

"I can't."

"Why can't you?" Joe asked.

"I have no access to the video files."

Joe frowned. "How can you be denied access? You're an electronic robot."

"It's the way things have been set up."

"I don't believe you," Joe said.

"Just because I have access to a few files doesn't mean I have access to all of the files in the whole world."

Joe sighed. "Okay, you're making a little bit of sense, so you're possibly telling the truth. We should see if we have access to anything else in here." He waved his hand at Moe, who walked to the left back corner of the room. Moe's flashlight lit up a closed metal door. Moe tried to open the door, but it was locked.

Joe turned to face Rob and said, "Open that door for Moe."

"I can't."

"You're a robot. You're supposed to do what people tell you to do," Joe said.

"I can't."

"Open that door, or I'll shoot you," Joe said angrily.

"I really can't open the door. When you fired your gun, the security system locked me out."

Joe sent two bullets into each of Rob's knees, but the robot was still standing and did not appear to be in any pain. Joe and Moe then both fired their guns on the metal door, but the bullets just bounced off the thick metal surface.

Joe frowned before saying to Rob, "Unlock that door, or I'll shoot this lady." Joe waved his gun backward toward Heidi.

The robot stared at Heidi, whose eyes were blinking back at him in an anxious way. He then asked her, "Aren't you one of the thieves?"

"No, they kidnapped me, and they're holding me as a hostage." She pointed to the rope that was connecting her to Joe. "I can't escape."

Joe said, "Rob, you can't let an innocent person like Heidi be hurt. You need to unlock that door."

Rob paused for a few seconds before saying, "Okay, I'll unlock it." Rob started to walk toward the front section of the office.

Joe asked, "Why are you walking away from the locked door?"

"I need to log onto one of the computers over here to have access to that door."

"No computers are on that desk." Joe raised his gun and pointed it at Heidi's face. She raised her shoulders, breathed in heavily, held her breath, and then exhaled with some jittery noises. Finally, she asked, "Can I just have a few seconds to pray?"

Joe lowered his gun slightly. "Okay, as long as it's just a few words."

Heidi looked upward and said, "Please stay with me and help me, Lord. In Jesus's name I pray, Amen."

Rob stared at Heidi as he said, "The computer's right here inside the desk."

"I don't believe you," Joe said.

"I'll show you." Rob reached out to the top right corner of the desk. He grabbed onto the pen holder and twisted it several times. The holder then made a snapping noise, and a part of the desk's top slid sideways. A computer screen and keyboard moved upward. Rob sat down, typed in a password, and opened up some security software. In less than a minute, the metal door in the back corner of the room made a scraping noise as it opened up.

Joe said, "While you're on that computer, turn on the lights."

Rob typed in a few words before clicking onto a light bulb image. The lights in the front office and the ones on the other side of the metal door turned on at the same time.

Joe, Heidi, and Moe moved to the back of the room and looked through the now-open metal doorway. The front of the room had a table with drones and control panels on it. Multiple different kinds of robots were standing quietly and motionless in different sections of the room. Instead of heads, most of the robots had video cameras or computer screens. Joe, Heidi, and Moe moved to the right corner of the room, where another metal door was locked. Moe went to the front office and talked to Rob, who quickly opened up the second metal door.

The just-unlocked room had three different levels. The first level was where people would be standing when they first walked into the room. The second level was in the middle of the room and was about six feet higher than the first level. The third level was at the back of the room; it was only a few feet higher than the second level. The three levels were connected together by escalators. The left side of the room had escalators moving upward; the right side of the room had escalators moving downward.

"It's a little strange that escalators are being used here. Stairs would have made more sense," Joe said.

"Maybe the robots can't walk up a regular staircase," Heidi said.

"You could be right," Moe said as he walked over to the left side of the room and jumped onto the moving escalator. In a few seconds, he had stepped off of the escalator and was standing on the room's second level. "Well, that's working almost like a regular escalator. It's just a little bit small and possibly too fast." Moe glanced down at the floor next to his feet. "It looks like there's an opening here."

Joe and Heidi walked over to the escalator and jumped onto the moving stairs. When they stepped off, Joe helped Moe to open up a compartment in the floor. Joe said, "This looks like a control panel, maybe for the escalators."

Moe pointed to the furthest corner of the panel and asked, "What's that?"

Joe stared at the back corner. Something was written on the back section. "It's a little too far away for me to read, but I think it's a bunch of numbers."

Heidi glanced briefly at Joe. His eyes were squinting as he tried to figure out the control panel's numbers. She stepped sideways a few inches and looked at him again. He had not noticed that she had moved. Heidi slowly raised her right hand up to her glasses and pressed one of the frame's buttons a couple of times. Her glasses were now magnifying everything in her viewing range; she was able to read four of the numbers on the control panel: 4666. She pressed a different button on the frame of her glasses; the lenses reverted back to their previous appearance.

Joe moved his head partially through the control panel's door and rested it against an electric motor; he was now closer to the numbers. He said, "I can figure out three of the numbers."

Moe asked, "What are they?"

"They're '666.'"

Heidi opened her mouth, made a noise, and then quickly closed her mouth.

Joe stood up, turned around, and stared at Heidi. "What were you going to say?"

"I was just shocked at the numbers."

"Why are they so shocking?" Joe asked.

"You've read the Bible, right?" Heidi asked.

"No, I haven't." Joe paused and then added, "What does the Bible say about '666'?"

"That number refers to the devil. Revelations 13 has some information about an evil beast with that number," Heidi said.

"So, you think this number must be evil?" Joe asked.

"If it's referencing something bad, then of course it's evil," Heidi said.

"I think you're wrong about the number being evil. It's just a number." Joe glanced down at the control panel's door and then added, "Plus, there were other numbers or letters with '666' in that panel."

Moe said, "We should take the engine out of the control panel. Then we'll be able to see all of the numbers."

"That sounds like a plan," Joe said as he turned Heidi around and took a wrench out of the backpack that was still connected to her back and shoulders. He handed the wrench to Moe, who was seated on the floor in front of the control panel.

Moe disassembled the engine and other elements in the control panel. He also took out each disconnected part from the panel. After only about five minutes, the control panel was nearly empty.

Joe turned Heidi around again and reached into the backpack. He pulled out some paper and a pencil before asking, "Can you see the numbers well enough, Moe?"

"Yeah, I can, but there are seventeen numbers here. You'll need to write them down." Moe looked up at Joe and said, "Oh, I see you already have some paper. That's great."

Moe read nine numbers out loud as Joe wrote them down. Pausing in his reading, Moe said, "There's a space now, so I think the first nine and the last eight numbers have been separated in some way."

"Okay, I'll write the next eight numbers on a different line on my paper."

Moe said, "02054666." He stood up, stared at the two groups of numbers on Joe's paper, and asked, "What do you think the numbers mean?"

The suddenly blank expression on Heidi's face suggested that she was hiding something and probably knew what the numbers meant; however, Joe and Moe did not notice her facial expression.

Joe said, "For an office like this one, I would guess the numbers could be a user name with a password." He put the piece of paper with the numbers on it into his shirt pocket.

"You could be right, Joe, but a password in a robot office like this one should be a little bit better. That eight-digit number doesn't have any letters or symbols in it."

"Since the numbers were hidden away in a control panel, they have to be related to some kind of security for something expensive. Maybe the numbers will open up a safe." Joe smiled at Moe. They then each walked over to one of the walls in the room. Joe—with Heidi being pulled after him on the rope—began walking around the left side of the room. Moe began on the right side. They walked twice around the whole room before Joe said, "I think we're looking for a safe in the wrong place."

Moe stopped moving and then stared at the higher-level escalator's control panel. He pointed at it and said, "We could try the other control panel."

Within a few seconds, Joe, Heidi, and Moe were all standing near the higher-level panel. Joe was the first one to kneel down; he opened the panel's door. Inside were multiple metal parts for the escalator. Joe knelt down and looked inside the control panel. After a few seconds, he said, "There's nothing here."

"Are you sure?" Moe asked.

"Yeah, you can look for yourself." Joe stood up, waved at the control panel, and watched as Moe checked it out.

After examining everything visually, Moe reached his right hand into the panel and carefully touched multiple places behind the engine before saying, "You're right, Joe. There really is nothing here."

"Instead of just guessing about everything, I think we should get Rob to come in here and tell us what those numbers mean," Joe said.

"Yeah, he can also tell us if there's a safe anywhere in this office." Moe waved as he went back into the previous office with the silent robots in it. Rob was seated at one of the desks while staring silently into the air; he looked as inert as the other robots did.

Moe walked up to Rob's desk and said, "We need you."

Rob ignored Moe and continued to stare off into the air.

Moe pushed Rob's chair away from the desk and shoved his gun into Rob's left shoulder. Nothing happened. Rob did not even move within his chair, but rather stayed inert and unresponsive.

"Are you dead?" Moe asked. After listening to silence for a few seconds, he pulled his gun upward and fired multiple times at Rob's chest.

Joe, with Heidi attached, walked into the room and yelled, "What are you doing?"

"The robot is acting like he's dead when he logically has to be alive," Moe said.

Joe shook his head sideways. "He's being controlled by a computer, so he's probably been turned off."

"Are you saying he's dead?" Moe asked.

"Yeah, I am." Joe turned around and looked at Heidi. "What do you think?"

Heidi stammered slightly as she said, "Well, I'm not a computer expert, but if I were in charge of the computers in here, I would just turn them all off." She stared at the multiple torn parts of Rob's shirt and some dents in his metallic skin before adding, "If he wasn't already dead, he's probably dead now."

Joe glared at Moe. "You need to put down your gun and stop wasting our ammunition."

"Okay, okay! I'll stop shooting the robot."

Joe looked at the items on Rob's desktop: a laptop, a drone, a cell phone, a checkbook, and a stack of bills. He picked up one of the bills and compared it with the checkbook. The same person's name, Robert Robertson, was on both items. Joe asked, "Hey, Moe, do you think Rob the robot is the same as the Robert whose name appears on these checks and bills?"

"How can a robot get a checking account?" Moe asked.

"I don't think a robot can get a bank account," Joe said.

"Rob told us that he had the same name as a person," Moe said. After scratching his chin, Moe added, "Robert Robertson is probably that person."

Joe looked closely at the topmost check in the checkbook. He then laughed. "Guess what I might have just found out?"

"What?" Moe asked.

"Do you remember those numbers that you read from the wall of the control panel?" Joe pulled the piece of paper with the numbers on it out of his pocket. He compared the numbers with the ones on Robert Robertson's check before saying, "They match. Those numbers on the control panel's wall were the bank routing and account numbers for Robert Robertson's checking account."

"How much money is in that account?" Moe asked.

Joe opened up the checkbook, turned a few of the pages, and silently read some of the transactions. He then said, "According to these numbers, there's over a hundred thousand dollars in the account."

"That's really neat, especially since we might be able to get access to his account through his cell phone," Moe said.

"These bills might be helpful too." Joe put the checkbook, bills, and cell phone into the backpack that Heidi was wearing. He then turned on the laptop and checked out some of the items. "There's nothing helpful here." He turned off the laptop and smiled at Heidi. "That's one less item that you'll have to carry."

Heidi sighed. "I'm really thankful that you're not adding the laptop into this backpack, which is already pretty heavy."

Joe said, "We should get moving again." He started walking forward. Heidi followed him, but Moe did not move.

"Aren't you coming with us, Moe?"

"I'm a little thirsty, hungry, and tired. Can we find somewhere to eat supper and rest for a while?" Moe asked.

Joe looked at his watch. "It's after nine o'clock, and I'm a little hungry and tired, too." He reached into the backpack and withdrew some cereal bars. After he gave one to Moe and one to Heidi, he began eating his own cereal bar.

Moe said, "I wonder if this refrigerator has any soda in it." He walked over to the refrigerator; only bottled water was there. He took a bottle for himself, one for Heidi, and one for Joe.

As Heidi was eating her cereal bar and drinking her water, Joe waved his hand at Moe and said, "Let's get moving. I want to be close to where we need to be tomorrow morning."

Moe took another cereal bar out of the backpack and then said, "Okay."

Joe started walking; Heidi and Moe followed him. Joe then said, "At least this time, we'll be walking down the stairs."

"Where are we going to now, Joe?" Moe asked.

"There's a place that was very quiet when I walked past it a couple of days ago."

"What's the company's name?" Moe asked.

"I don't know," Joe said.

"When you walked past the windows and doors, didn't you see some kind of name, product, or pictures?" Moe asked.

"The window was being replaced, so nothing was visible, except for the glass itself and some giant folders."

"The folders probably contained the company's name," Moe said.

"I think so. I could see a letter 'y' sticking out of one of the folders."

Joe, Heidi, and Moe had reached the stairwell; they began moving down the stairs. When they reached the tenth floor, Moe asked, "Can we stay overnight at the doughnut shop? We'll probably be able to make some coffee in the morning."

Joe smiled. "That's a great idea. Also, a blanket and curtain store is next to the doughnut shop. We can stop there first and find something to sleep on."

They exited the stairwell, walked past the printing office, and stopped in front of the store with blankets and curtains in the front windows. Moe shot out one of the front windows, climbed inside, turned on the lights, and unlocked the front door. Heidi followed Joe inside. When Joe gestured for her to sit down on the couch, she did. Moe withdrew Heidi's Taser gun from the backpack. He then walked behind Heidi. A few seconds later, she was shot by her own gun, fell forward, and hit her head on the floor. She quickly lost consciousness.

Dreaming with Pilgrims

Heidi's blurry vision suddenly improved. She was standing in front of the Plymouth Rock Canopy Building in Plymouth, Massachusetts. She turned around, looked across the road, and up the hill.

A lady walked over to Heidi. The lady was dressed in a long brown dress and was wearing several necklaces made from shells. She said, "As a descendant of Massasoit, I come here often."

"As a descendant of Brewster and Dexter, I love being here, too," Heidi said.

"I especially love that hill in front of us—the one that's looking at us, as well as at Plymouth Rock," the Massasoit descendant said.

"Don't you mean the hill's overlooking us?" Heidi asked.

"No, I think it's actually looking at us."

"I don't see any eyes," Heidi said.

"The Massasoit statue up there has eyes."

Heidi hit one of the buttons on the frame of her glasses, so the lenses were more focused on distant objects. "Oh, now I can see what you're talking about. The Massasoit statue has eyes that are moving around to look at different objects and people."

"I think the Massasoit statue is watching me," the Massasoit descendant said.

"Massasoit does seem to be watching you." Heidi's eyes moved down and across the sidewalk to the Bradford statue. She then added,

"I thought the Massasoit and Bradford statues were bronze. How can they have eyes that are moving around?"

"You're not awake right now; you're just dreaming."

Heidi looked at her watch, glanced away, and then looked at it again. After repeating the process a few times, she said, "You're right. I just did some reality checks, and my watch displays different times whenever I look at it."

"You now know that you're really in a dream."

"Yes, I am, and it's so great that you're here with me. Your relative, Massasoit, was the leader of the Wampanoag, right?"

"Yes, he was. I love seeing his statue, as well as the Bradford statue. The proximity of these statues to Plymouth Rock symbolizes the historic connections between Massasoit and Bradford."

Heidi said, "I want to go up that hill and visit with the Massasoit statue."

"I want to go up there, too. We can walk up the hill together."

"I'd love that."

Heidi and the Massasoit descendant turned around, crossed the street, and began to walk up the cement stairs that were on the hill. Near the top, Heidi's left foot slid on a pebble. With her right hand, she gripped onto the railing more tightly. Her right hand slid a few inches down the railing. She leaned more to her right and tried to twist her forearm around the railing. However, she was falling, and the railing was rising upward. After a few seconds, she was no longer able to reach the railing.

As Heidi slid backward, the Massasoit descendant grabbed onto Heidi's left arm, held her tightly, and helped her to regain her balance.

While Heidi was still breathing quickly from her fearful experience, she hugged the Massasoit descendant. They then held each other's hands as they finished walking up the stairs. On the upper-level sidewalk, they hugged each other again.

Tears formed in Heidi's eyes as she said, "My name's Heidi. As a descendant of Elder William Brewster and Gregory Dexter, I'm so thankful for a descendant of Massasoit to be here to help me."

The Massasoit descendant squeezed Heidi's hand. "My name's Betty. It's such a blessing for us to meet each other like this."

"We need to trade information, so we can remain friends."

Betty and Heidi took out their cell phones. They traded phone numbers and emails, as well as connecting through Facebook. Heidi said, "You're about to be one of my 'favorites' in my listing of phone contacts."

Betty laughed. "You're already number one in my phone listing."

A deep voice to their left said, "You both are my favorites."

Heidi and Betty turned in the direction of the voice. Only the statue of Massasoit was there.

Betty asked, "Did you say something to us, Massasoit?"

"Yes, I did," the statue's bronze mouth said. "I'm so happy every time I see peace between descendants of Massasoit and the Pilgrims." Massasoit's eyes moved back and forth several times between Heidi and Betty.

"Can you really see us?" Betty asked.

"Yes, I can." The bronze eyes were still moving.

Betty asked, "Has this type of meeting ever happened before?"

"Yes, multiple times, I've watched as descendants connect to one other." The Massasoit statue looked at the tourists on the sidewalk and then added, "All of the meetings have been peaceful ones. No wars have happened."

Betty said, "We need more peaceful encounters in our century."

Heidi shook her head in agreement. "Wars have been happening too much in every century."

Betty said, "I prefer to just think about peace. I completely love the 1621 peace treaty that happened between the Wampanoag and the Pilgrims."

Heidi's cell phone flew out of her purse, turned sideways, and grew in size until it resembled a large screen in a movie theater.

Some tourists at the bottom of the hill looked up at the screen.

Heidi asked Betty, "Can you help me to reach up into the middle of that screen?"

"Sure, I'd love to." Betty joined her hands together in front of her stomach, knelt down, and gestured for Heidi to step onto her hands.

Heidi carefully stepped on Betty's hands. Betty then moved Heidi upward to the middle of the screen.

Heidi swiped the screen with her entire arm. A description of the 1621 peace treaty came up onto the screen: "The agreement, in which both parties promised to not 'doe hurt' to one another, was the first treaty between a Native American tribe and a group of American colonists ... [T]he two peoples signed a peace treaty that lasted for more than fifty years."[31]

Betty said, "The treaty also said that they would help each other if attacked by other tribes."

"One of my ancestors, Williams Brewster, was actually there when the peace treaty was finalized and signed by Massasoit and Governor John Carver," Heidi said.

"So, our ancestors actually met each other," Betty said.

"They really did." Heidi stepped off of Betty's hands, and they hugged each other.

Betty said, "That meeting between our ancestors happened in the Bradford house, right?"

"Yes, it did," a new voice said.

Heidi and Betty both turned to look down at the new speaker. It was the William Bradford statue, which was below them and across the street. The bronze statue's hand waved. The statue then said, "Everyone back then liked Massasoit. In September 1623, Emmanuel Altham said in a letter that Massasoit 'is as proper a man as ever was seen in this country, and very courageous.'[32]"

Betty said, "Massasoit was so great!"

Heidi shook her head in agreement.

Betty's cell phone rang. She listened to someone, glanced at Heidi, and said into her phone, "I'll be right there." After turning off her phone, Betty said to Heidi, "I'll need to leave for a few minutes." She then flew off of the left side of the hill.

Heidi tried to see Betty but was unable to do so. Multiple times, Heidi tried to refocus her glasses, but Betty was still nowhere to be seen. Finally, Heidi touched the bottom part of the giant cell phone screen; her phone shrunk into its normal size. She then put her cell phone back into her purse.

A man's voice suddenly said, "Hi."

Heidi turned her head toward the voice. A man who was dressed like a Pilgrim was standing several feet to her left. She said, "Oh, I thought I was talking to myself. Thanks for listening to me."

"You're welcome." The Pilgrim man smiled. "I thought you were talking to the water."

"Oh, there is some water in front of me." Heidi had somehow moved back down the stairs, across the street, and close to Plymouth Bay. "The water seems to be listening to us." Heidi stared at the water.

The Pilgrim man looked beyond the shore and said, "You're right."

"Thank you, water, for listening to us."

One of the waves formed itself into a word: "Thanks." The Pilgrim actor said, "I'm so thankful to you and the water for listening. When I talk like a Pilgrim, people sometimes have problems understanding what I'm saying."

"You sound like you're talking in regular English. Shouldn't you be using words like 'thee' and 'thou'?"

"I'm in your dream, and you're the one who's making me talk like someone in the twenty-first century." The Pilgrim man paused for a few seconds and then added, "Normally, when I'm at work and dressed like a Pilgrim, I do talk like a Pilgrim."

"Where do you work?"

"I'm usually at Plimoth Plantation, but I sometimes help out on the *Mayflower II* or with tours in Plymouth."

"So, you work at a living history museum."

"Yes, in your dream, I'm really at work." The Pilgrim man stared at the water, which had changed in its size from a bay area into a small brook.

Heidi stood up and also stared at the water. "Am I still asleep?"

"Ay, thou art."

"Now you're talking like a Pilgrim." Heidi smiled.

The man asked, "What cheer?"

Heidi said, "I don't know what that expression means. I'm going to look it up in the "Pilgrim Language" section of *Mayflower Dreams.*" Heidi reached into her purse, pulled out the historical novel, and looked up its meaning. "According to the last section of *Mayflower Dreams,* 'What cheer?' means 'What is making you happy?'[33]"

The man smiled and lifted his eyebrows; he expected Heidi to answer his question about her happiness.

"I'm really very happy about being here with you. As a descendant of a Pilgrim, I love being able to interact with a Pilgrim actor in my century." Heidi smiled and then added, "Also, you're really doing a great job."

"I thank thee."

A lady walked up the Pilgrim man and whispered to him. He whispered back to her. Their talk was so soft that Heidi could not hear a word of what was being said. She could only hear some flowing water noises. After a minute of indecipherable noises, the Pilgrim man waved at Heidi and walked away.

The lady said to Heidi, "He's needed on the *Mayflower II.*"

"It's nice that he's working so hard at his job."

"You're right. He's really a hard worker."

The soft flowing water noise suddenly became loud.

Heidi looked at the water and asked, "What's happening with this water? Is it the Town Brook or Massachusetts Bay?"

"In a way, it's both. The Pilgrim actor who just left is following the brook to get to Massachusetts Bay and the *Mayflower II.* If you follow the brook in the opposite direction, you'll find Brewster Gardens."

The lady turned around and took a step toward the *Mayflower II,* which was now visible in the water.

Heidi said, "If I'm still asleep and know that I'm dreaming, I must be having a lucid dream. I might be able to control some of what is happening."

The lady kept on walking; she did not seem to have heard Heidi say anything.

In her dream, Heidi closed her eyes and fell asleep. A half an hour later, she opened her eyes and was uncertain if she was awake or dreaming again.

Heidi tried a reality check. She opened up her purse and found five twenty-dollar bills inside. She closed her purse and then opened it up again. The five bills had grown into a two-inch stack of fifty-dollar bills.

"I guess I'm lucid dreaming." Heidi sighed and then added, "I might be in the same dream or in a new dream. Either way, it's too bad I'm not actually awake with this much money in my purse."

"You don't need any money," a watery voice behind a bush said.

"Everyone needs money. Otherwise, we won't have any houses, cars, food, clothing, cell phones, or other essentials."

"Here in this dream, you don't need to worry about money."

"I often worry about money in my dreams," Heidi said.

"Why do you do that?"

"In my real life, worrying about money is just a part of my reality." Heidi sighed and then continued, "When I fall asleep, I often am thinking about money problems, so I bring some of the ideas from my conscious mind into my dreams."

"Because this is a lucid dream, you can change things. You managed to change me."

"Did I really?"

"Yeah, I'm just some water, but I've been talking to you."

"Oh, if I can change water, maybe I can use my imagination and change other things," Heidi said.

"You can change your own life."

"What things can I change?" Heidi asked.

"You can change your actions, so you're not always hiding."

"I'm a spy. I sometimes have to hide."

"That's true, but you're sometimes hiding yourself and your ideas with no reason for it."

"Okay, I think you're right," Heidi said.

"Do you need my help with anything?"

Heidi gazed at the water in front of her for a few seconds and then said, "I love water, especially when I'm really thirsty."

The water responded to her with its movements. One of its waves shook itself horizontally, like it was saying "no."

Heidi walked closer to the water, which now had the appearance of a brook. The wave that had just said "no" moved itself back and forth even faster. It seemed to be yelling "no" and to be gesturing for her to stop walking.

"Your water looks really clean, and I'm really thirsty." Heidi walked quickly up to the very edge of the brook. She knelt down, formed her right hand into a cup position, and moved it into the water. Before she could withdraw her hand, a wave hit it really hard.

Heidi asked, "Why are you trying to hurt me?"

The wave backed away and then hid itself inside the rest of the brook's water.

"I'm really thirsty," Heidi said, but the water remained hidden. After waiting for a few seconds, she added, "You also know about me being thirsty. That's why you're trying to hide from me."

The water remained quiet as it again shrunk itself backward and into a smaller area.

Heidi moved her hand softly across the top of the water. "I need some water, and I promise not to bite you. I'll just keep you warm inside my body. If I promise to be nice to you, can I please have just a little bit of water?"

A wave moved upward in a sweet fashion. Heidi put her hand into the water again, and the wave flowed gently into her hand. She put the water into her mouth, swallowed, and then said, "You taste as sweet as you look."

The remaining water in the brook had some additional waves raising themselves up and down; they appeared to be saying "yes."

Heidi said, "I guess you just needed me to ask for some water in a nice way, rather than acting like I was stealing water from your brook."

A wave formed its top section into the word "yes."

"I'm so sorry for acting like a thief and being mean to you." Heidi sighed and then added, "Maybe I'm doing this in my dream just so I can figure out why Joe and Moe are stealing things."

Another wave said "yes" through its movements.

"Okay, I'll think some more about these thieves when I wake up. For right now, I'm looking at you, so I'm wondering more about you. I remember my mom told me about a brook. Are you the Town Brook that was the source of water for the Pilgrims?"

A wave moved quickly up and down; it was saying "yes."

"Did you help the Pilgrims, or was it your ancestors who helped them?"

Two different waves raised themselves up and then came downward while pointing in two different places.

Heidi looked in the directions being pointed to by the waves. "I think you're trying to reference the *Mayflower* and Brewster Gardens."

Heidi walked backward, sat down on the ground, stared at the brook, and tried to decide where to go. Four of the waves in the Town Brook formed themselves into the numbers "1620." One of the waves in the brook was moving in conjunction with a gust of wind. The gust reached out to Heidi, picked her up, and flew her over to the Bradford statue.

The statue asked her, "Are you a bird?"

"No, I'm just a person who's lucid dreaming, so I can sometimes do some unusual things." Heidi paused and then added, "Being a descendant of William Brewster, though, is one thing that I wouldn't want to change."

The Bradford statue turned sideways to look at Brewster Gardens. The statue then explained to Heidi, "Your ancestor, William Brewster, was so wonderful. He was a great elder for the Pilgrims."

Heidi looked up at the hill. "The hill over here reminds me of the Pilgrims trying to create their own city on a hill."

"Rather than hiding our faith, I and the other Pilgrims wanted to establish a city in which we could share goodness and faith."

"The Bible describes a city on a hill as being seen by everyone. I'll read you the verses from my version of the Bible." Heidi turned on her cell phone, clicked onto a Bible app, found the Bible verses that she wanted to read, and read them out loud to Bradford:

> You are the light of the world. A city built on a hill cannot be hid. No one after lighting a lamp puts it under the bushel basket, but on the lampstand, and it gives light to all in the house. In the same way, let your light shine before others, so

> that they may see your good works and give glory to your Father in heaven. (Matt. 5: 14 – 16 NRSV)

A beam of light streamed down from the sun, landed on the hill, and made the hill look like a giant green lamp that was moving its beams of light around to multiple people and places.

"I've heard many people in your century call the whole city of Plymouth 'the city on the hill,'" the Bradford statue said.

"The metaphor of a city on a hill showed the Pilgrims' expectations that people would be looking at them, so the Pilgrims wanted to act in a positive way and establish a great city." Heidi glanced at the statue as she added, "People today are not just looking at the hill, Bradford; they're also looking at you."

"People remember that I was the governor of Plymouth for over thirty years."

"A lot of people know about what a great governor you were." Heidi paused for a few seconds and then added, "People admire you not just because you were a great governor, but also because you were the author of the greatest book about the Pilgrims."

"I'm not the only one who was a Pilgrim leader. In my book, *Of Plymouth Plantation,* I tell everyone about Brewster's great personality. He was 'wise and discreet and well-spoken, having a grave and deliberate utterance, with a very cheerful spirit.'[34]"

"I love being an ancestor of Brewster." Heidi sighed. "He was a publisher who sometimes had to hide before he left England for the New World. His experiences probably helped him to know when to be discreet and when to be well-spoken."

"Brewster was really good at talking, especially about religious matters. I also say in my book about Brewster's ministry as the elder to the Pilgrims: 'When preaching, he deeply moved and stirred the affections, and he was very plain and direct in what he taught, being thereby the more profitable to his hearers. He had a singularly good gift of prayer, both public and private, … '[35]"

"It's really nice that he helped other people so much with his preaching and his gift of prayer." Heidi paused and then added, "I wish I were more like him."

"You have your own gifts from God, and you've been using them nicely."

"Do you really think so?"

"Of course, I do. I'm alive in your dream. You've made a statue come alive, so you're very creative."

"Well, I guess I really can help people to be more alive—at least sometimes. That's been happening over the past two days."

Betty all of a sudden appeared and hugged Heidi, who said, "You also, Betty, have been helping people. You saved me from possibly falling down those cement stairs."

"Thanks, Heidi."

"Thank you, Betty."

Heidi and Betty again hugged each other.

Some loud noises of clapping hands and ruffling leaves were heard on the side of the hill.

The Bradford statue said, "I think Brewster Gardens is talking."

"How can 'Brewster Gardens' be talking?" Heidi asked.

Betty laughed. "If statues are moving and talking, then parts of the park can also move around and talk."

The Bradford statue said, "When the Pilgrims were assigning parts of Plymouth Colony to different people, the Elder William Brewster received that section over there for his gardening area."

Betty asked, "Do you mean William Brewster, back in the seventeenth century, actually had a garden in the same place that's now Brewster Gardens in Plymouth?"

Heidi said, "Yes, he really did have a garden over there."

"I'm so glad his garden is still here with us."

"I don't think his garden looked exactly like this one does, but his garden was in the same spot."

"You're right. Brewster probably had vegetables in his garden, rather than a lot of grass, bushes, flowers, and statues."

Heidi and Betty held hands, flew across the street, and landed in front of the pergola entrance to Brewster Gardens. They walked under the roof and between the columns.

Betty said, "I love this brick walkway."

Heidi shook her head in agreement and then pointed to the Town Brook. "That's the brook used by the Pilgrims for their drinking water." She went over to the brook, placed a cupped hand near the water, and asked, "Can I please have some more water?"

A wave moved upward, landed in her hand, and appeared to be smiling.

Heidi placed the water into her mouth. "It still tastes so great."

Betty said, "This brook has a beautiful bridge, so people can easily get across to the other side."

"There are so many beautiful parts of Brewster Gardens." Heidi turned around and faced the back section of the garden area. "I especially love *The Pilgrim Maiden* statue. It was created by Henry Hudson Kitson in 1922. When I was a child, I drew a picture of that statue, and I still have the picture."

"Do you have the picture with you?"

"No, I've been keeping it in a folder with my birth certificate."

"If this is a lucid dream, you should be able to retrieve it right now."

"You're right." Heidi closed her eyes. When she opened them again, the paper that she had colored as a child was being displayed on the water fountain in front of *The Pilgrim Maiden* statue.

Betty ran up to the section of the Town Brook with the water fountain in it. She jumped into the water and rescued the paper from the water. When she brought the page to Heidi, the warmth of Betty's hands had dried the wet paper.

Heidi said, "Thanks so much. The picture still looks like it did when I first drew it."

Betty smiled. "You must come here often."

"I do."

"I come out here often, too." Betty looked over at the right section of Brewster Gardens. "I think the Immigrant Memorial statue is very interesting. It's a stainless-steel statue made by Barney Zeitz in 2001. The intent was to remember the many immigrants who came into this country over the last few centuries."

"The seventeenth-century Pilgrims were not the only ones who helped to create and develop our country's communities," Heidi said.

"I know." Betty stepped up onto the bridge. "I can see why so many people get married here."

Heidi sighed. "I so want to get married in this historic garden."

"With your ancestry, I can understand your feelings." Betty paused and then asked, "Are you engaged? I don't see any rings on your fingers."

"No, I'm not even officially dating anyone right now, but there is someone whom I would love to be dating." Heidi looked at the bridge going over the Town Brook in Brewster Gardens. She then said, "If I'm still lucid dreaming, can I make someone appear in my dream?"

"Maybe you can. You should at least try and see if it's possible."

Heidi slowly inhaled and exhaled. Kevin suddenly appeared in the center of the bridge that was going over the brook.

Heidi ran toward Kevin. Before she stepped onto the bridge, she looked at her feet. She was wearing slippers. Inhaling, she glanced at her arms and legs. In the wind, her pajamas were fluttering around her body and acting like they were trying to tell her something. She looked at Kevin. He was dressed in a tuxedo and was moving an engagement ring toward her left hand.

"Yes, I would love to marry you," Heidi said. "However, I'm not yet ready—I'm dressed up all wrong and shouldn't be out here on a nice date with you."

The Town Brook said to Heidi, "Why don't you change your clothing?"

"That's a great idea!" Heidi closed her eyes for a few seconds. When she opened them up again, she was dressed in a long white gown. She smiled at Kevin and said, "Now I'm ready. People often get married out here."

Kevin slid an engagement ring onto Heidi's ring finger. He then took out a wedding ring. Before he had a chance to place it on Heidi's finger, some loud, splashing noises were heard. Kevin and Heidi both turned around to face the water below the brook. As they watched, the water changed into pieces of glass.

Quiet Censorship

Heidi opened her eyes to see some broken pieces of glass on the floor next to her.

Joe said, "Get up."

Heidi stood up, and Moe attached the backpack to her shoulders. They then walked through the broken glass window into a doughnut shop. Coffee had already been brewed by either Moe or Joe. Moe put some coffee into three large plastic cups, threw some doughnuts onto a plate, grabbed some napkins, and put everything onto one of the shop's tables.

Heidi looked at the cups with coffee in them. She then touched her watch, slid it slightly outward, and tried to take the two pills out of its back section. Before she had a chance to remove the pills, Joe and Moe had sat down. Joe stared at Heidi while Moe grasped onto his coffee cup.

Heidi sighed, moved her watch back to its regular position, and sat down next to Joe. She then joined Joe and Moe as they quickly ate their breakfast. Before Heidi had even finished a whole doughnut, she was pulled into the restroom and then told to bring her coffee and doughnut along as they exited the shop.

After placing some food into the backpack, Joe led the way down the corridor and into a stairwell. They began to walk down the stairs. On the seventh level, Joe stopped walking and said softly, "It's a little too quiet here." He opened the door from the stairwell into the corridor. No light was visible in the corridor, and no offices could be seen. Joe used his flashlight to find a light switch, turned on the corridor's lights, and stepped forward. The rope between him and Heidi suddenly became tense. Heidi was not moving. When he pulled on the rope, she yelled, "Okay, I'm coming."

Joe angrily responded, "You yelled like that on purpose!"

"No, I didn't." In a softer voice, Heidi added, "I'm just a little bit nervous."

"You yelled on purpose, so you could warn people about us." Joe placed his right hand on the side of his gun.

Heidi touched one of the buttons on the frame of her glasses. The lenses on her glasses became completely clear and let all of the LED lighting go through to her wide-open eyes. Immediately, her eyes reacted in negative ways to the intense lighting. They blinked multiple times, and tears began to form. She then said softly, "I'm really sorry about that. I'm just psyched out. How would you feel if everything was too quiet when you were tied up to a kidnapper with a gun?"

Joe looked at her eyes, which were watery and blinking. "With those tears in your eyes, you're either telling the truth, or you're a very good liar."

"I'm not a very good liar." Heidi blinked intensely for a couple of times, and a tear fell down her left cheek. "I promise to not yell again."

Joe sighed and removed his hand from his gun. "Okay, you're safe for the moment. Just try to behave better."

"I'll try."

Joe turned around and stared at Moe, who was laughing. After a few seconds, Joe asked him, "What's so funny?"

"You just censored her."

"No, I only told her what to do; I said to be quiet," Joe said.

"That's censorship."

"It's only censorship, Moe, if she's saying something bad."

"She really was saying something bad. She was yelling warnings to people and backstabbing us."

For a few seconds, Heidi remained silent as both Moe and Joe stared at her. She then put her right hand over her mouth, wiped away a smile that was forming beneath her hand, and said, "To make both of you happy, I'll try to censor myself."

Joe sighed before starting to walk down the corridor. Heidi and Moe followed him. When they arrived in front of the first office, they stopped moving. An eight-foot-wide window was on the left side of a wooden door. Joe pointed to the door and waved at Heidi to open it. She turned the handle, but nothing moved because the door was locked. When Joe tugged at her arm, she stepped backward. He then pulled up his gun, but before he could fire it, Moe stepped in front of him.

Joe lowered his gun and asked, "Why are you standing in the way?"

"I'm trying to keep you from making a lot of noise. There are quieter ways of breaking into this office."

"Now you're telling me to be quiet. That's censorship," Joe said.

"I'm not censoring you," Moe said.

"Yes, you are. I have every right to make as much noise as I want to."

"Then you'll be telling people that we're here," Moe said.

"Everyone already knows there are shooters in this building. Plus, they've probably been hearing us talking." Joe shoved Moe out of the way, fired six bullets into the door handle, and kicked the bottom of the door. It still would not open. Joe turned his gun toward the window, which shattered after the first bullet. He waved his hand at Moe, indicating that he could be the first one to go inside.

Moe put on some gloves and slowly climbed through the window. He immediately turned on the lights. He then moved to stand behind the door, so Heidi could not see what he was doing. Some sliding noises were heard from where he was standing. Moe opened the front door. When Joe and Heidi entered, they both paused to look at a bookcase near the entrance.

Heidi asked Moe softly, "Was that bookcase blocking the door?"

"Yeah, it was. I just slid it sideways."

Heidi watched as Moe touched one of the books on the middle shelf of the bookcase. The book had bright yellow words and pictures. A piece of rope was wound around the book. A padlock connected the rope to one of the nails in the back section of the bookcase.

Heidi looked at the rope attaching her waist to Joe's. "That book being tied to the bookcase makes me feel like I'm not alone."

Joe tugged gently at the rope connecting his waist to Heidi's. "I'm tied up, too." He then laughed at her expression. "You're not alone here, but I think you'd prefer to be alone."

Heidi stared at the tied-up book as she said, "Maybe that book's expensive."

Joe was silent for a few seconds and then asked, "Why do you think that book's expensive? It doesn't look like an antique. There's no leather cover or anything else interesting on it."

"It's tied to the bookcase."

"Why would someone tie down a book?" Joe asked.

"People can't just pick up and read a book that's tied onto the bookcase, so the book is probably expensive or important in some other way." Heidi paused and then added, "Perhaps the book is like a reserved book in a library. It's supposed to stay here and not be taken home by anyone."

Joe walked closer to the book and looked at its cover. "You're right. This book is an employee manual. The boss probably wants it to stay in here, so the employees can read it at any time."

Heidi looked at the book's size and smiled. "That's a very large manual. I'm guessing some of the employees have only read a few of the pages."

"Where did you get your knowledge about tied-down books?" Joe asked.

"That tied-down book might be like the books that historically used to be chained onto shelves or tables. Before Gutenberg's invention of movable type for printing presses, books were so expensive that they were often chained to keep them safe."

"This book doesn't really seem expensive. The company could make multiple copies of it. Maybe someone's censoring this copy," Joe said.

Heidi smiled. "Chaining up a book can be a form of censorship. If the book is chained in a way that people can't open it up, then the book's content is being hidden."

"I guess you're right. If people can't just pick up a book and read it, then censorship is happening," Joe said.

"Sometimes parents have books that they don't want their children to read," Heidi said.

"Those would probably be locked up in a desk drawer, instead of being chained up somewhere." Joe looked at the rope connecting himself to Heidi.

"Chaining, though, does say something," Heidi said.

"What can a chain say?" Joe asked.

Heidi looked at the rope around her waist. "A chain, like a rope, can be a symbol for a lack of freedom. People who chain up a book might also be saying something negative about the book and want everyone to see the book in a bad way."

"Chaining a book is different from hiding it," Joe said.

"You're right. If a book is being censored, the company can just hide it," Heidi said.

Joe smiled. "They also could be saying that the book must be read in the place where it has been chained up."

Moe said, "That makes sense."

Heidi shook her head in agreement. She stared at the rope connecting her waist to Joe's as she said, "They used to burn books that were censored." She sighed and then added, "At least today, books are a little bit safer, whether they're chained up or censored."

Joe looked at his section of the rope that was tying him and Heidi together. "Even today, censorship still happens."

Heidi was still looking at the rope as she said, "Sometimes censorship is necessary to avoid harassment and other problems. At other times, censorship might just be limiting someone's freedom of speech. Our justice system is helpful in lawful determinations of what should be free speech and what should be censored."

Joe said, "People can say what they want to online, right?"

"No, there are federal and state laws related to cyberspace," Heidi said.

"How can rules tell people what to say on the internet? The internet's for the whole world to enjoy," Joe said.

"Sometimes people harass or bully each other. Freedom doesn't mean that one person can hurt someone else." Heidi gripped the rope tightly and then let it go.

"Even so, I think freedom is essential. Doesn't the American Civil Liberties Union do anything to help with freedom?" Joe took a step away from Heidi.

"Yes, the ACLU sometimes helps. Its website says, 'The ACLU's nationwide network of local affiliate offices is ready and willing to counter state attacks on your right to speak freely online.'[36]"

Joe said, "You have a lot of knowledge about online information and books, Heidi. Do the books over there tell you anything about what kind of office this is?"

"I don't know." Heidi glanced at the bookcase and then at the pieces of glass on the floor before adding, "Some of the glass pieces have ink on them. The front window must have had a company's name and possibly some pictures on it."

"Now everything's unreadable," Joe said.

"Maybe it was also unreadable before we got here." Heidi looked away from the pieces of glass and glanced briefly around the office. The front room was small, containing only three desks, six chairs, and a few bookcases. As Heidi watched, Moe walked into the middle of the room and looked under two of the desks. No one was hiding under them, but there were some interesting books and articles on top of the left desk.

Heidi followed Joe as he walked over to the desk with the books and articles. One of the books was very thick. Heidi opened up its front cover. Inside were some pages that had been partially cut out, so a smart phone was now hidden inside its empty rectangular space.

Joe grabbed the phone and turned it on; its power was at ninety-two percent. Joe went to one of the news apps and started to laugh.

Moe asked, "What's so funny?"

"This news app is saying that we're 'shooters.'"

Moe shifted his gun. "Why do you think we aren't shooters?"

"We haven't shot anyone yet."

"Yes, we have. Don't you remember the guy with the scratched arm and the feet that we shot?" Moe asked.

Joe smiled. "Yeah, I do. Judas's bumpy feet were interesting."

"I think they were even more interesting after we shot them," Moe said.

"While we did shoot Judas, we didn't kill him. We aren't really shooters."

"Why do you think that?" Moe asked.

"Shooters shoot and kill people. We're just trying to steal a few items. We're not really here to kill people."

Moe sighed. "You're right, but if we have to, then we will."

"The big problem with killing anyone is what might happen if we're caught," Joe said.

"We won't be caught," Moe said.

"You're right. It's very unlikely we'll be caught, but just in case we're unlucky this time, it's better to be caught as a thief than as a murderer."

Moe shook his head up and down. "Thieves are able to get out of jail in a year or two."

"If we're ever in jail again, then we can worry about getting out. For right now, we should just worry about getting out of this room." Joe walked to the back of the room, where an old-fashioned wooden door was closed. "We should check out where this leads to." He pushed at the door; it was unlocked, and the lights were on.

Heidi followed Joe as he went down a short corridor that ended with a door opening into a kitchen area. A window at the back of the kitchen was wide open. A cabinet next to the window had one end of a rope wound around its base. The rest of the rope went out through the window.

Joe went over to the window, looked outside, and said, "I can't believe people climbed down seven stories on that rope."

Moe said, "Maybe they only went down one or two stories and then climbed into a different office."

"Even that seems unlikely," Joe said.

Heidi walked closer to the window, put one of her hands on the rope, and tried to look outside.

"No, don't you dare!" Joe yelled as he pulled Heidi away from the window. "Are you trying to escape?"

"No, I wasn't."

"I think you were." Joe's right hand touched the side of his gun.

"I'd never do anything as stupid as jumping out a window this high up while I was only holding onto that rope." Heidi inhaled, exhaled, and then added, "I just wanted to see where that rope led to."

"I don't believe you." Joe stared at Heidi as he closed the window.

Heidi felt vibrations on her glasses. Kevin had sent her a message, but she was unable to read it with Joe staring at her. She started blinking her eyes and shaking her hands slightly. "I really didn't mean to do anything. I'm sorry. I'm just scared all the time, so I'm not always acting logically."

Joe stared at her for another few seconds and then said, "Okay, you do look a little bit upset. Maybe you're telling me the truth."

Joe removed his hand from his gun. He then stepped over to help Moe check out some items in the cupboards and drawers. In one of the cupboards were some pictures on frames. Joe frowned as he asked Moe, "Why would someone hide pictures like these? Shouldn't they be placed on people's desks?"

Moe picked up one of the pictures. "This one has a picture of someone's house."

Joe pointed at one spot in the picture. "There's a street address on that mailbox. Maybe the owner is trying to keep the house's location secret."

"What difference does the address really make? Why would someone come into an office and try to find out where the employees live?" Moe asked.

Joe stared at a large garage that was standing next to the house in the picture. "Maybe the person who owns this picture is doing something illegal, like dealing drugs."

"Then he'd want everyone to see and to know about his home address, so he could sell drugs," Moe said.

"He might be trying to hide his address from some cops," Joe said.

Moe shook his head. "That could be why he's hidden the picture in this cupboard."

"The owner of that picture could be a woman," Heidi said.

"You're right about that." Joe picked up a different picture from the cupboard, turned it around, and opened up the back of its frame.

Moe asked, "Does that frame have any money hidden inside it?"

"No, there's just this one picture, but perhaps we should check all of these frames, just in case something is hidden somewhere." Joe handed Moe half of the framed pictures. For the next few minutes, they opened up and looked inside of each frame. Nothing was found.

The picture frames were now stacked up in the back section of the counter beneath the cupboard. Most of the pictures had been placed in front of the stacks of frames.

Joe moved one of the pictures and placed it next to one of the other ones. He suddenly said, "Oh, I know what's happening here."

Moe asked, "What? I don't see anything."

Joe placed four of the pictures next to each other. "These pictures are all from the same place."

Moe shook his head. "You're right. These houses are right next to each other."

Joe smiled. "Maybe someone's planning on buying these houses and then building something different."

"Do you think it would be worthwhile if we tried to buy a few of these houses first?" Moe asked.

"It might be a way to make some easy money. However, an easier way to make some money would be if we just sell this information to someone else."

Joe moved all of the pictures around until they were organized into a rectangular block with sixteen houses in it. He then took out his cell phone and took some pictures.

"Do we need to put the pictures back into the frames?" Moe asked.

"I think we should. We don't want anyone to know that we figured out what's happening here." Joe glanced at Heidi and then waved his hand at her. He was obviously telling her to help reframe the pictures.

Joe, Moe, and Heidi put all of the pictures back into the frames before placing the frames into the cupboard.

Joe then opened up another cupboard.

"Are you looking for anything specific?" Heidi asked as she stood behind Joe.

"We just need anything that's worth enough money to take up some space in that backpack you're carrying," Joe said.

"I think candy would be nice," Heidi said as she pointed to a bag of chocolates. "I won't even mind the added weight in this backpack."

Joe picked up the bag and handed it to Heidi. "Just don't eat all of it. Moe and I will need some, too."

Heidi opened up the bag of candy, ate one of the chocolates, and waved the bag in front of Joe and Moe. They both grabbed the bag and ate a few pieces of the candy.

Joe said, "I don't think that candy will last too long in the backpack."

Heidi laughed as she placed another piece of candy into her mouth. "It might not even last long enough to be put into the backpack."

Moe took the bag of candy out of Heidi's hand and said, "I'll carry this for a little while."

Heidi smiled as she asked, "Can I look for some soda or bottled water in the refrigerator?"

"That's a good idea," Joe said as he led Heidi over to the refrigerator. He then stepped away to look into a nearby cupboard as Heidi opened the refrigerator's door. The interior of the refrigerator was not cold, so it must have been unplugged. Inside the refrigerator was a small dog. Its collar had a nametag on it that read "Harley." The dog squeezed past the opening in the door and started to bark at Heidi, Joe, and Moe. Joe lifted up his gun. Before he could place his finger on the trigger, Heidi moved her hand to the top shelf of the refrigerator, grabbed some luncheon meat, and waved it in front of Harley. The dog stopped barking and stared at the meat in Heidi's hand. He then wagged his tail as she gave him a piece of the meat.

Joe put his gun down and asked Heidi for some of the luncheon meat. She split it up between him and Harley. Moe pulled out some bread and crackers from one of the cupboards. Joe shared his meat with Moe, who then asked if there was anything else good inside the refrigerator.

Heidi took out some cheese, as well as some cans of beer and soda. "There's some bottled water in here too. After we eat lunch, we can take it with us."

With their food and drinks on the countertops, they ate quickly. Harley watched them and kept on begging for more food. Heidi found some dog food in one of the cupboards and gave it to him.

After they had all finished eating and grabbed some bottled water from the refrigerator, Moe asked, "Should we put Harley back into the refrigerator?"

Joe said, "I wonder why someone put him in there."

Heidi said, "Well, the refrigerator's turned off, and his owner probably didn't want him jumping out the open window."

Joe said, "I think you're right. Now the window is closed, though, so the dog should be fine running around in here."

As Moe, Joe, and Heidi started to walk out of the kitchen, Harley barked. Heidi noticed that he was looking up at the light in the ceiling. She changed the focus of her glasses by pushing one of the buttons on the frame. She was then able to see a shadow moving above the ceiling's light fixture. At least one person had somehow climbed through the ceiling's tiles and was now almost invisible. Heidi's eyes jumped around to different spots on the ceiling. The ceiling tiles above a vent in the furthest wall were loose and incorrectly aligned with the other tiles.

The rope around Heidi's waist pulled at her and then stopped moving. Heidi glanced at Joe, who had stopped walking forward. She quickly turned her head downward to look at Harley. With a wagging tail, the dog was staring at the ceiling's light fixture. Heidi reached her hand out toward the dog. He ran over to her hand and licked it.

Joe was now watching the dog. He said, "Heidi, do you think Harley wants us to stay here with him?"

"He's probably just lonely and worried about being hungry again." Heidi was patting Harley.

From the corridor, Moe said, "Are you two coming, or are you both going to stay there with that dog?"

Joe began to move toward the corridor; Heidi started to follow him, but paused long enough to glance up again at the kitchen's ceiling light. Above the light was a small shadow that looked like a waving hand. Heidi smiled and shook her head slightly; she was trying to say "hi" to the ceiling person without Joe or Moe noticing anything. She then waved at the dog, rather than at the ceiling, and closed the door to keep Harley in the kitchen.

Joe, Moe, and Heidi went through the office area and out into the large corridor that led to the elevator and stairs. Rather than checking out the other offices on the seventh floor, Joe started walking straight back to the stairs.

"Where are we going now?" Moe asked.

"There's a store on the floor below us that might have some expensive products," Joe said.

"Is it a bank, by any chance?" Moe asked.

"No, it's just a store with musical instruments."

"Would those really be worth that much money?"

"Some instruments are really expensive," Joe said.

"They're also going to be sort of heavy." Moe paused and then added, "Pianos, especially, will be a little heavy for Heidi to carry around."

Joe laughed. "I wasn't planning on any of us carrying pianos around."

"Many other musical instruments will also be a little too heavy for me to carry," Heidi said.

Joe sighed. "We might or might not grab one or two of the smaller instruments. What's more important, though, is to look for some cash."

"Cash is always nice," Moe said.

"It's also easier to carry than metal instruments. Because of the repair work the store does, some cash might be hidden away somewhere," Joe said.

Moe asked, "Did you look up this store on the internet, or did you actually go there?"

Joe glanced quickly at Heidi and then looked back at Joe. "I did some research."

Joe, Moe, and Heidi went down to the sixth floor and then walked out into a hallway. The first office was very quiet; there were no noises and no lights. The second office had lights, and music was being played. Moe and Heidi followed Joe as he walked over to the musical office.

Free to Be Noisy

The door had a large sign: "Repairs with Music." On both sides of the door, the windows had interesting decorations. Along the lower sections of the windows were some photos of children and families playing different musical instruments. In the middle parts of the windows were large paintings of a band and an orchestra. Other sections of the windows had drawings of different instruments; the various parts of the instruments were labeled.

Music, possibly from a violin, was emanating from the interior of the store. Moe pushed heavily on the front door. Because it was not locked, it flew open quickly while making a loud metallic noise.

Joe asked, "What's that noise?"

Moe walked into the room, turned on the lights, and looked behind the door. "There's a trumpet over here." He picked it up and showed it to Joe and Heidi, who were now also inside the store.

Joe said, "That trumpet must have been placed against the door on purpose."

"Someone wanted the door's motion to make noise." Moe put the trumpet on a table in the front section of the room. He turned around, gazing intently at different sections of the room. "This room was noisy just a minute ago. Now everything's quiet."

"There must be some people in here. They were using that trumpet's noise to tell them when someone was coming into the shop."

Moe frowned. "I don't know if that makes sense. The front door wasn't locked. Wouldn't the people working here have a key to lock the front door?"

"Whenever the doors are locked, people like us always try to break glass windows." Moe stared at the photos and paintings on the windows. "Maybe the musical repairers are artistic—they don't want the windows to be shot out."

Joe was also gazing at the windows on both sides of the door. After a moment of looking at the photos, drawings, and paintings, he moved his gun forward and placed his finger on the trigger. "I'm taking this window, Moe. You can have the other one."

Moe raised up his gun before asking, "Heidi, which one of us do you think is the fastest shooter?"

Heidi swallowed as she kept on staring at the windows. "I don't know."

Moe said, "Well, let's find out." He looked at Joe, who shook his head in agreement.

Joe moved over closer to Moe. They both raised their guns to the same height. Moe then said, "On the count of three, two, one, go!"

Both windows were shot multiple times until no glass remained in the window frames. The pictures were torn apart as they fell with the broken-up pieces of glass onto the floor.

Joe said, "I guess I won."

Moe shook his head. "You're definitely faster." He then looked down at the tip of his gun and added, "However, we both know about my accuracy. I think I used fewer bullets than you did, but I did more damage."

Heidi was still staring at the pieces of pictures, photos, and drawings that were scattered on the floor near the windows. One of the photos was broken into two pieces; both parts had fallen right next to each other. On the left piece of the photo were three children playing different musical instruments: a flute, a drum, and a guitar. On the right part of the torn photo were two adults who were obviously the parents; they were smiling while watching their children.

Joe pulled on the rope attached to Heidi as he said, "Let's see if anyone's on the other side of that door." He pointed to a door in the right corner of the room.

Moe followed Joe past several tables. One of them had a violin next to an open toolbox. The violin was missing its tuning pegs and strings. Its chinrest had a crack with some splinters sticking out. Moe said, "That violin will be tough to play."

Joe laughed. "It will be tough to even just rest one's chin on that chinrest."

Moe picked up the violin, dropped it on the floor, jumped on it, and said, "Now it'll be even tougher to play." He then frowned while looking down at the side of his right leg.

"Is your foot okay?" Joe asked.

"I think so." Moe bent over and shook the bottom part of his jeans back and forth. A one-inch splinter fell onto the floor. Moe then pulled up the bottom part of his jeans and moved the sock outward and away from his right ankle. After looking at and rubbing his ankle, he said, "Everything's okay now."

"Are you bleeding?" Joe asked.

"Just a little bit, but it should stop quickly." Moe stood up, glared at the indented violin, and then kicked it across the room. Some bits of wood fell off as it flew under a table.

Joe took the backpack off of Heidi's back. After he found a bandage, he gave it to Moe, who put it on his ankle. Moe then followed Joe and Heidi over to the door in the back corner of the room.

Joe put his ear up against the door.

Moe asked, "Should I shoot at the door?"

Joe frowned as he put a finger in front of his lips. Moe realized that he was supposed to be quiet; he put a hand over his mouth, showing that he was silencing himself.

Joe listened very intently to what was happening on the other side of the door. After a minute, he said, "I thought I heard some music, but it's very quiet in there right now."

Moe asked, "Should we shoot through the lock?"

"Let's see if it's locked first." Joe grabbed the door's handle and tried to turn it. Nothing happened. "Yeah, it's locked." He stepped backward, took out his gun, and shot at the door's handle. After only a couple of shots, the handle fell off the door. Joe tried to push the door open, but something heavy in the next room was keeping the door shut.

Joe waved at Moe to come over and help. They both pushed against the door at the same time. Slowly, they opened the door. As soon as the opening was large enough, Moe squeezed through the doorway. Joe and Heidi followed him. No other people were in the room, but multiple desks, tables, chairs, speakers, and musical instruments were present.

Joe said, "If they had put multiple desks in front of that door, we might not have gotten in here."

On the interior side of the door was a desk with several computers on it. Moe said, "I think people put these computers on the desk in order to make it heavier. They probably thought these computers on a single desk would make it heavy enough to keep us outside of the room."

Joe said, "I'm sure you're right. Multiple desks, though, would have been heavier."

At the other end of the room was another door. Joe started walking toward it. Moe did not follow him, but rather asked, "What kind of walls are these?"

Joe stopped, looked at one of the walls, and then walked up to it. After touching its surface, he said, "It feels like foam or cork."

Heidi said, "I think it's some kind of special insulation or maybe soundproofing."

"Soundproofed walls make sense. When we were in the other room, I heard some kind of music, but it wasn't super loud." Joe paused and then added, "The music sounded like someone was playing an instrument, but the sound was too weak for me to figure out what the instrument was."

Heidi's eyes moved from the walls to a table and then to a musical instrument's case. "Since this place is a musical sales and repair shop, maybe people play their instruments in this soundproofed room."

Joe walked over to the other door again; Heidi and Moe followed him. This door also was locked. Moe shot off the handle and then pushed on the door. Nothing was blocking the door, so it was easily opened. Moe, Joe, and Heidi walked into a corridor, which led to two restrooms and an office area with several desks.

Joe opened the door to the men's room. Inside were two men. The one standing nearest the door was around fifty years old and had long straggly hair. He was wearing jeans and a tee-shirt with a guitar image on it. The other man was about thirty-five years old with short hair. He was dressed more formally with a buttoned shirt and a tie.

Joe moved his gun slightly sideways before asking, "Which one of you is the owner of this shop?"

The older man spoke almost too quickly when he said, "I am. My name's Charles."

The younger man frowned. "No, you're not the owner. I am."

Charles looked at the younger man and said, "Please, Roger, let's tell the truth here. I'm really the owner."

"No, I'm the owner." Roger sighed. "You know how much I've been helping this company."

"You've been hiring your relatives to do the painting and electrical work," Charles said.

"My relatives can be trusted," Roger said.

Charles opened his mouth to say something, looked at Roger's face, and then was quiet for a few seconds. He finally said, "Whether your relatives are trustworthy or not, you still should have gotten repair estimates from multiple companies and then hired the cheapest one."

"The cheapest one sometimes uses the worst materials." Roger paused briefly before adding, "You might be against me hiring companies owned by my family members, but there are some other things that you can't debate about my leadership. I've been making some good stock market choices to help our company financially."

Charles frowned. "My choices would have been better."

"No, I don't think so." Roger's face turned red as he added, "Stock market trends are so debatable, but something that you can't oppose is how I created that new contract."

"I didn't like some of the content and wording," Charles said.

"Even so, everyone—including you—signed it."

Charles said, "Sometimes I need to sign things that I don't agree with."

"Why would you do that?" Roger asked.

"I need to sometimes try and make people happy."

"I'm the one who really should keep the employees happy, so they don't all quit," Roger said.

"A lot of them have quit anyway," Charles said sarcastically.

"That might be true, but I've also been promising to initiate a lot of improvements to make our work environment better," Roger said.

"The quiet room could have been a better work environment."

Charles and Roger stopped talking and just glared at each other. They were still in the restroom, and Joe took a step forward into the doorway of the restroom. Joe looked back and forth between Charles and Roger before saying, "You two sound like a pair of politicians."

Roger laughed. "Charles and I are both descendants of seventeenth-century politicians. We must have some of their personality traits."

Joe asked, "Who were your ancestors?"

Roger said, "I'm a descendant of Roger Williams, who founded Rhode Island."

Joe turned to Charles and asked, "Were your ancestors the ones who banished Roger Williams from the Massachusetts Bay Colony?"

"No, I'm descended from British kings: Charles I and Charles II."

Joe asked, "Was one of those kings killed?"

Charles said, "Yeah, Charles I was executed by the British parliament in 1649. Eleven years later, Charles II became the British king."

Roger said, "While I don't like kings, Charles II signed the 1663 Rhode Island Charter, which made my ancestor, Roger Williams, very happy."

Joe looked back and forth between Roger and Charles. "If a document signed by Charles II made Roger Williams happy, why are you two fighting? Your ancestors must have gotten along, at least sometimes."

Roger said, "It doesn't matter what century we're talking about. People don't always get along, especially if we're talking about political leaders."

Charles pulled a bunch of his straggly hair back and forth along his left ear. "Everyone talks, but not everyone listens."

"Sometimes people don't want to listen to each other," Roger said.

"Back in the seventeenth century, people were supposed to listen to the king, even if they disagreed with him. Charles II was the one big British boss in the seventeenth century, and I'm the big boss in our century in this office," Charles said.

Roger's eyebrows moved close together as he stared angrily at Charles. He stroked his tie and then asked, "Why do you keep on lying about who's the boss?"

Charles's eyes moved down to the floor. He sighed heavily before saying, "I'm not lying. I'm really the boss." His eyes, twittering and blinking, moved upward and looked at Roger.

"Do you want to get fired?"

Charles frowned. "You're the one who's trying to get fired. I'm just doing my job."

"If you were really doing your job well, you'd be dressing better," Roger said.

"If you were paying me better, I'd have more money for better clothes."

Roger laughed. "You just admitted that I'm the boss."

"No, I didn't do that," Charles said.

"Yes, you did. You said that I should be paying you more money," Roger said.

Charles looked over at Joe, Moe, and Heidi. Moe and Heidi had blank expressions on their faces and remained quiet.

Joe's eyebrows were raised upward, and his right hand moved to the handle on his gun. Joe then asked, "Why are you lying about being the boss, Charles?"

After thinking for a few seconds, Charles said, "Roger should be paying me more money, but not because he's the boss. He just started doing the payroll, and he's been messing up."

Joe said, "Maybe we can have Roger write us some big checks."

Roger sighed. "I could write out checks for millions of dollars, but that doesn't mean any bank will cash them for you."

Charles laughed. "I wonder if my signature on million-dollar checks would be approved by banks."

Roger glared at Charles. "Your signature on a one-dollar check wouldn't be approved."

"You're wrong; my signature would be approved."

Roger said, "You told me yesterday that you were denied a credit card."

"That wasn't my fault. The credit-card company just messed up," Charles said.

"What about the fact that you can't even get credit to buy a new car?"

"Roger, I don't even want a new car anymore. The payments would be too high."

"You're paying over four hundred dollars a month for a car that's ten years old!" Roger said.

"Some old cars are really nice."

"Yours isn't, though, Charles. You told me that you hated your car."

"Even with all of the scratches in the paint, I still love my old car," Charles said.

"You're lying again." Roger looked at the other people in the room before adding, "He's a real liar."

"No, I'm not a liar!"

"Well, then, tell the shooters here that I'm your boss."

"There's no way you're the boss, Roger. I am." Charles closed his mouth tightly with his jaw extended outward; his facial expression showed his stubbornness. He then said too loudly, "I really am the person in charge here."

Roger took a step toward Charles and yelled out, "Stop your lying!"

Charles glared angrily at Roger before yelling back, "You're the one who needs to stop lying!"

Roger took another long step forward. Even though he was now only two feet away from Charles, his close proximity did not make

Charles step backward. Instead, Charles moved his chin up high and looked like he was going to stand steady in the same spot, no matter what happened. He then clenched both of his fists and raised them upward slightly.

Roger moved his right hand up to the height of his shoulder while clenching his fist. "Do you actually want to fight with me, Charles? We've been working together for years."

"Yeah, let's fight!"

"After our fight, do you promise to tell the truth?" Roger asked.

"I've been telling the truth." Charles moved his chin even higher.

"Will you admit that the winner is the boss?"

"The winner possibly will be the boss," Charles said. After thinking for a few seconds, he added, "We'll just have to decide on that after we see who wins."

"You know that I'll be the winner, so you'll have to just tell the truth about my being the owner of this shop," Roger said.

"Why do you think you'll be the winner?" Charles asked.

"I'm younger than you are."

"Age doesn't determine someone's strength." Charles moved both of his arms upward until they were stretched sideways out from his shoulders. He pointed his nose to his right arm; he then turned his face and pointed his nose to his left arm. "You know I've been exercising at a gym for years. You can see it in my biceps. My body is actually telling everyone here about all of the exercise that I've been doing."

Roger moved his right hand up above his head and stretched his fingers as high as possible. "I don't know if I've told you this, but I've been working out with weights at home nearly every single night." He pointed his left index finger over to his right arm's bicep muscle. "My body also says things to people. It's called body language."

Laughter filled the room. Charles then clenched his fists and asked, "So how should we fight? Should we be boxers, wrestlers, or something else?"

"We could wrestle," Roger said. He looked over at Heidi and asked, "What do you think we should do?"

"I love wrestling," Heidi said. After pausing for a few seconds, she added, "Love and Wrestling are really great together. They were both children of my ancestor, William Brewster."

Roger smiled. "That's so neat. As a descendant of Roger Williams, I know a little bit about the history of the Pilgrims."

"Brewster came over on the *Mayflower* with Love and Wrestling, as well as with his wife, Mary. I know Roger Williams came over later," Heidi said.

"He came over on the *Lyon* in 1631," Roger said.

"If you and Charles really want to fight, Roger, you should definitely wrestle. Arm wrestling might be the best kind," Heidi said.

Before Roger could reply, Charles said, "I think arm wrestling would be too easy. Boxing would be a more exciting way for us to fight, especially since we don't have any gloves or other equipment."

Roger frowned. "Do you really want to hit me like a boxer would, but with a gloveless hand?"

Charles shook his head affirmatively. "We should have a real fight. It will help us to feel less angry."

Roger's eyes widened. "Are you really going to feel better when you do something like hit me in the face?"

Charles looked at Roger's face, inhaled deeply, exhaled slowly, and said, "You're right. Boxing might not be the best idea."

"Do you really want to fight against me physically?"

"Yeah, I do." Charles paused for a few seconds before adding, "I think fighting will make both of us feel less stressed out."

Roger sighed. "Okay, we should have a real physical fight."

"Wrestling might be good. We can probably have a nice fight without hurting each other too much."

"We could start with arm wrestling, like Heidi wants." Roger looked over at Heidi and smiled. "After we arm wrestle, if you need something more intense, we could do some other kind of wrestling."

Charles pointed to the door leading out of the men's room. "We should arm wrestle in the next room."

Everyone walked into the small office area.

Roger said, "This room is nice, but our quiet room is better for arm wrestling. It has some nice tables and chairs."

Joe asked, "Does that room have some kind of soundproofing in its walls?"

Roger shook his head up and down. "Yes, it does. That's the room where people show us problems with their instruments."

Charles said, "It's also where our customers check out their repaired instruments to make certain they're happy with everything."

Roger smiled as he said, "You know what that room is also used for, don't you, Charles?"

Charles's face turned red. "Okay, we call it our 'quiet room' because we go there if we're upset about something."

Joe asked, "How can going into a quiet room make people feel better?"

Roger said, "We can yell, scream, play loud music, or do some other noisy things to reduce our stress. People in other offices won't hear too much of what someone is doing in the quiet room."

Charles said, "Okay, I often have to use that room during a normal work day."

Roger laughed. "For once, you're actually telling the truth, Charles. You even use that room too much."

Charles frowned. "I think you're just trying to pick on me for some reason."

"No, I'm not. You're the one who's always angry."

"I have good reasons to be angry." Charles raised his chin up and waved it back and forth toward Roger.

"So, you're blaming me for all of your problems, Charles."

"No, I'm blaming you for some of my problems."

"Let's go next door and fight it out," Roger said.

"Yes, let's do that."

Joe opened the door and walked into the quiet room. Heidi, Moe, Roger, and Charles followed him. Charles glanced around the room at the tables and chairs. He then moved a violin off of the central rectangular table and onto a different table that already had some other musical instruments on it. The table in the room's center now was already for an arm-wrestling fight. Its top area was empty, and a chair was on each of its four sides. Charles sat down in one of the chairs, and Roger sat in the chair on the opposite side of the table.

Roger asked, "Do we need to look up some rules on the internet, or should we just get started?"

Joe, Moe, and Heidi were standing on the left side of the table. Joe said, "I think we all know the basic arm-wresting rules, but if you mess up at all, I'll tell you about my rules." He raised his gun slightly and waved it back and forth.

Roger and Charles put their right elbows on the table, lifted their hands upward, and then clasped their right hands together. As they stared at each other, they tightened their jaws and their fists.

The sound of scraping metal made both Roger and Charles look to the side of their table. Joe was scraping the end of his gun against one of the metal table's legs. Joe then asked, "Moe, which one of them do you think will win?"

"Charles has the longest forearm and seems to know more about wrestling. However, Roger probably has the best muscles in his forearm, wrist, and fingers."

"I think you're right, Moe. They probably both have about the same chance of winning," Joe said.

Moe's face looked thoughtful for a few seconds before he said, "Charles will probably win because he's upset and has his anger to give him additional strength."

Joe smiled. "I know Charles has been lying, and Roger is the real boss. Therefore, Charles will probably respect his boss by giving up instead of actually winning."

Charles looked at Joe and frowned. "I'm the real boss, and I'll never give up!"

Joe laughed. "Moe, do you think we should bet some money on who the winner will be?"

"We could." Moe took his billfold out of his pocket and opened it up. Only a few one-dollar bills were inside. "Another possibility would be to shoot the loser of the arm-wresting fight."

Joe moved his gun slightly higher, showing more of its metal strength. "Okay, if Charles wins, you will also be a winner because you would have correctly figured out who would be the winner. You will win the chance to shoot Roger."

Moe moved his gun even higher than Joe's and said, "I think that sounds fair. If Roger wins, you can shoot Charles."

Heidi pressed against the frames of her glasses and sent a text message: "Possible upcoming shooting."

After just a few seconds, her glasses vibrated because of an incoming message. Heidi pressed a button and read the message: "We know. We're watching through a video system in the room."

Heidi moved her hand down to her waist. She quickly glanced at the walls and ceiling. Her eyes then stared at an air vent in one of the walls. Something inside the vent, possibly a camera lens, was reflecting light. Heidi smiled and sent a text message to Kevin: "Are Roger and Charles federal agents or police officers?"

A minute later, Kevin's response came through on Heidi's glasses: "We think Roger and Charles are undercover agents. They have been sending code messages to each other with their body language. Roger and Charles also are keeping the shooters from leaving the Repairs with Music office."

Heidi sent another message to Kevin: "Distracting and slowing down the shooters is a good way to save other people."

"You're right, and I know you're helping. I've been praying," Kevin responded.

"Thanks. I've been praying, too," Heidi said in her next message to Kevin.

Joe looked at Heidi, stepped closer to her, and asked, "What are you doing to your glasses?"

Heidi moved her glasses up onto her head and then back down in front of her eyes again. "These are new glasses. I think they're a little heavy for my nose."

Joe grunted and turned his eyes to focus on the arm wrestlers again.

Heidi also looked at Roger and Charles. Their left arms were resting on the table. Their right arms were positioned for wrestling. The elbows and biceps appeared strong; however, the forearms and hands were no longer firm but rather seemed anxious. Roger's and Charles's facial expressions were increasingly becoming even more anxious.

Roger opened his mouth and then closed it. Charles heavily inhaled and exhaled while Roger opened and closed his mouth again. Finally, Roger said in a stuttering voice, "We're really doing this fight just to keep you guys entertained, not to get killed."

Charles shook his head in agreement. "We're just trying to make you happy, so you won't kill us or some other people."

Joe asked, "You aren't trying to stall us until some police officers come up here, are you?"

Roger's eyes partially closed as he moved his head downward. The tone of his voice was higher than usual, so he sounded like he was lying when he said, "I wouldn't do anything like that. I'm not a police officer or some kind of a government agent."

"Then why are you acting like this?" Joe asked.

"A little while ago, Charles and I planned what to do if shooters came into our office. We were going to have a fight, just to keep you busy thinking about other things, instead of thinking about shooting us."

"It sounds like you made up a strange plan." Joe shifted his eyes away from Roger and over to Charles. Joe then asked, "Charles, how about if you tell me what you two guys supposedly planned?"

Charles pulled his hand away from Roger's clasping hand. "We're really just trying to be nice to you by having a wrestling show. If you like us as arm wrestlers, then we thought you wouldn't shoot us."

"We're only thinking of shooting one of you," Joe said.

Charles sighed. "If Roger and I are worried about being shot, we won't be able to arm wrestle in a great way. We'll look like amateurs, rather than two real athletes."

Joe frowned and then said to Moe, "If neither one of those guys actually tries to win while arm wrestling, then we'll have no real winner."

"If there's no winner, we'll have to make Heidi shoot them both," Moe said.

Roger, Charles, Joe, and Moe all looked at Heidi. Her left hand was tightly gripping the rope that connected her to Joe. She took a step backward, which made the rope tense up and pull at Joe's waist.

Joe frowned and tugged at the rope, pulling Heidi forward again. She opened her mouth to say something, but was unable to talk.

Joe said, "The only problem is her gun is in the backpack and should probably stay there."

Moe kept his machine gun attached to his shoulder as he took a nine-millimeter pistol out of his pocket. "I can let her borrow this one."

"Do you really think it's a good idea for us to put a gun into Heidi's hands?"

Moe laughed. "I was just kidding. There's no way I even want her to touch a gun."

"Maybe she knows how to find some other guns and more ammunition for us to use," Joe said.

Joe and Moe both looked at Heidi, who shook her head side to side before saying, "I don't know where there are any more guns."

Joe stared into her eyes. "I think you're lying."

"No, I'm not lying." Heidi paused while staring back at Joe. She then added, "Why would I lie about something like that? If I could lead you to some guns, I'd logically want to do so."

"Why would you want to give Moe and me some more guns?"

"I wouldn't really want to give you some more guns; I would rather want to give myself a gun. Then I could possibly pick it up and shoot it."

Joe asked, "Are you saying that you want to shoot us with a gun?"

"You've kidnapped me. Of course, I want to shoot you with a gun, but I'd only do it if I thought I was saving someone else's life."

Joe moved his gun close to Heidi's forehead. He then asked, "Moe, do you think it's better if we keep her alive as our kidnapped victim or kill her now?"

"We do need a person to use as a shield, just in case we get cornered somewhere," Moe said.

"We could kidnap a different person to use as a shield," Joe said.

Moe looked at Charles and Roger. "I don't really like these two men. They've been fighting too much."

"I agree with you," Joe said.

"Heidi has been following our directions most of the time," Moe said.

Joe lowered his gun. "For right now, we should keep her alive, just in case we need a shield." He looked at Roger and Charles, who were still seated at the table. Their hands were no longer connected together, and they were no longer facing each other. They had turned sideways; they were now watching Joe, Moe, and Heidi.

Moe said, "I'd still like to see the arm wrestlers do some wrestling."

Joe shook his head affirmatively. "If we plan on doing some minor damage, such as shooting the loser's little toe, they'll probably do a real arm wrestling match for us to watch."

Roger slid his hand up into an arm-wrestling position. "How about if the loser becomes another kidnapped victim for you guys to use? Then you'd have two shields—one for each of you."

"No, we can't do that," Joe said.

"I think having two shields is a good idea. In an emergency, we could shoot one and still have a shield," Moe said.

"There's one problem with having two shields," Joe said.

"What's that?" Moe asked.

"We don't have another long-enough rope, so we couldn't tie the second shield to one of us," Joe said.

"That would make things tough." Moe shook his head up and down.

"Plus, we already have too much to do, so watching over two people to use as shields will be a little bit too much," Joe said.

"You're right about us having a lot to do." Moe walked closer to the table where Roger and Charles were seated. He then turned toward Joe and said, "If Charles wins, I'll shoot Roger's little toe. If Roger wins, you can shoot Charles's little toe."

Joe walked closer to the table and said, "Okay, let's do that."

Roger and Charles moved their elbows onto the table and slowly clasped each other's hand. Their slowness and blinking eyes showed their anxiety about the upcoming match.

Joe said, "I'll be saying 'one, two, three, go.' When I say 'go,' you both need to start the wrestling match."

Roger and Charles clasped each other's hands more tightly.

Joe took a step closer to the table and studied their arm and hand positions. He then said, "One, two, three, go."

Roger's hand moved forward first. Then Charles's slanted palm was able to push Roger's whole hand backward several inches. Roger licked his lips, and Charles licked his own lips in the same way. Roger's eyes blinked three times; Charles blinked his eyes once and then glanced up at the ceiling. The movements on their faces showed that they were communicating in some kind of code system. As soon as Roger's eyes blinked again, they both started to stand up together. Their hands were still clasped, but their elbows were no longer on the table's surface. Instead, their elbows were more than a foot above the top of the table.

Joe yelled, "Stop right now! You're not following the rules."

Roger pulled his hand away from Charles and asked, "What are we doing wrong?"

"You both have to keep your elbows on the table's surface," Joe said.

Roger and Charles sat back down again, put their elbows on the table, and clasped each other's hand. Roger then asked, "Is this okay?"

Joe closely examined their elbow, arm, and hand positions before shaking his head. "I also want you both to remain seated while wrestling."

Roger raised his eyebrows and glanced quickly at Charles, who shook his head slightly up and down, showing his approval for Roger's idea. Roger let go of Charles's hand, folded his own hands together, and then said, "The arm wrestling will be more interesting if we can stand up. We then will have more leverage, and the fight will be more fun for you to watch."

Joe frowned. "I was thinking of a real arm-wrestling match, not a pushing match." He looked over at Moe. "What do you think, Moe?"

"If they can stand up and take their elbows off of the table, it'll be almost like a real wrestling match, rather than just arm wrestling."

Joe shook his head in agreement with Moe, but before he could say anything, Heidi took a step forward. Everyone's eyes turned toward her. She opened her mouth to say something and then paused when she saw Roger's facial expression. He obviously wanted Heidi to be quiet. She closed her mouth without making any noises.

After a few seconds of silence, Joe asked Heidi, "Do you know anything about wrestling?"

Her face turned pink, showing her embarrassment. She then said, "I'm not an expert, but it might be fun to see both kinds of wrestling."

Joe laughed. "Let's do that. Two wrestling matches sound like fun."

Moe asked, "Joe, who do you think will win? Will it be the real boss in a suit or the fake boss in jeans?"

"I'm guessing the real boss will win at least one of the matches."

Moe looked at Charles's biceps and Roger's hands before saying, "I think Roger, the real boss, will win the real arm wrestling match, and Charles will win the stand-up fake version of the arm wrestling."

Joe and Moe both laughed. Joe then said, "For the first match, your elbows need to stay on the table, and you'll both need to stay seated."

Charles and Roger moved their elbows forward and clasped each other's hands. After Joe examined their positions, he said, "One, two, three, go."

Roger and Charles began pushing against each other's palms.

Charles suddenly asked, "If I let you win, will you give me a raise?"

Roger looked surprised. He thought for a few seconds before saying, "After today, no matter who wins, you'll be getting a raise."

"Will I really?" Charles asked.

"Yes, you'll really be getting one. After this fight is over, I'll even write out and sign a note for you. Then if I'm killed, you'll have proof of my promise for your raise," Roger said.

Charles was smiling as he asked, "Do you know how much my raise will be?"

"You deserve at least an extra dollar per hour, but we'll have to talk about your added job responsibilities before deciding on a definite amount," Roger said.

"Are you promoting me?"

"Yes, you'll be the new assistant manager."

With tears of joy in his eyes, Charles said, "Thanks so much. You've made today so much better."

"Even bad events can have good outcomes," Roger said.

"I'm so thankful."

"I am, too. This fight between us is bringing us closer together," Roger said.

Charles shook his head in agreement and then bowed his head slightly. "I pray that you and everyone in this building will be okay."

Roger said, "According to the Bible, 'Rejoice always, pray without ceasing, give thanks in all circumstances; for this is the will of God in Christ Jesus for you' (1 Thess. 5:16 – 18 NRSV)."

Joe laughed. "Why would anyone be thankful in a situation like this one?"

"I'm really thankful for the wonderful life that I've lived." Charles glanced at Joe's gun before moving his eyes in vertical and horizontal lines. He had just drawn a cross with his eye movements.

Roger also moved his eyes into a visual depiction of a cross. He then said, "Even if we're killed, our Lord will stay with us and help us to live eternally in his paradise of goodness and love."

Above the middle of the table, the clasped hands of Charles and Roger now looked like they were praying together, rather than fighting with each other.

Heidi softly said "Amen." When Charles and Roger both looked up at her and smiled, she said in a louder voice, "May God bless you both. You're standing strong, being visible, and sharing your faith and your love."

Joe shoved Heidi backward. He then angrily punched at Charles and Roger's pair of clasped hands before yelling, "You're supposed to be wrestling!"

Charles looked at Joe while saying, "We really are arm wrestling."

Joe frowned. "You're lying again."

"No, I'm not. You can see our hands pushing against each other," Charles said.

"There's no way your hands are even weakly pushing against each other. Toddlers would be able to fight better than you two are." Joe stepped backward and placed his right hand onto his gun.

Moe also placed his hand on his gun. "Should we shoot them now?"

Joe's angry face was staring at Charles when Heidi suddenly said, "Maybe they'll still do the arm wrestling."

Joe glanced briefly at Heidi and then looked back at Charles. "What do you think we should do, Charles?"

Charles inhaled deeply and then exhaled slowly. He appeared to be purposefully trying to calm himself. He then looked at Roger. "Should we show them a real fight, Roger?"

"Of course, we should. I love arm wrestling. Let's really do it."

Roger and Charles both looked up at Joe, who turned toward Moe. Moe shook his head, showing his desire to see the arm-wrestling match.

Joe then said, "Okay, we'll let you try a real wrestling match just one more time." After he watched their arms and hands go into correct positions, he said, "One, two, three, go!"

Roger and Charles began pushing at each other's palms. Their biceps appeared large and straining. After a minute, they were both sweating, but neither one seemed to be very close to winning. Charles moved his chin downward and blinked his eyes twice. Roger also blinked twice. Charles's hand then started to relax slightly while still being positioned against Roger's palm. In just a few seconds, Roger's hand pushed Charles's arm backward onto the table. Roger was the winner. He pushed his fists upward toward the ceiling, showing his victory, while Charles bent his head forward, showing his defeat.

Joe slammed the end of his gun onto the table. "Did you really lose that game in an honest way, Charles, or did you just give up?"

Charles stretched out his right arm, pointed to it, and said, "Look at this sweat on my arm. I tried very hard to win."

"I don't believe you." Joe raised his eyebrows in disbelief.

"Why do you think I'm lying?"

"Everyone here knows you're a liar," Joe said.

"My boss said he'd give me a raise."

"We're not talking about your raise. We're talking about the arm-wrestling match, which was supposed to be a real fight," Joe said.

"I really did try."

"No, you really didn't try." Joe stared at Charles's hand and added, "When you were wrestling, your hand suddenly stopped pushing hard enough, and you lost too quickly to Roger."

"What's wrong with that? I'm older than Roger."

"Just because you're old doesn't mean you're weak. You already told us that you exercise at a gym," Joe said.

"My arm was just too tired." Charles stretched his right arm outward as he said, "Plus, I have arthritis, so my elbow and wrist were bothering me."

"Are you trying to make me shoot more than just your little toe?" Joe asked.

Charles inhaled, pulled his arm back close to his chest, and stared at Joe's gun. "I'm really just trying to save other people in this office. If someone's going to be shot, even if it's just a toe, I really want it to be me."

Everyone in the room looked at Charles.

"Is that really why you want to be shot—to save other people?" Roger asked.

"I'm divorced," Charles said. After pausing for a few seconds, he added, "If I'm hurt, my wife won't be too upset."

"That's not a reason to be hurt or possibly to even die," Roger said.

Joe laughed. "Charles won't die, unless we shoot more than his little toe."

Charles sighed before saying, "Even a small injury like that might result in a lot of blood loss, possible infection, and maybe death."

Joe said, "There could be problems, but wrapping up your foot tightly will probably stop any really extreme blood loss."

Charles said, "Thanks for assuring me that you'll probably just be hurting my little toe." Charles took off the shoe and sock from his left foot. He then rubbed his little toe. "Even with just a minor injury, though, if I'm hurt or die, my ex-wife won't care very much. However, if Roger is hurt or dies, his wife will truly be upset."

Roger took a step closer to Charles before saying, "That's very kind of you to try to help me in this situation, but you have children, brothers, sisters, and many friends."

"My children are older than yours."

"Your children still need you," Roger said.

"I'm older than you. If I die, fewer years will be lost than if you die."

Joe tapped Charles's shoulder, pointed to a chair, and said, "Okay, you convinced me, Charles. Sit down right here."

Heidi's eyes widened. She then inhaled and said, "You're not really going to shoot him, are you, Joe?"

"Would you rather be the one to shoot him?" Joe asked.

"No, I don't think I could, even if I wanted to," Heidi said.

Joe pointed his gun downward toward Charles's left toe.

Heidi said, "Wait a minute, please." Joe and Moe both looked at her. After pausing for a few seconds, she asked, "Don't you want to watch them do another arm-wrestling match? They were going to do a second one while possibly standing up, so it'll be more exciting to watch."

Joe sighed. "I don't think Charles and Roger will actually do a real fight. Right now, they're too happy with each other." Joe moved his gun again, put his finger on the trigger, and pulled it.

Charles's left toe was scraped by the bullet; he grabbed onto the top of his foot as his face showed his pain.

Roger took his jacket off and knelt down next to Charles's foot. "I'll wrap my jacket around your foot. It looks okay right now, but just in case it gets worse, I want to keep you safe."

Before Roger could touch Charles's toe with his jacket, Charles said, "No, please don't use your jacket, Roger. Something else, like my shirt, is cheaper and would be better."

"Money doesn't matter right now. Your health is more important." Roger put Charles's left foot inside of one of his jacket's sleeves. He then wrapped the rest of the jacket around Charles's foot, took off his belt, and wrapped it around the jacket.

Charles said, "I really didn't need that much cloth to cover such a small injury."

Roger said, "Actually, just to be safe, you do. Now, if we have to walk somewhere, all of the cloth under your foot will be helpful."

Moe pulled his gun upward. "I think we should shoot Roger, too." He smiled before adding, "I'm volunteering to be the shooter."

Joe said, "I think keeping Roger alive and well is important. That way, if we're caught by the police, we can prove that we're not real shooters who are running around shooting everyone."

Moe sighed. "I guess you're right. Theft, assault, and battery charges aren't as bad as attempted murder and murder charges." He then looked at Heidi. "There's also kidnapping."

Heidi said too quickly, "I'll be really quiet and won't tell anyone about this."

Joe and Moe both laughed. Joe then said, "We have another liar here."

Moe looked at Heidi. "If we weren't in such a hurry, I know who'd be shot next."

Joe said, "We should really get moving right now. We haven't found any of the items I wanted, so we probably need to go back to that jewelry shop."

Heidi and Moe followed Joe out of the Repairs with Music store. As soon as they were in the corridor, Heidi felt a slight vibration in her glasses. She knew it was an important message and immediately asked, "Can I use the restroom? I'll be really fast."

Joe shook his head.

Moe said, "I also need a quick break."

Moe walked into the nearby men's room; Joe and Heidi went into the ladies' room. As soon as Joe let her move into one of the stalls and partially close the door, Heidi pushed one of the buttons on her glasses. The words "Now is the time to bring the shooters into our office" streamed across the lenses. She responded by pushing one of the buttons a single time, which meant "yes."

A minute later, Joe, Heidi, and Moe were walking toward the stairwell. Two machines in the hallway had cans of soda and food items. They paused for a minute while Joe put some cash into the machines and withdrew soda, crackers, and candy items. He then gave some of the items to Heidi and Moe.

Heidi said, "Thanks so much."

Joe smiled. "I used your money."

"Thanks anyway," Heidi said.

"You're welcome."

They slowly ate while walking down the hallway. After a few minutes, Moe asked, "Where are we going?"

Heidi said, "I know one office that you might want to visit."

"Which one would that be?" Joe asked.

"You'd probably love my office, which is on the ninth floor."

"Does it have anything nice, like cash, jewelry, gold, or weapons?" Joe asked.

"The weapons will be locked away, but there's a small vault with some money in it. I might be able to open up the vault."

"Is there really some cash?" Joe asked.

"Yeah, we sometimes use the cash for operations."

"How much money is there?" Joe stopped walking and stared at Heidi.

"I don't know the current amount for sure, but there's always over a hundred thousand dollars."

Moe also stopped walking. Moe turned to look at Joe. They both shook their heads at each other.

Joe asked Heidi, "Where's your office?"

"It's on the ninth floor."

Joe said, "That's what I thought."

Heidi and Moe followed Joe as he led the way into the stairwell and up to the ninth floor.

H.I.D.E. Again

When Joe opened the door to leave the stairwell, Heidi said, "We should instead go through this hidden door over here." She walked up to the center wall panel, pushed it backward, and slid it to the side. Before she stepped through the doorway, the frame of her glasses vibrated. Heidi's right hand started to move up to her glasses. She glanced at Joe, who was staring at her. After hesitating for a few seconds, she moved her hand away from her glasses and stepped through the doorway into a narrow corridor. After walking around two turns, they arrived in the last section of the hallway. Wooden artwork and paintings were displayed on the walls.

While Joe looked at the art, Heidi pressed a button on her glasses. The following message from Kevin appeared: "Slow them down by talking about the pictures."

Heidi responded by pushing "yes" on the frame of her glasses. She then turned to look at the items on the wall and said, "Every day when I come into work, I love pausing to look at these paintings."

"This art is really neat, but why is it all placed in an ugly narrow hallway, instead of inside of a nice office?" Joe asked.

"I think the artwork makes this hallway look nicer. It's also a great way to begin a day at work," Heidi said.

"Are these originals?" Joe ran the index finger of his right hand along one of the frames.

"They're only copies, but even so, I always love looking at them."

"It's too bad these are only copies. They aren't worth too much money." After pausing, Joe added, "I still might want to take one or two of the paintings with us."

Heidi was standing in front of a copy of the title page for *A Key into the Language of America,* written by Roger Williams and published by Gregory Dexter. "As a descendant of Gregory Dexter, I love seeing pictures of what he published. The format of this title page is so neat."

"I like the way the letters look. That's a part of the format, right?" Joe asked.

"Yeah, it is. The words 'LANGUAGE' and 'AMERICA' are in all capitals and big on the page. The writer and the publisher were trying to show the importance of these two words," Heidi said.

"I can understand the importance of 'America,' but why is 'language' so important?" Joe asked.

"The word 'language' refers to how people communicate with each other. It is really important in its ability to create new ideas, to help people connect to each other, and to show social and cultural elements of society," Heidi said.

"Did the publisher of that book come over with the Pilgrims on the *Mayflower?*" Joe asked.

"No, Dexter didn't come over until later," Heidi said. After pausing for a few seconds, she added, "Roger Williams gave him some land."

"When did this happen?" Joe asked.

"Dexter was probably in Rhode Island in 1640, but he went back to England and worked at his publishing company. In 1644, he had to flee from England and move to Rhode Island because a book he published for Roger Williams was ordered to be burned," Heidi said.

"Why were books burned back then?" Joe asked.

"It was a form of censorship. If the government didn't want a book to be sold to anyone, then the book would be burned," Heidi said.

"What book did the politicians dislike?" Joe asked.

"Its title is really interesting: *The Bloudy Tenent of Persecution.*"

Joe smiled and moved his gun upward. "So, Roger Williams liked blood?"

Heidi frowned. "No, he was against bloody things, especially things like persecution."

"If his book wasn't about blood, then what was it about?" Joe asked.

"Roger Williams didn't want people to be hurt for their religious beliefs. *The Bloudy Tenent of Persecution* was a dialogue between Truth and Peace. The book also talked about the separation of church and state," Heidi said.

"When your ancestor came to this country, did he keep on printing things for Roger Williams and other Pilgrims in the New World?" Joe asked.

"No, Dexter didn't own any printing presses in the New World."

Joe turned away from the wall and took four steps further into the hallway.

Heidi was pulled one step forward by the rope attaching her to Joe. She then said, "Look at this one."

When Joe looked at her, she was staring at one of the paintings on the corridor's wall: *Embarkation of the Pilgrims,* by Robert Weir.

Joe turned around, stepped backward, and asked, "Does that painting have the Pilgrims in it?"

"Yes, it does. Another one of my ancestors, William Brewster, is the Pilgrim who is holding the Bible. He was the lay minister for the Pilgrims."

"Are the Pilgrims in that picture on the *Mayflower?*" Joe asked.

Heidi glanced at the picture for a few seconds before saying, "No, they're at a farewell service on a ship called the *Speedwell.*"

"Why were they on the *Speedwell,* instead of on the *Mayflower?*" Joe asked.

"The Pilgrims initially were planning on crossing the Atlantic Ocean in both ships, but the *Speedwell* had problems and had to go back to England." Heidi again pointed to the *Embarkation of the Pilgrims* painting before adding, "This is one of my favorite paintings. I've often thought about buying a copy of it, just so I could have pictures of Pilgrims on one of the walls in my own office."

"I like that painting, too, but it's not my favorite one," Joe said.

Heidi's raised eyebrows showed her surprise. "Do you really feel that way, Joe?"

"Yes, I do."

Heidi said, "That picture of the Pilgrims appears on the back of the 1918 version of the $10,000 bill."

Joe laughed. "I just changed my mind. I'd much prefer a picture on a $10,000 bill to the other ones here."

"If you didn't know about the $10,000 bill, which artwork would you prefer the most?" Heidi asked.

Joe moved a step forward and pointed to the next work of art. "My favorite one is the wooden American flag. I love this 3D version."

Heidi glanced anxiously at where Joe's hand was positioned. He was not touching the wooden flag, but his index finger was only an inch away. Heidi's glasses vibrated. Joe and Moe were in front of her with their backs facing her, so she pressed the button to see the following text message: "Walk forward fast, so he'll follow you away from that flag. Slow them down by unlocking the door into the reception area and then by making the door lock itself. Finally, when we tell you it's the right time, bring them back here, and walk them through the flag entrance."

Heidi pressed "yes" on her glasses.

Joe was touching the left side of the flag as he said, "I'd take this with us, but it's probably a little bit too heavy, and it definitely won't fit into the backpack."

Moe said, "We could maybe try to carry it after finding money in the office."

Heidi shook her head in agreement. "I should be able to open up that doorway at the end of this corridor."

Heidi started walking forward quickly; Joe and Moe followed her. When they arrived at the door to the reception area, there was only one visible security camera.

Joe touched Heidi's shoulder, waved at her to move behind him, raised his rifle, and shot several bullets into the camera.

While Joe was shooting, Heidi typed into her glasses' frame a text message: "Which vault will have just a little money?" She then looked slightly upward and to her left. The invisible security camera was located there. No bullets or pieces of metal had hit that section of the ceiling. While Heidi couldn't see who was on the other side of the security camera, she knew that multiple people would be watching what was happening to her. Her glasses vibrated. She immediately read the reply to her question: "We'll empty out most of the money in vault C and leave just a few dollars."

Heidi raised her chin upward, smiled at the camera, and then glanced at Joe. He was trying to open the door, but it was locked.

Heidi said loudly, "I'll need to unlock the door by entering in a security code."

With upraised eyebrows, Joe stared at her. He then asked, "Why are you talking so loudly? Are you trying to warn people in your office about us?"

"No, I wouldn't do that." Heidi glanced quickly at Joe and then looked past him at the door's handle. "I'm just a little bit nervous about the locking mechanism."

"You said that you can open the door," Joe said.

Heidi's right hand was shaking slightly. The shakes were a little bit too strong to be due to anxiety. She was rather just trying to look anxious as she said, "I'm just a little nervous about changes in the security code."

"Well, you should probably still try your code." Joe said. After a few seconds of silence, he added, "If people in your office ran away really quickly to a different place, they might not have bothered to change anything."

Heidi was staring at the door handle as she said, "I'll try it." She entered some numbers into the control panel. After the last number was entered, a red light lit up in the bottom of the panel. The door opened. Heidi looked backward. Joe was about to walk past her and through the door. Moe was standing five feet away with his gun pulled upward; he was obviously watching to see if anyone was going to come up behind them.

Joe took another step forward. Before he could walk into the room, Heidi's hand moved toward the control panel.

Joe pulled her away and asked, "What are you trying to do? The door's already open."

"I'll show you what the problem is." Heidi took a pen out of her purse and threw it into the room. The door to the room closed. "Do you see what's happening?"

"The door's closed. I can't see anything," Joe said.

"That's right. The door's closed, but now it's also locked, and I won't be able to open it up again from here," Heidi said.

"Why did you make the control panel lock us out?" Joe asked.

Heidi sighed. "Once the door opens, another code has to be entered into the panel. Otherwise, if someone just walks through the doorway, the door will automatically lock itself. Then the person who has walked into the room will be locked up with no way to exit."

"I guess the security system also locks up pens inside the room," Joe said sarcastically.

"Yeah, it does." Heidi smiled. "Actually, that room is a reception area, and I'm sure the people there can always use an extra pen."

"How come no one was in that room when the door was open?" Joe asked.

"I don't know. They must have gone over to one of our other offices," Heidi said.

"Is there a different way to get into the vault?" Joe asked.

Heidi's glasses vibrated. She turned around, so Joe would not be able to see her glasses. She pressed the button and read a message: "The flag entrance and Vault C are ready."

Heidi started moving to her right. "We can get to the money vault by going back this way." Joe walked behind Heidi. Moe stayed about fifteen feet further back and kept on turning around as he watched for other people.

Heidi walked for more than twenty feet back into the corridor. She stopped in front of the wooden carving of the American flag.

Joe asked, "Why are you bringing us back here to this same spot?"

"The other way wasn't working," Heidi said.

"We were over here before. What's going on?" Joe raised his gun up onto his shoulder.

Heidi moved her thumb toward one of the flag's stars, but Joe shoved his left hand out in front of her hand, so she had to stop.

Heidi stared at Joe while asking, "Do you want to get into that vault or not?"

"Yes, but I want you to first tell me why you made us go into that other room," Joe said.

Heidi sighed and then looked squarely into Joe's face. "Okay, I'll tell you. That other room had a hidden video camera in it."

Joe pressed his lips together in an angry expression. He silently glanced over at Moe, who also appeared angry.

Heidi said, "You shouldn't be getting upset. I think the camera wasn't even working."

"Are you sure about that?" Joe asked as he lifted up his chin in a powerful stance.

Heidi said, "Well, I didn't see any changes in the lighting in different places of the room. Normally, there's a slightly brighter section where the video camera is pointed."

Joe said angrily, "I don't care about the lighting. Why did you bring us in front of a video camera?"

Heidi hung her head slightly downward as she said, "You already know I'm a spy. I was just trying to do my job."

Joe touched his gun. "You shouldn't be doing your job right now. You're supposed to be helping me and Moe with our job."

Heidi sighed. "I'll try to be more helpful. What do you want me to do?"

"Just do what I say without doing other things," Joe said.

Moe had been silently listening to the debate between Joe and Heidi; now, he asked, "What if we stop fighting and just see if there's something nice in the vault?"

Joe looked at Moe, shook his head in agreement, removed his hand from his gun, and stepped out of the way. He then waved at the control panel, indicating to Heidi that she should do something to the panel.

Heidi moved closer to the control panel, pushed her index finger onto one of the buttons, and paused for a few seconds. Her glasses were vibrating. She said to Joe, "I can never remember the whole security code. However, one section of that painting always helps me to remember it."

Heidi moved a few feet to her left and stared at the *Embarkation of the Pilgrims* painting. She then pointed to the Pilgrim holding onto the Bible and said, "William Brewster, the one holding the Bible, is my ancestor. I also really love the Bible in that picture. It's so large."

Joe and Moe moved close to the painting and stared at it. While they were both not watching her, Heidi looked at the text message on her glasses: "Wait another minute and then get moving."

Heidi replied "yes" on her glasses.

Joe was still looking at the picture when he asked Heidi, "What reminds you of a security code?"

"It's the number of people praying, the number of hats, and the number of metal objects."

"What metal objects are you talking about?" Joe asked.

"The guns and armor are added in together for a total metallic number," Heidi said.

"The armor and guns in that painting are very interesting." After pausing for a moment, Joe added, "I thought Dexter was your ancestor."

"William Brewster is also my ancestor."

Joe frowned, but before he could say anything, Moe started laughing.

Joe turned to face Moe and asked, "What's so funny?"

Moe walked up to the painting and pointed at the Bible and the weapons. He then said, "I think it's so interesting how Heidi was first looking at the Bible and you were first looking at the armor and the weapons."

Joe asked, "What difference does it make?"

Heidi said, "The Pilgrims needed both the word of God and their weapons." After pausing for a few seconds, she added, "They actually needed God a lot more than they needed their weapons."

Joe asked, "Do you have the security code numbers now?"

"Yes, I do," Heidi said.

"Then let's just get moving." Joe took a few steps to the right and stood in front of the wooden flag. He then pulled at the rope attached to Heidi, forcing her to walk over to stand next to him. Pointing at the flag, he asked, "Where do you enter in the security code?"

Heidi pressed one of the flag's stars. A small rectangular section of the wooden flag opened up. On the right side of the flag, a control panel came forward out of the wall. Heidi typed in a series of numbers. On the left side of the flag, a door opened into a new hallway. Heidi held her palm upward, indicating that people should not yet enter. After waiting a few seconds, she entered another code into the panel and said, "It's okay now; we can go in."

Joe entered first and quickly walked down the hallway to another door. "Is this the next door we should be entering?"

Heidi said, "Yes, it is. I was just trying to remember the code for this panel. I don't usually come in this way." She typed in some numbers, and the door opened. She then walked into the room by taking three steps forward, one partially to her left, one backward, and one partially to her right. Her steps had formed the letter "y," but her eyes had been moving to different places in the room, so Joe and Moe didn't notice.

Joe asked, "Don't you need to enter another code?"

"Only a single series of numbers is needed for that door." Heidi walked forward into the center of the room; Joe and Moe followed her.

Heidi moved sideways to the wall on the right side of the room. When she slid a wall panel to the left, a small door was visible. She said, "The vault's in here."

"What are you waiting for? Open it up," Joe said.

Heidi put her glasses on top of her head and moved her eyes close to the scanner on the front of the control panel. She then put her glasses back in front of her eyes, input some numbers into the panel, and opened up the vault. Joe shoved her forward, so she was inside the vault before he was. He then followed her inside, and Moe stayed outside with his gun drawn.

While she was in front of Joe, another text message came through her glasses. She moved close to some safety deposit boxes that were structured into one of the walls. With Joe behind her and unable to see her glasses, she pressed a button on the frame of her glasses. The following message from Kevin appeared on the lenses: "Moe is still outside of the vault, so locking them inside the vault won't work. Plan

B is for you to keep them busy for at least five minutes. We'll then have your office rigged with a tripping wire and security people."

Heidi pressed the "yes" button. She then turned around.

Joe's eyes were moving around the interior of the vault. He finally asked, "Where's the money?"

"It's inside these safety deposit boxes," Heidi said.

Joe walked up to the drawer with the number "eighty-one" carved into its metal. He tried to open it, but the drawer was locked. He asked Heidi, "What are you waiting for? You need to open up these boxes."

"I wish I could, but I don't have the codes," Heidi said.

Joe's face turned angry as he said in a loud voice: "Why did you say you could help us to get into the money vault?"

Heidi looked anxious as she said, "I did help you to get into this money vault. Usually, some money will be up against the wall over there."

Joe's left hand moved up to the left side of his face and began to rub his tattoo.

Heidi stepped over to a different deposit box and pulled at its handle. The box was locked. "We should try all of these deposit boxes. Sometimes, one of them is left unlocked by mistake."

Joe pushed Heidi out of the way and then tried to open each of the three hundred deposit boxes. All of them were locked. He went over to the vault's door and said to Moe, "We might need that second bomb right now for this vault."

"I heard you say something about not finding any money, but I didn't hear the other things you said. What's happening?" Moe asked.

"The money is supposedly inside the safety deposit boxes, but so far, they're all locked," Joe said.

"Can't Heidi unlock the boxes?"

Heidi was standing just behind Joe, but she did not respond to Moe's question, but instead remained quiet.

Joe said, "I don't know if Heidi can unlock the boxes or not. She says she can't, but I don't know if I believe her."

Moe said, "Heidi works here. Logically, there should be at least one box that belongs to her."

"I think you're right, Moe. She should be able to open at least one box."

Moe glared at Heidi. "We could use our second bomb to try and make her talk."

Heidi opened her mouth to say something, but no words came out. Her face was very pale, and her eyes were wildly blinking. She folded her two hands together and said a silent prayer.

Joe was quiet while she prayed; he then said to Moe, "If we put a bomb next to her, we'd have no hostage."

"We do sort of need her alive for when we exit this building," Moe said.

"What we really need right now is some money," Joe said.

"We could use our last bomb to try and unlock a few of these deposit boxes," Moe said.

Joe looked around at the interior of the vault. "We could put the bomb in the left corner, where the largest deposit boxes are."

Moe switched places with Joe, so Moe was inside the vault with Heidi. Joe stood just barely outside of the vault, and the rope connecting him and Heidi together was stretched out to its maximum length. Moe moved over closer to Heidi, turned her around, and retrieved the bomb materials out of the backpack. He then pushed her slightly forward and waved toward the vault's door; he was telling her to go outside the vault and to stand near Joe.

Heidi stepped next to Joe. A vibration in her glasses told her that a text message had been sent to her. She stepped backward slightly, so Joe would not see it. After pressing the correct button, Heidi read the message: "There's nothing in the deposit boxes. Also, don't worry about the bomb; it's too small to cause any serious damage to that steel vault."

Less than three minutes later, Moe was finished setting up the bomb in the left corner of the vault. Joe and Heidi walked away from the vault; Moe closed the vault's door and set the timer for the bomb. He then joined Joe and Heidi. All three of them moved quickly down the corridor. After the bomb went off, Joe pulled Heidi back to the vault. Moe stood outside of the vault with his gun in a firing position while Joe and Heidi walked inside and looked at the damage. Several of the deposit boxes were scraped, but otherwise, everything seemed okay.

Joe tried to open up the scraped boxes, but they were still locked. He rubbed his tattoo while staring at Heidi for a few seconds. One section of his tattoo looked slightly indented. The tattoo had obviously been done to cover up a scar.

Joe then said, "We've been nice to you. We've let you live. The least you can do is to open up one or two of the boxes for us."

Heidi hesitated and then said, "The only box that I can unlock is my own, and I already know my box has nothing in it."

Angrily, Joe asked, "Why did you bring us in here when you knew we couldn't get any money?"

"I thought there would probably be some money in here. Plus, I didn't want any innocent people in other offices to get killed by your guns."

Joe raised his right hand and slapped the left side of Heidi's face. His thumb hit the bottom edge of her glasses. Heidi moved her left hand upward and partially covered the left side of her face. Her eyes had tears in them, but her voice was silent.

Joe raised his hand again and swung it toward Heidi's forehead. Heidi stepped backward, and Joe's hand missed hitting her. She then said, "Please don't hit me again."

"Why should I stop?" Joe asked.

"I know where there's some money, but if I'm unconscious, I won't be able to tell you about it."

"Where is it?" Joe's fists were clenched at his sides, but they appeared to be too anxious to remain in that one position for very long.

"There's a few hundred in my office."

"Do you really have some money there, or are you lying to us again?" Joe asked.

"Why would I lie when you're hitting me?"

"You're a spy, so you may want the truth to remain hidden," Joe said.

Heidi looked up at one of the lights in the ceiling. "In some ways, I love lights because I want everything to be visible."

"I thought your eyes were extremely sensitive," Joe said.

"They are."

"So, your eyes get tears in them whenever there's too much light," Joe said.

"Sometimes, lights are too bright for my eyes, but that doesn't mean I hate lights." Heidi paused and then added, "According to the Bible, 'No one after lighting a lamp hides it under a jar, or puts it under a bed, but puts it on a lampstand, so that those who enter may see the light. For nothing is hidden that will not be disclosed, nor is anything secret that will not become known and come to light' (Luke 8:16 – 17 NRSV)."

"Spies like you always have secrets," Joe said.

"When something's classified, we need to be quiet, at least for a while. If a lamp has already been lit, though, rather than remaining in the dark, the light needs to be placed where people can see it," Heidi said.

"That makes sense. Hidden things won't be lit up, but they will instead remain in darkness," Joe said.

"There are some things that I can shed some light on without breaking any laws," Heidi said.

Joe's eyes widened as he said, "You just made me really curious. Tell me one of these things."

"You already know this is really an office for a bunch of spies," Heidi said.

"Tell me something I don't know," Joe said sarcastically.

Heidi thought for a few seconds before saying, "I'm a brand-new spy, so I don't know everything yet."

Joe laughed. "Okay, I believe you really are new in the field, especially since I sometimes have noticed when you've been lying and when you've been telling the truth. An experienced spy would be better at hiding facial expressions."

"Thanks for letting me know about that. I'll have to practice making the expressions that I logically want to make, rather than just showing how I feel with my face's expressions."

Joe said, "Let's go to your office, Heidi. I'm curious to see if you really do have some money there."

Heidi led the way through a new corridor, into the round conference room, and finally around the circular conference room over to her own office. She unlocked the door and waved her hand, indicating that Joe could walk in first. As he took a step forward through the doorway, a wire flew across the doorway's floor. Joe tripped on the wire and landed on his hands and knees inside of Heidi's office. The door quickly began to close, separating him from Heidi and Moe, who were both still in the conference room. The middle section of the closing door had a serrated razor edge. Heidi stretched the rope tightly; she then moved up and down, sliding the rope against the sharpness of the door's edge. In just a few seconds, the rope that was tying her to Joe was cut in its middle.

Heidi yelled "I'm free" as she stepped away from the closed door. Before she was able to run, Moe hooked his left arm around her neck; his right hand placed his gun above her right ear. He then yelled, "What did you do to Joe?"

Heidi tried to talk, but she only managed to grunt and then cough. Moe loosened his left arm's grip on her neck. She swallowed several times before saying, "Joe's okay. He's only locked inside of a room."

While keeping his arm around Heidi's neck and his hand on his gun, Moe walked up close to the door. He used one of his elbows to knock on the door. From the other side, a softer, different knock was heard.

Moe's elbow then knocked again while Moe's voice asked, "Is that you, Joe?"

Hidden in Heidi's office on the other side of the door, Joe said, "I'm stuck inside of this office, Moe, and everything's locked up."

Moe said, "We'll try to get you out of there."

Joe replied, "Thanks. I really hate being stuck in such a small place."

Moe rubbed his chin against his shoulder. "I hate small places, too, but that room is probably bigger than a jail cell would be."

"No, I've been in jail before. This office is tinier," Joe said.

Some bumping noises were heard coming from inside the office. Moe asked, "Are you okay, Joe?"

After a few seconds, Joe yelled, "I'm fine."

Some low murmuring noises suggested that Joe was talking softly to one or more other people, who were probably inside the office with him.

Moe breathed heavily into Heidi's face while saying, "Open that door and let him out."

"I can't. The door's been locked," Heidi said.

"Isn't that your office?" Moe asked.

Heidi hesitated and then said, "Yeah, it is."

"Then unlock the door with your keys," Moe said.

"I can't. The locking mechanism would have been changed, so my keys will no longer work."

"Where are your keys?" Moe asked.

"They're in my purse, which is inside of the backpack."

Moe kept his gun pointed at Heidi's face while he removed his left arm from around her neck. He then reached into the backpack, pulled out Heidi's purse, and handed it to her. "Now you can give me your keys."

Heidi reached into her purse, pulled out her keychain, and gave it to Moe. With his gun still pointed at Heidi's head, Moe tried to unlock the door with each of the keys on Heidi's keychain. As he was trying the different keys, Heidi looked at a message on her glasses: "Keep Moe busy. We're questioning Joe."

She pushed the "yes" button as her response to the text message.

Moe was soon finished trying the keys. Not a single one of them worked.

Moe asked, "Do you have some more keys in your purse?"

"No, I don't think so, but I can check, just in case one fell off of my keychain," Heid said.

"Please check in your purse right now."

Heidi opened up the top part of her purse and put it in front of Moe's face. Moe looked inside the purse before he said, "I can't see everything in there. Just dump it all out onto the floor."

Heidi slowly removed items from her purse, starting with a small Bible, a calendar, and a checkbook. She next removed her billfold and gave Moe the money and her credit cards. He put the items into the backpack.

Moe then asked, "Don't you have some other things in there, like a pen or a pencil?"

Heidi opened up one of the zippered compartments and dumped out onto the floor several pens, pencils, and a jump drive. "Do you want to see what's on the jump drive?"

"No thanks. It's probably just some encrypted files."

Heidi opened up another zippered compartment, carefully took out some make-up, and put some lipstick on her lips.

Moe said, "It's interesting how women can so easily hide so many things inside of their purses. What else are you hiding in there?"

Heidi pulled out of her purse some tissues, hand cleaner, hand cream, and pictures. She showed each picture to Moe before shaking her purse and saying, "There are some more items in here. Do you want to see them all?"

"Of course, I do. I heard some kind of scraping metal noise in your purse."

"I think I know what you heard." Heidi reached inside her purse and took out a necklace, earrings, and several other jewelry items. Moe put the jewelry into the backpack and then asked, "Is anything else in there?"

Heidi tipped her purse upside down, shook it, and said, "You can see there's nothing else left in here."

Heidi handed her purse to Moe and then felt a vibration in her glasses. Moe was looking inside her empty purse, so she pushed the button on her glasses and read a text message from Kevin: "Joe told us about the third criminal and the location of the hidden bomb. We have the bomb situation under control, so it's okay now for us to arrest Moe. You should run away—or jump away—and then hide. We'll distract Moe with some music right before we start fighting with him."

Heidi replied by pushing the "yes" button on her glasses. She then threw herself to the ground, knocked a chair sideways, shoved it under the conference table, and crawled under the table and behind the chair.

Music by Zach Williams suddenly began to play from the ceiling.

Heidi's eyes lit up in happiness when she heard lines about freedom and chains from the song *Chain Breaker:* "If you need freedom or saving / He's a prison-shaking Savior / If you've got chains / He's a chain breaker."[37]

Moe glanced briefly up at the ceiling, raised the back part of his gun onto his shoulder, and quickly jumped next to the table. He was now closer to Heidi. She moved further under the table. His hand clasped his gun, and his index finger placed itself on the trigger. Before he could fire at Heidi, noises from multiple guns were heard. Moe's gun, knees, right arm, and right hand were all hit by bullets fired from the ceiling. For a few seconds, Moe's face looked shocked. He dropped his gun before falling backward and grabbing onto his knees. He then screamed in a hoarse, anxious voice.

Scraping noises were heard from the ceiling. Several of the ceiling's lights were partially opened; guns were pointing downward.

A voice from the ceiling said, "Move away from your gun, or we'll be shooting at your chest and your head."

Moe glanced up at the different openings in the ceiling, slid a few feet away from his gun, and raised his hands until they were above his head.

Several ceiling lights were moved sideways. Kevin and six police officers jumped down into the room. While the officers put ankle cuffs on Moe, he asked, "How is Joe? Is he okay?"

"He's fine," a female officer said.

"Can you also tell me what happened to Judas—that person who runs Below Low?" Moe asked.

A tall male officer said, "Judas is a person of interest for us. He's at a hospital, but he's going to live. He only has minor injuries."

"Those drugs in my backpack were put there by Judas, not by me or by Joe," Moe said.

"No, you stole some of Judas's drugs and put them into your backpack," the tall male officer said.

"You can't prove that," Moe said strongly.

"Yes, we can," the tall male officer said. After thinking for a few seconds, he added, "We have a video tape of you stealing some of the drugs from the basement, so your drug crimes will make things more difficult for you and your lawyer."

As Moe was escorted out of the room, Kevin walked over to where Heidi was lying under the table. He knelt down and slid next to her. Without even saying a word, they both stared at each other for a few seconds before kissing. Their hands joined together while their voices hummed sweet sounds that people in the whole room could hear.

Tears began to flow out of Heidi's eyes. Kevin asked, "Are you okay?"

She smiled broadly while saying, "I'm more than okay. I'm completely joyful now that you're here with me."

"Are your eyes okay?" Kevin asked.

"Yeah, they're fine. Do they look funny?"

"You're crying," Kevin said.

Heidi laughed. "My eyes are crying tears of joy, not tears of sadness."

Kevin hugged her as they again kissed. A tear from Heidi's right eye crawled out from under the lens of her glasses and bounced with joy onto Kevin's mouth. His tongue touched the tear's moisture and curled around it in happiness.

A voice several feet away from the table asked, "Hey, Kevin and Heidi, what are you two doing under there?"

Kevin looked out from under the table and said, "Hi, Mark. We're both just so thankful to be alive and healthy."

"I can tell you've been kissing."

"How do you know that?" Kevin asked.

Mark said, "You have lipstick on your lips, which means two lovers have been kissing, rather than two co-workers kissing."

Heidi said, "Love happens in many ways. This table that we're under is even telling us the importance of love." Heidi pointed up to the center area of the table. A Bible verse was written on the underside of the table, and only people who were under the table or who were looking under the table could see it: "And now faith, hope, and love abide, these three; and the greatest of these is love" (1 Cor. 13:13 NRSV).

Mark asked, "What do you mean the table is talking about love?"

Heidi and Kevin both looked upward at the Bible verse. They then smiled at each other, moved backward, rose up onto their knees, and turned the table upside down. Every person in the room could now see the Bible verse about faith, hope, and love.

Mark asked, "Do you know who wrote that Bible verse on the underside of the table?"

Heidi shook her head sideways. She then said, "It's a little bit strange that someone wrote something on that table. With the security cameras in here, we'll be able to tell who did it, though."

Kevin smiled with sparkling eyes and raised eyebrows.

Heidi immediately realized that he was the one who had written the Bible verse. She widened her eyes and smiled, showing Kevin that she knew he was the writer.

Kevin asked, "Does it really matter who wrote on the table? Aren't the positive feelings we have from reading those words more important?"

Heidi said, "Love is most important: my love for God and his love for me will always be with me."

Kevin said, "I love how you're sharing your love by sharing your faith."

Heidi looked at Kevin. "You're sharing your love and faith, too."

Everyone in the room looked at the Bible verse, and then a pair of hands started to clap. Kevin, Heidi, and all of the other people in the room also began to clap their hands. When the clapping stopped, Kevin said, "I think we should leave the table upside down, just like it is, so everyone can see that Bible verse."

Heidi said, "That's a great idea. An even better one would be to write the Bible verse on the top upper section of the table. We can then turn the table right side up, keep it as our conference table, and still see the Bible verse about faith, hope, and love."

Kevin and several other people turned the table right side up. They then found a permanent marker and used it to take turns writing all of the words of the Bible verse onto the top center part of the table. The two "love" words were written by Heidi and Kevin, who each held onto the other's hand, so they could write the letters in the "love" words together.

Heidi said, "Some things are classified and will remain hidden in our office. However, faith, hope, and love are now in the center of our conference table with wonderful lights from the ceiling beaming brightness onto their importance."

Suddenly, Matt walked into the room. He was the immediate boss for Kevin, Heidi, and about half of the other people in the room. Everyone stared at him as he walked over to the conference table and silently read the new words that had just been written on the table's center section. He said, "I can tell these words were written by different people."

Mark asked, "How can you tell?"

"The handwriting is different for each word." After a pause, Matt added, "Some of the words were actually written by two people working together."

Kevin gave Matt the permanent marker and asked, "Do you want to censor what's on the conference table, or would you prefer to add your own view?"

Matt extended his hand and accepted the marker from Kevin. "Yes, I'd love to add my own view. This is a conference table, where people confer with one another. Different views are needed here." He smiled broadly at Kevin and Heidi before writing on the table: "Love is unhidden at H.I.D.E."

Kevin and Heidi both extended their hands out to Matt. He took a step closer to them and clasped their hands. Everyone else in the room joined hands, so a circle of people now encircled the conference table.

Matt said, "Okay, freedom of speech is definitely in the workplace today." He clapped his hands, and everyone else joined in.

Heidi said, "I'm so thankful to be working with so many wonderful people."

Everyone in the room clapped their hands again. Kevin then reached his hand out to Heidi, who slid her hand into his. They smiled at each other as the other people in the room silently watched them.

Matt cleared his throat. After everyone looked at him, he said, "You all have been really great in helping to catch those shooters. I'm so thankful that no one was killed or seriously injured."

People in the room shook their heads and smiled. Matt then said, "After what Heidi has experienced over the past two days, she definitely needs some time off." He looked at Kevin and added, "Kevin has also had an exhausting two straight days of work. You both will come in for a debriefing tomorrow morning. Then you'll have the rest of the week off."

Kevin said, "Thanks so much, Matt. You're really the best boss. You're always so helpful, positive in your suggestions, and understanding of people's real-life situations."

Before Matt had a chance to say anything, Heidi said, "I'm thanking you, too, Matt. I'm also so happy about how you and all of my colleagues have helped me to get through the past two days."

Matt smiled as he said, "You should both go into Heidi's office for a minute. After that, you can take the rest of the day off."

Kevin said, "Thanks so much, Matt. We'll just be a few minutes in Heidi's office."

Heidi asked, "Is something strange going on in my office?"

Kevin smiled. "You'll see in a minute."

Kevin and Heidi both waved at their colleagues and then walked over to Heidi's office.

HEAVENLY CONNECTIONS

KEVIN PUT HIS HAND on the door to Heidi's office. "There's a surprise in here for you."

Heidi smiled. "Should I unlock the door, or should you?"

"It's already unlocked."

As soon as Heidi stepped through the door, she noticed two new items on the blank wall: *Embarkation of the Pilgrims,* by Robert Weir, and a copy of the title page for *A Key into the Language of America,* written by Roger Williams and published by Gregory Dexter.

After gasping in delight, Heidi turned to Kevin and hugged him. "How did you know I completely love these two items?"

Kevin raised his eyebrows. "During the JoeMoeNoGo Case, I was watching you every second on every possible video camera."

"Oh, I love that name for the case! Did you create it?"

"Yeah, I did," Kevin said.

"I also love how you must have been watching me all the time, especially when I was talking to Joe in our 'artistic hallway' with all the pictures."

"I didn't just see you. I also heard what you were saying." Kevin paused and then added, "I heard every single word you said and every single noise you made."

"That's so neat."

Kevin took a step closer to Heidi, lifted up her right hand, and pressed it against his lips. "I'm so thankful you're okay."

While Kevin was still holding onto her hand, Heidi slid her glasses above her forehead and onto the top of her head. She moved her lips upward and softly kissed Kevin's lips. His lips were initially as soft as hers. After a few seconds, his lips became stronger, as did hers. Her hands moved up his biceps and landed on his shoulders. He moved his hands onto her shoulders; then Heidi and Kevin moved in closer together.

While their lips were still attached to each other, noises from outside of Heidi's office were initially ignored. A throat being cleared was followed by several coughs. Then two people began to argue with each other.

A man's voice said, "We should leave them alone." The loudness of his voice suggested that he wanted Heidi and Kevin to hear him and to stop their long kiss. They did not stop, but only moved even closer together.

A lady's voice from the hallway said, "I just want to thank Heidi for what she did with Joe and Moe. She probably saved a lot of lives."

The loud-voiced man in the hallway said, "She also helped a lot of innocent people to be less anxious."

The lady said, "Everyone here is so happy about what Heidi did."

"They are. When Kevin asked us about moving those two historic items onto Heidi's wall, we all agreed that Heidi should have them."

"We should let Heidi have Kevin, too." The lady paused before adding, "Kevin should also have Heidi. Let's not say anything to anyone about what we're seeing here."

The man said loudly, "We have to say something to our boss." In a much softer voice, he added, "You know that Heidi's glasses are videotaping what they're doing."

The lady's voice was barely hearable as she softly said, "The video function probably is not on right now. It uses up too much of the battery to keep it running all the time."

"Oh, you're right. After the past couple of days, the battery in her glasses is probably really low."

"The video has to be shut off, unless she just forgot because she's busy right now."

The line phone rang on Heidi's desk. The man and the lady in the hallway looked at the phone and then stared at Kevin and Heidi. After the phone rang a third time, Kevin stepped backward and asked Heidi, "Should I get that call for you?"

Heidi sighed. "I really should answer it before it goes to voice mail." While still looking at Kevin, she stepped over to her desk, picked up her phone, and said, "Hello."

After listening for a minute, she said, "Thanks again, Matt. I could really use a couple of days off." With a smile on her face, she then handed the phone to Kevin.

He smiled back at her while accepting the phone. After saying "hello," he listened to Matt while staring at Heidi. Several times, Kevin shook his head up and down while saying "okay" into the phone. Finally, he said "good-bye" and hung up the phone.

Heidi asked, "Did Matt tell you the same thing he told me?"

Kevin laughed. "He probably changed the content a little bit."

"What did Matt say? Did he talk about me?"

"Yeah, he did." Kevin hesitated and then added, "He talked about us going into work tomorrow for a little while, preferably about nine o'clock, just for a short debriefing. Then you'll have the rest of the week off. Matt also wanted me to stay with you and to keep in touch with you." Kevin touched Heidi's shoulder.

Heidi smiled as she touched one of Kevin's shoulders. She then said, "You're so good at maintaining contact with people by touching them."

"You're great at that, too." Kevin stroked Heidi's forearm as he added, "We'll be able to have fun on our vacation days this week."

Heidi shook her head in agreement. "I'm really looking forward to spending some time with you this week." After pausing for a few seconds, she asked, "Did you tell Matt anything about us going out on a date?"

Kevin reached out, touched Heidi's glasses, and raised his eyebrows.

Heidi laughed. "They're turned off. We're free to talk and to say whatever we want to say."

Kevin sighed. "I didn't tell Matt anything, but I think he still knows how we feel about each other."

"That definitely could be a problem." Heidi frowned.

"I don't think we need to worry about the non-dating policy—at least, not yet. Matt's acting like he doesn't know anything."

"He's hiding what he knows," Heidi said.

"Yeah, he is. He'll probably be telling people that we're helping each other to recover from a tough situation." Kevin's face was blank; he was hiding something.

Heidi frowned. "So, are you really just trying to help me as a co-worker, instead of wanting to go out with me on an actual date?"

"I asked you out before the shooters began their rampage."

"I know that." Heidi pressed her lips together, raised her chin, and then asked, "Did you ask me out just to help me as a new field agent?"

A noise was heard out in the hallway. Kevin and Heidi both turned around to see a tall lady and a short man walking away from the doorway and down the hallway.

As soon as the lady and man were far enough away, Kevin smiled at Heidi and asked, "Are we ever really completely free to say whatever we're thinking?"

Heidi sighed. "I have multiple editors and censors in my brain. They sometimes make me hide my thoughts, so only I know what I'm thinking."

"Doesn't God also know?" Kevin asked.

"You're right, He does."

With a blank look on his face, Kevin said, "Even though God knows what we're thinking, people often have blank looks on their faces when they're trying to hide their thoughts from other people."

"You're showing me a nice example of that," Heidi said.

"I'm doing it for a good reason."

Heidi's eyelids fluttered. "What's your reason for hiding something from me?"

"I don't want to tell you right now, but I will in a little while."

Heidi's eyelids stopped moving as she stared blankly at Kevin. He stared back at her with an even blanker look on his face. When Heidi realized Kevin knew she was hiding her thoughts, she blushed. She then opened her mouth, but before she could say anything, the tall lady and short man were again walking near the doorway of her office. They were moving more slowly and appeared to be trying to hear what she and Kevin were saying. After pausing for a few seconds at the doorway, the lady and the man waved; they then walked through the corridor and away from Heidi's office.

Heidi asked, "Who was that?"

"I don't know for sure, but they might be two of the people from our Boston office."

"I wonder how much they heard."

Kevin sighed. "Whatever they heard doesn't really matter. Even if they say something to Matt, he'll just tell them about the two of us needing a chance to recover."

"A lot of people may just think we're being super-close to each other because of the stress we've been through." Heidi stared at Kevin, but his face remained blank.

Kevin blinked his eyes quickly. He then stood up in a super straight manner and said, "A lot of people think they know how we feel because they've seen how we've been looking at each other."

Heidi put her index fingers on each edge of her mouth and smiled broadly. Her mouth appeared to have smiled because of the motions of her index fingers. She was trying to add hand gestures to her face gestures, so her smile would appear happier.

Kevin softly brushed Heidi's chin with the index finger of his right hand. Closing her eyes, Heidi breathed in and out deeply. Her lips appeared to be asking Kevin to kiss them. Kevin's mouth moved close to hers. His lips then gently brushed against hers. When he pulled away, his face no longer looked blank; instead, he was glowing with a joyful expression that he was unable to hide.

A noise was heard from the hallway outside of Heidi's office. Matt, their boss, was standing just outside the doorway. He asked, "Are you two okay?"

While in a state of shared happiness, Kevin and Heidi both turned to face him.

Kevin said, "Thanks so much, Matt, for stopping by."

Matt's eyes went back and forth several times between Kevin and

Heidi. He then asked, "How are you both doing? Do you have any physical anxiety symptoms?"

Kevin said, "We're both fine. Thanks for asking."

Matt asked, "Heidi, do you like the new artwork on the wall of your office?"

Her smile was really large as she looked at her wall. "I'm so happy to have some artwork in here. As a descendant of William Brewster and Gregory Dexter, nothing could make me happier."

Kevin's hand reached behind Heidi and began to write an invisible message on her back with his index finger. Heidi silently focused on reading what was being written on her back as she kept on watching the artwork on the wall in front of her. In less than a minute, the following message was written by Kevin onto Heidi's back: "Would you like to go to Brewster Gardens with me?"

Kevin's writing could not be seen by Matt because of where Matt was standing. Matt had opened up a folder that he was holding onto and was silently reading one of the papers inside the folder.

Heidi stepped slightly sideways and wrote an invisible message onto Kevin's back: "Yes, I would love to go there with you."

Kevin wrote on Heidi's back, "As soon as Matt is done, can you go to Brewster Gardens right away?"

Heidi wrote on Kevin's back, "Yes, I'd love to."

Matt noticed what Heidi was doing and said, "Oh, you're rubbing Kevin's back."

Heidi blushed. "Yeah, I am. After the tough time he had today, I just want him to relax a little bit."

Kevin touched Heidi's elbow and said out loud, "Thanks, I really needed that."

Matt stared at Kevin's hand on Heidi's elbow for a few seconds before saying, "You both need to relax. I'll bring this file to your office, Kevin, and leave it on your desk. You can look at it sometime next week."

Kevin asked, "Should I look at that tomorrow morning when I come in for the debriefing?"

"No, this file is only an update on an already-closed case. Plus, I really just want you and Heidi at work for a little while tomorrow. You both need some time off."

Kevin said, "Thanks. I'll be sure to look at that folder next week."

Matt looked at Heidi and said, "If you need some additional time off, besides just the rest of this week, please let me know."

"Thanks so much, Matt. I'll probably be fine and back at work next Monday." Heidi smiled at Kevin and then added, "If I stay at home too much, I'll get lonely and bored."

Kevin and Heidi stared at each other. Matt shook his head, showing he understood what Heidi had just said, but neither Kevin nor Heidi saw Matt's head motion. Matt then said "good-bye," but Kevin and Heidi did not listen to him because they were focused on listening to each other's breathing.

Several minutes after Matt had walked away from Heidi's office, Kevin turned to face the doorway. He noticed Matt's absence and said, "Heidi, Matt has left."

Heidi looked at the empty doorway. "That's great. I guess we also can leave now."

As soon as they exited Heidi's office, Kevin picked up his briefcase, which was still sitting right outside of the doorway. "I have some food in here for us to enjoy at Brewster Gardens, but if you prefer, we could instead stop at a restaurant."

"Brewster Gardens will be great, and I'll really love to eat whatever you've planned for our first date together."

As soon as they reached the elevator, Heidi pushed the "down" button. When the doors opened, Kevin and Heidi paused before entering. Four employees from Amusement Plus—Bera, Gama, Mira, and Nira—were already in the elevator. All four of them stepped backward, and Nira's shoulder touched Mira's arm. Neither one of them moved away, but they rather stayed close together.

Bera waved at Kevin and Heidi. She was telling them to step into the elevator, which they did. The first floor button had already been pressed, so Heidi and Kevin were able to immediately turn around and talk to the other four people.

Heidi asked, "What happened in your store? Was everyone able to leave okay, or were some of you hiding when the shooters were running around the building?"

Mira said, "We were so blessed to be able to run away, instead of having to hide or fight."

"How did you all manage to escape so quickly?" Heidi asked.

"As soon as we knew about the shooters being in our building, we all went down one level by using the stairway. We then ran out into the corridor, down the stairwell, and out of the building," Mira said.

"Why did you return to the building?" Kevin asked.

"We found out the shooters were captured, so we went back to the Amusement Plus store to make certain everything was okay," Mira said.

"Is everything okay?" Heidi asked.

"Yes, it is. Nothing's been stolen or broken. The slide, though, hasn't been fixed yet, so it'll probably still vibrate if someone jumps on it," Mira said.

"Did all four of you need to go back to the store today?" Kevin asked.

"Yeah, we did, so we could check everything out more quickly. Plus, I really wanted us all to go out tonight and eat dinner together. That way, people would be less nervous about working tomorrow." Mira looked at her three colleagues, and they all smiled at each other.

Kevin, Heidi, and the Amusement Plus employees talked some more about the shooters. When the elevator arrived at the first floor, the doors opened. Everyone exited the elevator. Kevin and Heidi waved good-bye to the Amusement Plus employees, who left the building quickly.

While still in the lobby, Kevin and Heidi paused to speak with several people from the Below Low basement store. Skipper, Diva, and the living manikin appeared happy but tired.

After greetings were exchanged, Skipper asked, "Did you hear about what happened to Max?"

"No, what happened to him?" Heidi asked.

"Even though he wasn't at work today, he was questioned about the credit-card theft problem," Skipper said.

"Did he actually steal customers' credit-card information?" Kevin asked.

"I think he probably did," Skipper said.

"Was he arrested?" Heidi asked.

"Yeah, he was, but the police released him after only a few hours," Skipper said.

"How do you know about all of this?" Kevin asked.

"One of Max's neighbors is a relative of mine. Just a few minutes ago, I received a text message about Max going into his house, rather than being kept by the police," Skipper said.

"There might or might not be enough information to prosecute him, but I'm glad he's being questioned and thought of as a 'person of interest,'" Kevin said.

Heidi asked Skipper, "Is your boss, Judas, okay?"

Skipper started shifting his weight back and forth between his two feet. "He was sent to the hospital. He was then supposedly arrested and released on bail."

"I heard about that. I'm so glad when justice works," Kevin said.

Skipper's shifting motions continued as he asked, "Were the shooters okay, or were they shot when they were captured?"

"They had minor injuries but are now in prison. I'm also so glad that there's enough evidence to keep them in prison without being released on bail," Kevin said.

After saying good-bye, Kevin and Heidi left the Pilgrim Office Building and walked close to the window of the Drive-through Technology office. Even though there was still damage to the wall that had been done a couple of days ago by Joe's car, the actual window had been partially repaired. The drive-through window now was operating like usual. Jim was inside and waved at them.

Heidi waved at Jim, stepped closer to the window, and asked, "Is everyone in your office okay?"

"Yes, everyone's fine." Jim paused and then added, "I know you were kidnapped by the shooters. Were you hurt at all?"

"I'm actually doing great. I have a few minor injuries, but I'm just so happy to be free."

"Did that rope hurt you?" Jim asked.

"The shooters tied a rope around my waist, but my hands and feet could move. I also was forced into climbing up a lot of stairs while wearing a backpack. I think I'm now a little bit skinnier, especially around my waist."

Everyone laughed. Kevin said, "Even before you were kidnapped, Heidi, you were so perfect." He touched her waist before adding, "Now, you're even better than perfect."

"Thanks so much, Kevin; you're the one who's really better than perfect."

Jim looked at Kevin and asked him, "Are you also okay?"

"I'm great, and I'm so thankful no one was killed or seriously injured."

"I heard some people were shot," Jim said.

"A few people had minor injuries from being shot. However, they should all be fine within the next few days."

"I'm glad about no one being seriously hurt." Jim rubbed his eyes, which had dark circles under them from a lack of sleep. "Two days of worrying about crazy shooters is a tough experience, though. I'm completely exhausted."

"It really is tough to move past such an experience. People will need time to recover emotionally," Kevin said while rubbing his own forehead.

Heidi looked at Kevin and then added, "We're taking some time off from work, Jim, so we can relax and recover from all of the stress."

Kevin shook his head. "Jim, I think it's amazing you can be so conscientious and still be at work right now."

"Working helps me to keep my mind off of the negative things that happened." Jim glanced beyond Heidi and Kevin. A blue car was trying to pull up to the drive through window. The car stopped five feet away. A lady was driving the car; she turned off the car's engine, stepped out of the car, and walked over to the drive-through window.

Heidi immediately recognized the lady and said, "Hi, Tina. How are you doing?"

"I'm fine. How are you two doing?"

Heidi looked at Kevin, smiled, and said, "We're doing great."

"I'm so happy about that. I was really worried about you, Heidi."

"Thanks for caring about me."

"You're welcome. When I heard about everyone being alive and those thieves being captured, I was so thankful to God. Even though I don't pray too much, I immediately said a prayer of thanksgiving to God. I even promised to him that I would start going to church every Sunday, rather than just two or three times a year."

"We were so very thankful, too. We read and talked about a Bible verse at work," Heidi said. Her eyes shifted toward Kevin, whose eyes connected to hers and twinkled with joy.

Tina said, "Because of the help you gave me and everyone else in that building, Heidi, I'm planning on giving you those two necklaces that you wanted."

"I'm getting a raise, so I'll be buying them," Heidi said.

"No, you'll be accepting the cross and heart necklaces as a personal gift from me," Tina said.

"My job won't let me accept gifts, but I'm really happy that you want to help me," Heidi said.

"I'll sell you the necklaces at a great price: five dollars for each one. That's the price that I paid for them."

"That price is still a gift. You must have paid a lot more than that when you purchased them from a wholesaler," Heidi said.

"Actually, I really just paid about five dollars for each one. I bought them as a part of a special order." Tina's voice and raised eyebrows showed that she was telling the truth.

Heidi smiled. "Thanks so much. I'll stop by your store in a couple of days."

"I'll save the necklaces for you."

Heidi hugged Tina and then asked her, "What happened to the other people in your store? Did they run away before the shooters came in and stole some of the jewelry?"

"No, they actually had to hide in that locked-up office."

Heidi scratched her right ear. "Why didn't you hide there with them?"

"I was trying to put some of the jewelry into the vault."

Heidi frowned. "Don't you have insurance that will pay for stolen items?"

"I do, but there's a ten-thousand-dollar deductible."

"That's too bad." Heidi paused before asking, "How's everyone else in your office? Was anyone injured?"

"They're all okay."

Heidi asked, "Are you also okay?"

"Yeah, I am." Tina hesitated and then added, "I'm physically okay, but I do have one problem."

"What's that?" Heidi asked.

"I'm not sleeping too well. I just had a nightmare last night. It was about the shooters actually killing a lot of people."

Jim stared at Tina as he said, "I'm also having problems sleeping. I had a dream about this drive-through window being shot, blown up, and burned by a fire."

Heidi's eyes moved back and forth between Tina and Jim. Heidi then said, "I'm so sorry about both of you having nightmares, but there are a few things you can do to have better dreams."

"What do you suggest?" Tina asked.

"Lucid dreaming techniques can help you to focus on positive things. The end result will be fewer nightmares in the upcoming weeks and months," Heidi said.

"What's lucid dreaming?" Tina asked.

"Lucid dreaming is to be aware of yourself while you're dreaming," Heidi said. After glancing at Kevin and smiling, she added, "Many people can also control parts of their dreams."

"I don't think I can control what I'm dreaming while I'm dreaming, especially if it's a nightmare," Tina said.

"Even if you can't control your dreams while sleeping, there's a helpful technique you can use while you're awake," Heidi said.

"What's the technique?" Tina asked.

"You can try to make your dreams more positive," Heidi said. After pausing to look at Kevin again, she added, "Right before you go to sleep, Tina, try to focus your thoughts on something nice. Then you might dream about what you're thinking about."

Tina's eyes widened. "Oh, that's very interesting. If I'm thinking about shootings, then I'm telling my mind to dream about shootings."

Kevin shifted his eyes toward Heidi while his mouth and voice appeared to be talking to Tina: "Yes, you're right, Tina. If you think about something positive, like going to the beach on a summer day with family members, then one of your dreams might be about that visit to the beach."

Heidi and Kevin stared at each other for a few seconds. Heidi then said to Tina, "Some people can also control the content of their dreams while they're in the middle of a dream. If you're dreaming and suddenly realize that you're dreaming, you might be able to control parts of that dream."

"I've never noticed that I'm dreaming while I'm dreaming, except when I wake up in the middle of a dream," Tina said.

"That's okay." Heidi shifted her eyes from staring at Kevin to briefly glancing at Tina. "Most people can't easily control the content of their dreams while they're dreaming. However, everyone can use the technique of positive thinking before falling asleep."

"So, if I don't realize I'm dreaming while I'm dreaming, I can still control my dreams before I go to sleep by thinking of something positive," Tina said.

"Yeah, you can," Heidi said.

"I think your ideas are helpful, but I don't know if I can think about positive things right now. I'm really depressed," Tina said.

"Then you should speak with your doctor or a counselor," Heidi said.

Tina sighed. "I guess you're right."

Kevin said, "I agree with the different suggestions you have, Heidi. I have another one that might help."

Tina asked, "What's that?"

"Prayer really helps me."

Tina thought for a few seconds and then said, "Earlier today, I actually did feel more at peace when I prayed to God about being thankful."

At the same time, Kevin and Heidi both said, "That's wonderful!"

Tina smiled and then asked, "Did prayer help you to sleep last night?"

"Yes, it really did." Kevin looked at Heidi and added, "I was especially worried about Heidi, so I prayed for her. I then knew God would take care of her. My mind, heart, and soul were immediately happier and more at peace."

Heidi reached up and touched Kevin's shoulder. "My prayers were for you, too, as well as for myself and the other people in the building."

Kevin smiled at Heidi. "Our prayers were answered."

"Yes, they were." Heidi paused and then said, "My prayers have always been answered."

Tina asked, "Whenever you ask God for something, does He really give it to you?"

Heidi said, "Sometimes He gives me exactly what I ask for. At other times, He helps me in ways that He thinks are the best for my life and my soul."

"So, God doesn't always answer your prayers?"

"He really does always answer my prayers, but He does so in whatever ways He thinks are the best." Heidi thought for a few seconds and then added, "One day, back when I was younger, we didn't have a lot of food. My mom prayed for some help and told me that God would answer her prayer. She prayed that maybe we'd be able to get some more food from our church or from the Rhode Island Community Food Bank. Then she went outside to go to both places. Before she entered her car, a twenty-dollar bill flew through the air and landed at her feet."

"Did this really happen?" Tina asked.

"Yes, it did. I saw the bill. My mom picked it up with tears of joy in her eyes. She then looked around to see if anyone had dropped the money. There were no other people or cars on the street. My mom got into her car, took us to the store, and bought us enough food for the rest of the week."

"So miracles do happen," Tina said.

Heidi, Kevin, and Jim all said at the same time: "Yes, they do."

Heidi asked, "Wasn't it a miracle that no one was killed during the shootings in our building?"

Tina said, "I guess it was. I still can't believe everyone's okay."

Heidi gave Tina a hug and then said, "I'll pray for you, so you'll be able to get some sleep tonight with no nightmares happening."

Tina had tears in her eyes. "Thank you so much. I haven't been praying enough for years, but tonight, I'll be praying."

Heidi smiled. "Let's say a prayer right now." She bowed her head, folded her hands, and said, "Please, Lord, help Tina to have positive, peaceful dreams tonight. Please also help us all to be safe and loved by your grace. We're praying in the name of our Lord and Savior, Jesus Christ." All four people said "Amen" at the same time.

Tina said, "Thank you so much for your help."

Heidi said, "You're so welcome." After pausing for a few seconds, she added, "If you want to, we can trade emails. Then we'll be able to talk about things some more."

Tina said, "I'd love that. We can also become friends with each other on Facebook."

"I'll send you a friend request," Heidi said. She and Tina found paper and pens in their purses. After Heidi, Kevin, Jim, and Tina had all written down and traded their email addresses, Heidi said, "Thanks so much. It's so nice that we can talk to each other as friends."

"Yeah, it's great to have a new friend." Tina smiled broadly at Heidi. "I also love being able to send people messages on my smart phone or computer."

Everyone said good-bye. Heidi and Kevin walked away from the drive-through window. Tina got back into her blue car and drove forward to the still-open window. She then started talking to Jim about the kind of technology help that she needed.

After Heidi and Kevin had walked past five lines of cars in the parking lot, they paused. Kevin's car was on the right, and Heidi's car was further away. Kevin asked, "Would you like to go in my car?"

"Yes, I'd love to."

"After we come back from our trip, I'll plan on bringing you to your house. Then tomorrow morning, I'll pick you up at your house and take you back here for the brief debriefing. You'll be able to take your car back home tomorrow, unless we decide to go out on a second date right away," Kevin said.

"A second date sounds really great."

"We can figure out what to do on our second date during our first date." Kevin smiled.

"I love that plan."

Kevin opened up the passenger's door on his car. Once Heidi was inside, he put his briefcase in the trunk, let himself in, and started up his car. Within a minute, they had begun their trip to Plymouth, Massachusetts.

When they were on interstate ninety-five, Heidi asked, "Is it okay if I send a text message to Providence?"

"How can you send a message to a whole city?"

"I meant that I'd be texting the lady who works in the Dexter historic house. Her name is Providence."

"Oh, that's right. Her name is Providence. Are you planning on sending her a coded message about our first date?" Kevin asked.

"Yes, that's exactly what I was thinking of. As long as you're okay with it, I'll send her the following message: 'Love connection is happening now.'"

Kevin glanced at Heidi, smiled, and said, "I think that's a really great message."

Heidi typed in the message on her cell phone and sent it to Providence. Within a minute of sending the message, Heidi received a response that said, "Love was happening when you two were here in the Dexter house. It was probably also happening in many other places, but I'm so happy that you're now no longer trying to hide your love."

Heidi read the response message out loud to Kevin, who said, "You probably shouldn't respond to that response."

"Why should I be trying to keep our love a secret? Love is positive. It shouldn't be hidden."

Kevin hesitated and then said, "Okay, I guess you're right. We shouldn't hide our love from Providence, especially since she already knows about us."

Heidi sent a reply on her cell phone: "We've decided to tell you that we really do love each other."

The text response from Providence said, "I'm so happy for you!"

Heidi smiled and then said to Kevin, "We actually haven't been able to hide our love anyway. People have been noticing how we feel about each other."

"You're right about that. I've had so many questions from different friends of ours at work."

"How many of them do you think know about us?" Heidi asked.

"We haven't done anything wrong."

"You're right. We haven't been on a real date—at least not until today." Heidi smiled.

Kevin reached out and touched Heidi's wrist. "Even today, we haven't done anything wrong. How can love be wrong?"

"You're right. Especially since this is our first date, we can just say that we were relaxing after running, hiding, and fighting shooters."

"At times, we were also standing strong, being visible, and sharing our faith and our love."

"You're so right about that."

"Sharing our faith and our love is a lot more positive than fighting."

Heidi sighed. "I so agree with you. However, I've been trying to figure out what we should say to our boss. I don't want one or both of us to be fired for dating a colleague."

Kevin thought for a few seconds and then said, "He already knows how we feel about each other."

"Do you really think so?"

"I know so. He asked me about whether or not we were dating yet," Kevin said.

"What did you say?"

"I explained that we liked each other as friends and had not yet been on any real dates."

"What did he say?" Heidi asked.

"He told me to not update him about any changes. He said that he was too busy to keep on hearing about every time something might be happening. He also said that married people could work together in the same office; dating people would have to work in different offices in different states."

Heidi smiled. "That's a really interesting difference. If people share their love of each other, then they'll need to separate themselves from each other and work in different states."

"Well, at least we don't have to hide our love of God while we're at work."

Heidi shook her head in agreement. "I love the support that we received at the conference table today. Even if one of Matt's bosses wants to hide the Bible verse with a tablecloth, people will often lift up the tablecloth and show the Bible verse to each other."

"I think some people might just remove a tablecloth and keep it off."

"That's a great idea," Heidi said.

"I'd remove such a tablecloth. I really love the fact that our love for God can be on the visible, top section of the conference table, rather than on the invisible, hidden underside of that table."

"Love for God is now unhidden—and will remain unhidden—at H.I.D.E.," Heidi said in a strong voice.

"I even remember the Bible verse that was written on the table. It's actually my favorite verse, and one that I've loved for years: 'And now faith, hope, and love abide, these three; and the greatest of these is love' (1 Cor. 13:13 NRSV)."

"Were you really the one who initially wrote that verse on the hidden side of the table?"

"Yes, I was," Kevin said.

"Even before you told me with your facial expressions, I knew you were probably the one sharing your love for God with the courage and strength of a Pilgrim."

"You have the courage and strength of a Pilgrim, too," Kevin said.

Heidi sighed. "I wish I actually did. I sometimes hide my love for God when I should be sharing it."

"A lot of people do that. They are sometimes worried about how others will react."

"I was bullied a lot as a child, so I do worry a lot about people's reactions to whatever I say." Heidi thought for a second and then added, "There are some easy ways to share one's faith, though, and I've been doing many of them."

Kevin said, "I know you're been sharing your faith. You always do so with your friends. Even when we were just acquaintances, you were the first one of us to mention that you were going to church on Sunday."

"Just going to church on Sunday shows that one believes in God. Hopefully, all of my neighbors have noticed that I go to church almost every Sunday."

"People can also have a cross hanging on the rearview mirror of their cars." Kevin touched the cross that was hanging on his car's mirror.

"I have a religious tee shirt that I sometimes wear."

"I love that shirt, Heidi. You've been wearing it during our Saturday morning exercise classes."

"Thanks, Kevin. Many people wear tee shirts showing their love for a football team, a political party, or a pet."

"If people can share their love for a football team, then they should also be free to share their love for God," Kevin said.

"Some situations might require people to hide their views. For example, would you wear a tee shirt favoring the Boston Red Sox while in another team's stadium?"

Kevin said, "People do that, but I think I know what you're trying to say."

"I guess I'm comparing hiding one's faith with respecting other people's views."

Kevin said, "Hiding one's faith and showing toleration for different faiths are two different things."

Heidi thought for a few seconds before saying, "I think you're right."

"My sister's a teacher in a public school, and she has said before that it's sometimes tough for her. She doesn't want to make her students think that they need to be religious in order to get a good grade."

"Some students might then pretend to be religious, rather than really believing in God."

"You're right." Kevin paused and then added, "Lying about one's faith happened a lot in earlier centuries."

"Yeah, it did. That's why Roger Williams thought separation of church and state was so important. He wanted people to worship God because they actually believed in him, not because the state was telling them how to worship God."

"My sister does allow her students to have religious freedom," Kevin said.

"How does she do that in a public school system?"

"When her students write, she lets them use religious topics, as well as other topics. She gives them freedom by not telling them what religion she is or what religion to write about."

"That's interesting because it supports both freedom of speech and freedom of religion," Heidi said.

Kevin and Heidi talked about their families and their hopes for the future. They both wanted children and a home near their workplace. They enjoyed listening to peaceful, relaxing music on the car's radio while talking to each other in words, facial expressions, and body language. They often touched each other's hands, arms, and shoulders.

When Kevin's cell phone vibrated, he let Heidi answer it. One of their colleagues was wishing Kevin a happy vacation time and was hoping that he and Heidi were spending some relaxing time together. Heidi then sent some text messages to Kevin's family members on his phone, as well as some messages to her family on her phone.

After a trip of a little more than an hour, Kevin and Heidi arrived in Plymouth, Massachusetts. Kevin parked the car near the Plymouth Visitor Center. He then asked Heidi, "Do you want to just sit down somewhere and eat, or do you want to walk around for a little while?"

Heidi said, "I'm not really hungry yet."

"Neither am I."

"I would like to walk around just a little bit for maybe an hour or so," Heidi said as she and Kevin got out of the car and stretched their legs.

"We could make believe we're Pilgrims and walk along the same path that they did."

Kevin opened the trunk of his car. He then moved some picnic items from his briefcase into a backpack. After placing the backpack on his back, he walked with Heidi to the *Mayflower II*. Only about thirty other tourists were on the ship, but the *Mayflower II* was still crowded. As Heidi and Kevin looked inside the Captain's cabin, a group of four people walked up behind them.

Heidi said to Kevin, "This reproduction of the original *Mayflower* feels really crowded today, and there are a lot fewer people here today than were on the *Mayflower* in 1620."

A bearded man in the group of people laughed. He pushed his glasses onto the top of his head before asking, "Can you imagine living on a ship like this one for sixty-six days, like the Pilgrims did?"

Heidi said, "Their voyage across the Atlantic actually was sixty-six days, but they also were on their ship while they tried to determine where to set up their colony."

"I know about that. The Pilgrims initially travelled on the *Speedwell* to get to England and were planning on journeying across the Atlantic on two ships: the *Speedwell* and the *Mayflower.* Because of problems with the *Speedwell,* the Pilgrims wound up travelling on just the *Mayflower,* so they had to squeeze a lot of people onto a single ship," the bearded man said.

"There were a hundred and two passengers and about thirty crew members. One of my ancestors, William Brewster, was one of the passengers on the *Mayflower,*" Heidi said.

"Brewster Gardens is right over there, just beyond that hill." The bearded man waved his hand toward the hill.

"Thanks. We're planning on going there in a minute or two. We'll obviously be looking at Plymouth Rock on our way." Heidi and Kevin waved good-bye to the man. They then left the *Mayflower II* and walked down the sidewalk toward the canopy building that enclosed Plymouth Rock. Other groups of tourists were already standing in the enclosure and staring at the rock.

Heidi said to Kevin, "This piece of granite was possibly a part of the rock that the Pilgrims first stepped on when they arrived in Plymouth."

"Other parts of the rock are at the Smithsonian and the Pilgrim Hall Museum," Kevin said.

One of the tourists moved his cell phone forward and took a picture of thc rock. He then looked up some information on his phone and said to Heidi, "Plymouth Rock is claimed to be a 'world famous symbol of the courage and faith of the men and women who founded the first permanent colony in New England.'[38]"

"I love a granite rock being a symbol of courage and faith," Heidi said.

The tourist looked at his phone again and then said, "This website, *seeplymouth.com* says that '[i]nterpreters from the Massachusetts Department of Conservation and Recreation are often stationed at Plymouth Rock, sharing its history and answering visitors' questions.'[39]"

"I've never met any interpreters yet. Have you?" Heidi asked.

The tourist waved his hand toward a lady in a Pilgrim outfit. "I think that lady over there is an interpreter or some other kind of tourist guide."

Heidi walked over to listen to the lady, who was explaining the history of Plymouth Rock.

After listening for a few minutes, Heidi said, "There are a lot of people here today. Is this the normal number?"

The Pilgrim lady looked around before responding, "Yes, this number seems to be about right. Around a million visitors from all over the world come to Plymouth every year."[40]

"I guess people just love to connect to their history," Heidi said.

"They do. I think the history of our nation is so interesting," the Pilgrim lady said.

"It is, and I love to see historic items like Plymouth Rock," Kevin said.

"Actual physical objects help us to envision what happened to the Pilgrims," the Pilgrim lady said as she pointed toward Plymouth Rock.

"I know the Pilgrims had a tough journey. Even today, some of us have very tough journeys." Heidi stepped closer to Kevin and added, "Right now, I'm feeling so thankful for just being alive."

Kevin said, "I'm so thankful about being alive and here with you."

Heidi and Kevin waved good-bye to the Pilgrim lady. They then looked across the street and up the hill. Heidi said, "The Pilgrims thought of their city as a city on a hill. They thought a lot of people would be watching them and seeing how successful their city was."

"Even today, centuries later, we're reading their texts and watching their historic actions," Kevin said.

"The Pilgrims had so many obstacles to overcome. Like I've been doing over the past couple of days, they also had to 'run, hide, and fight.'"

"You're right. They were being persecuted and had to run away from England and other places," Kevin said.

"Some of them, like my Dexter and Brewster ancestors, had to hide what they were doing."

"So many publications were illegal back then, so the publishers often had to hide their identities."

Heidi shook her head in agreement. After a few seconds, she said, "The Pilgrims also often had to fight for their lives and their liberty."

"The *Mayflower* had cannons, in case pirates attacked them," Kevin said.

"Once the Pilgrims landed in the new world, they often carried guns around, so they could hunt for food, as well as have weapons to protect themselves."

Kevin gazed at Heidi as he said, "Like you, Heidi, the Pilgrims didn't just 'run, hide, and fight.' With their city on the hill, they also stood their ground, became visible, and shared their faith and their love."

Heidi smiled. "You're so sweet to compare me to my ancestors, Kevin."

"Thanks."

"I know my ancestors were able to initiate their city on the hill and stood their ground multiple times to keep their city on the hill," Heidi said.

"They not only stayed visible while being on the hill, but they also shared their faith and their love with others."

"One example of their shared faith and love happened when they joined together with the native people to celebrate the first Thanksgiving in our country," Heidi said.

"I'm so thankful we're both alive and can be here together." Kevin gave Heidi a kiss. He then held onto her hand as they crossed the street. They entered Brewster Gardens by stepping under the pergola. The pergola's ten pillars were holding a lattice roof, which partially shaded the brick walkway.

Kevin said, "I'd love to eat right here under the pergola."

"So would I, but too many people like to walk through this area."

"Even if we get kicked out, I'd love to stay here just for a few minutes with you."

Heidi smiled. "It really would be so nice to be here with you, even if it's just for a little while."

Kevin placed his backpack on the ground. He then withdrew two wine glasses, some wine, and a small box. "I have a surprise for you, Heidi."

Kevin bowed down on his knees, opened up the box, and asked, "Will you marry me?"

Heidi's face initially showed her complete surprise. A few seconds later, her joyful facial expression was saying "definitely yes" while her voice was saying the word "yes." She looked inside the box. An engagement ring was sparkling as it reflected the sun's bright rays.

Kevin took the ring out of the box and put it on Heidi's ring finger. He then stood up and hugged her. They kissed with an intensity that blocked out the clapping noises of a crowd of people who were circled around the pergola's pillars.

After a minute, one of the men in the crowd walked under the pergola and up to Kevin and Heidi. When the man touched Kevin and Heidi's shoulders, they both looked at him.

He said, "Hi, my name is Maul. You need to see the video version of what just happened. I recorded it on my cell phone." He showed them the video.

Heidi said, "I love that video." After pausing for a few seconds, she added, "You resemble someone I knew as a child. His name was Maul, too."

Maul stared at Heidi for a few seconds before saying, "You're Heidi, right?"

"Yes, I am."

"I think we knew each other back in elementary school," Maul said.

"Do you remember what you did to that picture of mine?" Heidi asked.

"No, what did I do?"

"I had drawn a picture while our class was here in Brewster Gardens, and you ruined it by drawing lines and other things over my images."

"Oh, I'm really sorry about that. When I was younger, I wasn't always behaving too well. My mom told me that I was bullying other children." Maul frowned, showing his own unhappiness with his actions.

Heidi said, "You were bullying me, as well as many other children."

"I remember some of the bullying things that I did, like calling you 'ugly.' However, even though I was mean to you, you still helped me a lot."

"Did I really, Maul? I can't remember anything that I did to help you."

"You interacted with other kids in very positive ways. Even though some of them also bullied you, just like I did, most of the kids really liked you," Maul said.

"I guess I did have a lot of friends back then," Heidi said.

"I saw how they liked you, so when my family moved and I switched to a different school, I started trying to be better behaved, just like you were."

Heidi said, "That's right; I remember your family moved away to a different city. After you moved, I never even talked to you until today."

"Right after we moved, I asked my parents if they believed in God.

They told me 'yes.' We then talked about the importance of going to church, so we could connect to and worship God."

"Did you start going to church, Maul?"

"Yeah, even though we were really busy, my family and I started going to church. This happened all because you shared your faith with me," Maul said.

"I remember praying in front of you one time—when we were at Brewster Gardens. Did I do other things to share my faith?"

"Yeah, I sometimes heard you talking to your friends about your belief in God. You and your friends talked about worship services, your Sunday school classes, and many fun church activities."

"I never realized you were listening," Heidi said.

"I often was. Whenever you talked to your friends about your church family while I was nearby, you were also communicating indirectly to me," Maul said. "Your dialogue with your friends helped me to understand that many people went to church in order to worship God."

"Thanks so much, Maul. I didn't realize how much I was helping you by talking to my friends."

"You really did help me a lot. Now I'm able to live a very positive life."

"I'll be praying that your life will continue to be positive," Heidi said.

"I'll be praying for your life to also be positive, especially with your new fiancé." Maul smiled at Kevin. They both shook hands. Maul then said, "I also want to officially ask you, Heidi, for forgiveness of the things that I did to you as a bully."

"Of course I forgive you. Thanks so much for asking. You can also ask God for His forgiveness."

"I've already done that, and He has forgiven me. I've been joyfully going to church for so many years because of your help."

Heidi hugged Maul, and he hugged her back. They both then hugged Kevin.

Maul said, "I'll send you a copy of this video. Please just let me know your email address." Heidi, Maul, and Kevin all traded email addresses.

Heidi said, "It's so great that you've created a wonderful video for me and my fiancé."

Maul smiled. "Thanks so much. I'm really happy to be able to do something positive for you, Heidi."

Kevin, Heidi, and Maul waved good-bye to each other. Kevin and Heidi walked out from under the pergola and over to the bridge that crossed the Town Brook. While holding hands, they crossed the bridge together. They next walked over near the Pilgrim lady statue. They sat down in front of the fountain, and Kevin pulled out some sandwiches and water from his backpack.

Heidi asked, "Do you think there will be problems at work because we're engaged?"

Kevin kissed Heidi's hand and then asked, "Are you asking about hiding your engagement ring?"

"I don't know whether I should or not. We're technically not supposed to be dating each other."

"Interestingly, everything's okay if we're married, though," Kevin said.

"You're right. Married people can both be working together at our company."

Kevin gazed at Heidi and asked, "Should we get married right away?"

"We could try to, but I'm guessing our families would want to go to our wedding. If we have to wait a few weeks, I could always hide my engagement ring while at work by putting a bandage over it and claiming an injury."

"That's an interesting idea. You'd still be wearing your ring, but it would be hidden from people at work until we're officially married."

Heidi thought for a few seconds and then frowned. "I don't really want to hide my engagement ring, especially by using a bandage."

"I completely agree with you. I don't want to hide our love for each other." Kevin paused and then added, "Hiding our love would be like hiding our faith by covering it up with a tablecloth in a conference room."

Heidi shook her head. "I don't want a bandage to hide my love, and I really don't want a tablecloth to hide my faith."

Kevin said, "If we share our love, one of us will probably have to leave and go to work in a different state. As you know, employees in the same department of our company are not supposed to be dating each other."

"I'm fairly new, so if I have to, I can probably easily switch to a different state. I can then try to get my Rhode Island job back again after we get married."

Kevin was silent for a few seconds. He then said, "You're right. It'll probably be easier for you to switch to a different state, but the need to switch to a new state might not even happen. If your engagement ring is unhidden while you're at work, it's possible our boss will be quiet about it and make believe he doesn't even see the ring."

"If he asks about our engagement, I can explain that I'm just waiting until the next pay period in order to give him two weeks' notice of changing to a different job in a different state."

Kevin smiled. "Logically, that makes sense. If you have to give two weeks' notice right away, we can then just get married immediately."

"We could also do something like make believe we're breaking up until the actual wedding date arrives."

Kevin bent forward, kissed the engagement ring, and then said, "I don't want to do that."

"I don't either. I was just trying to be funny." Heidi laughed.

"I'm guessing our boss will just make believe he can't see the ring."

"I think you're right."

Heidi looked over at the pergola section of Brewster Gardens. "I've always wanted to get married here. It might be possible for us to set up a date and time that would work for this venue and our minister's schedule."

"I'd also love to marry you right here."

"I've actually dreamed about getting married to you in Brewster Gardens, Kevin."

"I've dreamed about marrying you in many different places, Heidi, including in Brewster Gardens on a beautiful spring day."

"It's so neat that both of us have been having similar dreams."

Kevin said, "We're in love, so it makes sense that we're having some of the same dreams."

"What makes even more sense is for our dreams to become our reality."

"Within a few weeks, Heidi, we'll be married. Then our dreams will have become our reality."

Kevin and Heidi kissed in a way that had never happened to either one of them before: his tongue touched her front teeth while Heidi's tongue touched his bottom teeth. Their tongues enjoyed touching each other while also touching the other person's teeth. After they were done kissing, they made more plans for their second date, their wedding, and their future life together. They ate their ham and cheese sandwiches and drank their wine. They then enjoyed the sweetness of each other while eating some fruit and chocolate.

After Kevin and Heidi were finished with their lunch, they stood up to leave Brewster Gardens. Light from the sun bounced off of the Pilgrim maiden statue and landed upon their faces. The fountain's streaming bits of water were bursting into large, happy bubbles. Kevin reached out to hold onto Heidi's left hand. Rather than hiding her engagement ring with the presence of his hand, he placed his hand beneath her palm. He then raised her left hand and its ring up high. The sun's rays lit up the diamond; hundreds of people saw the symbol of shared love. Many of them hugged and kissed their own loved ones with whom they were sharing a reality.

Illustrations

Roger Williams Statue in Roger Williams State Park, Providence, RI

Jeremiah Dexter House, Providence, RI

Fireplace in the Jeremiah Dexter House, Providence, RI

The National Monument to the Forefathers, Plymouth, MA

Back View of the National Monument to the Forefathers, Plymouth, MA

Mayflower II, Plymouth, MA

Plymouth Rock, Plymouth, MA

Top of the Hill Overlooking Plymouth Rock
Canopy Building, Plymouth, MA

William Bradford Statue, Plymouth, MA

Massasoit Statue, Plymouth, MA

The Pergola at the Entrance of Brewster Gardens, Plymouth, MA

The Pilgrim Maiden Statue in Brewster Gardens, Plymouth, MA

The Immigrant Memorial Statue in Brewster Gardens, Plymouth, MA

The Bridge over the Town Brook in Brewster Gardens, Plymouth, MA

Endnotes

[1] Legal Information Institute, "First Amendment," *U.S. Constitution,* Cornell University Law School, accessed September 1, 2016, https://www.law.cornell.edu/constitution/first_amendment.

[2] Jocelyn Hargrave, "Disruptive Technological History: Papermaking to Digital Printing," *Journal of Scholarly Publishing* 44, no. 3 (April 2013): 221-236. *Academic Search Complete,* EBSCO*host,* accessed December 4, 2015, 231-232.

[3] "The Pilgrim Maiden Statue sculpted by Henry Hudson Kitson, Brewster Gardens, Plymouth Massachusetts Dedicated in 1924," FamilySearch, *familysearch.org* accessed July 29, 2016, https://familysearch.org/photos/artifacts/1216851.

[4] George F. Wilson, "Introduction to the Modern English Version of Bradford's *Plymouth Colony* for the Classics Club edition," quoted in Dorothy Brewster, *William Brewster of the Mayflower: Portrait of a Pilgrim* (New York: New York University Press, 1970), 105.

[5] Elizabeth L. Eisenstein, *The Printing Press as an Agent of Change: Communications and Cultural Transformations in Early-modern Europe,* vol. 2 (Cambridge: Cambridge University Press, 1979), 690.

[6] Fran Rees, *Johannes Gutenberg: Inventor of the Printing Press* (Minneapolis, Minnesota: Compass Point Books, 2006.), 82.

[7] Katharine Habe, "Johannes Gutenberg," *World History: The Modern Era,* ABC-CLIO, (2015), accessed December 4, 2015, http://0-worldhistory2.abc-clio.com.helin.uri.edu/Search/Display/1938390?terms=gutenberg.

[8] Fran Rees, *Johannes Gutenberg: Inventor of the Printing Press* (Minneapolis, Minnesota: Compass Point Books, 2006.), 73.

[9] Jeremy Norman & Co., Inc., "Gutenberg Prints the 42-Line Bible (1455-1456)," *Historyofinformation.com,* (Nov. 14, 2014), accessed January 4, 2017, http://www.historyofinformation.com/expanded.php?id=344.

[10] Mary B. Sherwood, *Pilgrim A Biography of William Brewster* (Falls Church, Virginia: Great Oak Press of Virginia, 1982), 10.

[11] Pilgrim Hall Museum, "The Pilgrim Press," 2016, accessed Oct. 25, 2016, http://www.pilgrimhallmuseum.org/pdf/Pilgrim_Press.pdf.

[12] Rev. Ashbel Steele, *Chief of the Pilgrims: or the Life and Time of William Brewster* (Freeport, New York: Books for Libraries Press, 1970), 367.

[13] Ibid.

[14] Bradford F. Swan, *Gregory Dexter of London and New England 1610-1700* (Rochester: The Printing House of Leo Hart, 1949), 10-11.

[15] "William Prynne," *Encyclopaedia Britannica, Encyclopaedia Britannica Online,* Encyclopaedia Britannica Inc., 2016, accessed August 2, 2016, https://www.britannica.com/biography/William-Prynne.

[16] Roger Williams, "Introduction," *A Key into the Language of America,* quoted in Edwin S. Gaustad, *Roger Williams: Lives and Legacies* (Oxford: Oxford University Press, 2005), 47.

[17] Karen Petit, *Roger Williams in an Elevator* (Mustang, Oklahoma: Tate Publishing and Enterprises, LLC, 2016), 50.

[18] Bradford F. Swan, *Gregory Dexter of London and New England 1610-1700* (Rochester: The Printing House of Leo Hart, 1949), 85.

[19] Library of Congress, "The Gutenberg Bible," *Library of Congress Bible Collection,* Library of Congress, accessed Oct. 24, 2016, https://www.loc.gov/exhibits/bibles/the-gutenberg-bible.html.

[20] Garry Bryant, "History of Rev. Gregory Dexter (1610-1700), Family Search, *familysearch.org,* October 8, 2014, accessed September 8, 2016, https://familysearch.org /photos/artifacts/10698027.

[21] Bradford F. Swan, *Gregory Dexter of London and New England 1610-1700* (Rochester: The Printing House of Leo Hart, 1949), 31.

[22] James Russell Wiggins, "Afterword: The Legacy of the Press in the American Revolution," *The Press & the American Revolution,* eds. Bernard Bailyn and John B. Hench (Worcester: American Antiquarian Society, 1980), 372.

[23] Grier, Peter, "Civil Order vs. First Amendment (Cover Story)," *Christian Science Monitor,* (June 25, 1991): 1, in *Academic Search Complete,* accessed March 24, 2016, http://0-search.ebscohost.com.helin.uri.edu/login.aspx?direct=true&db=a9h&AN=1965635&site=ehost-live.

[24] Cox, Archibald, "First Amendment," *Society* 24, no. 1 (November, 1986): 15, in *Academic Search Complete,* accessed January 6, 2016.

[25] Rev. Joseph Hunter, quoted in Rev. Ashbel Steele, *Chief of the Pilgrims: or the Life and Time of William Brewster* (Freeport, New York: Books for Libraries Press, 1970), 35.

[26] Barack Obama, "Obama at DNC: Our Path 'Leads to a Better Place,'" *Transcript: President Obama's DNC Speech, ABC News,* Sept. 6, 2012, accessed January 13, 2017, http://abcnews.go.com/Politics/OTUS/transcript-president-obamas-democratic-convention-speech/story?id=17175575.

[27] Murry Dry, "The First Amendment Freedoms, Civil Peace and the Quest for Truth," *Constitutional Commentary* 15, no. 2 (Summer 1998): 325, in *Academic Search Complete*, EBSCO*host*, accessed June 14, 2016.

[28] The Afters, "Lift Me Up," *Light Up the Sky, musixmatch.com,* accessed August 20, 2016, https://www.musixmatch.com/lyrics/The-Afters/Lift-Me-Up.

[29] William Bradford, (1651), quoted on *National Monument to the Forefathers* NRHP reference # 74002033 (Plymouth, Massachusetts, 1889).

[30] Wolfgang Dobras et al., *Gutenberg Man of the Millennium: From a Secret Enterprise to the First Media Revolution,* Abridged version of the Catalogue of the exhibition staged by the City of Mainz (Mainz, Germany: City of Mainz, 2000), 124.

[31] "Apr.1, 1621: The Pilgrim-Wampanoag Peace Treaty," *This Day in History, history.com,* accessed August 28, 2016, http://www.history.com/this-day-in-history/the-pilgrim-wampanoag-peace-treaty.

[32] Emmanuel Altham, letter written in September, 1623, quoted in "Massasoit Ousemequin," 2016, *MayflowerHistory.com,* accessed August 28, 2016, http://mayflowerhistory.com/massasoit/.

[33] Karen Petit, *Mayflower Dreams* (Mustang, Oklahoma: Tate Publishing and Enterprises, LLC, 2014), 395.

[34] William Bradford, *Of Plymouth Plantation,* Rendered into Modern English and with an Introduction by Harold Paget (Mineola, New York: Dover Publications, Inc. 2006), 208.

[35] Ibid., 208-209.

[36] American Civil Liberties Union, "Online Censorship in the States," *ACLU.org,* 2017, accessed January 2, 2017, https://www.aclu.org/other/online-censorship-states.

[37] Zach Williams, "Chain Breaker," *ktis.com,* Essential Music Publishing LLC, accessed January 5, 2017, http://myktis.com/songs/chain-breaker/.

[38] Destination Plymouth County, Massachusetts, "Pilgrim Memorial State Park," *seeplymouth.com,* 2012, accessed August 26, 2016, http://www.seeplymouth.com/beaches-and-parks/pilgrim-memorial-state-park.

[39] Ibid.

[40] Executive Office of Energy and Environmental Affairs, "Pilgrim Memorial State Park," *mass.gov,* Commonwealth of Massachusetts, 2016, accessed August 26, 2016, http://www.mass.gov/eea/agencies/dcr/massparks/region-south/pilgrim-memorial-state-park.html.

About the Author

Dr. Karen Petit is the author of four Christian novels: *Banking on Dreams, Mayflower Dreams, Roger Williams in an Elevator,* and *Unhidden Pilgrims.* This author has a large family, including her son, daughter, brothers, sisters, aunts, uncle, cousins, nieces, and nephews. She received her bachelor's, master's, and doctorate degrees in English from the University of Rhode Island. She loves to write, in addition to helping others to write.

As a descendant of the Reverend John Robinson, the pastor to the Pilgrims, Dr. Petit loves to write about history, religious freedom, ancestry, dreams, reality, and our Lord and Savior, Jesus Christ. In addition to writing novels, Petit has been writing poetry and academic documents. She also has been a presenter at multiple academic conferences, including at the CCCC Conference in 2005 and at the NEWCA Conference in 2013. Some of this author's presentation topics are available on her author website: www.drkarenpetit.com.

Dr. Petit not only enjoys writing, but she also loves to help other people to write. For more than nine years, this author has been the full-time Writing Center Coordinator and an adjunct faculty member at the Community College of Rhode Island. Before starting full-time at this college, Petit worked as an adjunct faculty member for over twenty years at many area colleges: Bristol Community College, Massasoit Community College, Rhode Island College, Worcester State University, Quinsigamond Community College, Bryant University, Roger Williams University, New England Institute of Technology, the University of Massachusetts at Dartmouth, and the University of Rhode Island.

Dr. Karen Petit is very thankful for her wonderful life. She has been enjoying her author events, as well as a large number of writing and educational activities. Her family, friends, and God have been the focus of her dreams and her reality for many years.

Printed in the United States
By Bookmasters